TERRY KAY

THE

KIDNAPPING

OF

AARON

GREENE

AN AVON BOOK

AVON BOOKS, INC.
An Imprint of HarperCollins*Publishers*
10 East 53rd Street
New York, New York 10022-5299

Copyright © 1999 by The Terry Kay Corporation
Inside cover author photo by Robert Lowery
Published by arrangement with the author
Library of Congress Catalog Card Number: 98-33817
ISBN: 0-380-72905-9
www.harpercollins.com

Published in hardcover by William Morrow and Company, Inc.; for information address Permissions Department, William Morrow and Company, Inc., 10 East 53rd Street, New York, New York 10022-5299.

First Avon Books Printing: February 2000

AVON TRADEMARK REG. U.S. PAT. OFF. AND IN OTHER COUNTRIES, MARCA REGISTRADA, HECHO EN U.S.A.

Printed in the U.S.A.

WCD 10 9 8 7 6 5 4 3 2 1

Also by Terry Kay

The Runaway
Shadow Song
To Whom the Angel Spoke
To Dance with the White Dog
Dark Thirty
After Eli
The Year the Lights Came On

For Tommie

Author's Note

————◆————

Once I was a sportswriter and, later, the theater-movie reviewer for *The Atlanta Journal,* and I think of that rich experience as an apprenticeship for the years of fiction that would follow.

In fact, this story was first imagined as a screenplay during those years. I wanted to write something that was action driven yet unusual in nature, and I settled on the idea of a kidnapping. But it was mostly thought and talk (as so many stories are). And then, in 1974, Reg Murphy, an editor for *The Atlanta Constitution,* was kidnapped. A ransom demand of $700,000 was paid by the newspapers (the kidnapper was later caught and convicted), prompting a humorous remark by a copyboy: "I wonder if they'd pay that much for me?" Personally, I think the newspaper would have responded exactly as it did for Reg, yet the remark did pose an interesting question: What is the value of a life?

For years, the idea of such a story remained just that with me—an idea. Other subjects led to other stories. Still, the concept of the kidnapping of a "nobody" lingered. Now it is on paper.

In this novel, I have used *The Atlanta Journal-Constitution* as the newspaper involved in the action out of respect for the memorable years I spent in those offices, though none of the characters are based on former coworkers. I realize, of course, that the daily routine of newspaper publishing has changed, and I admit to relying considerably on how it used to be, rather than how it is.

ONE

———◆———

ON THE MORNING THAT HE WOULD BE KID-
napped, Aaron Greene left his umbrella at home.

His mother had warned of rain. It was in the forecast,
she had said in her small, fretting voice. She had urged him
to wear his raincoat and to take his umbrella, but he had
forgotten the umbrella in the rush of leaving, and now he
thought of the five blocks he would have to walk from
the Omni station to the Century National Bank, and of
the morning crowd that would push against him in its
hurried dash through the fine mist of the rain that had
begun during the train ride from Decatur.

Aaron did not like the morning crowd. The morning
crowd was impersonal, sleep-drugged, somber. The
morning crowd moved to the pull of job clocks. The
morning crowd did not speak.

The morning crowd was there each day at the Decatur
train station, and at each stop on the ride into Atlanta—at
East Lake, Candler Park, Inman Park, King Memorial—
it invaded the train, pressing into the aisles, hovering over
filled seats, their hands curled around ceiling handrails like
somnolent birds. In the city, the train emptied stop by stop
and the morning crowd flowed out onto the sidewalks and
divided itself into thin streams at crossing lights.

Aaron was part of the train ride and the crush of bodies
and the hurrying, and he did not like it. He did not have

1

the bravery for crowds. Had never had it. He had always felt uncomfortable and awkward and embarrassed. His mother had explained that it was not an affliction, but shyness—that shy people were gentle (too gentle, she said) and that someday he would accept the tranquillity of his nature. His mother was also shy; she would not leave her home alone.

An older man in an expensive raincoat over an expensive suit sat beside Aaron on the train seat, reading the morning newspaper. The man had an umbrella wedged between his legs and Aaron's legs, and Aaron remembered the morning—it was in November—that a woman's eye had been stabbed by the metal rib of an umbrella opened quickly and carelessly. The man who held the umbrella had stared irritably at the woman and then had turned and walked briskly away from the sound of her screaming.

In the rain, the morning crowd was always more violent.

Aaron stared at the window beside his face. He saw his pale reflection simmering in the wet glass. A string of water, like a clear, bloodless capillary, ran across his mirrored forehead, through his eye, and over the corner of his mouth. From the seat behind him, he heard the voices of two boys. They were talking of the Atlanta Hawks.

"Man, they ain't got Mutombo, they ain't got nothing."

"What about Mookie?"

"He's all right, but Mutombo's the man. Best thing they ever done was get Mutombo."

"He's good. I ain't saying he ain't."

"That's who I play like: Mutombo. You come down the middle on me, I kick ass and do the finger-wave."

Aaron turned his head slightly and looked into the window behind him. In the reflection, he saw the boys. One was black, tall, broad-shouldered, his nose braided with a gold pin. The other was white, a slight build, his hair pulled into a pigtail. They were laughing, bobbing their bodies to an unheard music. Aaron knew the black boy.

His name was Doobie. That was what he was called. Maybe not his real name, but his called name. Doobie. He had played on the high school basketball team and had been in Aaron's algebra class. Once, he had borrowed a pencil from Aaron, but never returned it.

"Yeah, Mutombo," the white boy said. "You Mutombo, all right. You more like Spud Webb."

The two laughed easily. The boy who would be Dikembe Mutombo, the giant, made a motion of dunking a basketball, his long arm flying up and downward in the wavering reflection of the window. "Swissssh," he said.

Aaron turned his face from the window and listened to the laughter behind him crawl over the seat and fall on his shoulders. Though the house that his parents had bought ten years earlier had a basketball goal in the backyard, Aaron had never owned a basketball. He had never taken a shot at a basket. He had only dreamed of being a basketball player. Sometimes when he saw basketball games on television, he imagined that he was a player, leaping with grace through the shout-filled air of a gymnasium, the ball leaving his fingertips in a splendid arc. And in those moments—in the flickering, slow-motion beauty of his dream—Aaron understood the breathless sensation of celebration, the song of joy from people seized by awe.

There goes Aaron Greene.

Aaron Greene can fly. He has wings.

Aaron, Aaron, let me touch you. Let me touch you.

The people would reach with their fingers of praise as he walked among them and their fingers would slide over him like a warm wind.

In the flickering, slow-motion beauty of his dream, Aaron Greene was a god.

Aaron looked again at himself in the rain-streaked window of the train. The person he saw could not fly. There were no fingers of praise clawing for him. The person he saw was small and afraid.

The train stopped at the Five Points station, the doors

slid open. Part of the morning crowd spilled out of the opened doors, bubbled into a wad, rushed away, streamed together again at stairwells. The man next to Aaron folded his paper, looked out of his window, leaned back and closed his eyes as the train pulled away.

At the Omni station, the man's eyes snapped open, his body tightened. He stood and pushed himself rudely into the aisle, clutching his umbrella like a weapon. The scent of his shaving lotion coated the space where he stood.

The rain was a thin March mist, a Southern winter-spring rain—dark, rolling, wind-whipped, lightning-charged, quick-in, quick-out. The rain was cold on Aaron's face and hands. He walked cautiously near the edge of the sidewalk. He could sense the cars in the street, close enough to touch, barely moving on the slick skin of the pavement. And he could hear the rhythmic slapping of windshield wipers and the sharp, metal squeal of brakes and the muted drumming of idling motors. At his feet, he could see the jelly-quivering of car lights in water pools.

The rain matted his hair and seeped across his face. He could feel the wind from the funnel of office buildings on Marietta Street whipping hard against him, causing his eyes to tear unexpectedly. He pushed his hands deep into the pockets of his raincoat.

At the corner of Marietta and Spring, a large woman with a puffed, red face shoved into him roughly, forcing him off the curbing and into the street. He stepped quickly back onto the sidewalk and the large woman glared at him.

"Watch where you are," the woman snapped.

"Sorry," Aaron mumbled in apology.

He stared at the crossing light, watching an impatient few sprint across the street, weaving among the cars. He had never crossed against the light. Never. The wind twisted the mist over his face and swept against his ears and neck. The abdomen of the large woman brushed his hip. Her face was near his shoulder and he could smell the dead skin of her wet scalp and the grease of her thinning hair. The woman had the odor of old, damp clothing.

The light changed and he crossed the street, walking rapidly in front of the woman. He slowed with the knotting crowd waiting for buses in front of the Journal-Constitution Building. He did not see the car roll to a stop near him, and the voice from the car window startled him.

"Aaron?"

He turned to the car. He could see a woman wearing a brown raincoat and a man's rain hat. Large sunglasses covered her eyes. She was sitting in the passenger seat. A man was driving. Another man was in the backseat.

"Aaron Greene? Is that you?" the woman asked.

Aaron looked quickly around him. He saw the large woman with the puffed red face approaching him, laboriously pushing her weight. He turned back to the car. The woman had lowered the car window.

"You look like you're drowning," the woman said pleasantly. "Come on, get in. We'll give you a lift."

Aaron did not know the woman who spoke from the car. He smiled uneasily. He could feel his face flush with embarrassment.

The woman laughed. "You don't recognize me," she said lightly. "I work on the third floor. Alyse Burton. You deliver our mail."

Aaron stared at the woman in bewilderment. Her face was not familiar, but Aaron did not look at the faces of the people in the bank. He sorted and delivered their mail, but he did not look at them.

"Uh—hello," he said hesitantly.

"Get in," the woman urged. "No reason to get soaked."

"That—that's all right," Aaron stammered. "It's not far."

"It's far enough. Come on, Aaron. I won't take no for an answer."

Aaron could see the crossing light flash at Fairlie Street

and the crowd began to move sluggishly around him. He heard the large woman mutter a curse.

"Traffic's moving, Aaron," the woman named Alyse said. "Quit worrying about it. Get in." There was command in her voice.

He saw the back door of the car open and he stepped reluctantly toward it. A car horn bellowed in the snarled traffic.

"Better hurry," Alyse sang. She laughed again. "We'll be dragging you like a rag if you don't."

Aaron ducked his head and slipped into the backseat of the car and closed the door. Alyse turned in the seat to face him and the car eased forward. "You don't remember me at the office, do you?" she said softly.

Aaron blushed. He turned his eyes to avoid her face.

"That's all right," Alyse said. "It's a big place. Hard to remember everyone. You're the quiet one. That's how I remember you. Always quiet. Very quiet. Very nice."

"Nothing wrong with that," the man driving the car said. "It's a good trait. People talk too much. I'm for you, Aaron."

The woman named Alyse smiled gently. She said, "Meet some friends of mine, Aaron. Robert—" She motioned with her face to the man driving the car. The man wore a rain hat. He had a full beard, bronze-red in color.

"How you doing, Aaron?" Robert said. His voice was jovial. He eased the car back into the traffic.

"Fine," Aaron mumbled.

"And this is Morris," Alyse said, turning her face to the man beside Aaron. "He's a lot like you. He's also quiet."

"Hello," Aaron said uncomfortably. The man beside him was younger than the man named Robert. He had blond hair and a slender, pale face. He wore a tan raincoat over a blue turtleneck shirt.

"Hello, Aaron," Morris replied. His voice was cold.

Alyse half-turned in her seat and looked through the windshield. "It's not the kind of day to be walking around," she said. "I hate this kind of traffic. Bumper-to-bumper. It's a wonder more people aren't killed, run down like dogs." She was talking rapidly, giddily. "You can't stop in time. It's almost like being on ice, skidding around. Almost as bad as those ungodly snowstorms we have, except they're not snow, they're ice. Have you ever driven in this kind of traffic, Aaron?"

"Uh, no, ma'am," Aaron said quietly.

"The first time I did, I thought people were going to run me off the road," Alyse chattered. "I think I drove two miles an hour." She laughed again, again giddily, and Robert also laughed. "I've never been that frightened. I sometimes wish I lived downtown, right in the middle of everything. Then I'd ride buses, or take cabs, or walk when it didn't rain or snow. I'd never own a car." She glanced back at Aaron. "Would you like that, Aaron? Would you like to live downtown?"

"I—don't know," Aaron replied. "Maybe."

"I would," Alyse said. "Yes. Definitely. But we live where we live, don't we?"

The car passed through the clogged line of traffic at Forsyth Street and glided into the right lane in front of a Volkswagen. The Century National Bank was across the street from them. Aaron shifted restlessly in his seat. He wondered why the man named Robert was driving away from the bank.

"We can't help where we live, can we, Aaron?" Alyse said. She sounded tense. "If we had the money maybe we could afford to live where we wanted, but without it we have to take what we can."

Aaron looked at the digital clock recessed in the dashboard of the car. It was four minutes before eight.

"Maybe—maybe I'd better get out here," Aaron stammered. "I have to be at work at eight."

Alyse turned to face Aaron. He could see a flattened image of himself in the amber tint of her sunglasses and he remembered his reflection from the window of the train.

"No, Aaron, not now," Alyse said. "I want you to stay in the car."

Aaron looked instinctively out of the back window of the car. In the distance, he could see the large woman with the odor of old, damp clothing on the street corner, her huge, puffed face lifted in the rain, reading a street sign.

"I want you to stay with us, Aaron," Alyse said calmly.

Aaron saw a movement from the man sitting beside him, the man who had been introduced as Morris. The flap of his tan raincoat opened and Aaron saw the dark, slender barrel of a pistol pointed at his waist.

"Please do as I ask," Morris said.

TWO

———————◆———————

CODY YATES SAT WITH HIS FEET CROSSED ON the corner of his desk, reading the morning edition of *The Atlanta Constitution*. He held a cup of coffee, balancing it on the metal of his belt buckle. The coffee was bitter and burned in his stomach. His eyes and temples ached from the cigarette-and-bourbon hangover that had left him listless and angry at the unplanned indulgence of an afternoon beer that had extended into the night and had not ended until two o'clock in the morning. He looked at his watch. It was eight-twenty. He would need a metro edition follow-up for the *Atlanta Journal* half of the hyphenated twenty-four-hour newspaper that seemed to flow nonstop from high-speed presses hidden in the belly of the building. He had time. The story was on the police precinct for Underground Atlanta. He could fake waiting on a phone call if Halpern complained. Halpern would not understand a hangover. Halpern believed in sobriety. Halpern believed his job as city editor was a holy ordination.

Cody moved the coffee from his belt buckle to his desk and fingered a small bottle of Mylanta from his coat pocket. He opened the bottle and shook free two tablets and popped them into his mouth and began to chew them. Funny, he thought. I like the taste of these things. He leaned back, closed his eyes, chewed, listened to the monotonous quiet of the newsroom at his back. He was pleased he had been moved near the wall, in the most remote corner of the room. Halpern had said he was being a nuisance, that he talked too much, that he disturbed others who preferred work to chatter. Halpern could kiss his ass. Halpern knew nothing about newspapers. Halpern knew keypads and icons. It pleased Halpern that no one talked. And they didn't. No one. Not anymore. No one talked. They had stopped talking when the typewriters were removed and were replaced first by simple word processors and then sophisticated computers. Now everyone sat mesmerized in front of screens—blinded by the monitors that faced them head-high—and they punched delicately at soft-clicking keys and read with fascination the words that appeared silently before them, like eyeblinks, in the electronic spitting of black letters across a dull gray background. They had become mutes, speaking in an electronic finger code to machines. They had forgotten, or had never known, the energy of noise—the laughter, the pure, unbridled joy of a hollered discovery that once had made journalism a living opera, played to the gunfire music of mechanical key faces on long mechanical key arms striking against paper.

Before the computers, they—those who had been there, those who remembered—had been able to look over their typewriters, across the newsroom, and see and hear one another, and because they could see and hear, they better understood the world they wrote about in spurts of minutes with the dogbite of a deadline snapping at their heels. The goddamn computers had blocked the seeing. And the hearing. And the newsroom that he had loved had become a noiseless, boring, pathetic place to Cody Yates.

Cody picked up his coffee cup and drained the coffee from it in a single swallow, and then he shook a cigarette free from its package and put it between his lips and sucked on the filtered tip. The unlit cigarette was his flag of defiance against a no-smoking policy that had been in effect for years. He would take his cigarette outside the building and he would huddle with other smokers, like vagrants, in the designated area when he wanted to smoke, but damned if he would let anyone tell him he could not hold a cigarette in his mouth. Unlit. Once the newsroom had had the scent of tobacco; now it smelled of toilet water and perfume.

He could feel his throat tighten against imagined smoke. Got to quit smoking, he thought. Got to. Jesus, nobody smokes anymore.

He wiggled the cigarette in his mouth and glanced around the newsroom. He saw the disapproving gaze of Freda Graves. Eyes that seemed both sad and cold, he thought. A body that Michelangelo would have kept beside his bed to fondle on sleepless nights if he had been talented enough to sculpt it, but a personality too aloof for anyone, which was probably the reason she was unmarried. She turned her face back to her desk. Damn her, Cody thought. Damn the whole damn place.

Maybe he was wrong in staying all these years, he reasoned. He was forty-eight years old. Burnout age. Ten pounds overweight. Rogue gray-white hair streaking through the red-brown. Spiderweb lines of eyestrain.

He no longer felt six feet tall.

He wondered if he had osteoporosis.

He rolled his shoulders, heard a cracking.

Jesus, he thought.

He had twice been nominated for the Pulitzer Prize, had been a Nieman Fellow, had enough awards and plaques to fill a basement, but what good was any of it? Once he had been a star, better known than most of the people he wrote about. Now he was considered as antique as the manual portable typewriter that he kept on his desk as another act of defiance.

Maybe he should have left journalism for some plush public relations job with some money-grubbing company, where he could have faked anxiety over writing a brochure

a month. Christ, plenty had done it. Sellouts. The preening gentry of the corporate world, kissing kneecaps of the
executive nobility and feeding wide-mouthed egos with
sweet, select words of worship. There was a secret to it,
the Sellouts confessed: Never disagree, but never sound as
though you were a yes-man. And there was one other
thing: The executive nobility hated journalists. If you
wanted to make it as a Sellout you had to deny journalism
as vigorously as Peter denied Christ. The Sellouts were
accomplished liars. Sometimes Cody saw them in bars or
on the street and they always spoke kind, sympathetic
words to him. "Hey, Yates, how's it going? Still at it, huh?
Well, I admire that. I miss it sometimes. You've got guts.
You stayed with it." Sometimes they added, "Why don't
you take a weekend and come up to our condo on the
lake?" The condo line was not kind, or sympathetic.

Cody smiled wearily and twirled the unlit cigarette in
his fingers. Guts? he thought. Maybe staying did take guts.
And maybe that's all he had. Guts. He sure as hell didn't
have the pressed suits and two-hundred-dollar shoes and
company credit cards. They did. The Sellouts. Because
they got out, took the plush jobs, faked anxieties, kissed
kneecaps—maybe more. Maybe he should have left when
they took away the typewriters, when he was still young.
Maybe he should have started a weekly newspaper in the
mountains, where he could have hired housewives and
high school teachers to be reporters, and headlines could
have been about church raffles and reunions. He could
have had a flatbed press, slick with ink, and he could have
had a Linotype and a Ludlow and a handpress for business
cards. And noise. Enough noise to live it. And ashtrays for
fellow smokers.

He looked at his watch again. It was eight-thirty. Maybe
he should tell Halpern that he was sick and wanted to go
home. He needed sleep. He was getting too damn old for
partying. He could go home and sleep through the day
and, at night, watch reruns on television until he slept

again, and tomorrow he would feel better about Halpern and Freda Graves and the noiseless newsroom and the goddamn computers. Halpern could have Temple do the story on the police precinct for Underground Atlanta. Temple was always hanging around, wanting to work the police beat, and there was nothing to the precinct story. A moron could write it blindfolded.

The phone rang and Cody swiveled in his chair and lifted the receiver from its cradle. "Yeah?" he mumbled.

"Yates, get up here."

Cody recognized Harry Dilliard's voice. Harry was the managing editor of *The Atlanta Journal-Constitution*. Harry had authority.

"Yeah, sure," Cody said.

He took the elevator to the seventh floor and walked slowly to Harry Dilliard's glass-enclosed office. He could see Harry and Jack Halpern inside the office, huddled over Harry's desk. Shit, he thought. Halpern's bitching. Probably about his comments over Frank Barton's thumb-sucking retrospective on the Olympics. Frank was a joke. His story had been as deep and as fuzzy as a peach peel.

"You want me to wait?" Cody said in the doorway of the office.

"No," Harry said irritably. "Get in here and close the door."

Cody pushed the door closed and stood before the two men. He could feel the queasiness of his stomach and the rawness of his throat.

"What kind of car you got, Yates?" asked Harry.

Cody's eyes darted warily between the two men. He wanted to tell them it was a Rolls-Royce, but he knew better. It was a joke that he drove disposable cars, but it was also the truth. "Pontiac," he answered. "Why?"

"What's the license number?"

"BDM zero-three-one," Cody said.

"Where's it parked?" Jack Halpern asked.

"In the company lot. What the hell is this? Somebody hit it?"

"Could you tell if they had?" Jack said cynically.

Cody turned to Harry. "What's this about?" he asked.

Harry sat behind his desk. He picked up an envelope and held it. He said, "This was left downstairs this morning. It had my name on it, marked personal."

"So?" Cody said.

"Nobody knows who left it," Harry told him. "It was just there, on the corner of the guard's desk. It could have been anybody."

"And?"

"The note inside said there would be a cassette tape left on the left front tire of your car. It said we were to get it and play it."

"My car?" Cody said. "I just got here thirty—maybe forty—minutes ago."

"Your car," Jack said. "Red LeMans. License number BDM zero-three-one."

"Well, don't look at me, for Christ's sake," Cody said angrily. "I didn't do it."

"We're not saying you did," Harry snapped. "Maybe somebody wants to see us get our ass wet, but we'd better see if there's anything to it."

"Want me to send somebody for it?" Jack Halpern asked.

"We'll all go," Harry said.

The cassette tape was on the top of the tire of the car, protected from the rain by the fender and a plastic sandwich bag.

"Well, that part of it was right," Harry said. He stood under his umbrella and held the bag that Jack Halpern had handed him. The rain rolled in strings of water from the dome of his umbrella.

"I've got a tape deck in the car," Cody told him. "You want to listen to it here?"

Harry glanced into Cody's car, saw the rubble of magazines and books and newspapers and stained coffee cups. "No," he said, slipping the plastic bag into the pocket of his raincoat. He looked hard at Cody. "If we get back and play this thing and it's nothing but Slim Whitman yodeling in high C, I swear I'm going to kick your ass from here to Valdosta."

"Kick what you want," Cody replied bitterly. "I don't know the first damn thing about it."

"Come on, it's wet out here," Harry said.

"Wet? Christ, Harry, you got the umbrella," Cody complained.

"I know," Harry mumbled. He turned quickly and walked away. Cody and Jack Halpern followed, lowering their faces against the rain.

Cody sat in Harry Dilliard's office, drying his face and hair with paper towels he had taken from the men's room. He drank from a second cup of coffee and watched as Harry took a tape recorder from his desk drawer and slipped the tape from the plastic bag into the slot, closed it, and pushed the play button.

There was a long leader of silence, then the popping of static, then the voice: *"This morning a boy named Aaron Greene was abducted near your office building. He is eighteen years old, is five feet eleven inches tall, weighs approximately one hundred and fifty pounds. He lives with his parents at one-one-zero-six Willow Branch in Decatur. He attends Georgia State University in the afternoons and at night, and works at Century National Bank as a mail clerk during the day."*

There was a pause, the sound of tape scraping against the tape head, then: *"You can check this out. It's true. There will be a ransom demand for the boy's safe return. That demand, and all future correspondence, will be made to you, the media. Please understand this is serious. You should confirm our information as soon as possible. Also understand that he will remain in danger until the terms we demand are met. Good day, gentle-men."*

The tape continued to roll, with only the whisper of static. All three men stared at the machine.

"My God," Jack Halpern whispered.

"Am I crazy, or did I hear what I think I heard?" Harry Dilliard said.

Cody nodded once, slowly.

"Jesus, Yates, am I right?" Harry asked anxiously.

"Yes," Cody answered. "The level jumps all over the place, but that was me. That was my voice."

THREE

———◆———

THE ROOM WAS LARGE AND RICHLY AP-
pointed. A king-sized bed was centered against one wall.
The bed was covered by a thick, quilted comforter in the
color of amber, with decorative pillows leaning against the
walnut headboard. Night tables containing slender ceramic
lamps with brass trimmings were at each side of the bed.
Portrait art imitating the period of the Old Masters was
selectively spaced on the walls of the room in heavy, distinctive framing, with ceiling pinspots subtly lighting each
painting.

Four doors led from the room—one into the corridor,
one into a spacious bath and dressing room, one into a
steam room, and one into a library walled by bookshelves
filled with leather-bound books. A full bay window in the
library overlooked a garden of weeping willow with pale,
unfolding spring leaves and redbud with purpling tips and
sculptured boxwood and azalea and a tall statue of a nude
woman resembling a work from the Roman period. A
writing table and two cushioned reading chairs were beneath the bay window.

Of the four doors leading from the bedroom, the one
leading into the corridor was locked. The door leading
from the library to the garden was also locked.

Aaron Greene sat on the foot of the bed, his arms
crossed tight against his chest. The room intimidated him.

The room was too large, too expensive. He did not know how long he had been in the room. Hours. No one had spoken to him since he had been led, blindfolded, into the house and into the room. He had heard the barking of dogs and the subdued playing of music from somewhere beyond the walls. And voices. He had heard the voices of men and of one woman. The woman would be the one who called herself Alyse, he thought.

They had not spoken on the long, blind ride to the house. The man in the backseat with him—the man named Morris—had forced him to push his face into the crease of the seat and his body had been covered with a blanket. Then, out of the city, in a wooded area, they had stopped the car and blindfolded him. But they had been careful not to hurt him. He had sensed surprising kindness from the people who had taken him from the street.

Aaron moved on the bed, sitting forward. He folded his hands, left palm over right thigh, right palm over his left hand, in a gesture of anxiety that had been his habit since childhood. It was a gesture mimicked from his mother. He looked at his left wrist and realized he did not have his watch. He had left his watch on the dresser of his bedroom—a blunder of oversleeping. He did not know what time it was. Perhaps noon. The morning rain had stopped and a searing, brilliant sun had burned through the cloud cover, and outside, through the bay window, the day appeared warm and comfortable. He wondered if his parents knew he had been kidnapped. Yes, he reasoned. Someone would have told them. Perhaps his superiors at the bank would have called, asking why he was not at work. Perhaps the people who had taken him from the street would have called, asking for a ransom payment. Someone would know. Someone.

It was strange that he was not afraid, but he wasn't. He was only tired.

He slipped from the bed and walked tentatively across the room and then into the library. The library was a warm, comforting room, paneled above and below the bookshelves in an aged mahogany. He felt protected in the library, somehow isolated from the uncertainty beyond the locked corridor door of the bedroom. He could smell the odor of books and the sweetness of new grass and new tree leaves seeping into the room through the unseen slivers of cracks around the glass of the bay window. The library calmed Aaron, made him feel oddly secure.

He stood behind one of the reading chairs, near the window, and stared outside. He saw a redbird fly into a lush matting of grass, peck aimlessly at the ground, then fly away. Why had they taken him? he wondered. His parents did not have money or valuables. And they had not taken him at random. The woman Alyse had called his name, knew where he worked, knew his job. They had taken him deliberately, with reason.

He heard, from the bedroom, a knock at the door and then the push of a key into the metal lock and the opening and closing of the door.

"Aaron?"

It was the woman, Alyse. Her voice was relaxed, almost playful.

"You in the library?" Alyse asked, calling. He knew she was crossing the room. He turned from the window and crossed his arms nervously over his chest. She stood in the doorway, holding a tray of food. She still wore the sunglasses. "You must be hungry," she said.

She entered the library and placed the tray on the reading table. "I'm sorry," she continued. "I didn't mean to leave you alone for so long. It's almost one." She pulled away a cloth napkin covering the tray. The tray contained a small soup tureen, two bowls, sandwiches, two glasses filled with milk, two plates, silverware, two neatly folded napkins. "I hope you like soup and tuna sandwiches," she added cheerfully. "It's what we're having." She lifted the covering from the tureen and began dipping soup into the bowls with a delicately curved ladle. "I thought I'd eat with you." She looked up. "You don't mind, do you?"

Aaron shook his head slightly. He mumbled, "No."

"Good," Alyse said. "I don't like eating alone. I don't think anyone does, really."

He watched her closely as she prepared the table for the meal. She seemed different. Her hair was deep red. In the car, her hair had been brunette, or it had seemed brunette. And she appeared older. In her late thirties, perhaps. In the car, she had appeared much younger.

"Let's eat," she said pleasantly. "And talk. I know you've got questions."

Aaron moved hesitantly to the table and sat in one of the cushioned reading chairs and watched as she tasted the soup in a ceremony that was theatrical.

"Good," she said in approval of the soup. "Maria made it. She's our cook. She makes an oxtail ragout you wouldn't believe. I'll have her make some this week. You'll see, Aaron. It's really something."

"Why—am I here?" Aaron asked suddenly.

Alyse looked up and smiled. "Do you know what we know about you, Aaron? Almost everything. But we don't know what you like to eat. We simply couldn't find a good way to research it. You'll have to tell us. Whatever it is, Maria can prepare it. Whatever you want."

"Why am I here?" Aaron asked again.

Alyse leaned forward in her chair and laced her fingers. Her sunglasses were aimed at his face. She said quietly, "You were chosen, Aaron. Two years ago, when you were a junior in high school."

"I—I don't know what that means," Aaron said.

"It means you were selected over other candidates. You were the person we wanted."

"Why?"

"A number of reasons. Who you are. Your childhood. Your parents. Your work. A number of reasons. You'll understand more about it later."

"My parents don't—have any money," Aaron said nervously.

Alyse smiled. "We know," she said gently. "They're good people. We know a lot about them also. Don't worry, Aaron. This has nothing to do with your parents. They won't be bothered."

"Do they know?" Aaron asked.

"Yes," Alyse told him. "We saw the police go to your house earlier. Around ten. They know."

Aaron sat back in the chair and looked away from the woman named Alyse and from the eyes he could not see behind the sunglasses. The sensation of his parents—their confusion—made him shudder.

"I know you're worried," Alyse said quietly. "We can't stop that. But you don't have to be. You don't have to worry. Nothing will happen to your parents, or to you, regardless of what you hear or think. You'll understand that later. I promise."

Aaron did not reply. He moved uncomfortably in the chair, placed the palm of his left hand on his right thigh, with the palm of his right hand resting on his left hand. He could not quell the chilling convulsions of fear that fluttered in his body.

Alyse stood and walked to him and kneeled beside his chair. She touched his arm and stroked it gently. She said, "We took you, Aaron, not only because of *who* you are, but *what* you are. What all of us are. I could tell you all of it, but you wouldn't understand. Not now. And maybe you never will. Maybe we're wrong about things." Her voice became a whisper. "There are a lot of maybes, Aaron. But you must understand that we're committed to this. We know the risks. We're willing to take them. All of them." She stood and moved to the window and looked out into the garden.

"Who are you?" Aaron asked after a moment.

Alyse turned back to him. "People, Aaron. You've seen Morris and Robert. But there are others. It's almost—

almost like a club. You may or may not see the others."

"How—long will I be here?"

"A few days, a few weeks. We don't know. It depends on other people. People beyond our control."

"Can I—?"

"What, Aaron?"

"Call my parents?" he said.

Alyse shook her head. "No," she answered. "Not directly. The lines would be monitored. But we'll want you to make some tapes, say whatever you wish. We'll do that this afternoon. That'll let them know." She smiled again, a bright, comforting smile. "Look, I promise you'll be well taken care of. I know it's hard, but I want you to relax. In the dressing area of the bathroom, in the closet, you'll find clothes. Your size. You have the bedroom, the steam room, the library. Later, we'll go outside for walks. You'll like it here. I do. It's a wonderful place. Now I want you to eat. I'll leave you and come back later. If you need anything, just pick up the telephone and push zero. Someone will answer." She added, "It's only an internal line, though."

"Are you—?"

"What, Aaron? Ask it."

"Are you going to kill me?"

The smile on the face of Alyse faded, became sad. She crossed to Aaron and touched his face and then lightly kissed him on the forehead. "No," she whispered. "I told you: You won't be harmed." She turned and left the room.

FOUR

———◆———

THE BAR-S CORRAL WAS A TAVERN ON Steward Avenue, south of downtown Atlanta, a street with a reputation well earned and never overstated. The tavern was small and dimly lighted and smelled of stale cigarette smoke and spilled beer and lingering cologne. It had a jukebox beside the cigarette machine and a dance floor in a dark corner. Its motif was imitation Western. Saddles and holsters and ten-gallon hats and lariats and chaps and spurs hung from wooden pegs jabbed into clapboard walls. A large print of Indians chasing buffalo in the red dust of a canyon was behind the bar, above a row of bottles with metal pouring spouts curving from the tops like silver beaks on caged birds. The bartender, in his sixties, wore jeans and a Western shirt with pearl snap buttons. His hair had a dyed orange tint. A flowered bandanna was draped around his neck. The waitresses wore low-cut Western blouses with uplift bras to hold the flabby, teasing flesh of their breasts. Their jeans were skin-tight, tucked into Western boots.

Cody Yates had never been inside the Bar-S Corral. He had selected it by whim. He cared only that it was south of Atlanta, away from his apartment on Highland Avenue. He did not want to be at his apartment. Or at the newsroom. Or at any of the bars he often frequented at night. He wanted to be alone, a stranger in a remote place. The

Bar-S Corral was remote. In its imitation dressing, the Bar-S Corral could have been in any city in America.

It was late in the afternoon, the day dimming to sunset. Cody had a scotch and water on the table, but the scotch was inferior and tasteless and he ignored it. He did not want the drink, had ordered it out of habit. His early-morning hangover had eased only slightly. He had asked the waitress for six plastic swizzle sticks—sticks with round, flat heads on one end, the Bar-S logo imprinted on one side—and he held one and struck his lighter and played the stick over the flame until it began to curl, and then he picked up a second swizzle stick and carefully fused it to the first. In a few minutes, working with his lighter to bend and shape the sticks, burning the tips of his fingers, dipping them in the scotch to cool them, he had fashioned together a rough likeness of a stick man that he called Don Quixote. It was Cody's way of avoiding boredom. In the years that he had wasted time alone in bars, he had created enough Don Quixotes to open a museum.

He lit a cigarette and watched it burn in the cup of the ashtray. Got to quit smoking, he thought. Got to. Millie had bitched about it all the time, and now, when he saw her, Sabrina also bitched, bitched the way a ten-year-old bitches—with soft, pleading eyes and rote, learned-in-school lectures that were annoyingly sensible.

The burning cigarette mesmerized Cody. He saw in the blue-silver screen of its swirling smoke the faces of Millie and Sabrina. He wondered what they would say about the thing with the voice when the news got out. Maybe I should call Millie, tell her, he thought. And maybe that would help. They were friends. Sometimes, when there was no reason for bitterness, they talked for hours. She had a way of reviving him.

The song from the jukebox was Kenny Rogers's woeful tale of a philosophic gambler. Cody heard rough laughter from a table across the room and the sassy, practiced voice of the perfumed waitress: "Wishing's as far as you're gonna get."

He was tired. He had spent the day being questioned about Aaron Greene. No one believed him. No one. Not Harry Dilliard nor Jack Halpern nor the heavy-faced agents from the Federal and Georgia Bureaus of Investigation nor the officers from the City of Atlanta Police Department. He had no idea how, or when, his voice had been recorded, or by whom. And certainly he had no idea why. But none of them had believed him.

"You doing all right, honey?"

Cody nodded to the waitress.

"You need anything, you let me know."

"Sure."

"That's a cute little man," she said.

"Thanks," Cody mumbled. "You can have him."

The waitress smiled and leaned across the table to pick up Don Quixote. The flesh of her uplift breasts quivered seductively. "You look done in," she said.

"Just a little."

"Honey, I know the feeling," the waitress said, turning to leave.

Cody fingered the rim of his drink glass. Not even Menotti believed him, he thought. Jesus, not even Menotti, and he had known Menotti for years. Menotti had been in his wedding. They had played poker together. He was one of the few people who ever addressed Menotti by his first name—Victor. Once he had written an article on Menotti after Menotti had taken an assault rifle away from a crazed woman determined to kill her husband's lover. The article had embarrassed Menotti. "Makes me sound like Clint Eastwood," he had complained mildly to Cody. "Next thing I know, some kid in grade school will be trying to take me out with a cap pistol."

He had requested that Menotti be present for the questioning about Aaron Greene—a familiar face among demanding strangers. Menotti had asked one question: "If you don't know this kid, and you say that's your voice on the tape, how the hell did you say his name?"

The question had angered Cody. "How the hell do I know?" he had snapped in answer. "I say a lot of names. I'm in the goddamn name business."

But it was a sensible question. The fact that his telephone had been tapped was hardly worth investigation. Had been for months, guessed the FBI. What was the man's name? Oglesbee. Something Oglesbee. He looked FBI. He was black, but he looked like Robert Stack, for God's sake. Something Oglesbee had said the use of his voice was the same as someone cutting letters out of magazines and pasting them together to make messages. "They had a damn good operation," Something Oglesbee had pronounced. "A good cutter. Whoever did that could edit a fart out of a tornado, so we know we're dealing with at least one pro."

Getting Greene would have been easy. He was sure he had said the word "green" over the past few months.

The grass is green.

I like green eyes.

I'm green with envy.

Greene would have been easy.

But Aaron? When in hell had he said the name Aaron?

George Jones moaned nasally from the jukebox. The Bar-S Corral thickened with smoke. Cody sipped from the tasteless, watery drink and turned in his chair to look across the room at the dance floor. He saw a couple grinding into one another, pelvis into pelvis. The woman's arms were locked around the man's neck and the man's hands stroked her lower back. The dance looked like a mating ritual from some television show on nature. He remembered what a friend had said about dancing to country music: "They don't dance to the music. They dance to the lyrics. The sadder it is, the closer they get."

Hank Aaron? Maybe that was it. Maybe he'd said something about Hank Aaron. Hank Aaron had been a prominent figure in Atlanta since breaking Babe Ruth's home run record with the Braves, and his picture constantly appeared in the papers. Maybe he had said something to Spence Waller about Hank Aaron. Spence had been obsessed with the Olympics, had tried to get a pool together on who would trot the torch into the stadium during opening ceremonies. Spence had guessed Aaron. Maybe he had said to Spence, "Aaron? Not in a million years." Something like that. Something to annoy Spence. It would have been enough. One clear, clean, plucked Aaron, scissored and stored, like a vital donor organ. Duplicated, it could be used a thousand times if necessary.

But Cody could not remember talking to Spence about Hank Aaron. Hell, he couldn't remember talking to Spence about anything. Spence was a boil on the butt of humanity. He had to be around Spence because of the newsroom, but he had kept his conversations limited to nods and grunts. It couldn't have been Spence, or Hank Aaron.

Maybe he had mentioned Aaron Copland. He loved Copland's music.

Cody lit another cigarette. He took his pen from his jacket and printed Aaron Copland's name on a napkin. Possible, he decided. More than possible. He had been talking about Aaron Copland recently. Where? With whom? He drew from his cigarette, traced over Aaron Copland's name again. Millie? Yes, it was Millie. They had talked about American composers. Millie had completed a course in music appreciation and had argued that only Aaron Copland could be considered a great American composer, and he had agreed, which had surprised him. He never agreed with Millie. Mostly on principle. Millie was remarkably passionate in her convictions. Arguing with her was like mainstreaming adrenaline. But he had agreed about Copland, and his knowledge of American composers was nonexistent. He liked Copland's music. Plain and simple. Just that.

It made sense. Snip. Snip. Splice. Splice. Aaron Copland had become Aaron Greene. He would have to ask Millie, make sure it happened during a telephone conversation. Millie would know. Millie remembered in exasperating, exacting detail everything she had ever said or everything ever said to her.

"Honey, you sure you all right?" The waitress stood beside him, balancing a drink tray on her spreading fingertips. "You look like you lost your best friend."

"Naw, not that," Cody told her.

"You not hiding from the law, are you?" she asked flippantly, but guarded.

"Not on purpose," Cody said. "Why? Do I look like it?"

The waitress took a damp cloth from her tray and wiped it over Cody's table, leaning close to him. She said in a whisper, "Man at the table near the door. He's been watching you for a half hour, I'd guess. Looks law to me. Just wondered."

Cody turned in his chair and looked across the room. Menotti. Menotti slumped in a chair, his deadpan face staring straight ahead. "You're a perceptive woman," he said to the waitress. "What's he drinking?"

"Brandy."

"Pour two and bring them over."

Victor Menotti's expression did not change as Cody slipped into the chair across from him at the table. He appeared oblivious to the noise of the Bar-S Corral.

"This coincidental?" Cody asked. "Or is this where you do your courting these days?"

Menotti snorted a laugh. "I'm invisible," he said. "You're not supposed to know I'm here."

"You should have left the neon tubing at home."

"Yeah, well, what the hell," Menotti sighed. He drained the brandy from his glass.

"I thought you had peasants to do your legwork," Cody said.

Menotti looked at him incredulously. "You don't think it was me that's been puttering around after you, do you? Good God, Yates. You've got one hell of an inflated sense of worth. All I did was show up when they called me."

The waitress placed the two glasses of brandy on the table. She smiled nervously at Menotti, then left.

"Great tits," Menotti said unemotionally.

"Nice enough," Cody replied.

"Never did understand how that works, exactly," Menotti mused. "Someday I'm going to take one of those bras over to the boys at Georgia Tech and see if they've got an engineer who can explain it."

"It's the effect that matters," Cody said.

"I guess," Menotti mumbled. He lifted his glass and saluted Cody and drank from it. "Lousy brandy," he said bitterly. "You'd think they'd bring out the good stuff for a cop. Ought to be some kind of law against swill."

"Make one up," Cody said. "You'd probably get by with it."

"My, my," Menotti clucked. "A little tense, are we? How's Millie?"

Cody's face colored in anger. "I have no idea," he said, controlling himself. "I haven't seen her in a couple of weeks, not since Sabrina's birthday."

"Talk to her much?"

"Is this an inquisition?" snapped Cody.

"It's a question, asshole," Menotti growled. "Chitchat. The kind of obligatory nonsense that people engage in to avoid saying something stupid."

"You still don't believe me, do you?" Cody said.

A smile cracked over Menotti's face. "Like I said," he replied lightly. "Something stupid. Sure I believe you. But they don't. They think you're some kind of glory-seeker." He looked at Cody and winked. "They don't know you as well as I do, Cody. You're too damn lazy to pull off something like this. But you got to admit, it's classic."

"You know anything more than I do?" asked Cody.

"Of course I do," Menotti answered. "I'm a cop. I know a lot more than you do. You're a goddamn typist. What do you expect to know?"

"Share the wealth, Victor," Cody said wearily. "I didn't crawl off to this end of town to get lost, only to hide for a while."

Menotti pulled up in his chair and shook a cigarette free from its package and lit it. He had the handsome dark face of an Italian, with dark eyes that flickered his moods like strobe lights. He leaned his elbows on the table and looked at Cody. "I know it's not a college prank. I know the boy's been jerked up by somebody, or a lot of somebodies, with an agenda. I know it's not because they can expect anything out of his parents. I went out there today. Nothing, Cody. I mean, nothing. House must have cost them seventy-five or eighty K. The old man makes about forty-five a year. Works for a department store, keeping books. One of those kind who never says a word. Brown-bags it every day. Eats at his desk. The mother's like a spook. She could barely talk."

"Maybe she's worried," Cody said bluntly.

"She's scared shitless. Wouldn't you be?" Menotti said. "But that's not the point. She'd be that way if Ed Mc-Mahon dropped ten million off on her front porch."

"What're you saying?"

"Whoever got the kid didn't do it because his folks are loaded. And they didn't do it because the kid's famous. Christ, I couldn't even get a good description of him out of his neighbors. I couldn't get the name of a friend from his folks—not one. Think of that, Yates. Not one good friend. I went to his old high school. Told them the same thing we told the neighbors, that we were running a check on him for a government job. Not a teacher over there remembered him until I showed them his picture, and even then they were vague."

"When did he graduate?" asked Cody.

"That's the kicker. Last year. It's like that scene out of

The Last Picture Show. Remember? The one at the football game, when the team's doing great, and this guy says something like 'I used to play,' and the other guy says, 'When?' and the first guy answers, 'Last year.' Jesus. I thought about that. Can you believe it? A kid that was there a year ago and they didn't remember him. Christ, they should have voted him Mr. Nobody, or Most Likely to Be Forgotten."

"Then why?" Cody said. "Why him?"

Menotti shrugged with a tilt of his head. "I guess we'll find out soon enough. But that's not the thing that keeps bugging me, old friend. There's another question, just as big."

"What?"

"Why you, Cody?"

"Me?"

"You." Menotti's eyes read Cody's face carefully.

Cody pressed his palms over the lacquered top of the table. He said, "I don't know, Victor. I wish I could tell you. You know me. You know damn well I didn't stage this."

"I know," Menotti said dispassionately. "But there's got to be something. There's got to be a reason." He stretched against the back of the chair and drew on his cigarette.

"What did you find out at the bank?" Cody asked.

"Nothing," Menotti answered. "We didn't even go over there. Oglesbee had one of his people call and say the boy was sick." He flicked ash toward the ashtray, missed. He added, "That's one thing we agreed on. No need to get those chest-thumping bastards on their high horse until we have to. The kid delivered mail. That was it."

"Could it have anything to do with the fact that he's Jewish?"

Menotti rolled his cigarette dead in the ashtray. "It's a thought," he admitted. "The African Prince is sniffing it out."

"Who?"

"Oglesbee. That's what they call him. Looks like a prince, like one of those Hollywood actors they'd dress up to play a field hand, but the guy speaks like Richard Burton doing *Hamlet*. Anyway, that's what they call Oglesbee—the African Prince."

"What about you? You think there's anything to it— the Jewish angle?"

Menotti wagged his head. He said casually, "We picked up there was a little trouble in the neighborhood when they moved in. Nothing serious. Used to be hard-line WASP out there. The principal at the school told me there'd been a little harassing of Jews—teenage Klan stuff—but he kicked some ass and it stopped."

"I see a skinhead now and then," Cody said. "They scare the shit out of me."

"Yeah, well, they just want some ink, Yates. Just like everybody else." He looked at Cody. "Story still coming out tomorrow?"

"Yeah," Cody told him. "But it's on hold, in case anything else happens."

"You write it?"

Cody glared at Menotti. "What do you think? Of course not. They gave it to Temple."

"Amos Temple? Bright young man. Hell of a writer. He's my favorite. That boy writes like an angel," Menotti said, smiling.

"You're loving this, aren't you?" Cody said.

"With passion," Menotti answered. "What I can't believe is that they actually went along with the African Prince and held off on it today." He laughed. "Maybe they think we'll nail you before the night's over and that'll make better print. I get the feeling, old friend, that your star has faded a bit in the hallowed halls of Fishwrapper, Inc."

"Kiss my ass, Menotti."

"And put a glow on your face? I don't think so. By the way, did the bureau boys tell you anything about the tap?"

"Nothing," Cody said sourly. "One of them said he guessed it was from my home phone."

"Well, now, that's what I'd call brilliant deducing. Must be J. Edgar's kinfolk," Menotti said. "You talk a lot of business at home?"

Cody rolled his shoulders. "Some. Yeah. Sure. I'd rather work there."

"Way you talk, Cody, they've probably got a thousand miles of tape to cut from."

Cody ignored the comment. He said, "I assume somebody's checking the studios in town. If whoever did the cut is as good as all of you seem to think, it ought to narrow the field."

Menotti smirked. "Yeah, I think they've got James Bond working on it," he said cynically. "No, my boy, they won't find him that way. Believe me. And the only prints on the tape belonged to you clowns. Otherwise, it must have been steam-cleaned. Now let me tell you a couple of things."

"Such as?"

"If I find out you're jerking me around, Cody, you're going to find out just how annoying I can be."

"I'm terrified," Cody said dryly.

"You better be. But I'm not finished."

"I'm listening."

"The best chance you've got to come out of this with even a shred of credibility is to trust me. You tell me everything that happens, and I don't give a happy hoot in hell what it is. You go around me to those pressed-suit assholes from the bureaus and I'll run your little pecker through so many wringers it'll look like parchment paper."

Cody's face flushed red. "Christ, Menotti, are you threatening me?"

Menotti nodded. "I am. That's exactly what I'm doing. One other thing."

"What?"

"You didn't see me tonight. I followed you like the

proverbial shadow, only better. I stayed in your pocket until after you left this godforsaken place and then I tucked you in bed and you had no idea it was me. I was so clever at all this horseshit you thought a bleached-blond whore had French-kissed you to sleep. And for that, you can have the joy of paying for these drinks. I'm going home. My ass is dragging."

"You're a good man, Menotti," Cody said wearily. "A saint."

"Yeah, I know. By the way, before you leave, see if you can find out how those bras work." He looked toward the waitress and flashed a smile. "Great knockers," he said. "Great knockers."

FIVE

———————•———————

THE MAN WHO SAT ACROSS FROM AARON AT
the writing table was Robert—had said to him, "Hello,
Aaron, you remember me, don't you? Robert"—but he
did not look the same as he had looked that morning in
the car. He wore half-glasses in a horn-rimmed frame. His
voice was clipped, the sound of someone from England.
He wore a tuxedo. The bud of a rose, its crimson petals
closed like a fist, was pinned to the lapel of his jacket.

"It's really simple, Aaron," Robert said. "It's a regular
tape recorder, just like the one you have at home." He
looked up from the machine and smiled at Aaron. "You
do have one?"

Aaron nodded. He looked at Alyse. She stood behind
Robert. She, too, was dressed formally—a white gown
with delicate lace covering the sleeves and gathering at her
throat. She smiled warmly.

"See, I knew it," Robert exulted. "All young chaps
have a tape recorder. Couldn't get along without one."
He handed Aaron a small microphone. "Now, I'm going
to turn it on and I want you to say anything you wish.
We'll make sure it gets to your parents."

"Just talk, Aaron," urged Alyse. "You don't have to
worry about how it sounds, or anything like that. And
take your time. If you want to stop and start again, Robert
can do that."

35

"Ready?" Robert asked.

Aaron bobbed his head slightly.

"Good," Robert said. He pressed the record button on the recorder. Aaron could hear the soft scraping of the tape against the tape head. Alyse watched him calmly.

"Uh, Mom, Dad," Aaron began. "I—I know you're worried about me, but—but it's all right. I'm all right. I'm in a—in a big place. The people are—" He paused and looked at Robert and then at Alyse. Both nodded approval. "The people are—have been good to me. I've got plenty to eat. Don't worry about me. I—don't know what's happening, but I feel—all right. I—I guess I'll talk to you again sometime."

Robert pushed the stop button on the recorder. "Very good," he said enthusiastically. "I told you it'd be easy. Next time, you can say more if you wish. Tell them about your new wardrobe, about the books, or the view. Do you like the view, Aaron?"

Aaron looked out of the bay window of the library. It was dark, but the garden was lighted. It seemed peaceful. "Yes," Aaron said.

"Good," Alyse replied. "Tomorrow morning we'll go for a walk. Maybe play croquet. Have you ever played croquet, Aaron?"

Aaron shook his head. He continued to look into the garden.

"No?" Robert said. "Well, then, we'll teach you. It's fun. You'll see."

Aaron turned to Alyse. "How long am I going to stay here?" he asked.

Alyse moved to the chair near Aaron and sat. Aaron realized that her eyes were green. He had not seen her eyes. She had always worn the sunglasses. She reached for his hand and held it, as she would hold a child's hand for comfort. She said quietly, "We don't know. Not long, I hope. But it could be. We'll know more soon. Very soon. Perhaps by tomorrow night. But while you're here, we want you to be as comfortable as possible. I'm sorry we have to keep you—secured. But you can do almost anything you wish, except read newspapers or listen to the radio or watch television."

"Why?" Aaron asked.

"We think it's best," Alyse answered.

"She's right, lad," Robert added. "No reason to get upset by all the goings-on outside these walls." He laughed easily. "You know how it is with the newsboys. They like to make horror stories out of everything, now don't they?" He stood and picked up the tape recorder. "Why don't you read a bit from one of the books, or take a rest? We're expected at dinner." He paused. "Have you eaten?" He looked at Alyse. "Has he had dinner?"

"Yes," Alyse said. "Earlier, though he didn't eat very much."

"It'll take time," Robert said merrily. Then, to Aaron: "But you're letting waste some of the finest food in the country. Believe me. If you want anything later—some ice cream or a piece of pie or something—just pick up your phone and tell them to send for Robert." He smiled. "And you know that's me."

Alyse stood and leaned to Aaron and kissed him tenderly on the forehead. "Rest," she whispered.

The dining room was large, with a high ceiling bordered by mahogany crown molding. A single Cézanne decorated one of the long sidewalls, a tapestry of a foxhunt dominated the other. A formal dining table was in the center of the room, with a large crystal chandelier above it. The chandelier glittered from a nest of clear, bright bulbs. The table was covered in a white linen cloth and contained three flower arrangements evenly spaced. There were five formal place settings of crystal and china and silverware—two settings on each side and one at the end of the table near a double door leading into a sitting room.

Alyse and Robert entered the dining room from the

kitchen. Two other people, both dressed formally, were already at the table, standing beside chairs. One was Morris, the other a small, delicate, youthful woman. Alyse and Robert did not speak. They crossed quickly, but quietly, to their places and stood beside their chairs. A servant, old and dignified, stood beside the double doors leading to the sitting room. He waited a moment, scanned the room, then turned stiffly and left through the double doors. A moment later, the doors opened again and the servant pushed a wheelchair with a high, ornately carved wooden back through them and guided it to the head of the table. The man in the wheelchair—also old, slightly bent at the shoulders, his white hair shining under the light of the chandelier—was dressed in a white tuxedo. He looked around the table. A smile eased across his mouth. He nodded once and the company sat obediently, men assisting the women.

"My back is giving me a little fight tonight," the old man in the wheelchair said. "Oscar insisted on wheeling me in." He looked up at the servant. "What's the soup, Oscar?" he asked hoarsely.

"It's an onion broth, sir," the servant named Oscar answered politely.

"Good, good," the old man enthused. "You may serve it."

"Of course," Oscar replied. He left the room.

The four people at the table with the old man sat erect in their chairs, their faces turned toward him.

"And how's our young guest?" the old man said, looking at Alyse.

"A little confused, but otherwise fine," Alyse answered. "He isn't eating well."

"That'll come, that'll come," the old man said. His body rocked in a body nod. "Did you get the tape?"

"Yes sir," Robert replied proudly. "He was a bit nervous, but he did it."

"And what did you do with it?" the old man asked patiently.

"Destroyed it, of course," Alyse answered.

"Very good," the old man said. "You've done a fine job with him," he added. Then: "What would you like to hear tonight, Alyse? I think you should make the selection."

A blush colored Alyse's face. She smiled joyfully. "Rachmaninoff," she said. "I love the way you play Rachmaninoff."

"Rachmaninoff. Yes, I enjoy Rachmaninoff," the old man said softly. "I met him once, when I was a boy. Yes, it's a good evening for Rachmaninoff."

Aaron lay across the bed and listened to the distant sound of the piano—a lulling, haunting sound, vigorous, but muted. The sound seeped into him, locked in his mind. He did not know that in another section of the house, in a spacious, richly appointed sitting room with a grand piano elevated as a centerpiece, Ewell Pender was playing a difficult selection from Sergey Vasilyevich Rachmaninoff as four people, seated comfortably in arm chairs, listened attentively.

SIX

———————◆———————

CODY YATES DID NOT SLEEP WELL. HE HAD called Millie at midnight, waking her, and she had screamed at him for missing Sabrina's softball game the night before and he had simply apologized and accepted the abuse. It was deserved. He had forgotten about the game. "You can go rot in hell," Millie had hissed, and she had slammed the telephone violently, leaving a shrill buzzing in his ear. He knew, as he sat on the side of the bed holding the telephone, that the rest of the night would be fitful, miserable. He arose early, showered, dressed, and drove into the city before the morning crowd began its invasion. He stopped at a McDonald's for coffee and an Egg McMuffin, wondering if he was still being followed by the City of Atlanta police or one of the bureaus. Probably, he thought, but he did not care. He had covered too many stories on the police beat to worry about it. Christ, how many times had he been with Menotti on a spy mission? Enough to be bored by it. It was tiresome work—sitting, watching, following, recording little tell-tale notes—and most of it was worthless, even when they cornered a drug lord with one hand on the money and the other on the goods, or when they pulled in some poor unsuspecting conventioneer for negotiating a moment or two of out-of-town pleasure with a sidewalk hooker. There was always an incensed lawyer sputtering about

40

technicalities, irritating the system until the system shrugged off the incident. If he was being followed, Cody concluded, let them note that I dribbled coffee on my shirt.

Of the coffee stain, Cody uttered, "Shit."

The story that Amos Temple had written of Aaron Greene's kidnapping was on Cody's desk, in an envelope marked "Private." He opened it and read. The story was straightforward, with a short sidebar on Ruth and Nathan Greene. By agreement, there was no mention of the tape of Cody's voice. The FBI agent Oglesbee—Temple's story gave his first name: Philip—had insisted that details of the tape be kept secret, at least until a second tape arrived. The decision did not bother Cody. He knew what would happen when the media learned that his voice had been used to communicate information. He would be hounded unmercifully. He would be accused of grandstanding. The callers to radio talk shows would offer suggestions that he had kidnapped Aaron Greene and the whole thing was nothing more than a stunt in a media war.

Amos Temple's story was as simple and as factual as it could be, but Cody knew the headline that would blare across the front page of the *Journal* with its loud, dark-lettered voice would make the story more sensational than its words merited, and the questions would begin. Why Aaron Greene? He was as nondescript as a human could be. And what did the kidnappers want? Was it anti-Semitic terrorism?

Cody sat at his desk and watched his coworkers wander into the newsroom. No one spoke to him and he spoke to no one. At least it's been kept quiet, he reasoned. That, too, was by agreement. No one except those necessarily involved would know of the kidnapping, not until the pressure of silence exploded, and that would be soon enough. Harry Dilliard had scheduled a meeting of his editors at eight o'clock, and he would tell them, and the story would then flutter across the newsroom like a flash fire. By nine o'clock it would be plated for the metro edition. The only thing that could change the schedule would be another message from Aaron Greene's abductors.

The soft clicking of a keyboard near him caused Cody to turn. Freda Graves was working on a story that was probably meaningless, her eyes narrowed on the terminal with an intense stare, and he wondered if he had ever been as intense. Maybe. He pinched a cigarette from its package and put it between his lips. He wanted to call Millie, to apologize. He made a promise that he would send flowers to Sabrina.

The wino appeared in the lobby of the Journal-Constitution Building at seven-ten. He had an envelope in his hand and he wandered self-consciously across the lobby to the guard's desk.

"Come on, buddy, get out of here," the guard growled.

"Got to leave this," the wino said.

"What is it?"

"Fellow said to leave it," the wino answered. He looked over the shoulder of the guard to two men in business suits. He knew they were from the police. "He give me ten dollars," he added, offering the envelope to the guard.

"Who's it for?" the guard asked.

"Fellow said leave it," the wino replied. He began to back away. His red, watery eyes stayed on the two men in business suits.

"Just a minute, friend," one of the men said. "Let's take a look at this."

The guard passed the envelope to him and the man read the name printed on it: "Cody Yates." He nodded and the other man beside him moved quickly from behind the guard's desk and took the wino by the arm. He said, "Come on, friend. Why don't you and I go have a little talk."

The wino's eyes squeezed in fright. He looked toward the door. His hands began to shake.

It was seven-forty when Philip Oglesbee arrived and the tape was played in Harry Dilliard's office. Cody Yates's voice said: *"By now you know we are not lying. We have the boy. We want ten million dollars from the Century National Bank, to be delivered at a time and site to be named later. This demand should be published or the next tape will go to radio stations throughout the area."*

The voice ended and Harry pushed the stop button.

"The bank," Harry said in astonishment. He sat back heavily in his chair. "They want money from the damned bank."

"The bank's got it," Philip Oglesbee said dryly. "Not the Greenes." He shook his head and sighed cynically. "This is a new one."

"The bank's not going to hand over ten million dollars for a mailboy nobody's ever heard of," Harry said. "Don't they know that?"

"Maybe they do," Philip Oglesbee said. "Maybe they know that better than we do." He looked suspiciously at Cody. "What do you think?"

"I don't think anything," Cody replied calmly. "I'm not the message, just the messenger."

"Sure," Philip Oglesbee said. "Sure." Then: "At least we know. I would have put money on some neo-Nazi thing. Those assholes are popping up everywhere." He paused, then added sternly, "That's not a quote. It's not even a thought any longer."

Harry was suddenly on his feet. He looked at the clock on the wall behind his desk. "Have we got time for a rewrite before the first edition?" he asked anxiously.

"Not for the first," Jack Halpern replied quickly. "We had it planned for the metro. You want us to try to re-plate?"

"I don't want anybody to call the bank before we can talk to them," Philip Oglesbee said.

Harry turned to face Philip. "I won't hold off on this any longer," he replied. "The tape came here. Both of them. One was addressed to me, the other to one of our employees. I believe that narrows the field of ownership."

"If we don't replate, if we wait for the metro, we've got a little time," Jack suggested.

"Give me until nine-thirty," Philip said evenly.

Harry turned back to the clock. He glanced through the glass wall of his office, saw the curious stares of office staff. "All right," he said after a moment. "Nine-thirty. We'll be on the phone then. It's going to take some time to put it all together anyway." He looked at Amos Temple. "How long do you need?"

"Thirty minutes," Amos answered. There was a tittering of excitement in his voice. "I can have it wrapped, everything but a quote from the bank. We can drop that in at the last minute, maybe even lead with it." Amos was young, talented, ambitious.

"Get it right," warned Jack Halpern.

"He will," Harry said coolly. He looked at Philip Oglesbee. "You know we have to do it," he added.

Philip tilted his head, shrugged. He was watching Cody. "You going to say whose voice is on the tape?" he asked.

"We have to," Harry told him. "I think Yates ought to do a sidebar, a first-person piece on his reaction. We can put it on the front, under the fold."

Harry was in command. The reporter's energy surged in him. A story was in his grasp and he was squeezing his fist around it. Harry had never liked being the managing editor. He wanted to report. A good story was like a good hunt, with the prey running itself into submission. Harry liked the hunt.

"All hell's going to break loose when it hits the street," Jack Halpern said fretfully. "Every radio and television station in town's going to storm this place."

A greedy smile cracked on Harry's face. He said, "We'll have a press conference, at twelve-thirty. The metro edition will be on the street by then."

Philip Oglesbee's dark eyes narrowed. He lifted his head regally. "No," he said, controlling himself. "If there's going to be a press conference, we'll have it, not you. We'll have it at our headquarters. I'll be damned if I'll permit this boy to be the slaughter for some goddamn media range war."

"Fine. Twelve-thirty," Harry said firmly.

Philip knew he had to concede. He did not care about the time for a conference. The media would be swarming his office anyway. "Twelve-thirty," he said. He pushed the eject button on the tape player and snapped the tape out. He slipped the tape back into the envelope and dropped the envelope into a plastic bag. "I've got a wino to talk to and then a bank president," he mumbled. He looked once again at Cody. "You be at the conference," he said. He walked briskly from the office.

"We've got work to do," Harry commanded. "And I've got a meeting in a few minutes. Any questions?"

"Yeah," Cody said. "One."

"What?" Harry was irritated.

"I've never seen a picture of Aaron Greene. Have we got one?"

Harry reached across his desk and pulled a photograph from beneath a paper. He handed it to Cody.

Aaron Greene was not smiling in the photograph taken from his high school yearbook. His plain, expressionless face seemed oddly absent of features. Cody turned the photograph over and tried to recall Aaron's face from memory. He couldn't.

SEVEN

———◆———

VICTOR MENOTTI DID NOT LIKE PLAYING tagalong to Philip Oglesbee, but he knew the rules: a kidnapping was as federal as the assassination of a president. And now there was more than a kidnapping; now a federally insured bank was involved. Menotti was with Philip Oglesbee to maintain appearances—a family-of-law portrait with a pose of harmony and happiness. If Menotti's smile was tight-lipped, it would not show in the portrait.

But the African Prince also needed Menotti, or someone like him. Philip Oglesbee had been assigned to Atlanta from Detroit in the late spring of 1996, a pre–Olympic move that had more to do with politics than precaution. In a city dominated by black influence, the Federal Bureau of Investigation needed a man who had the bearing, as well as the permission, of authority. It had been a hectic time, especially with the bombing at Centennial Park. Philip Oglesbee had barely learned the back roads from his home to his office, and he had never had experience with Southerners. He knew only the stories, and the stories had always angered him. In his first weeks—when his own agents had anointed him the African Prince—he had been a clenched muscle. To his surprise, most of the Southerners he met in Atlanta seemed oblivious to his disposition. They wanted to talk football, after learning he had played defensive end for Princeton. To Philip, such talk was the

blithering of obsession. He did not know it was the South-
erner's trick of casual conversation.

Menotti had been rush-ordered to Philip's office at
eight. He had listened to the tape and had sat quietly for
a second interview with the wino. The wino knew nothing. A very small man in a funny-looking beard had given
him ten dollars for walking around the corner and handing
an envelope to the guard in the newspaper office. The
wino was frightened. He trembled and stuttered his story,
and was then led away by a young agent to be fed and
rewarded.

"You know what pisses me off?" Philip had said to Menotti. "We found the funny-looking beard two blocks
away, in the middle of the sidewalk. It was one of those
things that hooks over the ears. Whoever's doing this has
got the balls of an elephant."

Menotti entered the Century National Bank behind
Philip, a tagalong who would show well in the family
portrait. It was eight minutes after nine.

Ethridge Landon's office was on the first floor of the
bank, in the northwest corner. Its entrance was protected
by an outer office occupied by his executive assistant, a
woman named Brenda Patterson. Outside Brenda Patterson's office was a small lobby with a secretary's desk. Rachel Segriest was the secretary. It was impossible to see
Ethridge Landon without permission from Brenda Patterson or Rachel Segriest.

Brenda and Rachel were discussing the agenda for a
board meeting at Rachel's desk when the two men approached.

"Yes?" Brenda said. Her tone was official, hard.

"Is Ethridge Landon in?" Philip asked.

"He's extremely busy," Brenda replied. "Unless you
have an—"

"It'll only take a few minutes."

"And what's the nature of your business?" Brenda asked
irritably.

Philip reached into the inside pocket of his suit and withdrew a wallet. He opened it and displayed his FBI credentials. "It's private," he said coolly.

"Oh," Brenda replied, startled. "Yes, of course. Follow me, please."

Ethridge Landon's office was ego-large and luxuriously appointed with leather chairs, a long navy-blue sofa fronted by a coffee table, a conference table with six chairs, an oversized executive desk with a heavy glass covering, and a matching credenza. Two tall houseplants in polished brass containers stood in one corner. Bookcases with leather-bound books lined one of the walls. Recessed video screens were inset in the wall near the conference table. Pictures of Ethridge Landon on hunting and skiing trips, expensively framed, decorated another wall. A book—*Who's Who in American Finance*—was on the coffee table, a silk ribbon marking the page of Ethridge Landon's name.

A short, trim man with thinning hair at his forehead was sitting behind the desk, reading *The Atlanta Constitution*. He wore rimless glasses. He looked up, annoyed, as Brenda Patterson led Philip Oglesbee and Victor Menotti into the office.

"Yes?" he said curtly.

"I'm sorry to interrupt, Mr. Landon," Brenda said nervously, "but these gentlemen need to see you."

Ethridge Landon swiveled in his chair and stood.

"Thank you," Philip said to Brenda, dismissing her with his voice. She nodded and backed out of the office and closed the door.

"Must be important if you got by Brenda without an argument," Ethridge Landon said.

Philip opened the wallet he held in his hand and extended it. "I'm Philip Oglesbee, FBI," he said. "This is Victor Menotti. He's a detective with the City of Atlanta."

Ethridge Landon's face clouded. "What can I do for you?"

"You have an employee by the name of Aaron Greene," Philip said calmly. "He's been kidnapped."

"Who?" Ethridge said after a moment. "I don't think I know that name."

"He's a mailboy," Menotti said.

Ethridge nodded as though suddenly remembering Aaron Greene. He said, "Kidnapped? That's—terrible. What is it? A custody fight?"

Philip shook his head. "You don't understand. He's been kidnapped by someone unknown. His parents have nothing to do with it."

"My God," Ethridge said. "They must be terrified."

"They are," Menotti replied.

Ethridge gestured with his hand to the two leather chairs in front of his desk. "Sit down, gentlemen, please," he mumbled. He sat again in his chair, sinking deep into it. Philip and Menotti sat. "Now, tell me about this. What can we do?"

"You can brace yourself," Philip said. "Whoever took the boy is holding the bank responsible for the ransom."

Ethridge's eyes flared behind his rimless glasses. He sat forward in his chair. "What?"

"They want ten million dollars," Philip said evenly.

"What?" Ethridge said again, his voice becoming shrill.

"That's the demand," Philip told him. "It happened yesterday. We just got the demand this morning."

"God almighty," Ethridge whispered. He sat back in his chair. He said again, "God almighty."

"The press knows about it—the *Journal-Constitution*. Whoever took the boy is communicating through them," Philip explained. "At nine-thirty, a reporter will be calling you for comments. We wanted to let you know before they caught you cold."

Ethridge glanced at his watch. It was nine-twenty. He reached for the telephone, touched one button. "Get me Littlejohn," he ordered. "Now." He dropped the receiver back over its cradle.

Menotti looked at the African Prince and smiled. Menotti knew Littlejohn. He was the corporate attorney for the Century National Bank. Once he had been a defender of petty drug dealers. Jason Littlejohn was an arrogant asshole.

"I know you've got things to consider," Philip said. He stood and Menotti stood. "We'll be back in touch with you. We'll want to talk to some people about the boy, look over his work record."

Ethridge nodded irritably. "Tell Brenda," he said in a tone of corporate command. "She'll handle everything." He looked up, a foolish expression on his flushed face. "I appreciate you letting me know. I hope to hell you've got everybody you can find working on this."

"We're taking care of it," Philip said. His African Prince gaze covered Ethridge Landon. "We'll be back," he added.

EIGHT

━━━━━━━━◆━━━━━━━━

THE QUOTE THAT ETHRIDGE LANDON GAVE
Amos Temple for the metro edition of *The Atlanta Journal*
was: "We deplore this act of terrorism against one of our
valued employees and wish to express our deepest sympathy to his parents. As members of Aaron Greene's extended family, we well understand the sense of shock and
fear they must be experiencing."

To the question of the ransom, the response was not as
emotional: "I have been advised by counsel not to discuss
this issue at this time. We have just received notification
of the kidnapping and the ransom demand, and must review it in more detail."

"Does that mean you will or won't consider meeting
the demand?" Amos had asked.

"I'm sorry, I can't address that at this time," Ethridge
Landon had replied.

Cody Yates read the final draft of the story, including the
comments of Ethridge Landon, and he laughed quietly at
his desk. It was what he expected, what he could have
written before the interview. A quick little tap dance, a
foot shuffle on a small stage. Lawyer bullshit. Or maybe
not. Maybe it was PR bullshit approved by the lawyers—
PR bullshit written by one of the Sellouts. Who was at

the bank? Roy Carnes. He had been a sportswriter with talent. No, not Roy. Roy was with an advertising agency. Cody shifted in his chair, gazed out of the window. Miriam, he thought suddenly. Miriam Finch. Miriam of the puffed blond hair and the seductive hazel eyes. Miriam had written features. Cody picked up the printouts on Ethridge Landon that he had punched up from internal files on his computer and he scanned the pages until he found the story written by Miriam. He remembered it. Miriam had made Ethridge Landon a god of finance. She had left the imprint of her lips on every word. It was a whore's free sample. Cody remembered the rumor that Miriam had spent a weekend with Ethridge Landon at a golf resort in North Carolina and had been hired shortly thereafter to fill a created position of Corporate Communication. He smiled and tossed the file on his desk. Perfect title, he thought. Perfect. But what the hell. The last time he saw Miriam, she was driving a Mercedes. It was not a disposable car.

Cody had written his sidebar feature in fifteen minutes. It began: "I do not know why I am involved in this."

It was the most precise lead he had ever written for any publication. And it was the truth.

The phone on Cody's desk rang and Harry Dilliard announced to him, "Paper's up."

"I'll be right there," Cody said.

Harry held the paper in his hands and beamed over the headline:

MAILBOY KIDNAPPED

The subhead, leading into Amos Temple's story and nestled next to a slender, one-column yearbook picture of Aaron Greene, continued the drumroll:

**TEN MILLION
DEMANDED
FROM BANK**

Cody's sidebar was under the fold in a wrap. Its headline was:

REPORTER'S VOICE USED BY KIDNAPPERS

"Good job," Harry said, smiling. He repeated, "Good job." He dropped the paper on his desk. "Boys, we kicked some ass today. Like we used to." He stood and began pacing. "God, I love it," he crooned, punching the air with his fist. "We'll have every black-tongued vulture who ever love-licked a microphone working overtime to find the crumbs, but that's all they'll get this time—crumbs. What time is it?"

"Ten-thirty," Jack Halpern said.

"All right, here's what we're going to do," Harry said. "As soon as it gets out that we've got the story, this place will look like the Alamo with John Wayne out front. We don't say anything—just that we've printed everything we know. Tell them we understand the FBI is having a press conference, and to check with them. Tell them we're co-operating fully. Tell them we had the story yesterday, but agreed to hold off until it could be investigated." He smiled again. "Don't pat the back, people—stroke it. Be as high and mighty as the occasion allows, but don't start preening. Just enjoy it." He laughed gleefully, turned to Cody. "Yates, you're the one they'll want. You I worry about, so get out of here. Go over to the FBI office and hide. Tell them you don't want to say anything until the conference. They'll put you in a closet if they have to. Believe me, the last thing they want is some half-cocked journalist taking the spotlight." He pivoted to Amos Temple and Jack Halpern. "Temple, you hound the bank. Hal-

pern, you get somebody over to the conference—
McArthur. He'll make them pucker just by showing up.
When we push this snowball off the hill I want to keep it
rolling. I'll be meeting with AP in a few minutes."

"What about the family?" Cody asked.

"The feds have them under wraps," Harry replied.
"We've got some shots of the house we'll run in the late
edition, but nobody's talked to them. Why don't you see
what you can come up with? Go out there when the
conference is over. Maybe they'll let you in, since you're
involved. Talk to that buddy of yours from the police—
what's his name?"

"Menotti. Victor Menotti."

Harry wagged his head enthusiastically. "Yeah. Menotti. Maybe he can get you in."

"I'll see," Cody said. He could hear Menotti's sarcastic
laugh.

Harry stopped his pacing. He sat on the edge of his desk.
"Look," he said seriously. "I know there's more to this
than a story. There's a kid out there who must be scared
to death. My God, I would be, and from everything we
know about him, he's been a loner all his life. I want us
to tell this story. I want us to ride it for all it's worth, but
I don't want to do anything to put that boy in harm's way.
Don't do it. Those assholes from television and radio may,
but you won't. Do you understand?"

The men listening to Harry Dilliard nodded gravely.

The story of Aaron Greene's kidnapping struck Atlanta
like an unexpected war. By one o'clock, every radio and
television station in Atlanta had broadcast its facts and had
begun the remarkable speculations that would elevate fact
to myth and myth to lunacy. Grave-voiced announcers,
in their rushed, this-is-a-bulletin seriousness, interrupted
programs to flash the news: Aaron Greene, an eighteen-
year-old boy from Decatur, a mail clerk at Century National Bank, had been kidnapped, the bank held

responsible for his ransom of ten million dollars. And, most puzzling, the kidnappers had communicated their demands through audiocassette tapes, using the voice of a newspaper reporter, Cody Yates.

At his press conference, Philip Oglesbee had distributed copies of the tapes of Cody Yates's voice and Cody had been assaulted by pointed microphones, aimed at his face like blunt spears. Cody could only say over and over, "I don't know why. . . . I've never heard of Aaron Greene until this happened. . . . Yes, it's my voice. . . . No, I don't know how long I was recorded. . . . No, I won't do a talk show. . . . No, I didn't stage this, damn it. Of course not. . . ."

Aaron Greene was news. News that could not be delayed.

"Not since the Atlanta child murders and the Centennial Park bombing during the Olympic Games has anything shocked this city as much as the kidnapping of Aaron Greene. What we want to know is how you feel about it. Though the FBI denies there is any evidence to support such a theory, there is a strong suspicion that this could be inspired by neo-Nazi activity, or diehard militia groups. What do you think? The story from today's edition of The Atlanta Journal *tells us very little about Aaron Greene himself, except to say he was shy and a loner. Why Aaron Greene? Or is this simply a hoax, a ploy on the part of the newspaper to increase sagging readership, as some have suggested? At this point, no one knows the answers. WJES's news reporters are, at this very moment, trying to piece together all the facts, the complete story, and we'll interrupt our programming when we know something more definitive. As always, we are first in the know, with exclusive insight into the latest news of the day. You can be assured of the latest details from the South's leading news department as they piece together this bizarre story. Perhaps we'll get an interview with Aaron's parents, Ruth and Nathan Greene. At this time, we understand they're being kept in seclusion by law enforcement officials, but you can be assured that as soon as*

we know, you'll know. Right now, we want to find out how you feel about this. Is it for real, or is it a hoax? The lines are now filled for The Katie Harris Show, *but keep trying and we'll get you on, with your opinion.*

"Brian, in Stone Mountain, you're on the air."

"Hey, Katie, how you doing?"

"Fine, Brian. What's your take on this Aaron Greene story?"

"There ain't nothing to it. It's just a hoax, like you been saying. All that trouble that newspaper's been through lately, it's got to be that. Just another gimmick to sell more papers. They're probably paying that boy's family to go along with it."

"What're you saying, Brian? This is a conspiracy?"

"Sounds like it to me. There's something else I don't understand."

"What's that, Brian?"

"If they was gonna use somebody's voice, why didn't they use somebody from a radio station, like you? They could've done the taping straight off the radio and wouldn't've had to tap no phone."

"Well, that's a question that's been asked also, Brian. Seems it would have been easier, doesn't it?"

"What I was thinking. Seems like they'd've done that. They ought to've used you. You got the best voice on the radio."

"That's sweet of you, Brian, but what if somebody really did kidnap Aaron?"

"Well, they'd have to prove it before I believed it."

"So it's a hoax vote for you?"

"Put me down."

"Good. Thanks for the call, Brian. Barbara from East Point, what do you think?"

"I haven't heard much said about the bank. What're they going to do?"

"We don't really know, Barbara. The statement that we received at the press conference simply says they're reviewing the issue with their lawyers and law enforcement officials. Maybe they're like Brian from Stone Mountain. Maybe they think it's a hoax."

"Don't sound like no hoax to me. I think he's been kid-napped. I just pray he's still alive."

"Does any of this sound anti-Semitic, Barbara?"

"Ah—what's that?"

"Against the Jews. Does it sound like someone wanting to attack the Jews? Aaron Greene is Jewish, you know."

"Oh, oh, yes. I didn't understand you. No, no, I don't think that. Not everything that goes on is against the Jews or the blacks. But it seems like it's always made out to be that way."

"So, you think it's real, Barbara?"

"I do."

"One for hoax, one for real. Eddie in Marietta, you're on the air. . . ."

When he returned to his desk from the press conference, Cody found a sealed envelope with his name and the word "Personal" printed on it, and beside the envelope a call-back message from Millie at Piedmont Hospital, where she worked as a counselor. He pushed the envelope aside and called Millie.

"Jesus, you all right?" Millie asked anxiously.

"Yeah. A little bushed, but all right," Cody told her.

"Is this why you called last night?"

"Yeah."

"Why didn't you tell me?" Millie demanded.

Cody could hear the dampness of tears in her voice. He saw Frank Barton watching him with curiosity, and he became suddenly aware of other people staring at him. He turned in his chair to face the window.

"Cody? Why didn't you tell me?" Millie said again.

"It was late. I'd already screwed up once."

"Forget that. Oh, Sabrina got the flowers at school. She's floating. Thank you, Cody. That was sweet."

"I'll try to remember her next game," Cody said. He picked up the envelope and turned it in his hand.

"Don't worry. Are they going to hang you out on this?"

"A little, I guess," Cody answered. "Radio, mostly.

Those goddamn talk shows." He looked at the printing on the envelope. It was familiar.

Millie spit a curse into the phone. "Cody, forget them. They're sad. The people who call those shows haven't anything else to do. My God, don't you know it's the cheapest thrill most of them have had since early masturbation? It's what Andy Warhol meant by fame. I ran into one of them at a meeting not long ago. She's a regular caller. Even has a nickname—Mama Dean, or something like that. She drove me crazy cooing about what she said and what was said back to her. Cody, Cody, it's the new subculture. Don't you know that? It's everywhere. All over the damned country. And we worry about street gangs. Spend an afternoon listening to any of those microphone midgets, then you'll worry."

Cody laughed. He thought of the sports talk program he listened to regularly. But he loved Millie for being so opinionated. He wished to hell he could have lived with her.

"You want to come over for dinner?" Millie asked softly.

"Maybe soon," Cody replied. "I can't tonight. We've got this thing to deal with."

"I understand. I just wanted to know if you were all right."

"I'm fine. Thanks for the call, Millie."

"I heard the tape on the news, Cody. You sounded like you were drunk."

"That's a possibility," Cody admitted.

Millie laughed easily. "What I thought, too. By the way, how did they do that?"

"I have no idea. It's a little more complicated than splicing tape, I'd guess. The FBI's working on it."

"Well, it was clever enough," Millie said. Then: "Look, I'm busy. I'll talk to you soon."

"Sure. Kiss Sabrina for me."

Cody put down the phone and opened the envelope.

It was a message from Freda Graves: *I just heard about everything. I'll be out on assignment the rest of the day, but want you to call me at home tonight. I've got something to tell you that may be of interest.*

There was a telephone number and in parentheses a note that she would be out until seven. Curious, Cody thought. The message from the great stone statue—Miss In-Control—seemed almost human. He slipped the message into his suit pocket.

NINE

A TALL, THICK STONE FENCE WITH A BRICK cap enclosed the garden, sealing it from the front yard and from the trees that Aaron could see growing in each direction that he looked. He could not see the front of the house, but knew it was large and impressive, like castles he remembered from children's books. And he knew it was isolated. He could not hear the familiar droning of traffic that he heard constantly in his own house.

The woman Alyse had served his breakfast—eggs, a small steak, orange juice, toast, coffee—and had stayed to eat with him and to talk casually about his studies. Aaron was not afraid of Alyse. She was cheerful and pleasant. She had listened intently when he told her that he wanted to be a certified public accountant, as his father was, and she had insisted that she admired people who were superior at mathematics.

After the breakfast, Alyse had said to him, "Why don't you spend some time in the garden this morning, Aaron? I promised you a game of croquet, but it'll have to be this afternoon if we have time. Still, it's a beautiful day—the prettiest yet. Go walk around the garden. Take a book and read, if you wish. You'll find some chairs. And by the way, if you want to use the hot tub, please do. It's in the gazebo, easy to find. You've got a pair of swimming trunks among your clothes."

"I—I've never been in—" Aaron had stammered.

"A hot tub? Really?" Alyse had enthused. "You don't know what you're missing. It's the most relaxing thing imaginable. You simply sit back and let the water massage you. You'll love it, I promise. You'll see the directions. It's easy. You turn a knob."

Aaron walked through the garden slowly, discovering it. The garden was magnificent. Manicured flower beds, shrubs trimmed so delicately they seemed scissored, white-pebbled walkways. He paused at the statue of the nude woman. Her arms were lifted and her fingers were pushed into the marble folds of her hair, like a woman standing under a waterfall. Her stone face was serene. Her small stone breasts were raised to the sunlight. The garden did not seem real to Aaron. It was as though he had stepped from the house into a painting, or a photograph.

The gazebo with the hot tub was sheltered by a circle of weeping willows, isolating it from the rest of the garden. The gazebo was surprisingly large, with a shower and dressing room inset in one corner. To Aaron, the hot tub was like a small pool. He stood at the edge of the gazebo and watched the rolling water in the pool and the skim of steam that drifted over the bubbled surface. His eyes wandered to a pattern of wet footprints leading from the hot tub across the wood decking to the shower and dressing room. The footprints were small, child-size. He glanced up quickly to the door of the dressing room. The door was slatted and through the slats he saw the shadowed outline of a lithe figure pressed motionless against the wall. It was the outline of a girl, someone he had not seen before. He turned and walked away hurriedly, retracing his steps toward the door leading from the library. Near the house, he heard a soft noise, a muted cough, and he stopped and looked toward the sound. He saw an old man dressed in work clothes, a wide-brim straw hat covering a mat of white hair, work gloves on his hands. The man was kneeling near a flower bed, working with a trowel in a strip of freshly turned soil. A gray cat stretched lazily in the shade of a plant beside him. The man looked up at Aaron.

"Could you pull that bag of potting soil over for me?" the man said. His voice was deep, but soft. He nodded toward a bag.

Aaron moved to the bag and lifted it and carried it to the kneeling man.

"That's better," the man said. "Meant to bring it over before I got down, but forgot it." He reached into the bag with the trowel and scooped the dark soil and mixed it with the dirt in the flower bed. Aaron watched him. The old man's gloved hands moved slowly, but expertly.

"A little bit of this makes it hold the water," the old man said. He did not look at Aaron. "You have to be careful when you're planting things. A lot of people don't think so. They think you can just drop some seed or cuttings and heap some dirt over them with the heel of your shoe, and they'll grow. Some do, I suppose, but that's not the right way. Plants are like people. They need nurturing." The old man raised his face to Aaron. "You're our young guest, aren't you?"

Aaron nodded. The old man's eyes were light blue. His face was age-lined with a red tint of blood pumped from the exercise of work, but his eyes were startlingly clear and young.

"Well, Aaron," the old man continued easily, "I'm glad to meet you."

"You—know me?" Aaron asked.

The old man dug another scoop of potting soil from the bag and began mixing it with the soil. After a moment, he said, "Yes, I know you. You're our guest. Have you ever worked in a garden, Aaron?"

"No—no, sir."

"Let me show you something."

Aaron kneeled beside the old man.

"Feel the ground, Aaron. Run your fingers in it." The

old man held a clump of dirt in his hand. Aaron reached hesitantly and pushed his fingers into the dirt and curled his fingers around it. The dirt was cool. "Smell it, Aaron," the old man said, pulling his gloved hand to his face and inhaling slowly. Aaron copied him. The dirt smelled clean, like the ground after a rain. "Now that's when you know you're going to get a good plant growing. When you can touch the earth and knead it with your fingers, when you let it know you're asking something special of it." He opened his gloved hand and let the dirt filter through his fingers. Aaron dropped the dirt he held and smoothed it with the palm of his hand.

"I love this place, Aaron," the old man said. He nursed a rosebush out of a plastic pot and examined it and then tucked it gently into a burrowed-out hole in the mulched ground. "It's the best garden I've ever been in. Fed with underground pipes that keep everything watered, and we can even add liquid fertilizer when we need it. You should see it later in the spring. So many flowers here you could be blinded by the colors."

Aaron touched the earth again with his fingertips. The old man did not sound like a gardener.

"Did you see the statue?" the old man asked.

Aaron could feel a blush on his face. "Yes sir," he answered.

"We call her Salome, after the woman in the Bible. A man came from Italy to sculpt it."

The old man planted another rosebush, then moved gingerly on his knees.

"Would you like to help me in the garden?" the old man asked.

"I guess," Aaron muttered.

"Well, I'd like that. Sometimes the others come out and work, but I know they're doing it just to make me feel that I'm not alone out here." He chuckled lightly, softly. "They don't know I like being alone most of the time. What about you, Aaron?"

"I—don't know," Aaron confessed.

"You're young. Young people like to be with other people. That's the way it should be. When I was young, I didn't get much of a chance to be with people my age. I guess I was too shy. When you get older, it doesn't matter that much."

The old man handed a potted rosebush to Aaron. "Let's see you plant it. Like I just did. Scoop out a place with your hand and ease the plant out of its pot and then sort of wiggle it into the ground and bring the dirt back around it and press it down with your fingers."

Aaron planted the rosebush as the old man watched.

"Good," the old man said. He reached and patted Aaron on his arm. "Good," he repeated. "Now, do me a favor. Go over to the gazebo and you'll see a watering bucket with a sprinkler head. Put some water in it and bring it to me. We need to water these."

"Yes sir," Aaron said. He remembered the girl hiding in the dressing room, and he looked for her at the gazebo, but he did not see her. The pumps from the hot tub had stopped and the water moved only from the slight breeze that slipped across its surface. Aaron could see the wet footprints drying on the decking. The dressing-room door was open. A single brown towel hung from a hook on the door. He saw the watering bucket and filled it from a faucet located on the side of the dressing room.

Aaron knew he was being watched. He could sense it. But he did not know who was watching, or from where.

At seven, the servant Oscar opened the door to the formal dining room and Ewell Pender entered and sat at the head of the table. The company of four awaited his nod to sit.

"You look lovely, all of you," Ewell Pender said warmly. He nodded, turned his face to Oscar. "Did the salmon arrive?" he asked as the four settled into their chairs.

"It did, sir. In time for the marinade."

"Good. Good. I've had a taste for salmon for a week. Give us a few moments before you begin to serve."

Oscar bowed slightly and exited into the kitchen.

Ewell Pender turned back to face his company at the table. His clear blue eyes wandered over them, a smile fixed easily in his slender, eroded face. "Our young guest seems to be getting on well enough," he said after a moment. He looked at Alyse. "Did he have his dinner?"

"Yes," Alyse answered. "He ate well."

"And did we get another tape?"

"We did. Earlier this afternoon. Robert has it."

"Good, good," Ewell Pender replied. Then: "I'm glad you're with us tonight, Robert." The smile on his face blinked in his eyes. "Though I presume you have an appointment later."

"For a short time," Robert said. "But I wanted to have the tape ready for you."

"Good. Will you play it?"

Robert lifted a tape recorder from beside his chair and placed it on the table and pushed the play button. Aaron's taped voice said:

"Mom, Dad. Uh—I'm—I'm still all right. The people I'm with are very nice. This is a pretty place I'm in. I wish you could see it. There's a garden outside with a big fence that goes around it. I walked out in it today and helped a man plant some plants. The food they give me is good and it's more than I can eat. I still don't know what's going on, but I hope you don't worry too much. The lady who takes care of me said to tell you that I'm not wasting time, but when I come back I'll know a lot more than I used to. She said just to do whatever they tell you, and don't worry about me. And—and I don't want you to. I'm not being hurt in any way. That's—that's all I can think of. I don't know if I'll talk to you anymore or not. Maybe I will soon." There was a long pause, a sound of the tape's quiet hiss, and then Aaron added, *"I love you."*

The tape ended and Ewell Pender folded his hands under his chin and smiled happily. He said, "Very good. He sounds better. Don't you think?"

The company of four nodded agreement.

"Did you get an edit out of it?" Ewell Pender asked.

Robert nodded energetically. "I did. And we added a little background." He ejected the tape and pushed another into the player and pushed the play button. Aaron's voice stammered:

"*Uh—I'm—I'm in a big fence. Do whatever they tell you. I don't want to hurt anymore.*"

Robert pushed the stop button. Ewell Pender nodded approval. He played his fingers over the corners of his mouth and closed his eyes in thought. After a moment he said, "Take the word 'big' out of it. Maybe it says more than we want it to."

"Yes sir," Robert said. "That's easy. One keystroke."

Ewell Pender's eyes remained closed. His fingers touched his chin. "There was a sound. What was it?"

Robert beamed. "I'm rather proud of that, sir," he said, "though I can't take credit. Morris suggested it. It's music from a jukebox. Old country tunes. On our digital readings, it has the exact sound of a jukebox maybe three floors away. It's the sort of sound that drifts through old structures."

"Very good," Ewell Pender said. He opened his eyes and looked at Robert. "Though I can't say I approve of the music."

"Of course not," Robert said easily.

"But perfect for this. Perfect. We should hold it until the right time. Do you think the authorities have the equipment to break it down?"

"I'm sure they do, but it'll take some time and they'll still have to follow up on it. If we get some radio play— and we will—it won't matter very much."

Ewell Pender nodded and smiled. His eyes drifted over the four people seated at the table. "Why are we doing this?" he asked gently.

For a moment, no one spoke, and then Robert answered in an even voice, "To bring the people out of their slumber, their apathy."

The smile held on Ewell Pender's face. He moved his eyes to the young woman seated at his right, near him. "Who are the people?"

"Those who are made to feel worthless," the young woman replied quietly.

"Very good," Ewell Pender said.

"The people like Aaron," Alyse added.

"Yes, like Aaron," Ewell Pender agreed. He turned to look at Morris. "Like all of us have felt. Is that right, Morris?"

"Yes," Morris said.

"Do we still believe we are doing a good thing?" asked Ewell Pender.

The four nodded.

"And the risk is worth it?"

The four again nodded.

Ewell Pender moved forward in his chair. "I'm extremely proud of each of you," he said softly. "Each of you is equally important in achieving our mission, which is why you have been selected to participate." He paused, then looked again at the young woman seated near him. "Carla, you were at the hot tub today, weren't you?" His voice was calm, but direct.

"Yes," Carla whispered.

"I thought the instruction was for you to remain unseen for the time being."

Carla looked quickly across the table to Alyse, then bowed her head.

Ewell Pender inhaled slowly in a soft rasping sound. He said, "I don't mind you using the tub. I like to see you enjoy yourself, but the boy was in the garden when you were there. I'm told he may have seen you."

"I—don't know," Carla said in a small voice. "I don't think so." She glanced at Morris. Morris saw everything, and his eyes were always on her. Morris stared at her solemnly.

"Maybe not," Ewell Pender said, "but we can't take chances, can we? You know that we've talked about it. It isn't time for him to see you."

"I'm sorry," Carla said softly.

"I think you need to be excused for the evening," Ewell Pender told her. "And maybe you should avoid the garden for the time being."

Carla stood without replying. A blush of shame colored her face. She stepped away from her chair and pushed it quietly underneath the table.

"I'll have Oscar bring you a cart," Ewell Pender said.

"Thank you," Carla replied softly.

Ewell Pender turned toward her. "Now, don't be frightened or upset. We have to be careful, that's all." He smiled. "This little reprimand is merely a reminder to keep focused, nothing more. Why don't you select the music for tonight? You'll be able to hear it in your room."

Carla looked at him. Her eyes moistened. She said timidly, "Mozart."

"Ah, Mozart," Ewell Pender whispered. "Yes, that's excellent. Mozart. Such wonderful power Mozart had. A genius, even as a child. You've made a good selection, Carla."

TEN

———————◆———————

CODY DID NOT HAVE TO MANIPULATE VICtor Menotti for a visit with Nathan and Ruth Greene; he
was invited.

It was early evening, the bluish gloaming of night, when
Menotti stopped at Cody's apartment building and impatiently blew the car horn of his unmarked department
Chevrolet. Cody joined him immediately.

"You're late," Cody said.

"Not by Menotti Standard Time," Menotti grumbled.
"You deal with the kind of red-tape bullshit I have to deal
with and you'd understand what late means."

"Been with Oglesbee?" Cody asked.

Menotti nodded sourly. "Son of a bitch is one picky
human being. Made his boys show him *exactly* how the
cutter picked your miserable voice apart. It took them
about two seconds to figure it out and about two hours to
describe it to the great Prince."

"So, how'd he do it? The cutter?" asked Cody.

"How should I know? It's all digital stuff. Underline a
word or a syllable, hit a couple of buttons, and it transfers
to another tape, or a CD, or something. Ask Sabrina. She
probably knows. Oglesbee's boys said a four-year-old
could do it if he had the right equipment."

"That's why the voice level's so different," Cody suggested.

69

"What they said," Menotti said. "But I told them they were sucking wind. I told them that's the way you talked when you were drunk. Told them you were at the bottom of all of it. Just a big publicity stunt."

"Yeah, you got me," Cody said wearily. "I confess. I did it. Snatched the kid off the street, paid him a couple of hundred, and put him on a Greyhound headed west. Probably in Vegas now, playing blackjack and screwing showgirls. And me, I'm basking in the glory of attention. Maybe you've heard some of the talk shows. They've got me dead to rights. Nailed my ass with all that man-in-the-street wisdom."

"What I figure," Menotti mused.

"Actually, part of it's a lie. The kid's at my apartment, locked in a closet."

"Naw."

"Naw, what?"

"Naw, he ain't. I looked."

"You've been in my apartment?" Cody asked irritably. Menotti laughed. He turned the car east on Ponce de Leon. "You couldn't tell?"

"No, you son of a bitch," Cody said.

"I've always been good at that," Menotti replied proudly. "Everything back in its right place, precisely. By the way, you need to pay your gas bill. You've got a second notice."

"Damn," exclaimed Cody. "You were there."

"Yep."

"What for?"

"Because, my friend, you're the answer, or part of it," Menotti said. He slowed for a traffic light. A car pulled beside him in the inside lane, driven by a boy wearing a blond crewcut. Hard rap music thundered from speakers embedded in the backseat headrest. The boy glanced at Menotti and smirked arrogantly. Menotti reached into his inside coat pocket and pulled out his wallet and snapped it open to display his police badge. The boy paled. His arm shot out for the volume control and the music died midnote. Menotti smiled and replaced his wallet. "Works every time," he said.

"You love power, don't you?" Cody said.

"I do. Yes, I do," Menotti answered. Then: "Why do they play that rap shit?" The light changed and he pulled away slowly, watching the boy.

"Why am I the answer?" Cody asked.

"To what?" Menotti replied.

"Damned if I know. You said I was the answer."

"Oh, that," Menotti said casually. "I don't know why, yet, but you are, or at least you're the scent this blood-hound plans to follow. The African Prince can run around in circles making a name for himself if he wants to, but you're mine." He looked again at Cody. "You want to tell me what it is, or do I have to find out for myself?"

Cody snorted sarcastically. "Menotti, the way I feel right now, I wouldn't help you find your ass if you were a one-armed blind man. I don't even know what you're talking about. Now, why do you want me to see the Greenes?"

"They wanted to see you."

"Why?"

"I guess to ask about their boy. Maybe they just want to look at you, see if they can figure out why it's your shitty voice that's so damned important."

"Did you tell them I'd write about this?"

"I told them it was a risk. Will you?"

"Wouldn't you?"

Menotti shrugged. "I guess. It's power, ain't it?"

Nathan and Ruth Greene lived in a small brick house near Decatur. The house had two bedrooms, a living room, a den, a dining room, a kitchen, and one bathroom. The lawns were well kept and thickly carpeted with Bermuda grass. In the far backyard there were five large oaks. Ruth Greene had bordered the lawn near the oaks with azaleas and with a selection of flowers that bloomed colorfully through spring and summer. A hurricane fence surrounded the backyard.

"They don't have diddly-squat," Menotti said as he parked the car on the street, behind another plain dark Chevrolet. Cody followed him up the driveway. Styrofoam cups and loose food wrappings were scattered over the lawn and lodged against the shrubbery at the base of the house, like pods of mushrooms. "What I love about your kind," Menotti grumbled. "Bunch of goddamn leeches. Showed up here an hour after the story broke, hanging around for one good glimpse of tears, until they knew nothing was going to happen and they got tired of waiting or talking to the neighbors. Look at this crap they left behind. You'd think they could have picked up after themselves, for Christ's sake."

Cody did not argue. There was an arrogance to the media that embarrassed him, a haughty sense of self-importance that contradicted promotional ads of integrity. Once journalism had had pride; now it was showmanship. Television had done that. Television had made celebrities of names and faces, and radio and the print media had tried desperately to cling to the gaudy bunting of the bandwagon. That was why the talk shows dominated and why newspapers had become bastardized versions of supermarket tabloids. Cody wondered how the tabloids would have handled the kidnapping of Aaron Greene. ALIENS KIDNAP BOY, INVADE REPORTER TO USE VOICE IN DEMANDS. That would sell a copy or two, he thought.

"You're sure you don't know these people? Never been here?" Menotti asked at the door.

"I'm sure," Cody told him. "Never been here. Never heard of them."

"We'll see," Menotti mumbled. He rang the doorbell. An agent in a dark dress suit opened the door.

"I've got Yates," Menotti said.

The agent nodded and stepped outside and closed the door.

"Anything new?" Menotti asked. He did not introduce Cody.

"A few drive-bys. People looking," the agent said.

"Calls?"

The agent looked warily at Cody. He said, "One more."

"The same thing?"

"Yes."

"All right. Keep an eye out here. There was a Pontiac following us from North Druid Hills. Maybe it's nothing."

Cody was astonished. He had not seen a car following them.

"Sure," the agent said. He opened the door and entered the house. Menotti and Cody followed. The agent disappeared through a door leading into a corridor.

Nathan and Ruth Greene were seated together on the sofa. They could have posed for a portrait of resignation. Both were thin. Both had the ashen color of sudden fear. Both trembled.

"I'm sorry about your son," Cody told them after introductions. "And I honestly don't know anything about this. I don't know why my voice is being used on those tapes."

"Why my boy?" Ruth Greene moaned sorrowfully. "He's a good boy. He's never hurt anyone."

"I don't know the answer to that, either, Mrs. Greene," Cody said. "It must be because he works for the bank. Maybe they simply picked him at random."

"But they won't pay for a boy like Aaron," Nathan Greene said anxiously. "Why should they? What does he do? He delivers the mail. There's nothing to delivering the mail."

"You must have answered this many times," Cody said carefully, "but how did Aaron get the job? Did he, or either of you, know anyone at the bank?"

Nathan Greene shook his head vigorously. "No. No one. Many years ago, before Aaron was born, I applied for a job there, but I met no one, only the people in the personnel office."

"You didn't get the job?"

"No, no, you must understand. There wasn't a job. I applied if one became available. But after that I went to work with the department store, and I've been with them since. There's nothing to any of that."

"But Aaron got a job there," Cody said.

"He was called by someone about it," Ruth Greene explained. "They said they were calling a number of people who had just graduated from high school. He made good grades. He was a good boy in high school."

"Who called him?" asked Cody. "Do you remember?"

"No," Ruth Greene answered. "It was a call for him. He talked to them, then went to the bank and made his application. We told that to the police."

Menotti nodded agreement. "We've kept all that information confidential," he explained.

"I didn't want him to take the job," Ruth Greene said quietly.

"Why?" asked Cody.

"He's never been away. He's very shy. He didn't know how things were outside."

Nathan Greene touched his wife's hand and held it. "I pushed him to do it," he said with regret. "I thought he needed to be out. He had to learn what it was like away from the home."

There was a pause, an expanding, wordless space that closed on Nathan and Ruth Greene. Outside a car passed the house slowly. Its light beams flickered across the living-room window.

"Did you put together the notes we talked about?" Menotti asked gently.

"Yes," Nathan Greene replied. He leaned to the coffee table in front of the sofa and lifted a magazine and pulled a folded piece of paper from it. "We tried to put down everything we could think of." He handed the paper to Menotti.

"Good," Menotti said. "I know that was hard to do, but it may help. We want to make sure we do everything we can, and the more we know, the easier it is." He pushed the paper into his coat pocket. "I think we'd better go now," he added. "Unless there's something else you want to ask Mr. Yates."

Ruth Greene turned her face to Cody. Her eyes were damp. "You have a child?" she asked.

"Yes," Cody told her. "A little girl."

"Then you know," Ruth Greene said.

"Mr. Greene?" Menotti said.

"No, no," Nathan Greene answered in an apologetic voice. "Thank you for coming. Maybe we wanted to know if you could tell us something that would help."

"I'm sorry I can't," Cody said. "If I learn anything, you'll know about it."

"Please," Ruth Greene begged. "Please."

Menotti and Cody rode in silence from the Greene home to a Burger King. Menotti guided the car to the drive-through. "Want anything?" he asked Cody.

"Coffee. Black."

"Two coffees, black," Menotti said to the machine.

A voice squawked and Menotti drove to the service window.

"What was that about the phone calls?" Cody asked.

"Nothing."

"Bullshit."

Menotti took the coffee and paid the check. He handed one of the coffees to Cody and eased the car away from the window and parked. Cody knew he was watching for the Pontiac that might have followed them earlier.

"Always got some nuts, Yates," Menotti said at last. "This time it's a Jew-hater."

"What does he say?"

" 'The Jew-boy's going to die.' That's what he says. Every call. Covers the phone with a handkerchief or something, and he tries to change his pitch, but it's the same voice."

"Jesus, no wonder they're scared," Cody whispered.

"His folks?" Menotti said. "They don't know about it. They don't answer the phone—we do." He turned his head to watch a car circle through the parking lot. It was an Oldsmobile.

"You think there's a tie-in?" Cody asked.

Menotti sipped from his coffee. He lit a cigarette and let the smoke billow from the opened window. "A tie-in?" he said. "I doubt it. But I'd like to get the bastard. Christ, I hate those bastards."

"Can I write about that?"

"No. No, you can't. Not now," Menotti said firmly. He looked at Cody. "I'll tell you when. I may even want you to do it in a day or so, but not now."

Cody knew that Victor Menotti was testing him, and teasing him. He also knew there was a reason. He said, "All right."

It was after nine when Menotti left Cody at his apartment, and, being tired, Cody poured a glass of wine and slumped into the ancient armchair that had fashioned itself to the contour of his body. It was a chair he had had since college, a chair that had followed him from apartment to apartment, into and out of a marriage, like a lazy but faithful dog. The wine he drank was good, a far more civilized drink than cheap scotch. He wondered if Nathan and Ruth Greene drank wine. Perhaps. Ceremonial wine at Passover, or one of the other holidays.

The telephone rang. Sabrina, he thought. She would be giddy over the flowers, then she would whisper into the phone and tell him who her mother was dating. Unlike children who developed the lucrative art of moping following a divorce, Sabrina loved the soap-opera intrigue of it.

It was not Sabrina on the phone. It was Freda Graves.

"I just got in," Cody told her. "Just a few minutes ago. I was about to give you a call, in fact. Thanks for the note."

"It's all right," Freda said. Her voice was direct and professional, but soft. "I didn't know if you went back to the office after the press conference. I didn't know if you'd found it."

"Yeah, sure. I should have called earlier, but I've been with the police. Went out to see the boy's parents."

"How are they?"

"Upset. And afraid. Don't think I've ever met anyone as timid as they are."

For a moment Freda did not speak, and then she said in a strangely quiet voice, "I've been thinking about them all day. I wondered about them, what kind of people they are. My father was timid. Not my mother. My father was."

Cody laughed easily. "Well, you won't believe it, but so was I when I was a child. Scared of my own shadow. Why I'm such a bastard today. Compensation. You had something to tell me?"

"Yes, but . . ."

"What's the matter?"

"I'm a little, well, reluctant to speak over your telephone about it."

"I guess I can understand that," Cody said. "Want to meet somewhere for a glass of wine?"

There was a pause—too long, Cody thought—and then Freda said, "I hope you don't take this too personally, but I'd rather not."

"Why?"

"Let's just say I don't think I'd feel comfortable in the places you must frequent," Freda replied. "If you wish, you can come here. I'm off North Druid Hills."

The invitation surprised Cody. And intrigued him.

Maybe he was wrong about the great stone queen. "Sure," he said. "Give me the address."

Freda Graves's apartment could have been a cover shot for an interior decorating magazine. It was immaculate and orderly. Its colors were soft greens and pinks. There were books, many books. Cody could smell the hot-wax vanilla fragrance of a burning candle, but he could not see the candle.

"Hell of an apartment," he said to Freda. "Makes me want to bomb mine."

"I'm sure it's exactly what you thought it would be. Everything in its place. And I know you. Yes, I'd want to bomb your place, too, without seeing it. Or at least have it disinfected. And if you want to smoke here, you have to do it on the deck."

Freda was dressed casually in slacks and a blouse. The blouse was pink, the slacks gray. She did not seem as tense as she did in the newsroom. Cody was staring at her, and she blushed and smiled.

"My God, what was that?" Cody said.

"What?"

"That. On your face. A smile. Damned if you didn't smile."

"Come on, Cody, don't be an ass. Yes, I smile. What do you want? I'm having a glass of wine."

"Wine's good. It's my drink, you know. Very fine wine, the expensive stuff. The only thing I drink."

Freda sighed a weary laugh. "If I know you, you'd drink vinegar if I poured it. Sit down." She directed him to a chair near the door leading to the deck, then poured the wine and sat on the sofa.

"You wanted to tell me something," Cody said.

Freda tilted her head to look at the glass she held in her hands. "I may have seen the person who left the tape on the wheel of your car," she said.

"Tell me," Cody urged.

"I was in the parking lot. I saw your car." She shrugged. "It's not hard to miss. Anyway, a girl—at least I think it was a girl—was crossing the parking lot and she went between your car and the one next to it. She had a briefcase, and she stumbled and the briefcase popped open and some things spilled out. She was kneeling there, gathering things up. And then she got up and rushed off. I didn't think anything about it then. It was raining."

"Did you get a good look at her?" asked Cody.

Freda shook her head. "She had an umbrella and a cap pulled down over her head. The cap was the only thing I remember."

"Why?"

"It was one of those old-fashioned things like airplane pilots used to wear in World War One. With the earflaps. Do you know what I mean?"

"Yeah, sure," Cody replied. "I'll be damned." He reached for a cigarette.

"On the deck, Cody."

"You mind?"

"Not at all. It's pleasant out."

Freda took the bottle of wine and followed Cody through the sliding glass door onto the deck. They sat in lounge chairs. The night was clear, clean, slightly cool. Cody lit his cigarette and watched the smoke swirl above his head and disappear.

"That's a nasty habit," Freda said.

"I know," Cody answered. "Why didn't you tell Halpern or Dilliard about the girl?"

"That would have been unfair," Freda said. "You're the one in the middle of this. Maybe there's nothing to it. Maybe the girl actually stumbled. And maybe you know her." She moved her face to look at Cody. "But she was a little young for you, or she looked young, wearing that cap. Do you know anyone who wears that kind of cap?"

"Nobody," Cody told her. "I'd remember that. Used to have one myself, when I was a kid, but then everybody

I knew had one. Boys. Not girls. And what do you mean, too young for me? I'm not ancient."

Freda laughed aloud, and the laughter surprised Cody. He could not remember hearing her laugh. The great stone queen had a personality.

"You know, I kind of like you like this," Cody said. "There's a soft spot in all that steel you wrap around you. Tell me about yourself, Freda Graves."

"I'm a very nice person," Freda said. "Very professional."

"I know about the professional part," Cody replied. "After eight years of watching you, it's a little obvious, to tell you the truth."

"People are not always the same away from their working environment," Freda said.

Cody rocked his body in agreement. "Interesting," he said. "Where did you live as a child? Where did you go to school? What did you study? How did you get in this business? Tell me those things."

"Boring stuff, really. I was born in Montgomery, Alabama, but we moved to Atlanta when I was five. I went to Northside High School, then to the University of Missouri to study journalism. I worked for a daily in Dayton, Ohio, before moving back home and getting the job I have now. See? Boring."

"Yeah, it is, the way you rattle it off," Cody said. "Why do I get the feeling you may be leaving out a few million facts?"

"You didn't ask about anything else. Besides, I don't believe in exchanging résumés."

"Sorry," Cody said. "It's the wine. Wine always makes me inquisitive. Anyway, I've learned a lot today."

"Such as?" Freda asked.

Cody drew from his cigarette, nudged the ash from its tip with the fingernail of his little finger. He shifted to look at Freda. There was an eagerness in her face, a look he had never seen from her. "I've learned you hang up the steel blouse when you quit being Brenda Starr," he said.

"Please, don't do that," Freda said quietly. She toyed with her wineglass, sipped from it. "I know my reputation."

"Do you?"

"Yes, I do." She looked at him, and the eyes that could be cold or sad were sad.

Cody leaned back in his lounge chair. He liked being with her. It bewildered him, but he enjoyed it. "You got a man?" he asked after a moment.

"That's none of your damn business," Freda said. Then: "No."

"Pity."

"It's late, Cody," she said abruptly. "I have to be in early. I'm not like you. I have to have my sleep." She stood.

"Sure," Cody said. He pulled himself from his chair. He wondered if Menotti's men had followed him and were watching from the street. "Thanks for everything," he added. "I sort of doubt that whoever you saw had anything to do with the tape, though. I've stumbled my way across that lot a few times myself. Besides, the boys with the badges are saying this is the work of a pro, and from how you described her, she was a kid."

"I guess you're right," Freda said.

"I'm glad she was there," Cody said. "Otherwise we wouldn't have had this fine meeting."

A blush tinted Freda's face. "I would be grateful if you kept it between us."

Cody tilted his head and gazed at her. He said, "Look, you don't have to worry about me. I know the rules, even if I do break one now and again. Sorry about prying. I'm also sorry we've spent all these years in the same space and barely tolerated one another. But I don't blame you. Lately I've been taking stock of myself, and I don't like me, either."

"I didn't say—"

"You don't have to."

The blush was still in Freda's face. She looked away. "I hope you get through this all right," she said. Her voice was formal, professional.

"I will," Cody told her. He turned away, then turned back. "The day you started working at the paper and we met, did we shake hands?"

"I don't remember," she answered. "It was a long time ago."

"I don't think so," Cody said.

"Probably not."

"So we've actually never touched?"

"No," Freda said coolly, "and I prefer to keep it that way."

Cody smiled a tired, exasperated smile. He shook his head, exhaled a slow sigh. "Why did you say that? I was enjoying this. It was almost like a real human encounter. But I was wrong, wasn't I?"

"I think you should leave," Freda told him.

Cody took a step toward her. "I will," he said, "but I'd like something first."

"What?"

"A hug. Just that. A hug. After the day I've had today— no, after the year I've had—I think a hug would be nice. But maybe you don't believe in such things. Maybe you're afraid of germs or something."

"I'm not that cold, Cody. And I do know this game you're playing."

"Game? What game? Hey, I just gave you an out," Cody said. "Tell me you're afraid of germs."

"That's not it."

"Then what the hell is it? Am I that offensive?"

"No. I—"

Cody stepped closer and embraced her gently. Her body became rigid. She turned her head.

"How old are you?" he asked against her shoulder.

"None of your business," she said.

"You're thirty-seven."

"If you know, why did you ask?"

"The reason I know is because on your last birthday there was a little office get-together after work, and Lillian Ferris bought you a card that made a joke of the fading thirties. I wasn't invited to the get-together, by the way. Lillian said I was too old."

"You've had your hug, Cody, now please let go of me," Freda said. She moved her body slightly against him.

"This is only half a hug," Cody insisted. "A real hug is when both people put arms around one another."

Freda raised her arms and embraced him weakly. He could smell the intoxicating air of perfume in her hair. He pulled his face back and looked at her.

"Thanks," he said.

"You're welcome."

He brushed his lips across her lips, held them. Her mouth parted and he could feel the moisture and the heat of her tongue. Her body rose to him, fit into it. He could feel the rush of her pulse beat.

"Jesus," he muttered.

"Cody—"

Cody left Freda Graves's apartment at two o'clock in the morning. The naked body of the statue that Michelangelo would have sculpted if he had had the talent was sleeping peacefully in her bed, the nipples of her breasts closed as gently as her eyes. Before he left, Cody blew out the vanilla-scented candle that burned on the night table.

ELEVEN

JASON LITTLEJOHN PACED IN A TIGHT CIRCLE in a corner of Ethridge Landon's office. It was a lawyer's pace, an almost prissy step executed on a mental runway the length of a jury box. His arms were folded against his broad chest. He was impeccably dressed in a dark blue suit with a faint stripe. A red silk power tie with a small diamond pattern was knotted in a single loop and pulled snugly at his throat, leaving a shallow, perfect trough below the center of the knot. His white button-down shirt had a sheen of starch. His black wingtip shoes were polished to a mirror shine, one of the many hangover rituals from his days in the military. His short-cropped hair was as sculpted as a model's, with a feathering of gray spraying back from his temples and touching at his ears. Jason believed that, at the age of forty-three, the gray made him look distinguished and sensuous. He often touched his hair with his fingertips when talking to people, a subconscious habit of vanity.

Jason paced and listened intently to Miriam Finch discuss with Ethridge Landon the public relations options of the kidnapping of Aaron Greene. He did not like Miriam. Miriam was a calculating whore who had early-morning locked-door meetings with Ethridge Landon, leaving the office reeking with the odor of sex. She had screwed her way into the job and she was screwing her way into security. And Landon, either blind or naive, had no idea that anyone knew of the affair.

"I don't give a damn," Ethridge Landon was saying angrily. "It's your job to handle those bastards, not mine."

"Of course I will," Miriam said confidently.

"It's nine-fifteen," Ethridge said, glancing at his watch. "I've been listening to this crap since seven o'clock, and I'm tired of it. I'm going into that boardroom in exactly ten minutes and I'm going to recommend to the board of directors that we pull the plug on this nonsense right now." He tapped his glass-top desk with his forefinger. "Ten million dollars for a mailboy? Christ. I still think that little son of a bitch is in on this."

Jason stopped pacing and unfolded his arms. He posed with both hands shoved into the pocket of his suit pants. "As your lawyer, Mr. Landon, I've got to caution you about making such statements outside this office. You don't need a libel suit to complicate matters."

Ethridge snorted a short laugh. "Do you really think I'm that stupid?"

"Of course not, but as your lawyer—"

Ethridge waved an interruption with his hand. "I know, I know," he said. "But it doesn't matter. We're on solid ground, I think. We're doing what the FBI recommends. Christ, we pay a penny and by tomorrow morning, this country would be overrun with janitors and cleaning ladies and secretaries and security guards locked away by some nut too damned afraid to walk into a bank with a gun. Think about it. This is a bank, for God's sake, not General Motors. No, we're all right. We're fine."

"Of course we are, Ethridge," Miriam said. She glared belligerently at Jason. "After all, we're only doing what the FBI wants us to do. How can anyone argue with that?"

"The media, I think, could have a field day with it," Jason advised evenly.

"So? Let them," Ethridge replied. "Sound business always wins out over emotion. I don't give a tinker's damn about emotion."

"I agree," Jason said. "I just think we need to be aware of the possibilities."

Ethridge turned to face his attorney. He said irritably, "That's what Miriam's been doing for the last hour. Going over them. I thought you were listening."

Jason's face colored in anger. "I was," he said. "But there's more to this than how the media are going to behave. I've been on the phone constantly with our outside counsel, both here and in Washington. They're concerned about adverse publicity."

"Why?" Miriam asked in a superior tone.

Jason pivoted to face her. He wanted to slap her. "Because it may cause a backlash, a thorough investigation of the books and of the investment practices of the bank. If you remember, we had that little disagreement with the examiners only a few months ago. Even if everything were antiseptic-clean, it could have an impact. As this company's attorney, I think it's my responsibility to advise you, Miriam, that whatever you release, it should have my approval."

"Somehow I knew that's what you were getting at," Miriam said calmly. "My God, Jason, sometimes you sound exactly like a child who's all huffy because he can't get his way."

"I resent that," Jason snapped.

"Calm down," Ethridge said harshly. "Both of you." He looked at Jason. "She's right, though. Good God, Jason, she knows we have to have the lawyers look at things, but you guys are always so tight-assed about what can and can't be done. How in the name of God anything ever gets accomplished in this country is a mystery to me."

"It's for your protection," Jason said.

Ethridge reached for the coffee cup on his desk. He picked it up and drained it. "You make that sound so— so genuinely personal," he said to Jason.

"It is."

Ethridge studied the face of his corporate attorney. He thought: You lying, greedy son of a bitch. He said, "Thank you, Jason. I need support right now."

"I hope you know you've got it from me," Jason said earnestly. His eyes flickered. He lifted his face dramatically. "And I mean more than just a lawyer-client privilege."

Ethridge wanted to laugh.

"You feel comfortable with the statement I've prepared?" Miriam asked.

"Yeah," Ethridge replied. "I glanced at it. You see it, Jason?"

"I did. Outside counsel is in my office, reviewing it now."

"Good. Did you have any trouble with it?"

"Not much. Maybe a word or two. We'll get our thoughts back to Miriam after the board meeting. I still believe we should be prepared to address the possibility of this being an anti-Semitic act. It's already an issue."

"It's also a cheap stunt," Miriam hissed.

"That's your opinion," Jason shot back. "We've got at least one board member, maybe two, who think otherwise, and I think it would be unwise not to address the question."

"Why, for God's sake?"

"Because Aaron Greene is Jewish. And before you become incensed about it, it's not just my opinion. Every radio show in this city's talking about it."

Miriam stared at Jason Littlejohn. His face was splotched red. She said, "That's unbelievable, even for you."

"As the corporate attorney, it's my job to look at possibilities that may be unbelievable," Jason said.

"All right, that's enough," Ethridge said. "I want to keep the Jewish thing out of this. We've got enough to worry about, starting with nine very distressed people waiting for us." He looked at his watch. "Let's go face them."

*   *   *

The nine members of the board of directors of the Century
National Bank listened attentively as Ethridge Landon re-
viewed the events of the kidnapping of Aaron Greene.
Philip Oglesbee was in the boardroom. He concurred in
Landon's recommendation to refuse to pay the ransom
demand of ten million dollars.

"It would set a precedent that could become uncon-
trollable," Philip explained. "This is not a normal kidnapping."

"What does that mean?" asked a board member.

"People who are kidnapped are usually associated with
great personal wealth or celebrity. This is more like a hi-
jacking, with one exception. Hijackings almost always involve governments. This involves a private, profit-making
institution."

"On paper, maybe," the board member retorted with a
hint of annoyance. "Funny how much a 'private, profit-
making institution' wallows in federal regulations."

Philip smiled, and the smile was the only reply he
needed. He loved being with the federal government. The
federal government was one hell of a big gorilla.

"What about all these bombings we've had lately?" another board member wanted to know. "Any tie-in?"

Philip shook his head. "We're fairly certain they're
unrelated. Our manpower's spread thin because of them,
but we can't find any connection at all."

"Do you think the boy—what's his name?"

"Greene. Aaron Greene," Philip answered.

"Jewish, right? Do you think he's involved? Or his family?"

"No." The answer was blunt, hard.

"Sounds suspicious, that's all," the board member said.
"I've heard a rumor of a kind of Jewish underground—
kids, mostly. They're supposed to be raising money to
keep the Middle East in an uproar. Bunch of militants, like
we had in the sixties."

"That's radio talk," Philip said. "If such a group existed, believe me, we'd know about it. It's rumor. Worse, it's jabber."

"I don't know," the board member replied in an annoyed voice. He was not accustomed to being rebuffed. "If—hypothetically—such an organization did exist, a bank would be a perfect target."

"Such an organization does not exist," Philip said emphatically. His glare made the board member look away.

"Just wanted to make sure that everything's looked into," the board member said.

"I'm satisfied that's taking place," said Ethridge. "I've had Jason Littlejohn reviewing everything with our outside counsel. They're comfortable with the way the case is being investigated. Jason, is that correct?"

"Essentially, yes," Jason replied seriously. "As the bank's attorney, and as legal counsel to the board, I have to caution that much of what occurs in such an investigation is privileged information, but from all appearances and from our discussions with Mr. Oglesbee and other law enforcement officials—some in Washington, by the way—we think matters are being handled as they should be." He paused, inhaled dramatically, let his eyes sweep the board members. "Of course," he added, "it's possible that this is related to an ethnic matter in some way, but we have nothing to substantiate that at the moment." He cleared his throat. His face was shining with his sense of authority.

Philip stared at Jason Littlejohn. He knew nothing of contacts with officials in Washington. Victor Menotti was right, he thought. Jason Littlejohn was an asshole.

"Now, what I'd like is a sign of approval," Ethridge said. "Please raise your hand if you agree with this plan of action."

Eight members of the board of directors lifted their hands in unison.

"I count eight," Ethridge said, his voice tensing. He looked at the man sitting at the end of the table opposite him. "You didn't vote, Mr. Pender. Did you understand what we were doing?"

Ewell Pender raised his face slowly and gazed calmly at Ethridge. He said, in a quiet voice, "I understand perfectly clearly, Mr. Landon. I think we're about to send a boy to his death, and I can't vote for that."

The Century National Bank issued its public statement through Miriam Finch at a ten-thirty press conference in the boardroom. Miriam was dressed conservatively in a gray business suit and yellow blouse. The blouse was accented by an extravagant bow at her throat, complementing the deep blond of her hair. She wore a plastic name tag that read "Miriam Finch, Vice President of Corporate Communications."

Ethridge Landon was not present, by his own choosing, but Jason Littlejohn stood in the back of the room, in a crowded corner, his arms crossed over his chest. His face was furrowed in worry. He did not like the prepared statement that had been approved by Ethridge Landon. It had not been written by his staff. It said too much.

"I want to read a brief statement," Miriam said into the microphone at the lectern, "but I must caution you before I do that we will be reluctant to address any questions not referenced in the statement."

Stupid bitch, Jason thought. She had agreed to do nothing more than read the statement. He moved uncomfortably and leaned against the wall. He wondered if anyone would ask about the Jewish matter, and how, if someone did, she would squirm out of it. Someday, he vowed silently, I'm going to bury her ass.

The statement was brief:

"Although the Century National Bank deplores the inhumane act of the kidnapping of one of its employees, it refuses to be a victim of such terrorist activities. The ransom demand of ten million dollars will not be paid. Depositors and stockholders should be assured that bank officials are cooperating fully with federal, state, and local investigators. The bank will issue no further statements on this matter during this investigation."

There was a pause, a wave of silence lapping around Miriam. Then, from a woman holding a microphone, "That's it?" Her voice was disbelieving.

"That's it," Miriam said. She tried to smile pleasantly.

Several hands shot up, voices crowded voices. Miriam pointed to Amos Temple.

"Does the bank think this is a hoax?" Amos asked indignantly.

"We're certainly not treating it that way," Miriam answered. "We're cooperating with the investigation."

"That's not an answer," Amos snapped.

"I think it is," Miriam said coolly. She moved her eyes from Amos and pointed to another reporter.

The questions spilled.

"Has there been any direct communication with the bank?"

"No."

"Have you talked to Cody Yates about his voice being used to issue demands?"

"We don't see any reason to. Perhaps you could ask Mr. Yates about that matter, but I don't think he's present."

"Have you talked to the boy's family?"

"Not directly. We've expressed our deep regrets, but we haven't met with them. I understand that law enforcement officials have kept them secluded."

"Have you started an internal investigation on the possibility of collaboration?"

"As I said, we're cooperating with the authorities on all phases of the investigation. Beyond that, we have no comment at this time."

"Jesus, Miriam," someone said in exasperation.

"I'm sorry," Miriam replied uneasily. "Please understand this is a delicate matter. I think the statement has been circulated now. Thank you all for coming."

Amos Temple raised his hand. He said, in a loud voice, "Just one thing, Miriam."

Miriam knew she could not ignore Amos Temple. She did not like him, but she could not ignore him. "Yes?" she said.

"How in the name of God did you do a press release without mentioning Aaron Greene's name?"

Miriam's face flushed crimson. She glanced at the news release in her hand, scanning it quickly. She looked up and saw Jason Littlejohn in the back of the room. There was a level, mean smile on his face. "Oh, I do apologize," Miriam said uneasily. "Talk about embarrassing typos. It simply got omitted. But all of you know the name. I'm sorry for the omission. We did this rather quickly this morning."

Amos pushed himself forward. "What *is* his name, Miriam?" he insisted.

"Why, you just said it, Amos. Aaron."

"What's his last name?"

Miriam swallowed. She smiled nervously, glanced at the nameless press release. "It's—" Her eyes flashed over the room, like a lost child searching for a parent. "It's—"

"You don't know, do you, Miriam?" Amos pressed. Then he added, "Greene. His name is Aaron Greene."

"Yes, yes," Miriam stammered. "I do know that. Aaron Greene. I'm sorry. I just had a lapse. We've been in something of a pressure cooker since all of this began, and—"

A ripple of cynical laughter flowed in the room, and a voice rose over it: "I have a question."

Miriam looked up to a man standing behind Amos Temple. He was older. His voice carried authority. The laughter faded.

"Olin," Miriam said. "I didn't see you."

Olin McArthur was the senior reporter in Atlanta, working special assignments for the *Journal-Constitution*. Even members of the electronic media respected Olin's privilege of closing press conferences.

"It's a surprising oversight, but I can understand an omission from a press release," Olin McArthur began, "and I can understand the need to control all the speculation that you get in these types of stories. I'm sure all of us do. But no one's asked the one thing that interests me the most."

"And what's that, Olin?" Miriam said. She was afraid of him. It was in her voice.

"What if this person who has been kidnapped, this Aaron Greene, had been Ethridge Landon? Would the bank take the same position?"

Miriam's face blinked in surprise. It was not a question she had expected. "I—I don't know what position the bank would have taken under those circumstances," she answered hesitantly. "Each incident of this kind, as you know, has its own conditions."

"Would the bank have paid the ransom?" Olin asked calmly. The room was silent.

Miriam glanced at Jason Littlejohn. The hard smile had moved from his face to his eyes. "I—certainly think the same action would—apply," she replied. Then: "I think that's all I can say about that." She flashed a bothered smile and started to move from the podium. Olin's voice stopped her.

"I know it's unfair to put you in this position, Miriam," Olin said gently, yet in a voice clearly heard, "but you must understand our dilemma, also. This story is basic, and it's simple: Is one person's life worth more than another? This Aaron Greene is an office boy, not even in the shadow of the corporate ladder. Does that make him expendable? And would Ethridge Landon also be expendable if he had been kidnapped? That's the question you should prepare to answer, Miriam. At least for me."

In the back of the room, Jason Littlejohn muttered, "Son of a bitch."

*   *   *

If none among the media had thought of Olin McArthur's pinning question, all adopted it eagerly.

In the afternoon, *The Atlanta Journal's* headline on Amos Temple's story was:

BANK REFUSES TO PAY RANSOM

The subhead read:

**VALUE OF LIFE
BECOMES ISSUE
IN KIDNAPPING**

The story, with its headlines, was shot with electronic swiftness across America.

And it was quickly answered by an aroused public.

"What we want to know from you, the Katie Harris Show audience, is this: Would the Century National Bank pay a ten-million-dollar ransom if the chief executive officer of the bank— if Ethridge Landon—had been kidnapped? Is this the case of a somebody versus a nobody? Of an Ethridge Landon versus an Aaron Who? Is one life worth ten million dollars and another life not? How do you feel about it? Has the corporate world become so unfeeling that it would make such judgment calls? Put yourself in Aaron Greene's place. An office boy who delivers the mail, runs errands, takes orders from anyone who thinks of something to be done. What is the value of his life? Is he expendable simply because he isn't the president of the company? And if that's true, how many of us would also be expendable? Our lines are open. Danny in Austell, you're on the air."

"Am I on?"

"Yes, Danny, you're on the air. What do you think?"

"You're damn right they'd pay, if it was a big shot."

"But not for Aaron Greene?"

"Not a penny. Not one red cent."

"Is that fair, Danny?"

"Fair? No, it ain't fair, Katie, but it's just the way it is. Don't nobody care nothing unless you a big shot. I guarantee you, they wouldn't pay a nickel if it was me."

"All right, Danny, thanks for your call. I think you'll get a lot of support. This is Katie Harris. Jackie in Decatur, what's your opinion? Would the bank pay a ransom for the kidnapping of its president?"

"I'm a first-time caller, Katie, but a long-time listener, and I agree with Danny. Yes, they'd pay. They'd find some way of making it seem right and they'd pay whatever it took. The rich always find some way of making things happen. It's like that boy that raped that woman last year, and his daddy owned all them car dealerships, and he got off with doing nothing but a month of community service. It's like O. J. Simpson buying his way off killing his wife and that boy that was with her. If it'd been my boy that was accused of rape, they'd have him strapped in the electric chair, and if it was me in place of O. J. Simpson, they'd have had me found guilty before I could turn around. They don't care nothing about that little boy. So what if he's been killed and buried somewhere? They can say anything they want to down at that bank, but if the shoe was on the other foot, it'd be a different side of the mouth they'd be talking out of."

"Frankly, Jackie, I think we've talked enough about the O. J. Simpson thing. That's old news. But what can be done about this situation with Aaron Greene, or Aaron Who, as people are now calling him? That's what I'm interested in."

"Do what I'm fixing to do. Take my money out of that bank. I don't have much. A few hundred dollars that I've scrimped and saved to have, but I'm going to take it out and put it somewhere else."

"You think that'll send a message, Jackie?"

"It would if enough people feel like I do."

"Well, maybe you've started something, Jackie."

"I hope so."

TWELVE

BY THE OUTFIT THAT SHE WORE—JEANS
stylishly torn at the knees, bulky sweater, high-top tennis
shoes, stocking cap, riding gloves—it was impossible to
recognize Carla Napier as a girl. Her hair was swept up
and back as a boy would wear his hair. Her delicate face,
without makeup, seemed only the face of a small teenage
boy. She had a knapsack strapped to her back and she rode
a bicycle with elevated handlebars. Among the crowds on
the street, Carla was an annoying, but smiling, presence.

She pedaled north on Forsyth, turned right at Marietta,
then veered left onto Edgewood and passed Central City
Park and continued to Georgia State University. She
parked and wheel-locked the bicycle and went into Sparks
Hall. Students mingled in the corridors, talking in the lan-
guid mood of late afternoon. She passed hurriedly among
them and went to a telephone. Nearby a couple argued
easily about an economics professor. She pushed a quarter
into the telephone and punched the sequence of a memorized number. After a moment, she said in a soft voice,
"Mrs. Dilliard?" A pause. Then: "Listen to me very carefully. Call your husband and tell him to go to Rich's at
Lenox Square, to the menswear department. Tell him to
look for a mannequin dressed in a blue pin-striped suit.
Look in the left inside pocket of the coat and he'll find a
tape. It has Cody Yates's name on it." She replaced the

receiver quickly, turned, and began walking out of the building. A voice calling her name stopped her.

"Carla? Carla Napier?"

She turned. The boy speaking to her was Ron Eaton. She had attended Carlton-Ayers School with him.

"Ron," she said. She was nervous. She had not expected anything to interrupt the schedule.

"It is you," the boy said enthusiastically. "I thought so. I was passing the telephone and heard your voice, and I knew it was somebody I knew. Damn, it's good to see you." He embraced Carla awkwardly. "What're you doing here? You in school?"

Carla wondered what he had heard at the telephone. She answered, "Three days a week. I've been in the library. Are you here now?"

"Just transferred. I was at Duke, but it was too far away." He laughed and said in a whisper, "The old Doc thought I'd make better progress in familiar surroundings—exactly the opposite of what he said a year ago. How are you, by the way?"

"Fine," Carla told him, smiling. "Much better. Believe it or not, I can even speak out in class." She studied the face of Ron Eaton. He reminded her of Aaron Greene— boyish, uncertain eyes, a posture that seemed always to step backward.

"And they thought we were a lost cause," Ron Eaton said. "God bless good old Carlton-Ayers. Cost our parents a fortune, but it made us quit sucking our thumbs, didn't it?"

"Yes," Carla replied. She glanced at her watch.

"Looks like you've got to go," Ron said.

"I'm sorry, but I do," Carla told him. "Maybe I'll run into you again, soon."

"Hey, I'd like that. You were my first date. Remember? Prom night at Carlton-Ayers. Ninth grade, wasn't it?"

Carla smiled and nodded. She remembered the night. Full of fear and dreams—fear and dreams mingling in a sour chemistry, the scent of it pasted on Ron Eaton like a rancid perfume.

"Are you still at home?" asked Ron.

"Ah, no," Carla said. "My—my parents finally divorced. I'm staying with friends. I'm sorry, Ron, but I really do have to run."

"I'll be on the lookout for you," Ron promised. "Maybe we can grab a sandwich for lunch. Make up for that prom night."

"Sure," Carla said. "See you." She turned and rushed away.

Outside, Carla unlocked the bicycle and began pedaling toward the state capitol. At the corner of Courtland and Martin Luther King Boulevard, she got off the bicycle and waited. A white van crossed Courtland and parked, and Morris got out and opened the back of the van. Carla pushed the bicycle to him and he placed it in the van.

"Get in," he said in a hard voice.

In the van, driving away, Carla said, "I'm sorry I was late."

"I had to circle the block three times," Morris said irritably. "What happened?"

"I was detained."

"How?" The question was sharply asked.

"I ran into an old classmate from school. I had to talk to him."

"Who is he?"

"Just a friend. His name's Ron Eaton. I haven't seen him in years. We were at Carlton-Ayers together."

Morris spat a sarcastic laugh. "The loony bin."

"You went there," Carla said icily.

"Yeah, and I was loony. Everybody was. They still are." He looked at her. "You get it done?"

"Yes." She looked out of the window, away from Morris's small, hard eyes.

"What's the matter?" he asked.

"Nothing, Morris. Nothing's wrong."

"It's that boy you just saw. Ron Eaton. You date him?"

"No. Yes. Once. We went to the ninth-grade prom together."

"Sounds lovey-dovey to me. You like him?"

"He's very nice."

"He take you to bed?" Morris asked bitterly.

Carla turned to face him. She said defensively, "I was in the ninth grade and terrified of even dancing with him. Why would you ask such a thing?"

"I'll bet he had you," Morris said. His voice was angry. "I'll bet he whacked off in bed every night, just thinking about you."

"Well, think what you want," Carla snapped. "He didn't make love to me, and I don't want you to say anything else about him. He was very timid. Now he's better, and that makes me glad."

"Are you going to see him again?"

"I don't know. He goes to State. Maybe I'll see him there."

"You wanted the other boy to see you, too, didn't you?" Morris said. "That's why you went into the garden. You wanted him to see you."

"Don't talk about him," Carla said angrily.

"You like being seen by boys, don't you?" Morris teased.

Carla turned to look out of the window again. She said, fighting for control, "Take me home, Morris."

"Sure. Sure, I'll take you home."

"What?" Harry Dilliard said.

His wife repeated the instructions she had been given. His wife's voice trembled.

"All right," Harry said, writing in his newsman's shorthand. "Listen, don't let this bother you. It means nothing. Go across the street and stay with Phyllis if you want to. I'll get in touch with you later."

"Are you going to tell the police?" asked his wife.

"Of course I am. Right now. In fact, you may have a policeman come out, just to check on things. Tell him what happened, exactly the way you told me. And quit worrying. It's not an epidemic, for God's sake. Nobody's going to throw a blanket over your head and take you off." He glanced at his notes, ran a checklist of questions in his mind, then asked, "Was it a woman or a man who called?"

"I don't know," his wife whined. "It sounded like a young girl, or maybe a boy. A girl, I think."

Harry made a note. "A girl?" he mumbled.

"A young woman," his wife replied.

"All right," Harry said.

"Call me," his wife whimpered.

"I will."

Harry replaced the telephone on the receiver. "Son of a bitch," he sighed. He lifted the telephone again, touched a single button. "Get Halpern in here," he said to Nina Clark, his secretary. "And find Yates," he added. "He's at the police station, or he'd better be. No, wait. To hell with Yates. Get me that detective—Menotti. And get Temple in here with Halpern. And when you finish with all that, get me Philip Oglesbee over at the FBI."

"You want him here, too?" asked Nina.

"No, Nina, I want him on the telephone, but after I talk to Menotti."

At the Atlanta Police Department, Victor Menotti took the transferred call from Harry Dilliard's office and then motioned for Cody to follow him.

"What's up?" Cody asked.

"Another tape."

"Where?"

Menotti laughed. "Rich's at Lenox. In the men's department. I like this. It's got style."

As they drove to the department store, Menotti asked, "You see anything in those files?"

"Nothing," Cody replied. He had been reading from file cases of alleged and real kidnappings, but the term was technical. Most of the cases were exaggerations of runaways or anger over custody of children. Not a single case demanded a ransom. Not a single case used recorded messages.

"Didn't think you would," Menotti told him. "At least it keeps you off the street."

"Right now, it keeps me out of the office. I called in earlier. You know this made every banner in the country, don't you? And it was the lead or second lead on every television station from Savannah to San Francisco. Quirky damn thing. You never know. Some days a broken fingernail on Dolly Parton gets as much play as Bill Clinton lusting after interns, other days the Pope could become a Southern Baptist and it wouldn't make the gossip columns."

"That's offensive," Menotti said dryly. "Maybe you forget, asshole, but I'm a Catholic."

"Sorry," Cody mumbled. "Anyway, everybody who ever took Journalism 101 wants the inside story, and more than a few of them are demanding that I come clean." He laughed. "That's the word Halpern used: *clean*. That son of a bitch is worse than you, Menotti. He told me that a New York publishing company left its number. Wants to talk a hurry-up book deal. And believe it or not, Sherlock, the networks are after yours truly. Maybe I could become a television star, jump mediums, make some money for a change."

"Go for it," Menotti said. "You'd be an ugly son of a bitch to have to watch, but go for it. By the way, do me a favor on your way to fame."

"What's that?"

"Get home a little earlier. My boys got a little tired of watching you play tag-the-tit last night."

Cody blushed. He was right. The bastards did follow him. He wondered if they'd seen him on the deck.

"Who was she?" Menotti asked.

"A coworker," Cody said nonchalantly. "We were talking business." He thought of sleeping with Freda Graves. He had tried to call her earlier, but she was on assignment.

Menotti cracked a short laugh. "You're a work of art, boy," he said.

"Look, why don't you let me give you a call every hour or so?" Cody said. "It'd save the city some money."

"Naw," Menotti replied easily. "Spoil my fun. I told you, Cody: You're mine. Besides, those boys following you are new at the job. They love it. I've got them believing you're the grandson of Al Capone." He glanced at Cody. "She really look as good as my boys say?"

"She's all right."

"Millie know about her?"

"No. And I'd prefer to keep it that way."

"Sure. Of course. Won't say a thing—until I need to."

"You're a prince, Menotti."

"Not me," Menotti said. "But we're about to see him."

"Oglesbee?"

"You got it."

The tape in the blue pin-striped suit, played in the privacy of a manager's office, said in Cody Yates's voice: *"The bank is playing with a life. If our demands are not met in one month from this date, we cannot assure Aaron Greene's safety. The bank should listen to the people. The people understand what it's like to be a nobody. People don't like being stepped on. People know how corrupt the powerful few are. No matter what the bank thinks, there are more people like Aaron Greene than like Ethridge Landon. This is not a game. Aaron Greene is in jeopardy."*

Philip Oglesbee pushed the off button on the tape machine. "Damn," he said. "It still amazes me, how they do that."

"At least you know it wasn't me this time," Cody said.

"I never thought you had anything to do with it anyway," Philip said. He shook his head. "I'm forty-four years old, and I'm out of the loop on this stuff. I can't believe how fast they can pull something like this off. Jesus, what they're talking about happened today, and here we are with a tape that's been edited as clean as a whistle."

"I still don't understand it," Cody said.

Philip pushed a button, popped the tape from the machine, picked it up with his handkerchief, and dropped it into an envelope. "Nothing to it, they tell me," he said. "It's the kind of stuff Bill Gates was probably playing around with when he was two or three years old. They tapped your phone, got a few miles of tape, probably transferred it to CD, fed it to a hard drive, and anytime they want to put together a message, all they do is type it in and whatever the hell it is inside one of those things puts it together, word for word, or syllable for syllable, and then they lift the sound. Kid's play."

"Your guys figure it out?" asked Menotti.

Philip Oglesbee laughed. "Shit," he said. "My thirteen-year-old son told me how it worked. My guys just confirmed it."

"Yeah, well, didn't they take one hell of a chance?" Amos Temple said. "I mean, leaving it in a suit? Somebody could have bought it."

Menotti shook his head. "Not likely. Not on a mannequin. Not in Rich's. And they picked the right one. Not a security camera on it."

"Okay, what do we do with it?" asked Harry.

The question surprised Philip Oglesbee. "Print it," he said. "I'll have some copies made and distributed to radio and television. I'd rather put it out up front than have somebody claim they were able to obtain a copy. God, I hate that, and I promise you, whoever's doing this will make sure it happens."

"We'd better let the Greenes know what's going on," Menotti suggested.

"Yeah," Philip agreed. "I've got a couple of boys out there. I'll drive out. You want to go?"

"No reason," Menotti said. "Your boys talking to the salespeople?"

Philip nodded. "No help. They've got a sale going. The store has been packed, which is probably why it was chosen as the place to leave the tape. Nobody ever seems to see anything in a crowd."

"You heard the news. A new tape has been released by the kidnappers of Aaron Greene. We have been able to obtain a copy of that tape through our contacts and we'll play it for you in a few minutes, but what we want to know now is how you feel about it, here on The Katie Harris Show. *One month. That's the threat. What does it mean? One month to live? What do you think? Should the bank reconsider its position and meet the kidnappers' demands? And if they do, will it be a precedent for more kidnappings from other groups? Can the bank, or any institution, afford to be terrorized? And what about the question that seems to be on everyone's mind: Would the bank pay the ransom if the kidnapped party happened to be the chief executive officer of the bank, or some other high-ranking official? Is it all right to put Aaron Greene in danger because he's a mailboy? Remember on yesterday's show, our unofficial poll—the first opportunity for you to respond to this tragic event—was overwhelmingly in support of the opinion that the bank would pay if Ethridge Landon had been the victim. How do we resolve this moral dilemma? Let us know how you feel. Mitzi in Duluth, you're on the air."*

"Katie?"

"Yes, Mitzi, you're on the air. What do you think?"

"I love your show, and I love you, but it makes me sick to my stomach to think we're even talking about this. They're going to kill that poor boy, Katie. I know it. I can feel it. I cried half the night, just thinking about it."

"It is upsetting, Mitzi. And it's hard not to feel he's in danger."

"That's the kind of country we are, Katie, and that's what makes me so mad. It don't matter about the little person. The little person will always come up on the short end of things. I

think the government ought to step in and do something about it. We pay enough taxes to have somebody up there in Washington care about the little people."

"Well, the FBI is working on the case around the clock, Mitzi. At least, that's what we've been told."

"Maybe so, but they don't seem to be getting anywhere, if you ask me. And what about that newspaper fellow? Has anybody looked into him? If it's his voice, he must have something to do with it. I'll bet you could turn up a rock in his backyard and find some answers."

"The report we have is that Cody Yates—he's the man you're talking about, Mitzi—has nothing to do with it. Apparently his telephone was tapped for a number of months to get the tape the kidnappers needed. But it is a question being asked by a lot of people. We've tried to get Mr. Yates on this show, but he refuses. I don't know why. You'd think he'd be eager to tell his side of the story. Maybe it's because he works for a newspaper, and the newspaper wants to keep all that kind of news for itself. This is a competitive business, Mitzi."

"Still seems funny to me. All I know to do is pray for that boy, and it don't matter to me at all that he's Jewish. I talked to my minister. He said he'd have a special prayer service for him on Sunday. I just hope every Christian church in the country does the same thing. If the government can't help us, the Lord can."

"Thanks for the call, Mitzi. Before we break for the weather report, let's hear from Douglas in Jonesboro."

Ewell Pender stood at the window of his second-floor study and watched the game of croquet on the lawn of the garden. Alyse and the boy. He could not hear Alyse's laughter, but he could see it. Her head lifted high, her face bright in the late-afternoon sun. She wore her hair back, clasped at the neck. He liked her hair that way. It made her seem girlish and happy. The boy was bending over the ball with the mallet in his hand. He tapped lightly at the ball and the ball rolled a few feet, sliding through a wicket. Alyse raised her hands and applauded. The boy seems to like her, Ewell Pender thought. And he should. Alyse was gentle and patient. She was the perfect companion.

He turned to a soft knock at the door. Oscar entered without an invitation. He pushed a serving cart to the desk and poured tea into a fragile china cup, then, using silver tongs, he placed two lumps of sugar into the cup.

"Will you be joined, sir?" Oscar asked in his courtly voice.

"Yes," Ewell Pender replied. "One other cup, please."

"I've taken the liberty of adding some small cinnamon cakes to the tray," Oscar said. He took another cup and saucer from a drawer in the cart.

"You know me too well, Oscar. I'm in a weak mood, I'm afraid."

"Yes sir. Will you need anything else?"

"No, thank you."

Oscar turned to leave.

"Oh, one thing," Ewell Pender said.

Oscar turned back. "Yes sir."

"Would you join us tonight for our small concert?"

"I would be honored, sir."

"I thought I would play a selection from Mendelssohn. I believe you have an appreciation for him."

Oscar smiled.

"Would you please ask Carla to join me."

Oscar dipped his head in a servant's acknowledgment and left the room quietly. Ewell Pender moved to his desk and took a cake and bit into it. It was exceptional. A trace of cinnamon. He sat at his desk and sipped from his tea. He was pleased that he had asked Oscar to join them for the music. Oscar was the most civilized person he knew, yet the most unlikely to be at all civilized—not with his youth, spent in the German military as a reluctant officer in the Schutzstaffel—the SS—during the Second World War. But youth was easily forgiven. Oscar had changed. He had faked his death and escaped to America, even taking the name Davenport, after an English soldier whose name tag he had found on a battlefield, and he had found employment at the Pender estate. He was now an old man, a faithful servant, a friend. Still, he kept the friendship in check. Oscar did not believe it was proper for a servant to behave in a familiar manner with his employer. He understood propriety. Propriety was not to be violated. It was almost impossible to believe that Oscar had once killed in rage, even if the killing had been deserved.

Ewell Pender knew the knock at the door, the timid rapping, was Carla's. She had made remarkable progress in the past year, though there was still uncertainty in her behavior. The scar of a debilitating fear of unworthiness was embedded in her like a hideous tumor. Still, he trusted her. He liked the caring she wore as an aura. It was a balance. She was not like Morris. Morris had become obsessed with his encyclopedic knowledge. Morris did not demonstrate the capacity for caring, only the potential for destruction. Morris was gifted, but he would always need to be watched—carefully watched.

"Please come in," he said to Carla.

Carla entered the room and closed the door. She wore a spring dress, brightly colored. Her hair framed her face perfectly. She was girl-woman pretty, with innocence and with sensuality. Carla had always reminded him of a character from a play by Ibsen. What was it? *A Doll's House?* He did not remember.

He stood. "Would you care for some tea?"

"Thank you, yes," Carla said. She sat in the chair before the desk.

Ewell Pender poured the tea and placed two lumps of sugar into it and stirred it. "Some cakes?" he asked, presenting the tea.

"I think not," Carla said after a moment.

"Then forgive me for indulging," he said. He took another cake and ate it, slowly, with great pleasure, then he sat at his desk. "How are you?" he asked gently.

"Very well, thank you."

"I hope you're not upset about that little disciplinary procedure."

"No. I was wrong. I deserved it."

"And perhaps I was wrong," Ewell Pender said. He moved out of his chair and back to the window, and motioned for Carla to join him. "Look at them," he said. "I think you should be out with them, having fun."

A quick, involuntary smile slipped across Carla's face. She watched Alyse strike the ball, saw the ball roll off-line.

"He's seen everyone but you and Maria and Oscar," Ewell Pender said. "Or I should say he hasn't seen you directly. I've kept you away from him because of your youth. I thought it might confuse him."

"I understand," she said.

"But he seems to have adjusted fairly well. I think he feels he's in a safe environment. Indeed, it may improve him to see you." He paused, looking through the window at Aaron and Alyse. "Perhaps you could help him through his awkward stage," he added.

The smile vanished from Carla's face. "Whatever you wish."

"Good. Now, why don't we finish our tea. I want you to tell me about today. I understand you encountered a former friend at the university."

Carla fought the surge of temper. She thought: Morris. She said, "Yes. We only spoke for a moment."

"Come, come, sit."

He guided her to her chair and sat near her. He did not want the desk between them, separating them.

"Tell me about him," he urged gently. "What's his name?"

"Ron," Carla answered. "Ron Eaton. We were at Carlton-Ayers together. Everyone thought he had a severe learning disability, but he didn't. It was all psychological. After the training, he was as aggressive as any of us. I think he must be very bright. He was at Duke, but returned to be at home."

"That's good. Very good. Once they thought the same about me, Carla," Ewell Pender said quietly. "That's why my grandfather founded the school, but, of course, you know that."

"Yes."

"Do you think he could have heard you making the call?" The question was calmly asked.

Carla could feel a blush swim across her temples. Morris had left nothing out of his report, not even speculation. "No," she said firmly.

"Are you sure?"

"Yes," she replied. "I know what I'm doing when I have an assignment."

"Of course. Of course you do," Ewell Pender said. "We have to be careful, that's all. Every question must be asked."

Carla did not reply. She sipped from her tea.

"You don't like Morris very much, do you?" he asked.

"I—like him," Carla said after a moment. "Sometimes he scares me a little. I think he's always watching me."

"I understand," Ewell Pender said. "Morris is business. He believes in it. He doesn't permit enough time for reflection or meditation. I watch him in our music hour. Sometimes I think he's simply being patient. I wonder if he hears at all. Do you think he dislikes the Jewish people?"

"I—don't know."

"Of course you don't. It's not something we bring up, is it?"

"I know he's valuable," Carla said.

Ewell Pender nodded agreement. "He is." He gazed at Carla, a long, thoughtful gaze. "But everyone is," he added. "That's what we learn in overcoming our handicaps, isn't it? Morris overcame his handicaps and he is, indeed, valuable. What we must guard against is developing new handicaps. We lose our value when that happens."

"Yes," Carla said.

"Now, I have a question for you: If you had to make the decision, would you have Morris deliver the letter?"

Carla was surprised by the question. She could not remember Ewell Pender involving any of the group in critical decisions. "I think so," she said after a moment. "I'm sure he's thought of every possibility. Yes. He would handle it well."

"Thank you," Ewell Pender said. "I think you're right. I think he will handle it well. In fact, he should be delivering it in a few minutes. The attorneys called earlier. Everything is as we want it. Now, why don't you run along. Change into something comfortable and go outside and join the play. I think you'll be good for the boy. I think you, perhaps more than any of us, can help him in his learning experiences."

Carla stood. She looked quizzically at Ewell Pender. Her clear blue eyes were glittering with the fluid of excitement. "I'll try," she said meekly.

Morris wore a chauffeur's uniform. He said to the guard at the lobby desk of the *Journal-Constitution*, "I'm to deliver this to a Mr. Harry Dilliard." He smiled at the two men in business suits sitting behind the guard. He knew they were agents—probably federal—and he knew they were bored.

"What is it?" the guard said.

"I think it's a letter," Morris answered politely. "It's from Mr. Ewell Pender. He asked that I deliver it personally."

"You work for him?"

"Yes. I'm his driver."

The two men in business suits stood and stepped forward. One of them said, "Would you mind opening it?"

"I'm afraid it's sealed," Morris replied.

"May I see it?" the man asked.

"Of course," Morris answered. He handed the envelope to the man. The man fingered it carefully.

"We'll deliver it," the man said gruffly.

"I'm afraid I—can't accept that," Morris said. He smiled easily. "I don't know who you are."

The man reached into his inside coat pocket and removed his credentials and displayed them with a flip of his fingers. A show, Morris thought. A gesture from television police programs. The man was with the Georgia Bureau of Investigation.

"Oh, I see," Morris said. He glanced at the guard, then back to the man. "I suppose it's all right. Mr. Pender insisted that I deliver it personally, but—"

"You can go with me," the man said.

"Thank you," Morris replied. "I'd feel better doing that. Don't want to get in any trouble about it."

"Yeah, sure," the man mumbled.

Harry Dilliard took the envelope from the agent. "Who's it from?" he asked, eyeing the chauffeur standing conspicuously at the secretary's desk outside of his office.

"Ewell Pender," he said, the agent answered. He bobbed his head toward Morris.

"Pender? That old eccentric? My God, I thought he was dead. Wonder what he wants?" Harry opened the envelope and read. Then he said, "I'll be damned."

THIRTEEN

———◆———

CODY DID NOT ANSWER THE TELEPHONE. TO hell with it, he thought. He was tired of the badgering. He had been home for two hours and he had talked on the telephone from the moment he walked through the door, except for two whizzing minutes in the bathroom. The questions were always the same, and all of the questions, rolled into a wad of words, asked only one thing: What can you tell us that you're not telling anyone else? Stupid questions. Why in God's name would they expect him to reveal something he would not first use himself? Didn't they understand that he knew their trick? Had used it himself. Many times. It was an old technique: Badger until surrender. But he knew the game. Had been at it a long time. Many years. Too many years. Bullshit. Maybe tomorrow he would have the number changed and leave it unlisted. In the meantime, he would let the answering machine take the punishment.

He knew he would have to leave his apartment for peace, but he did not want to go to the bars. The badgering on the street, by amateurs, was worse than the badgering over the telephone. He had to give television its due: Put up a face on the screen and people remembered it. He had stopped at the grocer's and had had to leave without buying. At the service station, he had been trapped against the pumps by two women who recognized him. The telephone was not as bad, but it was bad enough; he had to leave his apartment.

Millie, he thought. She'd invited him. Almost insisted. No, he couldn't. He had talked earlier with Sabrina and she had whispered that Millie was cooking dinner for a man who taught at Emory University. Philosophy, he guessed. Well, the poor son of a bitch would meet his match, and if he arrived horny, he would leave bewildered. Millie would nail his hide to the wall like a wild game trophy. She would serve him veal piccata and quote Alfred North Whitehead and if he opened his mouth to debate the views of Whitehead, she would make him feel like swamp slime. Cody smiled at the vision of a professor of philosophy sitting at a candlelit table, enduring the nonstop ravings of his former wife.

The vision of the candles made Cody think of Freda Graves. He had not been to the office and had not seen her, and when he called she was still out on assignment. He remembered touching her, remembered watching her undress with a slow deliberateness that was incredibly exotic. He remembered her breasts burgeoning from the thin, front-snap brassiere, and the slender, muscled abdomen shadowed in the candlelight. He remembered her standing before him, wearing white, V-cut bikini panties.

The telephone stopped ringing. Cody lifted the receiver quickly and listened for the dial tone. He punched Freda's number.

"What you are about to hear is a poor imitation of a primeval scream," he said when she answered on the second ring.

"What's wrong?" Her voice had an edge of concern.

"No privacy. The goddamn telephone. It won't stop ringing. I can't step outside without being assaulted. I went down to check the mail. Ted Koppel was waiting for me. He wrestled me to the ground and held me down while Dan Rather asked embarrassing questions about the size of my genitalia. I finally broke away and escaped to my own bathroom—to check on my genitalia, as you might expect, since it seemed to hold some interest for inquiring minds—and who do you think was there? Barbara Walters."

Freda laughed.

"Now for the beggar's imitation," Cody said. "I've got to get out of here. Can you stand some company? I'll behave. I promise."

"Then, no," Freda said coyly.

"Fine. I'll be a maniac," Cody told her. "I feel like one anyway. Can I bring anything? A bottle of wine?"

"Bring Ted Koppel. He turns me on."

"Sure. Why don't you put on one of those outfits you ordered through *Penthouse*? You know—black stockings and garter belt and spiked heels. I understand Ted's a fool for that sort of thing."

"Isn't that what you wear when you entertain?" Freda said, teasing.

Cody smiled. The warrior princess of the western world had thrown away her steel armor. The woman who remained was remarkable.

"See you in a few minutes," he said.

"Okay," Freda replied softly.

Cody was certain that Menotti's men had followed him, but he did not care. The car that had eased behind him from his apartment was so nondescript it was obvious. The only people left on planet Earth with no-option cars were the police. And Menotti's men had gotten clumsy; they followed too close. Perhaps they wanted him to know they were there. Perhaps it was their way of pleading for a short night. If so, they were going to suffer. Cody did not plan to go back to his apartment. Maybe he would order pizza for them in a few hours.

He sat on the deck of Freda Graves's second-floor apartment and smoked a cigarette and watched Freda turn steaks on the grill. The weather was cool, the wine superb, the odor of cooking steaks relaxing. Freda was dressed in jeans and a Hard Rock Café T-shirt from San Francisco. She did not wear a bra, and as she moved her arms to attend the steaks, Cody could see her breasts quivering beneath the shirt. I don't believe this, he thought. I've worked with her for eight years and despised her. Eight years wasted. He wondered who she had dated, what man had watched the ballet of her body rising magnificently above him in the amber light of candles. Certainly someone. She was practiced.

"Is rare all right?" Freda asked.

"Medium," he replied.

"Medium," she said.

"Where were you today?" he asked casually.

"Working on a feature."

"About?"

"A homeless woman with two children. It's part of the homeless series, but I don't want to talk about it."

"Not easy, is it?" he said.

"No. I never like those kind of stories."

"You do them well."

She looked up from the steaks. "You really think so, or is that an obligatory compliment?"

"Obligatory? No. You're a damn fine writer, lady, and I mean it. From what I read, you've only got one problem."

"Tell me," she said.

"You've never been really mad, you've never lost it," Cody said calmly. "You get upset and offended, but never pissed-off mad."

"I'll have to think about that," Freda replied. "But you do think I'm a good writer?"

"Yep. I've never liked you enough to tell you that, but you are."

Freda smiled and returned to her watch of the steaks. She asked, after a moment, "Why didn't you like me?"

"You can give off a chill that would make the *Titanic*

turn south," he said honestly. "I prefer my ice floating in scotch or tea, not in people."

"And, you, Cody Yates, can be a real ass. But you know that, don't you?"

Cody crushed out the cigarette in a cut-glass ashtray. "I guess."

"But I do have a confession to make," Freda said.

"Sounds interesting," Cody replied.

"When I was a senior in college, I wrote a paper on your series about prison conditions in the South, the one that should have won the Pulitzer. It was brilliant. It really was."

Cody blinked in surprise. "You did?"

"I did. I got an A. In fact, I still have the paper, along with your series."

"I'll be damned," Cody said in astonishment. "Why didn't you tell me?"

"To be truthful, I was a little awed by you when I first came to the paper, and then I got the word."

"What word?"

"I was told to avoid you, that friendship with you would automatically put me on a to-be-watched list with management."

Cody laughed. "So that's why nobody speaks to me. I thought it was my leprosy." He picked up his glass of wine, swirled the wine with a rocking of his hand. "Why are you taking such a chance now?"

Freda closed the top of the grill and watched the smoke swirl out of the vent. "Do you know why I became a journalist?" she asked after a moment.

"A misguided high school counselor?" Cody said.

Freda smiled. "Not hardly," she replied. "When I was fourteen I read a story about the reunion between a nurse and a soldier she had saved during the Second World War." She looked at Cody. "It made me weep. Not because it was sad, but because it was so wonderfully written.

I read it over and over, Cody, read it until I memorized it. Then I began to write it from memory. I wrote it so many times that I began to believe I had conducted the interview—not the writer whose name was on the story. And, finally, I believed I *was* the writer. That's why I do what I do, why I'm the kind of person I am. I've always wanted to write that story—for real."

Cody sat listening, watching the face of the woman he had considered cold and aloof. My God, he thought, she's telling me something she's never told anyone, and he believed, in that moment, that he understood her. As a journalist, she had learned to balance the romance of the profession with its startling reality. She had survived newsrooms because she understood the nature of newsrooms—moody, energetic, demanding, arrogant, comic, tragic. Her persona was her shield against the little uncivil wars that erupted with ease and with regularity around her. Her persona—her reputation—was absolute: Detached, cold as an iceberg. A neutron bomb could not melt the chill of her glare when she fixed it, with laser sharpness, on a target.

But the people who worked around her, those engaged in uncivil wars for the sport of battle, did not know that Freda was terrified. She believed that she had never written a story as grand as the story of the nurse who saved a soldier in the Second World War, and the awards and compliments and even the quivering regard of her cohorts could not assuage the fear that her greatest triumph as a writer had occurred at age fourteen, copying from memory the words of someone else.

"Thank you for telling me," Cody said quietly.

She turned from the grill to face him. "But that's not what you asked about, is it? You asked why I was taking a chance being with you."

"Yes, I did."

"I've been there eight years," Freda said. "I'm thinking

about leaving anyway. And I'm old enough now to believe that what I do on my own time is my business, and part of that business involves you. I've always been attracted to you, Cody Yates, but didn't want to admit it." She paused, looked toward the sliding glass door leading into the apartment. "Was that the telephone?"

"Could be," Cody replied. "But it's not mine, thank God."

"Watch the steaks," she said. "They're almost ready." She went into the apartment, answered the telephone, and returned to the door. "It's for you," she said, frowning. "A man named Menotti."

"Beautiful," grumbled Cody.

"I know the name, but I don't know why. Who is he?"

"Detective for the city. And an old friend."

"Now I remember. I'll get the steaks."

Menotti was laughing playfully when Cody answered the call.

"Pissant," Cody sneered.

"Got enough for a visitor?" Menotti asked.

"Kiss my ass," Cody hissed. "What do you want?"

"I want you, my friend. Got something to show you."

"What?"

"A letter. I'm out front, on my cell phone. Can I come up?"

"If you don't stay."

"Not over a couple of hours."

"While you're there, why don't you send your boys home," Cody said. "I'm sure they've got families, and I intend to be here considerably longer than their shift break."

Menotti laughed again. The phone clicked dead.

Cody walked back to the deck. "Better take them off the flame and put them in the oven," he said. "We're about to have a visitor."

"He's coming here? When?"

"In a minute or two. He was out front, on his cellular.

Look, if you want me to leave, I can meet him downstairs."

"No. No, it's all right. I'll put the steaks away. We can eat when he leaves. How did he know you were here?"

"I don't know," Cody lied. "Maybe he had me followed. The man's Dick Tracy in the flesh."

Freda put the steaks into the oven and went into her bedroom and closed the door. When she returned, she was wearing a bra beneath a loose blouse. She blushed at Cody's recognition.

"I—was a little casual, don't you think?" she said.

"I think you were close to perfection," Cody told her.

Menotti was in a frivolous mood. He met Freda with exaggerated courtesy, begging forgiveness for his intrusion. He explained that he had volunteered to find Cody, to deliver a copy of a letter from Harry Dilliard's office. "He tried to get you at your apartment," he said to Cody, "but all he got was your answering machine. I told him I was planning to see you."

"You're a kind man, Menotti," Cody said.

"It's my civic duty," Menotti said, smiling. "I'm high on civic duty." He handed Cody the letter.

"Would you like a glass of wine?" asked Freda.

"Thank you, no, I can't stay," Menotti answered. He looked smugly at Cody.

"I'm sure you haven't pried this open and read it, have you?" Cody asked.

"Of course I read it," Menotti replied. "But I didn't need to pry it open, as you put it. We all read it. We were called right after it was delivered to the paper."

"What is it?"

"You read it," Menotti said. He smiled pleasantly at Freda, a boyish smile, she thought, a smile of tarnished innocence.

Cody pulled the letter from the envelope and read aloud:

"Dear Mr. Dilliard:

"This is to inform you that the Ewell Pender Foundation has, on this date, established an account in the name of Aaron Greene (hereinafter called the Aaron Greene Fund) for the purpose of raising by public contribution the necessary amount of money to meet demands for the safe return of Aaron Greene to his family.

"This account will be audited by Thrasher, Dellgood and Dellgood, certified public accountants.

"To initiate contributions, the Ewell Pender Foundation has designated two hundred thousand dollars for the Aaron Greene Fund.

"As a citizen, I wish to encourage all concerned individuals to participate in this vital effort. It would be an unconscionable violation of human rights to condemn a person to death solely on the social status of that person.

"I am further instructing that advertisements of this announcement be placed in the nation's major newspapers, with detailed information on participation by the citizenry. The title of this campaign will be 'Wake Up America!'— chosen to inspire the public conscience in the treatment of defenseless members of society.

"In the event this campaign is unsuccessful, all money will be refunded at a cost to be borne by the Ewell Pender Foundation.

"Further, as the only dissenting member of the Board of Directors of the Century National Bank in the decision regarding Aaron Greene, I have, this date, tendered my resignation from that board."

The letter was signed in a clear script by Ewell Pender.

"I've heard the name, but I don't remember. Who is he?" asked Freda, as Cody folded the letter and slipped it back into its envelope.

"Old-line family," Cody explained. "Blood as blue as ink. More money than Midas. I did a profile on him a few years ago. Jesus, he must be eighty now, or close to it. Used to be on the front lines of anything that happened, but he dropped out of sight. I'd even forgotten about him being on the board at the bank, but that's to be expected. His grandfather was one of the founding partners. His grandfather was the money-maker. In the railroad business, but he didn't shovel coal, if you know what I mean. From what I learned, he was a tough son of a bitch. Got what he wanted, and he wanted a lot. His son—Pender's father—blew his brains out because he couldn't stand the heat in the shadow. Ewell had to have special schooling after that, and his grandfather founded a school just to provide it. It still operates today. Then somebody killed the old man. They never did find out who. Could have been a thousand people, the story goes. Every now and then, some magazine will do a piece about it, one of those unsolved mystery features."

"What's he like?" Menotti asked.

Cody shrugged. "Pender? Who knows? Hell, he's old. An old man. But this sounds like him. The downtrodden being picked on. It's right down his alley. Tell you the truth, I only met him a couple of times. His staff gathered most of what I needed. He didn't give a damn about the business, so he shopped it out. Paid top dollar for executives, and they made him more money than his grandfather ever dreamed of. Went from railroads to oil, banking, insurance, trucking, exports, software—you name it. I doubt if Ewell Pender even knows everything he owns. He never married, so he didn't have a family lapping up his money. He wanted to be a concert pianist. All he ever did was play the piano. Good, really good, but not good enough, I suppose. Collects art. Pours millions into symphonies all over the world, or he used to. That's the point: He's been out of the headlines for years. I really thought he was dead."

"And he can afford to pull this new stunt off?" Menotti said. He was sitting forward on the edge of the chair, his elbows propped on his knees, listening carefully.

"Afford it?" Cody replied. "He could pay the tab and give the boy a Rolls-Royce to drive home in."

"Did he like the piece you did on him?" asked Freda.

"I don't know," Cody said. "I suppose he did. I got a note from him, but I always assumed it was one of those little details that his secretary did for him. I remember her well. She was impressive—one of those totally devoted types. She really wanted it to be right. Had a great name— Alyse Burton. Don't know why I remember that, but I do. Maybe it had to do with the name Burton. She looked a lot like Elizabeth Taylor, back when Elizabeth Taylor looked like Elizabeth Taylor."

"Maybe I'd better have a chat with him," Menotti mumbled.

Cody gazed patiently at Menotti. "I know what you're thinking, old friend, and there's nothing to it. I'm not the key to this. It's just coincidental. I've done a lot of stories on a lot of people over the years."

"What are you talking about?" Freda said, puzzled.

"Nothing," Cody answered. His voice warned Freda not to press the question. Then, to Menotti: "What do you think will happen when this gets out—the letter? Will it do any good?"

Menotti slipped back in his chair. He laced his fingers over his chest. He said, "Remember when Oral Roberts went on the air and told everyone that God was going to snatch him up to heaven if his people didn't fill the coffers? Did that do any good?"

"That was different," Cody argued. "It was religious fanaticism."

"Different? How? Tell me a better ransom demand," Menotti said blithely. "None I can think of—except this."

"Why this?" Freda asked.

"Because it gets to everybody, not just a few. Because everybody knows what it means. They're just like that boy. Deep down in their souls they know they're a no-body."

Menotti stood and gazed out the window for a moment, then turned to look at Freda. "Don't you?" he said. "Don't you feel like a nobody occasionally? I do. Every day. Maybe for just a second, or if it's a bad day, maybe for hours. I think everybody does, even if they bounce around like a rubber ball and they've got a smile on their face that looks like an orchid in bloom. I think everybody has a little shiver of doom, of being totally worthless, that passes through them every day, and that's why they'll pay, why it'll roll in. They could be Aaron Greene." He turned his look to Cody. "Will it do any good? You watch. It'll be like a parade, with dollar-bill confetti. That's a two-hundred-thousand-dollar snowball that old man just pushed off the top of the hill. He's going to get a lot of credit, and people love that kind of recognition. In a couple of days, it'll be some television star, or some sports jock, and then some politician leaping on the bandwagon, and the rest of us poor slobs will fall in with our pennies and nickels. And I think that whoever did this knew it all along. They knew."

"You don't agree with it, do you?" Cody said.

Menotti smiled sadly. "Oh, yes, I agree. Probably give something myself. If I didn't, my wife would. But it won't work. I also know that." He turned to Freda. "I'm glad to meet you. You're a fine reporter." The smile turned bright. Boyish. "Much better than most people I know in your profession."

"Thank you," Freda said warmly. "Can you stay for dinner? We can put on another steak."

"Wish I could, but it's been a long day," Menotti answered. He glanced at Cody. "A couple of guys are waiting downstairs for me. We've got some things to do."

Cody understood the message. He stood. "Did Harry want me to call him?"

"He didn't say."

"I'll see you tomorrow," Cody said.

"Don't rush it," Menotti replied in a casual, coded voice. "Make it in the afternoon."

In bed, after they had made love, Freda said softly, "I know what he meant."

"Who?"

"Your friend. Menotti. When he was talking about people feeling worthless, feeling as though they don't exist. I saw that when I was interviewing that mother for the homeless story I've got to do. That's exactly how she feels." She moved against his arm. The candlelight flickered across the ceiling above the bed. "My father went through that. He was fired when he was fifty-three, from a company he had worked for for twenty years. They didn't care, Cody. They didn't care. All he'd done for them, and they didn't give a damn, and he was more loyal to that damn company than he was to his own family. They fabricated some ridiculous story about violating company policy in a political campaign, when he did nothing more than what he was asked to do. I checked it out. It was a setup. It almost killed him. Everything that's being said about Aaron Greene on those talk shows is true, Cody. It is. If it were the president of the bank who'd been kidnapped, they'd pay. No questions asked. They'd open the vaults and roll it out in a wheelbarrow. You know that. That's what I don't like. All that pious bullshit about not giving in to terrorism. They don't care anything about that boy."

Cody could feel her body shudder. He knew she was crying. He folded his arms around her and her flesh was warm against him.

FOURTEEN

HE COULD FEEL THE PRICKLING HEAT OF EX-
citement still on his throat and chest, a rash, like the pin-
dots of measles. He knew the rash would fade as he became
calm, but he did not want to be calm. Not yet. He wanted
to keep the cheering alive, wanted to feel it on his throat
and chest, wanted it to pump its joy through his blood-
stream.

His hand still clutched the folded pages of the paper,
and he was certain that his fingers could read the marking
of the grade like a reader of Braille. The grade was an A,
a large, jubilant painting on the front of his title sheet. The
tip of the *A* leapt up into his typed name, making a tent
over the *o* in Ron. Damn, he thought. A miracle. No one
got an A in one of George Holden's courses. Never. It
was George Holden's belief that the study of economics
was too complicated to be understood by anyone still an
undergraduate. But he had an A. Ron Eaton had an A.
And there was a single-word note on the front of the paper
from George Holden. *Brilliant.*

Damn.

It had been a paper on the effect of the Olympics in
Atlanta, particularly with street vendors. He had begun the
paper with the sentence "There were no pros for street
vendors during the 1996 Olympics in Atlanta; only cons."
He meant con as being conned.

Brilliant.

Damn.

He wanted to call his mother, but did not stop at the bank of telephones. He would wait and tell her at home, watch the bloom of surprise on her face. He needed to see that, to see the bloom. God, he had watched the wilting of her face often enough.

He pushed open the door to the building and stepped onto the sidewalk and inhaled slowly, deeply. The air smelled of oil, and he laughed involuntarily. He had wanted the air to be as clean as the air after a rain. He shook his head, crossed the street, and walked in a quick stride toward the parking lot. He was late. His mother would begin worrying. *I should have called her*, he thought.

His car was at the far end of the lot, on the lower deck, tucked into a corner space that left barely enough room to park without hitting one of the cement pillars holding the top parking floors. He had scraped the pillar before, but it did not matter. The car was old, an Impala that belonged to his mother. It had taken nicks and dents. Another nick, another dent, another scrape meant nothing.

He took his keys from his pocket and opened the door and threw his books and the paper with an A blazing on its title sheet like a flag on the backseat, and then he glanced down at the left front tire.

"Ah, shit," Ron muttered. The tire was flat.

He closed the door and kneeled beside the fender. A large nail was driven into the side of the tire, near the rim.

"Trouble?" a voice said.

Ron's head jerked up in surprise. He had not seen anyone in the parking lot. A man in a rough blond beard—a beard that seemed pasted to his face, rather than grown—stood at the rear of the car. He was wearing a pea jacket and a stocking cap rolled to fit the crown of his head. He had his hands in the pockets of the jacket.

"Uh, flat tire," Ron said nervously.

"Your car?" the man asked.

"My mother's," Ron answered. He did not move from his kneeling position.

The man smiled. He blinked once, slowly. "Don't look like much of a car for picking up girls," he said.

"It—it's my mother's," Ron said again.

"You ever get a girl in this car?" the man asked, his eyes leveled on Ron.

Ron could feel the queasiness of fear in his stomach. "I—I've got to fix the tire," he mumbled.

The man peered into the backseat of the car. A smile, a sneer, curled over his lips. "I'll bet you've had plenty of girls in this car," he said in a voice that sounded like a giggle. "Big backseat. You could wallow around all night back there." He looked at Ron. His smile blazed. "I'll bet if I opened the door and took a deep breath, I could smell the women you've had in that backseat. Like a dog, I could smell them. They always leave a scent, you know. It's like honey-heat." The man sniffed a laugh, looked around quickly. "Honey-heat," he whispered.

Ron started to rise. The man's hands flew out of his pocket and Ron saw the dull flash of a steel pipe, maybe a foot long. He froze. The man kicked suddenly, the point of his shoe catching Ron in the stomach, driving him backward. And then the man was over Ron. The pipe fell across his throat. A cry gurgled from Ron. He heard hard breathing, felt the moisture of a silly laugh spilling on his face from the man pinning him against the concrete, and then he lost consciousness.

It was Victor Menotti's habit, when bothered, when he needed to think clearly, to go into a public library with a notebook and sit at a reading table and draw straight lines on notepaper. The lines were lines of thought, labeled in a shorthand of his own invention. It was a habit he had obtained from his wife, who taught school and went often to libraries to work on lesson plans. She had begged him to accompany her in their first years of marriage. She had said, "Find a book and read. It'll be good for you, I promise. Calm you down." He had known, of course, that she merely wanted his company, wanted him to watch her at work and, by watching, to admire her. Both the promise and the motive had been realized. Victor Menotti did admire his wife—in fact, was in awe of her—but he also had discovered the therapeutic wonder of a library's orderly and quiet environment. It was exactly the opposite of his desk at police headquarters. He could work in chaos, but he could not reason, could not follow his straight lines on notebook paper, coded in an indecipherable shorthand.

He sat in the library, alone at the table, and looked at the lines. There were only two of them. One was for Cody Yates, one for Ewell Pender. He had intuitively written their names under the lines. There was no reason. It was as though the names were in the tip of the pencil and they fell off, under the lines. But Menotti trusted his intuition. His intuition was a voice that whispered to him like a knowing counselor. He had solved a number of baffling cases listening to that voice.

He looked at Ewell Pender's name, and traced over it again with the tip of his pencil, darkening the lettering.

He had not read the morning newspaper, but he knew the story of Ewell Pender's fund for Aaron Greene was on the front page, declaring in its black-lettered tongues the simple cry of equality—*Wake Up America!* It was a damn strong argument, Menotti thought. Could have been written by the Christian Coalition, or any splinter group of the so-called Moral Majority. Them vs. Us. The Haves and the Have-nots. And there were a hell of a lot of people on the Us and Have-nots side to join in the hissing and bellowing.

It would become ugly. It was an old story that grew like a rich harvest of bitterness in the overworked soil of the South. The Haves were forever getting their balls chopped off by religious leaders and politicians and journalists championing the cause of the Have-nots while posing as righteous arbiters of social unrest. Like the hell-raising over some very private clubs. When was it? A couple of years ago. Maybe longer. It had to do with excluding blacks and Jews and, implied in the stories, other undesirables. Yeah, Menotti decided. A couple of years ago. If his memory was correct, Ethridge Landon had been in the eye of that storm, defending the right of his club to its exclusive membership policy. The Haves—and Ethridge Landon—had taken a beating, had even closed the club, but they had endured. Arrogant bastards. Sitting pretty on the cushion of money, snapping their manicured fingers for service, peering down their surgically straight noses at riffraff.

And now one of the Haves—Ewell Pender—had joined the Have-nots, a Them had become an Us, but an Us with money. Why?

Menotti wrote beside Ewell Pender's name: *ec.* It was short for "eccentric." Eccentric was how Harry Dilliard had described him. But, what the hell. A lot of people were eccentric, yet only the wealthy were able to make such behavior an admirable trait. He had heard the word two nights earlier from his wife. She had been talking of Ted Turner and she had called him eccentric. She had said it not as condemnation, but as a compliment, and that was one of the privileges of being wealthy. The not-wealthy who were thought of as eccentric were also considered fanatics, troublemakers, mavericks.

Under the line with Cody Yates's name, Menotti wrote: *mv.* "Maverick." Interesting, he thought. If Cody was a maverick then he, too, was eccentric—mildly eccentric. But Cody was not a fanatic or a troublemaker, regardless of his irritating disposition at times. Cody was an idealist who believed that his profession was important, but the years of trying to make it behave importantly had taken its toll. Cody was like a fighter who had answered the bell too often. His skills were on automatic, but his heart had been bruised by the pounding.

Menotti tried to imagine Cody as a younger man, fifteen years earlier, during the first year they had known one another. It had been a comfortable relationship from the beginning. They had mind-boxed gently, in the expected friction of friendship. Little jabs, healed with smiles, with the jokes that men tell. He had attended Cody's wedding to Millie and had berated him for the divorce, and perhaps he had been too critical, had jabbed too hard. The closed-door life of a man and woman was never the same as the one portrayed at holiday parties. Maybe Millie was as over-bearing and demanding as Cody had claimed. Maybe her flirtation with higher education had dulled her flirtation with Cody. Whatever it had been, it had left Cody in need of attention—and he was getting that now. Freda Graves would not likely spend her time discussing the symphony or a traveling exhibit of Andrew Wyeth paintings, and if she did, it would not be while Cody had his hands on her breasts. If Menotti had read her right—and he took great pride in his talent for reading people—Freda Graves was too smart to worry about being smart.

Menotti casually drew a line from Cody's name to Ewell Pender's name—*mv* to *ec*, connecting them like a tie be-tween railroad tracks. The movement of his hand felt good, felt right. A tingle even. An electric shock. If it had been a Ouija board, he would have believed his hand had been mystically moved. He lifted his hand, stirred slightly in his seat, and drew another connecting line. The same sensation struck him again. Why? he wondered. Was there a relationship that not even Cody realized? He pushed the paper away and stared at it, narrowing his eyes on the lines. There *was* something. Had to be.

A librarian passed Menotti's table with books in her arm. She smiled pleasantly, nodded, and walked away. She must think I'm disabled, he thought, an idiot savant skilled at scribbling in straight lines on a sheet of paper, someone left by an attendant while the attendant browsed the li-brary. Or maybe she thinks I'm drawing diagrams for bombs, since Atlanta had become bomb-crazy. He looked again at the paper. Strange, he thought. There were only two lines—Cody's and Ewell Pender's. Why hadn't he drawn a line for Aaron Greene? Had he forgotten Aaron? He pulled the paper back to him and drew another line and wrote Aaron's name beneath it. He paused, holding the point of the pencil over the paper. Then, beside Aaron's name, he wrote: *nb. Nb* for "nobody." No, he thought. No. He rubbed the eraser over the *nb* and wrote *eb. Eb* for "everybody."

A message from Philip Oglesbee had been left for Menotti at police headquarters. It said: *Another anti-Semitic call this morning. You have any answers?*

"No answers," Menotti said over the telephone to the African Prince. "But I know where to ask some questions. Any luck with the tracing?"

"Nothing. We put a caller ID on the phone, and that tells us where they're coming from—pay phones, all of them. From all over. Not a matching set of prints on any of them. Whoever it is at least knows something about technology and rubber gloves."

"I'll get on it," Menotti said.

"Maybe my first hunch was right," Philip said seriously. "Maybe it is anti-Semitic, and they're trying to make a buck while they're at it. Did you see the paper this morning?"

"Not yet," Menotti told him.

"It looks like a London tabloid. I talked to Dilliard. He said the story on Pender's Wake Up America campaign had been picked up all over the country."

"I don't doubt it."

Philip chuckled. " 'Wake Up America!' " he mused. "Corny as Kansas, but damned if it's not getting more media play than Michael Jordan. We've already heard from all three networks, and CNN's moved in like a bad relative needing a handout. And that doesn't count being hounded by every independent radio and television station in the great forty-eight, or everybody with a laptop slung over their shoulder, pretending to be a reporter of integrity." He wanted to sound annoyed, but he did not.

"Do what I do," Menotti advised. "Lie to them."

Philip coughed a laugh. He said, "Yeah. No wonder you locals are so damned beloved. Let me know if you get anything on the calls. You want a couple of my boys?"

"Not yet," Menotti said. "I think we locals can handle it."

Philip ignored the slap. "I talked to the police commissioner," he said. "He pushed down the orders for you to be left alone over there. He wants you to report what you get directly to me, with copies to him of anything you put on paper."

"I figured as much," Menotti said. "Suits me."

"Good. Give me a call this afternoon," Philip replied. His tone was one of accustomed authority.

Menotti stopped his car in front of Howard Edwards's novelty store in a small shopping strip on Buford Highway. A bell at the top of the door jingled as he entered the shop. A man's voice in the back of the store, behind a partition, called, "Be right there, friend."

"Take your time," Menotti answered. He strolled the store, looking at displays of magnetic signs and bumper stickers and cups and glasses and pencils. It was a trashy store, poorly kept. The advertisements promoting Howard Edwards's selections were from a litany of redneck and racist slogans. Howard was proud of his fierce belief in the propaganda of the Klan and his arrests at civil rights gatherings over the years. He had boasted of hitting a black man with a rock during the march on Forsyth County, but Howard was not as vehement in his hatred of blacks as he was in his disgust for the Jews. To Howard, the Jews owned everything.

"What can I get you?" Howard asked in a booming,

friendly voice, coming forward from the back of the store.

Menotti turned to face him. "Hello, Howard."

Howard Edwards's face colored suddenly with anger. "Fuck you," he growled.

"You forgot about the horse I rode in on," Menotti said easily.

"What you want?" Howard snapped.

Menotti moved toward him, his eyes locked hard on Howard's face. "I want you. I want your miserable ass on a greased pole," he hissed. "I want to see you dead, you miserable son of a bitch."

Howard blinked in surprise. He had been arrested a half-dozen times by Victor Menotti, but he had never seen Menotti angry.

"What the hell I done now?" Howard demanded.

"You still love the Jews as much as you used to?" Menotti said forcefully. He was close to Howard.

"Kiss my ass, Menotti."

"I asked you a question, you bucket of rat shit."

"And I answered it."

Menotti heard a movement from behind the partition. He looked over Howard's shoulder and saw a large man with long, grease-caked hair and a billowing beard. He wore a work shirt with the sleeves cut off at the shoulders. The tattoo of a bar code, like the bar codes used in grocery checkout stations, was on the hard muscles of both arms. He was holding a pipe wrench.

"What's the trouble, Howard?" the man snarled.

"Not a thing, friend," Menotti said evenly. "It's private."

"Maybe it was, but it ain't no more," the man growled. He raised the pipe wrench and stepped toward Menotti.

Menotti's right hand darted inside his coat. He felt the tip of his handgun, a semiautomatic 9mm department-issue, and yanked it from its shoulder holster. He raised it and fanned the safety with his thumb in one motion. The man stopped in midstep.

"It's private, friend," Menotti said firmly. "Unless you still insist, and if you do, I'm going to blow a hole right through the center of your ugly face, and, to tell you the truth, I wouldn't mind that. It'd get me relieved of duty—with pay—while they conduct one of those godawful internal investigations over whether or not I acted in haste, or if I, in some way, offended your civil liberties." He swiveled the barrel of the gun toward Howard. "And, of course, if I kill you, I'm naturally going to have to kill Howard just to keep any conflicts out of my official report. But you know what, friend? I'll get a vacation that I sorely need and you and Howard will get a funeral that you both sorely deserve."

"Get back, Billy," Howard said. He did not take his eyes off Menotti. "I'll take care of it."

"Yeah, sure," the man named Billy mumbled. He started to step backward.

"Stay right there, friend," warned Menotti. "You put that wrench down real easy and I'll quit being so tense about this little hole-maker. Then I want you to stand there like you're a tree and you've got roots that run all the way to China."

The man slowly placed the wrench on the floor.

"Now, let me tell you who I am," Menotti continued. "My name is Victor Menotti. I'm a detective for the City of Atlanta, and if I ask questions, I want some answers. Do you understand that?"

The man nodded.

"Good," Menotti said. "When I leave here, the two of you can spend the rest of the day feeling each other's muscles and swapping lies about how you're going to whip my ass the next time you see me, but until I go, I ask the questions and you give me the answers."

"What you want to know?" asked Howard.

"You been making any phone calls about Jews lately, Howard?"

"What the hell you talking about?"

"You been making any threats?"

"I ain't had time. The niggers keep me busy," Howard sneered. He smiled smugly.

"You know about that boy that's been kidnapped?" Menotti asked.

"Why, no, I ain't heard nothing," Howard replied in a mocking voice. "Some little Jew-boy get hisself snatched up?" He glared at Menotti. "You know goddamn well I heard of it. Who ain't? But if you think I got that boy off somewhere, you full of shit."

Menotti lowered his hand holding the semiautomatic. He said wearily, "I know you don't have him, Howard. If I thought that, I'd have this place taken apart like it was Swiss cheese needing holes. You dumb shit. You're not smart enough to pull off what these people are doing. But somebody's been making calls, saying the Jew-boy is going to die. And that sounds like you, Howard. Playing games maybe. Showing off for Billy, or one of your other clones. We've already nailed your ass twice for spouting off, or have you forgotten those few tender moments in our welcome house? You just naturally pop up in my mind whenever I hear something like that."

The anger flushed again in Howard Edwards's face. He said, "I don't give a shit what happens to any Jew on the face of the earth, but you ain't gon' march in here and start on me when I ain't done nothing. Goddamn it, I got rights, too."

Menotti smiled. He had arrested Howard Edwards so many times he knew when Howard was lying. This time he wasn't.

"You remember the last time we had a little set-to, Howard?" Menotti asked.

"Yeah," Howard mumbled.

"Caught you trying to put the make on that transvestite, remember?"

Howard glanced back to Billy. "I thought the son of a bitch was a woman."

"Remember what you promised me?" Menotti said.

Howard nodded. His face was the color of ash.

"You promised me that if I drove your sorry ass home and let that drop, you'd owe me one."

Howard nodded again. He ducked his face to stare at the floor.

"Well, I'm here to collect. You hear anything about this, you give me a call," Menotti said. He looked at the man named Billy. "And that goes for your sophisticated friend there. Do you understand, friend?"

Billy wagged his head slowly. There was a look of bewilderment in his eyes.

"All right," Menotti said. He slipped his gun back into its holster, then swept the store with his eyes. "Why don't you clean this place up, Howard? Good God, man, you might actually make a sale or two if the place looked halfway decent. And take down all that racial shit. You want to sell it, put it under the counter. Put out some magazines with naked women in them."

Howard shrugged. A half-smile cracked on his face. He said, "Someday, you gon' get your fucking head blowed off, Menotti." Then: "You got any idea who's got the boy?"

"None," Menotti answered honestly.

"Well, one thing's sure as shit: The bank ain't gon' pay a plugged nickel for him. Everybody's dead right on that one. I don't care if he's a Jew or a nigger or a fucking circus midget. If he ain't worth nothing, he ain't got a chance."

"My God, Howard," Menotti said, "damned if you don't sound sympathetic."

"Fuck you, Menotti—and the horse you rode in on."

Cody had agreed to meet Menotti at the Rusty Nail at five o'clock. At five-fifteen, still waiting, he called Harry Dilliard at the newspaper and asked if there had been any new tapes.

"Nothing," Harry said. "Where are you?"

"At the Rusty Nail, out on Buford. Menotti wanted me to meet him here."

"Why?"

"He didn't say," Cody replied. "Maybe to have a drink. I don't know."

"So, what did you do today?" asked Harry.

"Avoided the world, like you ordered," Cody answered wearily. "I went fishing." Cody liked the lie. He had stayed in Freda Graves's apartment, away from the assault of telephone calls. Only Menotti—and his men—knew where to find him.

"Of course, Cody. Stupid of me to ask. I understand you're famous for fishing, another Hemingway at it," Harry said cynically. "I know I told you to stay out of sight, but you could have called in."

"I did," Cody said. "Halpern said it was a madhouse down there."

"He got that right. The whole damn world's on this, most of them looking for your sorry ass. A guy from *Newsweek* just left. The BBC had a stringer crew in here this afternoon. Sent in a correspondent from Washington to do the interviews. Damn, I love those Brits. They've got the greatest voices in the world."

"I caught *The Katie Harris Show* this afternoon," Cody told him. "It's still the subject of the enlightened."

"She still yanking at your gonads for hiding something?" asked Harry.

"Not too bad. The talk's about Pender. Well, split fifty-fifty, I'd say. Half of them think he's crazy and the other half think he's a saint. But they're talking money. All of them."

Harry laughed. "You're not going to believe it, Yates, but we're waking up with the rest of America. We're giving hard cash."

"You're kidding? The paper?" Cody asked in astonishment.

"You got it. The big boys upstairs sent down word a few minutes ago. Said we'd add twenty thousand to the kitty."

"Not a small sum," Cody said. "That surprises me."

"It's pretty much the amount that it cost Pender to run a full-page ad, splitting the difference between weekday and Sunday editions," Harry said. "You could call it a trade-off. Some newsprint and ink for some sizable PR."

"Ain't we something," Cody mused. "I've got to go. I'll see you in the morning."

"Be here, Yates, but don't say a damn word to anybody who tries to stick a microphone under your nose."

Cody returned to his table—a high-backed booth—and ordered a club soda with a lime twist. Menotti arrived at five-thirty. His face was fatigued. He slipped into the seat across from Cody and stretched his shoulders against the booth back.

"What do you want?" asked Cody.

"What're you having?"

"Club soda."

"Same."

Cody signaled the order to the waitress standing at the bar. "What's going on?" he asked Menotti.

"Talk to me about Ewell Pender," Menotti said quietly.

"I told you all I know."

"Why's he doing this?"

"Who the hell knows? He's old. He's got the money. Maybe he's tired of being out of the headlines."

"You know what a detective does, Yates?"

"Detects, I suppose," Cody said. He did not intend to argue with Menotti. Freda would be at her apartment in another thirty minutes. An argument would waste time.

"Good word," Menotti replied. "Detects. Do you know what the word 'detect' means? It means 'to come upon.' "

"I'll buy that," Cody said. "Where's this leading?"

Menotti leaned forward over the table and played with

a cigarette he had pulled from his coat pocket. "I've come upon the theory that there's more than a magazine story between you and Pender," he said evenly.

Cody sighed and tapped a cigarette from his own package and lit it, then held the lighter to Menotti. The waitress placed the two glasses of club soda on the table and asked if Cody and Menotti wanted popcorn.

"Not for me," Cody said pleasantly. He looked at Menotti. Menotti waved away the offer with his fingers. "We'll just stay with the heavy stuff," he added. The waitress smiled obligatorily and left.

"Well?" Menotti said after a moment.

"Jesus, Victor, why don't you drop this?" Cody moaned. "I thought you had something to tell me."

"I am telling you, Cody. I'm telling you that I can't shake the feeling that something's there. I like my feelings. They lead me around like I'm a dog on a leash. This time they're leading me straight to you and Pender, and they're yelping like they've treed a bobcat."

Cody drew from the cigarette and thought of its bitter taste. It was his first of the day, a break in his vow to Freda to go an entire day without smoking.

"Well, let me see if I can help you," Cody said. He dropped back against the booth and gazed at Menotti. "I don't know very much about him, except that he's my real father. You see, my mother was a domestic in his mansion and he was a horny bastard—not being married—and my mother was, and still is, a beautiful woman. He treated her like Cinderella at a Savannah cotillion, and she found him, and his money, irresistible. That's how I got to Yale. He paid for it. It's also why I secretly own the newspapers, and just piddle around the office, doing what I damn well please. Of course, I don't see him very often. I send him cards on Father's Day and at Christmas and on his birthday, and once or twice a year we go fishing, or to a Braves game, or we toss a football around in his backyard. It's not much, but I don't complain."

Menotti grinned. He gulped from the club soda and leveled his eyes on Cody. "I noticed the family resemblance," he said dryly.

Cody crushed out his cigarette. "That's because you're a detective. You may be the only person alive who's ever come upon that incredible fact."

"You don't know anything, do you?" Menotti asked seriously. "You really don't."

"No, Victor, I don't. I wish I did. I wish I could give you a book of facts linking me to Ewell Pender, but the truth is, I've only seen him a couple of times. I wrote one magazine story. That's it. Period. It's coincidence. Jesus, I barely remember it. That was when Millie and I separated."

Menotti rubbed his face with his hands and slumped deeper against the cushion of the booth back. He said, "Tell me how his father died."

"Killed himself, so goes the story. Not much argument there. He left a note saying he couldn't take the pressure any longer."

"And the grandfather?"

Cody shrugged with his shoulders. "Nobody knows the hard facts about that one. He was found dead, shot through the mouth, apparently with one of his own guns. He was a collector. The gun that killed him was a nasty little German Luger out of the First Great War. It was missing. They never found it. But whoever killed him wanted him to know he was going to die; that's pretty certain."

"Why?"

"They made him eat it. Barrel in the mouth, like I said."

"What year did it happen? You remember?"

Cody thought for a moment, turning his glass in his hand. "It was in the forties, after the war, I think, or just at the end of it. Pender was in his twenties, his grandfather was mid-seventies, I'd guess. Maybe I'm getting the dates confused, Victor, but I think I'm right. Pender's father committed suicide when Pender was nine or ten years old.

The mother died a couple of years later of a high-stress heart attack, and the grandfather bit the bullet—and I mean that literally—about fifteen years later."

"I haven't had time to check it out. They didn't arrest anybody, did they?" asked Menotti.

"Not according to what I read," Cody told him. "But, Victor, I have to confess that many great writers of literature accept the first thing they read about anything. We're poets, my boy, not archaeologists. The plain truth is, I don't know. I don't think they did. Like I said, I was a little out of sorts when I was doing that story—dealing with Millie—but if you're obsessed by it, you can look it up. Just remember, it was viewed by a lot of people not as the murder of an old man, but as an occasion to celebrate. He was a ball-buster."

"Very poetic, Cody."

"I try," Cody said. Then: "Tell me something, Victor: Why the hell are they using audiocassette tapes for this? That's horse-and-buggy stuff. I don't know diddly about it, but why not e-mail? Or some other whiz-bang toy?"

"Maybe they're old-fashioned," Menotti said. "You got me. The African Prince told me they didn't have anybody on their staff who knew a hell of a lot about audiotapes and they had to bring one of their fellows out of retirement to give them some advice. Old fart, Cody. Like you. But he does know an eight-track from a computer disk. From what the Prince says, the old fellow's having a blast. Claims that whoever's doing it is as fascinated with his game as he is with the money—maybe more so."

"Maybe he's right."

"I'd bet on it," Menotti said.

"So, is that all you wanted out of me?" Cody asked. "If it is, I've got an appointment."

"One other question."

"Ask away," Cody said.

"Talked to Millie lately?"

"You're an ass, Victor. A real ass."

"Look," Menotti advised, "I don't care who you diddle, or when, or where, or how often, but give the lady a call. Believe me, she's worried about you. I know. She called Arlene."

"Jesus."

"Just do it, Cody."

"All right, I will."

"When?"

"Today. Before I leave here."

"Good boy," Menotti said.

FIFTEEN

———◆———

JASON LITTLEJOHN SAT IN THE HOT TUB ON the deck of his home, his back pushed against a spewing jet of warm water. Bubbles sizzled around his chest and popped in the cool air. His back, strained from an early-morning game of racquetball with Ethridge Landon, relaxed. His arms were draped over the sides of the hot tub and his head was tilted backward. Strings of perspiration drained down his face out of his silvering temples. He was mind-weary from a conference that had begun at ten in the morning. The conference had been with three lawyers from the consulting firm of Raymond, Gaines, Albright and Detwilder. The three lawyers had discovered a possible violation in reporting material events to the Securities Exchange Commission and were frantically attempting to cover the involvement of Raymond, Gaines, Albright and Detwilder. With Ewell Pender's resignation, the attention of the New York god-makers would be intensified and their microscopic eyes would want to see everything remotely questionable. The afternoon had been spent bickering over highlighted words. It was an old trick of rolling blame into a ball and then battering it back and forth, hoping it would lodge immovably on the playing court of the opposition. One repetitive word kept ringing in Jason's head: *clearly.* It had been said a thousand times, a million times, a billion times, during the day.

"Clearly, this means . . ."

Clearly, Jason had a headache from it. Ethridge Landon had left Jason to negotiate the differences, implying by his absence and his refusal to address the issue that he, Ethridge Landon, was immune to whatever fault the Securities Exchange Commission or federal bank examiners might find.

So what else is new? Jason thought. He had stepped in the path of lethal accusations before, protecting Landon like a bodyguard conditioned to accept assassination attempts. The little set-to with Ewell Pender a few months earlier, the one regarding a poor performance rating on community investment loans, was an example. He had taken on Pender and the bank examiners, and had defended Landon and the bank with a legal pirouette that would have made George Balanchine gasp in admiration. Ethridge had walked away unscathed. It had been that way for three years, since he had been appointed corporate counsel for the Century National Bank. His predecessor, Frank Pair, had followed a philosophy of minimal risk, and it had cost him his position. Frank Pair had been too jovial, had not catered enough to Ethridge Landon, and he had been easy to push aside. But Frank's dismissal—a retirement ruse—had not been a personal matter with Jason; it was business, and business was more than a framed MBA; it was also being alert to opportunity and having the nerve to seize opportunity at the right time.

The glass sliding door leading into the house opened and Jeanne Littlejohn stepped onto the deck. She wore a bikini with a towel wrapped around her hips, folded into itself at her navel. Her breasts billowed over the cups of her bikini top. She had two glasses in her hand.

"I made you a drink," she said.

"Thanks," her husband replied. "I was sitting here thinking about one."

She handed him the glass and slipped the towel from her waist and eased into the hot tub opposite him. "God, that feels good," she sighed. She sipped from her drink and placed it on the deck. Then she stretched in the water, her legs reaching for him, touching his legs, her toes tickling him playfully in his groin.

"Come on," Jason said. "I need my rest. My back's killing me."

"You're getting old," Jeanne teased.

"Old? Christ, I'm forty-three. How do you get old out of that? You're only three years behind me, in case your mirror forgot. Do you feel old? Forget it. It's not my age, it's my back."

"Turn around," Jeanne purred. "I'll rub it."

"Not right now," he said. "The water feels good."

"Does, doesn't it?" Jeanne murmured. She pulled off her top and slipped deeper into the water, letting her breasts float teasingly at the surface. Steam rose from her pink nipples.

Jason could feel the bloodrush. His wife was stunningly beautiful. Golden hair. Chocolate eyes. Full, plump lips over a perfect mouth with perfect teeth. In the nude, Jeanne Littlejohn always made Jason weak with surprise. He was lucky and he knew it. Damned lucky. Yet, it was luck that carried a price. Jeanne Littlejohn used her body as a tease, as the only power she had or cared about. There were rumors about her, rumors that Jason ignored. Jeanne was an asset, and that mattered more than an occasional indiscretion.

"Don't you ever worry that someone's going to get a peek at you?" he asked.

Jeanne's foot nuzzled against him. "Not unless they can see through a fence," she replied. She rolled in the tub and moved her breasts just above the jet of water. The sensation pleased her.

"Did you call DeKalb Peachtree Airport?" asked Jason.

Jeanne hummed a yes.

"What did they say? When can I start taking lessons?"

"In May," Jeanne said, rolling to face him. "But I still think it's a little obvious."

"Obvious? How?"

Jeanne laughed and picked up her glass. She pulled back to sit on the underwater seat. Her breasts bobbed in the water. "You take up flying two months after Ethridge starts his lessons. Don't you think that's obvious?"

Of course, Jason thought. But Jeanne did not understand opportunity. Being obvious was the key.

"I've already said it was Ethridge who inspired me to do it," he said. "And that's the truth. He's been talking about it since his first lesson, trying to get everybody he knows involved."

"Are you the only one to follow his lead?" asked Jeanne.

"I guess," Jason said. "So what? And to cut through the bullshit, yes, I'm doing it in part because Ethridge is doing it. I learned a long time ago that advantage goes to the person who knows how to recognize advantage. You've just got to have the guts to do it."

"I'm kidding," Jeanne teased easily. She added, "After all, if Ethridge hadn't put in a hot tub, we'd still be without one. I think it's wonderful that he inspires you."

"Don't start it, Jeanne."

"I'm sorry," Jeanne said. "I'm just chattering." She flicked water at his face with the tips of her fingers. "So, what's new on the kidnapping thing? What was that boy's name?"

"Aaron Greene," Jason answered.

"I don't know why I can't remember that," Jeanne said casually. "What's the latest?"

"I've been in a meeting all day. I don't know. Pender's name is all over the paper, the old bastard. What a play. The old son of a bitch has no idea how much trouble he could cause. But I guess if I had that much money, I wouldn't bother about it, either."

"Darling, I know you wouldn't," Jeanne corrected.

"We're catching it from all four sides, that's all I know,"

Jason admitted. "Last I heard, we've got people closing out accounts faster than we're opening new ones. We can't take a lot of that."

"Little accounts, I'd guess," Jeanne said. "I don't think I'd start to worry until some of the big boys get involved."

"Money, my dear, is money," Jason countered.

"You really think it could have that much of an impact?"

"Of course it could."

"Should we transfer some funds to the bank in Arizona?" Jeanne asked.

Jason pushed himself up from the water and sat on the edge of the tub. The water dripped from him and steam coated his body. He said, after a moment, "Not now. It'd send the wrong signal to Ethridge. But I may in the next few days. I can say I need it for that land development project."

"Could this fold the bank?" Jeanne asked, suddenly worried.

"Technically, no," Jason answered. "You were right. Most of the withdrawals are from small depositors, the nickel-and-dime crowd. Doesn't mean much when you look at the whole, and I don't think the major accounts are concerned. I'm not as worried about them as I am the government."

"Why the government?"

"I don't want to talk about it," Jason said.

"Then don't," Jeanne said. "Let Miriam worry about it."

Jason snorted a cynical laugh.

"Not jealous, are you?" Jeanne said lightly. "She's getting a lot of attention."

"It's her job to get attention, not mine."

Jeanne smiled. She had never known anyone who could find the heat of the spotlight better than her husband.

"Want to go out tonight?" she asked. "Maybe we could

call Ethridge and Lydia. The four of us haven't been any-where together in a month."

Jason picked up a towel and began to dry the water from his face. "Not tonight," he said. "I've got some work to do. Besides, Ethridge's mood is as puckered as his ass. I see enough of that at work. I don't need it after hours."

"Just a thought," Jeanne said. "He's always sweet to me."

"You're a woman," Jason replied too quickly.

"What does that mean?"

"Nothing."

"You think he comes on to me?" Jeanne pressed.

"Of course he comes on to you," Jason shot back. "Je-sus, do you think I'm blind? And you invite the hell out of it. One of these days, the two of you are going to take it too far and Lydia's going to claw your eyes out, or I'm going to have to beat the shit out of Ethridge."

Jeanne laughed. She ran the tips of her fingers over her breasts and then turned in the tub with her arms and slipped across the steam-capped water until she was at his legs. "Would you really fight for me?" she cooed.

"Depends," Jason answered.

"On what?"

"On whether or not you're worth it at the time."

"Do you need proof?" she asked. She kissed his knees and the inside of his thighs, nuzzling her face against him, between his legs. He placed his hands flat on the deck and pushed his body forward to meet her face. He could feel her breath and the soft brushing of her breasts against his shins.

"In the water," she whispered, looking up at him.

Jason slid into the rolling, heated water. He felt the jet stream pound into him.

It was eight-forty when Menotti took the telephone call at his home. The caller was one of the FBI agents assigned to protect Nathan and Ruth Greene.

"We got another contact," the agent told Menotti.

"Same message?" asked Menotti.

"Same," the agent said.

"What did you get off the ID?"

"Same as before. A pay phone. This time off West Paces Ferry Road."

"Did you call Oglesbee?" Menotti asked routinely.

"He told us to relay to you," the agent said with an edge to his voice. "Said you were handling it."

"All right," Menotti replied. "I'll talk to him in the morning. Maybe we'd better send the tapes in tomorrow and let the experts take a listen. See if they can profile him."

"I'll have Denton bring them," the agent said.

"How're the Greenes holding up?" Menotti asked.

"The same. Still tense. They keep asking about the calls and why we're recording."

"They don't know, do they?"

"No. We tell them it's the media."

"I thought they were changing the number today," Menotti grumbled.

"Tomorrow morning," the agent said. "They wanted to give it another day. See if we could put together a pattern."

"All right. Get me the new number and let me know if anything else happens."

Menotti heard a tired mumble and the buzz of the disconnected call.

"Who was it?" Arlene Menotti asked her husband when he returned to the living room.

"Business."

"The Greene boy?"

"Yeah. The Greene boy."

"My God, that's sad," Arlene said in her worried voice. She was sitting propped against the end of the sofa, her knees up, a stack of papers balanced on her thighs. "I wonder if he's all right, if he's hurting or if he's afraid. He must be. He couldn't be that shy and not be afraid."

Menotti settled in his chair and picked up the newspaper he had been reading. He said, "I guess."

"You can't be picked on in class like he was and not suffer from it," Arlene continued. "I know. I've had students like that."

"Yeah," Menotti mumbled rotely, his eyes on the story of Ewell Pender's resignation from the Century National Bank and the Wake Up America campaign that was reverberating throughout the country like a war chant. Then he heard, in the echo of hearing, what his wife had said. "What was that?" he asked.

"What?"

"You just said something about him being picked on in class. What was it?"

Arlene lowered the pencil she held over the paper. "That he was picked on," she repeated. "A child suffers—"

"How do you know he was picked on?" Menotti asked.

"Didn't I tell you?" his wife replied. "Peggy Burns called me. You remember Peggy, don't you? We taught together in DeKalb County for a couple of years."

"Peggy? Yeah, sure," Menotti lied. He did not remember, but he did not want his wife to tell him in agonizing detail the history of Peggy Burns.

"She taught him a couple of years ago, when he was a junior, I think," Arlene continued. "She retired last year."

"Taught Aaron?"

"Isn't that who we're talking about?" Arlene said irritably.

"When did you talk to her?" Menotti said, ignoring her tone.

"This afternoon, about five, I guess. She'd noticed your name in the paper and called. I haven't talked to Peggy in five years, or longer."

Menotti slipped forward in his seat. He folded the paper

he was reading and dropped it beside his chair. "What did she say exactly?"

"My Lord, Victor, am I being interrogated?"

"Call it what you want," Menotti said. "I'm just interested."

"She said that some of the boys in his homeroom class nominated him for class president as a sick joke. You know how boys are. Put someone down and that's fun. But Aaron apparently didn't know it was a joke. He thought he was being nominated because he was liked by them. Then they insisted that he make a campaign speech and he couldn't. He tried. He stood before the class and tried, but he couldn't do it. They laughed him out of the room."

"Why didn't you tell me this?" Menotti asked, his voice sharp and demanding.

His voice angered Arlene. She *was* being interrogated, and she did not like it. She turned on the sofa and placed the papers she had been grading on the coffee table.

"First, Victor, I don't like being talked to like that. I'm not one of your prostitutes trying to claim virginity. I'm your wife, damn it."

Menotti's face colored in embarrassment. "Sorry," he mumbled. "I'm just a little on edge about this one."

"Good. Thank you," Arlene said triumphantly. "Second, the reason I haven't said anything is the simple fact that you were late coming home and I've been preoccupied with these papers, which happens to be *my* job, in case you've forgotten. Anyway, it was just a conversation with an old friend. A sweet person, but not anyone you'd want to have as your next-door neighbor. How can it possibly mean anything?"

"I don't know," Menotti said. "She's the first teacher I know of who even remembered him. The kid was that nondescript. There has to be a reason."

"A good one, in fact," Arlene said. "After that embarrassment in the classroom, she spent a lot of time with Aaron. She even tried to get him interested in that special school—Carlton-Ayers—but his family didn't want him to transfer for his last year. They were afraid of him being away. I think being shy must be genetic with them."

"Jesus," Menotti whispered. He bolted from his chair.

"What is it?" Arlene asked.

"I missed it. Damn it, I missed it," Menotti hissed.

"Missed what?"

"What did I do with my briefcase?"

"It's in the kitchen, on the counter, where you always leave it," Arlene answered.

Menotti moved quickly into the kitchen and found his briefcase and opened it and withdrew a file. He spread the file over the kitchen table. Arlene had followed him into the kitchen, and she stood at the door and watched her husband flip through papers. A worried frown cut into her face.

"What are you looking for?" Arlene asked.

"This," Menotti said. He ran his palm over a folded sheet. "I asked the boy's parents to write down everything they could remember about him." He tapped his finger on the sheet. "There it is. They had discussed Aaron going to Carlton-Ayers, but changed their minds. Just what Peggy said."

"What does that matter?" asked Arlene. "I'm sure a lot of parents go through the same thing."

"What I missed was *why* the subject of transferring ever came up." He looked up at Arlene. "I need to talk to Peggy," he said.

"Call her. I've got the number."

"Get her for me, will you? You know her. I just met her once or twice. I need an icebreaker."

"Dear God, Victor, why?"

"I don't want her to think she holds the key to solving some great mystery and wind up calling one of those talk shows," Menotti said patiently. "Trust me."

"Jesus, Victor." There was disgust in his wife's voice. She crossed to the telephone, turned over a letter about a guaranteed ten million dollars for Arlene Menotti *if* Arlene Menotti had the matching numbers. On the back of the envelope was Peggy Burns's number. She lifted the telephone from its receiver and punched the number.

Peggy Burns answered immediately.

"Peggy, it's Arlene," Arlene said. "Listen, Victor would like to ask you a couple of questions about Aaron. Is that all right?" She paused, nodded. "Good," she said. She handed the phone to Menotti. The look on her face was triumphant.

"I owe you," Menotti mouthed.

There was a moment of pleasantry in the conversation, talk of the lapsed years in communication, then Menotti said, "Listen, Peggy, Arlene told me about your efforts to get Aaron into Carlton-Ayers after the incident in the classroom."

"It would have been good for him," Peggy said over the phone.

"I'm sure," Menotti replied patiently. "Let me ask something about the incident in the classroom. Were any of the boys punished?"

"One," Peggy answered. "He was sort of the ringleader. He was expelled for the rest of the year, but that was because he roughed up Aaron in the hallway the next day, taunting him for being Jewish."

"Do you remember his name?"

"Harlow, I think," Peggy said. "Denny Harlow. Yes. That was it."

"Do you remember him?"

"Vividly. A troublemaker. A bully. Ask Arlene. She'll tell you about the type I'm talking about."

"Was he a skinhead?" asked Menotti.

"A—what?"

"A skinhead. It's a term for radicals, racists. Members shave their heads."

"Oh, that," Peggy said. "There were two or three boys like that in school, but, no, Denny wasn't one of them.

He was on the fringe, I'd say, but not one of them. I used to see him hanging around with them, though."

"This Denny. Was he smart?" asked Menotti.

"He could have been," Peggy said thoughtfully. "I think he could have been very smart, but I didn't see it in the classroom. He took great pride in being defiant. I hate to say it, but I think most teachers simply gave up on him and passed him on to the next class to get away from him. He took too much energy to discipline."

"Well, Peggy, thanks a lot. Maybe it's nothing, but you look at everything you can, you know."

"I hope they find Aaron, and he's all right," Peggy said softly.

"We'll find him," Menotti assured her. "It's too public. Too much at stake. They'll slip up somewhere."

"I hope they don't hurt him."

"Me, too, Peggy," Menotti said. "Listen, it was good talking with you. It's been a long time since we've all been together. Arlene and I were talking about setting a date, and she wants to discuss it with you. Just a minute, okay?" He handed the telephone to Arlene, who glared at him in disgust. Menotti shrugged and walked back to the kitchen table.

"Peggy," Arlene said sweetly, "what's your schedule?"

SIXTEEN

◆

AARON DID NOT KNOW WHO TOOK HIS clothes at night and left him with a new outfit for each morning, conspicuously hanging in the dressing room of the suite he occupied. He did not hear anyone enter or leave during the night, could not remember the presence of lights. He slept soundly, too soundly. He believed that his food contained a mild drug that numbed him. The first night, he had dreamed frightening dreams, but he did not remember dreaming since that night. If he did, the dreams had vanished with the weakening power of the drug.

The clothes were always there, each day a new selection, and he always examined them with wonder before dressing. They were from the latest collections of designer names. Aaron had never worn such expensive clothes, and the fit of them on his body felt surprisingly tailored. He believed that Alyse had selected them. He could sense her presence as he dressed, could imagine her compliment: *You look wonderful today, Aaron. Do you like the shirt? All the boys your age are wearing them.*

It was the fifth day of his abduction from an Atlanta street, and Aaron had adjusted to a routine that was oddly comfortable and intriguing. Alyse had urged him to pretend that he was on a special vacation in a special but remote place, with nothing to do but relax and to be curious about the place and the people he met. "Don't think

155

about the outside world," she had advised. "There's nothing to worry about. Your parents are fine; if they weren't, we'd tell you."

He thought of his parents and knew they were not fine; they were in agony. His parents were easily distressed, easily terrified. Still, there was surety in Alyse's voice. It was a light voice, always brimming with the possibility of laughter, and she treated him gently. On the morning of the fourth day, playing a game of chess with him in the library, she had picked up one of the chess pieces, a queen, and had said, "This is what you are, Aaron. You're the most powerful member in this game we're playing. But it's more than a game now—much more." It had been the only time he had heard her voice lose its gaiety.

Aaron was consciously aware that he had been kidnapped for a purpose he did not understand, and he knew that in the world outside the suite and the garden, there were people looking for him. He knew also that he would not be easily found. Who would look behind the locked doors and gates of a mansion? He had tried to memorize all that he could about his environment. One day he would have to describe it to the authorities and it would be important to be accurate. One day he would be freed, or he would find a way to free himself. He did not think of dying. Alyse could not kill him, or permit him to be killed.

The girl who had joined them for croquet had surprised him. He was certain it was the same girl who had been at the hot tub. Her name, she told him, was Carla. She was his age, or very near it, he judged. Maybe a year older. It was hard to tell. She had not laughed until she began to play the game, and then her laughter was that of a child. Alyse had left them to attend to an unnamed duty, and after the game they sat on the bench in the garden and Carla had talked guardedly about wanting to attend school in Paris to study French. Aaron had wanted to ask about the hot tub, but did not. He was sure that when he saw her again, she would not be the same. Her hair would be different, her makeup, the tint of her eyes. Each day, Alyse had changed appearances subtly, like a character from a movie. And the man Robert. His appearance also seemed different each time he visited and urged Aaron to speak freely into the microphone.

Only the old man in the garden—the man who called himself Ewell—had appeared the same for each slow walk among the plants and flowers he admired and tended. And one other person did not change—or seemed not to change: the man who was called Morris. It was not easy to tell about Morris. Aaron saw him only at a distance, only as a sentry keeping watch over the garden. From the distance, Morris seemed always the same. Aaron believed that Morris kept the gun in his hand, or near his hand. Aaron believed that Morris could kill him, if Alyse did not protect him.

Aaron showered, then dressed in the jeans and yellow pullover shirt and slipped his feet into the low-cut tennis shoes and went into the library to await his breakfast. The sun was up. Outside, the garden shimmered from light and from water spewed in a mist out of the watering system hidden in a covering of close-clipped grass. In the light, the mist had the look of a spider's web draping the plants. He knew it was later than usual for his breakfast. Could tell it by the light and by the gnawing feel of hunger. He took a book from the library shelf. It was Herman Melville's *Moby-Dick*. He opened it to the first page and read a few sentences, then closed the book and replaced it on the shelf. He had watched the movie *Moby-Dick* on television with his parents. The movie had impressed him with its mystery of the great white whale and the madman sea captain seeking to slaughter it. He went to the window and looked out at the garden. The face of the statue of the nude woman Salome stared into a tunnel of sun, and the delicately chiseled joy of her eyes and lips seemed real to Aaron.

A soft knocking sounded at the corridor door leading

into the bedroom. Aaron turned to it. The door opened and Carla stepped inside, holding a tray. She called tentatively: "Aaron."

"In here," he answered.

"Oh, good," Carla said. She entered the room and placed the tray on the reading table. She was dressed in gray slacks and a blue sweater, and the slacks and the sweater made her appear more womanly. "I'm sorry I'm late," she told him.

"Where's—the other lady?" Aaron asked.

"She had some things to do. They asked me to bring you your breakfast. Is that all right?"

Aaron shrugged. "Sure," he said. "I guess."

"Do you mind if I eat with you?"

Aaron shook his head. He sat at the table.

"Maria made waffles and bacon," Carla said lightly. "I hope you like them. I do. I love waffles. Sometimes Maria makes them for me late at night, as a snack."

"Sometimes my mother makes them," Aaron said. "I like them, too."

Aaron ate in silence, listening to Carla confess to favored treatment from Maria. He was surprised by the ease of her voice, by the relaxed nature of her conversation. She had the voice of girls at school, the girls he had overheard in the lunchroom and hallways. Giddy, glad, gossiping voices, words spilling from their mouths like water from fountains. It was hard to believe that Carla was one of the people who kept him prisoner.

"I hope you get to meet Maria soon," Carla enthused. "She's more like a mother to me than my own mother was."

"Where is your mother?" Aaron asked.

Carla pushed her plate aside. She gazed out of the window. "She lives in Canada now. She married a Canadian when she divorced my father." She looked back at Aaron. "I don't see her much."

"Your father lives here?"

"In Florida. He moved to Miami after their divorce. He's in exports. I don't know what, really. Everything, I suppose. I see him every couple of months. He comes in for business, or I fly down there. I don't think he'll ever marry again. The first one didn't work out, and I think he's afraid of making the same mistake. I don't blame him. I don't think I'll ever marry. Do you, Aaron? Do you think you'll marry someday?"

A blush crawled into Aaron's face. "I don't know," he said.

Carla smiled at the blush. "Do you have a girlfriend, Aaron? I've never asked Alyse about that."

"No," Aaron said. He stared at the floor.

"Did you ever like a girl, but were afraid to tell her?"

Aaron shifted in his chair. He tilted his head. "I—don't know."

"Don't know. Of course you know."

"Maybe. Maybe once," Aaron admitted quietly. He could feel the heat of embarrassment rising on the stem of his neck.

Carla sat up in her chair, her elbows resting comfortably on the table. "What was her name?" she asked eagerly.

"Ah, it was—Ginny. I—I think that was it."

"How old were you?"

Aaron tilted his head again. He swallowed. The blush burned in his face. "Maybe—maybe fourteen. Maybe I was fourteen."

"What happened to her?"

"Nothing," Aaron said. He paused and smiled slightly. "She liked a boy named Andy. He played football."

"I hate football players," Carla exclaimed. "They're arrogant. I hope he broke both his legs. Was she a cheerleader?"

Aaron nodded. His smile widened. He had never had such a conversation with a girl—with anyone. He felt foolish.

Carla laughed girlishly. "I knew it. She was a cheerleader and she was dumb as a worm. Pretty. Oh, very pretty, but dumb. All she did in the summer was sunbathe, and when she's forty, she's going to look like bad cow leather. I've known lots of girls like that, Aaron. They're all the same. They all date somebody named Andy. Half of them are pregnant before they get through their last rah-rah. I hate people that dumb." She pushed up from the table with her hands. "Come on, it's pretty out. Let's go out to the garden."

"All right," Aaron said. He glanced at the table. Alyse would have replaced the dishes on the tray and covered the tray with a napkin.

"Well, are you going to sit there all day?" Carla said lightly. "You don't have to worry about anything. Everyone's gone, except Maria and Oscar. Do you know about Oscar?"

Aaron nodded. Alyse had explained that he might see another older man in the garden. That man would be Oscar, Alyse had said. Oscar was in charge of the household staff.

"He's great," Carla said. "I love Oscar. Come on, it's too pretty to stay inside."

Aaron stood and followed her out of the library door and into the garden.

The air was crisp and green-sweet. Aaron's eyes swept the fence, pausing at the gate. He did not see the man named Morris. He wondered if Carla had told the truth inadvertently: Were they alone, except for Maria and Oscar? And if they were, could he climb the fence to freedom?

"Did you try the hot tub?" Carla asked. She did not wait for an answer. "You should if you haven't. I love it. When it's cold, you can sink down in the water and then when you come out, it takes your breath. I saw a picture of a man and a woman in one when it was snowing. Alyse took it at a ski resort near Denver. She thought the man and woman were lovers. The snow was falling everywhere, and they were sitting in the water and it was steaming, with steam all over their bodies like smoke. I want to do that someday. I want to go to Colorado and go skiing and then sit in a hot tub when it's snowing."

Aaron remembered seeing the watery footprints of Carla on the deck of the gazebo, remembered her silhouette through the slats of the dressing-room door.

"Why don't we do that?" Carla said suddenly. "Get in the hot tub?"

"I don't know," Aaron said. There was hesitation in his voice. "Maybe."

Carla stopped beside the marble statue called Salome. "Do you think the statue's pretty, Aaron?"

Aaron looked away, toward the gazebo. "It's—all right."

"Do you know that I posed for it?" Carla said lightly.

Aaron stared at her in astonishment.

"Oh, yes, I did." She struck the pose of the statue, her arms lifted, her fingers pushed into her hair at the temples, her mouth slightly parted. It was a startling imitation. She broke the pose and laughed. "Do you believe that, Aaron?"

Aaron did not answer. He turned to look at the statue.

"I had to stand that way for hours. In the nude, just like that. The artist did a painting and took photographs and then he did the sculpture. Sometimes I had to come down and pose again, because he couldn't remember what I was like from the painting or the photographs.

"It bothered me at first, posing in the nude. Then I got used to it, and I liked it. Everybody thinks it's awful, but it's not. It's natural. It's the best way to be. Someday I think I'll join a nudist camp." She paused. "Does that embarrass you, Aaron?"

Aaron nodded awkwardly. "A little," he admitted.

"I'm sorry," Carla replied. She moved near him and took his hand in her hands. "I understand that. I used to be like you. Really. Exactly. I used to be afraid of everything, or embarrassed by it. I went to a school to help me. All of us did. Everyone you've seen here went to school to overcome those—problems. And you can do it, too. It's easy. I'll help you."

Aaron's breathing was labored. The touch of Carla's hand and the sound of her voice telling him surprising truths frightened him.

"Will you let me, Aaron? Will you?"

Aaron's head bobbed a hesitant yes.

"Good." Carla dropped Aaron's hand. She turned back to the statue. "Now, the truth: No, I didn't pose for that statue. I wish it was me, but it isn't. It's Alyse. Can you see her in it? I can."

Aaron looked again at the statue. Yes, he thought. That was why the face of the statue was radiant: Alyse.

"Can you, Aaron?" asked Carla. "Can you see Alyse in it?"

"A—little," Aaron mumbled.

"She's beautiful," Carla cooed. "The first time I saw her I thought she was a model; then I learned she had been just like me. Think of that, Aaron. Alyse used to be shy and afraid, just like I was. Like you are now. But she's not now, not anymore. She's the reason I wanted to change. I thought if I could be like Alyse, I'd never want anything else. I still think that. She's like an older sister to me, or, sometimes, a mother. She's not really old enough to be my mother, of course, since she's only, like, thirty-seven." She paused, inhaled on a laugh, then added, "Well, she could be, but I don't think of her that way."

"It's pretty," Aaron said quietly. "The statue's pretty."

Carla stretched in the morning sun, then hugged herself. She said, after a moment, "Let's use the hot tub, Aaron. I want to be the first to show you how good it is. Will you let me do that?"

Again Aaron shrugged.

"I take that as a yes," Carla said. "Come on. I'll take the tray back and put on my bathing suit. I know there's one for you in the dresser. I helped Alyse select your things. I'll meet you back here in ten minutes." She caught his hand and pulled him and he followed her back into the library.

Aaron waited until he heard the lock on the door leading from the bedroom to the corridor, then he moved quickly from the dressing room back into the library and stood at the edge of the window. He knew the garden well. There was no one in it. His body trembled with uncertainty. Carla had said they were alone, except for Maria and Oscar. It had sounded like the truth. He had heard no sounds of voices, or of other activity, from beyond the wall. He could not wait. The wall was not high and there were chairs at the gazebo. If he could get over the wall, he could run and find someone and tell them who he was and ask them to call his parents.

He slipped quietly through the library door and into the garden, then ran across the grass to the gazebo. He had only a few minutes before Carla returned. He took a small folding chair with a wood seat and hurried back across the garden to the corner of the fence, where the ground curved up in a slight incline. Perspiration dripped from his face. He had never been as afraid, not even in the car with Morris pointing the barrel of the gun at his chest. He placed the chair on the ground and stood on it and reached up for the top of the fence. His fingers curled over the edge of the brick. He pulled hard and his feet lifted from the chair. He could feel his heart stroking against the wall of his chest.

"Oh, please, Aaron, don't do it."

Carla's voice was below him. It was a soft, begging voice. He turned his head over his shoulder and looked down at her.

"Don't do it," she said in a sob. "I don't want you to. Please don't make me call out for someone. Oh, God, I used to be just like you. I know how you feel."

Aaron lowered himself slowly. His feet touched the chair and he dropped his fingers from the fence. He turned cautiously and sat in the chair. He could feel tears burning in his face.

"It's all right, Aaron," Carla said gently. "It's all right. I won't tell. Nobody will know." She kneeled before him. "I saw you from my bedroom window. I can see the garden from there. The house was designed that way. Everyone's bedroom overlooks the garden." She touched his face with the fingers of her left hand. "I won't tell," she said again. "I know how you feel." She leaned forward and kissed his forehead gently. Her hand lifted his chin and she kissed his lips, then she held him.

From the shaded window of the study, Oscar watched Carla pull Aaron into the cradle of her arms. He blinked and the clear blue of his eyes narrowed on them. He nodded once involuntarily. Then his eyes caught a movement outside the wall and he turned to watch. He saw a figure slip from the shadows of a tree into the sunlight. It was Morris. He held a gun in his hand. He moved to the wall and stood pressed against it, listening. Oscar stepped away from the window. A frown cut into his face.

SEVENTEEN

———————◆———————

JOEL GARNER'S PRESS AGENT, QWEN MCMIL-
lan, had alerted the Atlanta media of his early-morning
arrival and of the announcement he would make regarding
Aaron Greene. She had said to them, "Joel thinks it's important that he come to Atlanta. He's very disturbed over
this." She had refused comment on the contents of Joel's
announcement, but did not deny that he would contribute
heavily to the Aaron Greene Fund. "I think you'll be surprised and pleased," she had said when pressed.

Joel Garner was an actor of extraordinary talent. He had
been celebrated by critics for his role in a half-dozen movies, earning praise for his sensitivity and versatility. He was
young and he was handsome, but not pretty. His eyes
dominated his face. His eyes were as commanding as
voices. His eyes stunned audiences, mesmerizing them.
When Joel Garner made an appearance, it was news. He
was successful and wealthy. He was a star.

Qwen McMillan stood in the wide corridor of Terminal
A at Hartsfield International Airport with the chauffeur
she had hired to transport Joel into Atlanta, and she
watched awed members of the media stammer with questions, their bravery subdued by the heat of Joel Garner's
penetrating eyes. It was an old scene for Qwen.

"I am here," Joel Garner said in his actor's voice, "because I must be here. I ache for Aaron Greene. I know he

must feel alone and lost, and I know how that feels. That is why I became an actor, to overcome those fears. Every role I do, I prepare for it by remembering those times when I felt alone and lost. I want to meet with your mayor, with the officials of the bank, with Mr. Ewell Pender, with anyone who may play a role in this tragic event. We cannot let Aaron Greene become a casualty of this senseless terrorism. Mr. Pender's campaign is exactly right: America must wake up to what is happening in our homes and communities. How can we lecture on human rights to other countries when, in our own nation, we treat people so shabbily? Now, are there any questions?"

"Will you make a personal contribution to the fund?" a voice from among the microphones asked.

"Yes," Joel replied with dignity. "I am prepared to match Mr. Pender's contribution of two hundred thousand dollars."

A collective gasp rose from the interviewers.

"And I am further challenging my fellow actors and coworkers in the entertainment industry to make their own contributions," Joel added.

"Any plans of making a movie out of this?" someone asked boldly.

Joel's eyes cut to the voice like weapons. He said softly but deliberately, "I think that question is tasteless and unnecessary. I am an actor, not a predator. I am here because I fear for the life of a human being, not because I want to further my career. This is not a movie or a play we're talking about. It's not make-believe. It's real."

At the newspaper, Cody watched the television interview with Joel Garner in Harry Dilliard's office. When it was finished, Harry pushed the off button on his remote control and settled back in his chair.

"Too bad he's not John Wayne," Harry said. "Old John would have been beating the living shit out of people the minute he stepped off the plane, and he wouldn't have stopped until he found the boy."

"Sure," Cody said. "Exactly what I was thinking. What we need is John Wayne. Or maybe Rambo."

"Another two hundred thousand," Harry muttered. "Nothing cheap about that boy. Makes our twenty thousand sound piddling."

"*Sound* piddling?" Cody said. "Harry, it *is* piddling, for God's sake."

Harry snorted. "It's ten times what the other so-called media are doing."

"Maybe it's because we've got first cut on the story," Cody suggested wearily.

"No, Yates, we have you," Harry replied. "What Joel Garner is to the silver screen, you are to us at this particular moment in time. Amazing, when you think of it. Your miserable voice has probably been heard by more people over the last few days than Joel Garner's. Jesus, that's hard to believe."

"I think he gets four or five million a movie," Cody said. "Just to show you my heart's in the right place, Harry, I won't be greedy. Say a raise of five thousand a year."

A smile curled on Harry's face. He said in a low voice, "Think of it this way, Yates: It saved your job. Now get out of here and try to keep it."

"I'm going to lunch and then to the station," Cody said.

"Check in with me later," Harry warned.

Cody wanted to have lunch with Freda, but she had left earlier with a photographer to direct a photo session on one of the homeless families she had interviewed. Maybe it was best that she had the story to occupy her, Cody thought. They had made an agreement about their behavior at the office. It would remain one of distance and dislike. Asking her to lunch would have violated the agreement and tongues would have wagged. Cody did not want anyone in the newsroom to know about Freda. He was certain that Freda felt the same.

He left the newsroom and drove to his apartment. He had been gone for two days and knew there was mail to be collected and bills to be paid. He knew also that he was no longer being followed by no-option policemen in no-option police cars. Menotti had pulled the surveillance, complaining that his men were bored. Menotti, Cody thought. Menotti was a bloodhound, but he had been right about the Aaron Greene Fund attracting attention. Joel Garner was big-time attention. Ten million in a month would be hard to raise, but Ewell Pender and Joel Garner and a few more like them would have purses unzipping from Maine to California. Maybe they could pull it off. Maybe.

Cody parked his car in his reserved, numbered slot and rushed quickly inside the building. Curious neighbors would be at lunch, but still he wanted to avoid anyone who might be outside. He unlocked his mailbox and pulled out the wad of envelopes and thumbed through them. Junk mail. A bank statement that would again bellow in its hard, bottom-line numbers the sad refrain of his spending habits. Three bills. A card from Sabrina. He opened the card. Sabrina had drawn a stick figure with stick-figure hands thrusting microphones toward the worried stick-figure face. Perspiration beads sprayed from the face. Printed at the bottom of the picture were the words *My Famous Father.* Cody smiled and slipped the card back into its envelope. Millie had taught their daughter well. She had imagination and humor.

He took the stairs leading to his second-floor apartment, bolting them two in a step. He opened the door. He could smell the faint odor of stale cigarette smoke and a beer he had spilled two days earlier. The odor was offensive and he vowed never again to smoke in the apartment. And not to spill beer. Freda's apartment smelled of flowers and perfume and scented candles—sweet, feminine fragrances.

His apartment was a locker room, a depository for discarded jockstraps, yellowed with perspiration. He wanted to gag.

He threw the letters on the counter dividing the kitchen from the living room and pushed the playback button on his answering machine. The recorder whirled the tape in reverse, stopped with an annoying squeal, then began playing. Cody looked at his bank statement as he listened.

NBC television had called. CBS. ABC. CNN.

Six radio stations, including a personal message from Katie Harris, asking for a casual meeting, a glass of wine, chatter. "I won't even bring up Aaron Greene," Katie said in a purr. "Promise. I'd just like to get to know the most wanted man in Atlanta."

Sabrina, asking if he had received her card. She giggled.

Millie, apologizing for Sabrina.

Harry Dilliard, saying Joel Garner was stopping by the newspaper.

The voices droned.

And then Cody heard himself.

"The people care more about Aaron Greene than the bank cares. The people may save his life. The bank thinks it is greater than the people, but it is not. The bank is putting Aaron Greene in danger. We are not to blame if Aaron suffers. Landon is. Tomorrow, there will be another message. It will be from Aaron."

A chill struck Cody. He pushed the stop button, then the reverse button, and replayed the message. The tone of his uneven voice seemed angry and deadly. He sat on his sofa and lit a cigarette. Why was it his voice? he wondered. Why? He pushed from the sofa and went to the telephone and called Menotti.

"Yeah," Menotti said gruffly.

"I got another tape," Cody told him.

"Where?"

"At home. On the recorder."

"Son of a bitch," Menotti whispered. "Good touch. What did it say?"

Cody played the message into the receiver.

"You want me to send for it or do you want to bring it in?" asked Menotti.

"Don't you guys want to look the place over?" Cody asked.

"What for?" Menotti said. "Nobody's been there. We may have stopped following you, old friend, but I've had somebody hanging over your place like a vulture. Nobody's been there."

"Is my phone tapped?"

"Nope. Didn't think we needed it, and I guess I blew it. You don't have an identifier, do you?"

"On my salary? Are you coming out here, or not?"

"Not me," Menotti answered. "I'm helping the homicide boys look over some old cases I handled a few years back."

"Homicide? You don't do homicide."

"I think I know that," Menotti said. "It just got a little messy here, that's all. Couple of elderly ladies down on the south side didn't make it out of bed this morning. Throats cut. I had a couple of cases with the same MO, so I'm taking a look."

"Jesus," Cody muttered. "I swear to God, I hate this town, Victor. I swear I'm moving to the mountains. I'd rather live with the goddamn bears than the rats in this place."

"Maybe I'll go with you," Menotti said. "I'll send somebody over. Oglesbee will want to hear it."

"Call me later, all right?" Cody said.

"Where?"

"Probably here. I'll call Harry about the tape and let them get started on the story, but I'm not going back in. I've got to see Millie and Sabrina. I think I'd better give the other address a night off. I hate tension."

"Then why do you cause so much of it?" Menotti said sarcastically.

*   *   *

The tape was taken from Cody's apartment by an agent from the FBI, eagerly dispatched by Philip Oglesbee after Menotti's call to him. Cody slipped a new tape into the machine and turned it on. He knew the calls would begin again as soon as Philip finished his press conference. Harry had accepted the news of the tape with unusual calm; it was too late for any edition of the *Journal* and he knew the *Constitution* would use it as the lead for the following morning. He ordered a sidebar from Cody to accompany Amos Temple's news coverage, which would be a rewrite of Olin McArthur. The only thing fresh would be Cody's story, another of his first-person accounts, and that was enough for Harry. He knew that Cody's first-person stories were increasing street sales of the *Journal* by ten to fifteen thousand copies.

"First edition," he emphasized to Cody. "Have it here by seven, and get lost until then. Disappear. I don't want anybody prying anything out of you. We've got to have something the rest of them don't have."

On the six-o'clock evening report, Philip Oglesbee's announcement of the new tape upstaged Joel Garner's dramatic arrival in Atlanta, and it amused Cody. The African Prince had scored one for the workingman. The African Prince also looked good on television. He knew how to handle the press.

At six-ten, Cody called Freda. She was not distant, as he had expected, and he wondered if he could no longer read her signals of irritation. Maybe what he had been told since childhood was correct. Maybe sex made a man blind.

"I'll stay here tonight and work on the sidebar," Cody told her. "But I'll call you later. I won't be long with Sabrina, but I need to see her. She's caught up in this thing of her father being in the news."

"You don't see her enough," Freda said. "Do you have anything for her?"

Cody had not considered a gift. He lied. "A box of candy. A small box."

"That's a terrible gift," Freda said. "Next time, put some thought into it."

"She likes candy," Cody protested.

"Of course she does. She's a child. Call me when you get in."

The drive along Ponce de Leon to the community clustering around Emory University was crowded with late-afternoon traffic, and Cody turned left at Druid Hills Country Club to weave through the side streets. He had promised Millie he would be there at seven for a quick dinner, but he had stopped for the candy and he was late.

The familiar streets leading to the home he had shared with Millie and Sabrina always depressed Cody. He was an idealist. He had believed that he would marry, have children, tend his lawn, mingle with his neighbors, and be blissfully happy. The bliss had ended with absurd arguments over absurd things, and not even the remarkable ritual of forgiving sex had repaired the damage. Thankfully, when the razor of divorce fell across them, the severance had been kind and polite. Divorced, they seldom argued. They were grand friends. On occasion, they were uninhibited lovers. And they had Sabrina. Sabrina was a link more powerful than steel.

Cody pulled into the driveway of the house and jumped from the car and caught the leaping Sabrina in his arms, feeling her squeal flutter through him. He saw Millie watching from the front door, a patient smile covering her face.

"Who do you love the most, me or Mickey Mouse?" Cody said.

"Mickey Mouse," Sabrina kidded.

"Don't blame you, baby. He's richer. Is Mama mad?"

"Not much. She said you're always late."

"You're not late if you get there before it's over," Cody whispered. He growled into her ear.

Sabrina giggled. She rolled her head against his shoulder.

"Got you a gift," Cody told her.

"What?"

"Well, actually, it's for you and your mother, but you can't have it before dinner."

"What?" demanded Sabrina.

Cody released her and reached into the car and gave her the box of candy. It was not a small box. It was the largest he could find in the drugstore.

"Great," Sabrina cried. She sprinted to her mother, holding the candy before her.

"Not before dinner," Millie warned. She watched Cody approach the house. "Go on in," she said to Sabrina, "and put it up."

"Hello, lady," Cody said. He kissed Millie lightly. "How are you?"

"Good," she answered simply. "Dinner's a little cold, but I'm fine."

"Sorry," Cody said. "I had to call Harry." It was a lie, one often used with Millie, but one always accepted.

"I saw the news," Millie told him. "Have you met Joel Garner?"

"No, but if I do, I'll get his autograph for you."

"Get his phone number while you're at it," Millie said dryly.

"You'd be disappointed, love. Actors have to have somebody in a director's chair call action before they can do anything."

Millie smiled. "I do have that old director's chair you used to take on fishing trips, and I do have a voice," she teased. "Come on. Let's eat. Talk to me. Tell me everything that's going on in the life of the famous journalist Cody Yates."

Cody knew from the dinner that Millie meant for him to eat and leave, that she had other plans. The dinner was the quick one—fettucine Alfredo, with a spinach salad and a light, dry wine. Whenever Millie prepared it, she pro-

nounced it his favorite. It wasn't, but it was a decent sub-
stitute. It was the kind of meal that had the appearance of
careful planning, but was turned out in minutes by Millie.
She was a superb cook, a natural. Millie could sprinkle
basil over cornbread and feed kings.

"Thought I'd serve your favorite," Millie said as he sat
at the table, near Sabrina.

"I noticed," Cody replied too politely. "Must be a special occasion. I didn't forget a birthday or anniversary, did
I?"

"You're a star," Millie said, serving the fettucine. "Isn't
he, Sabrina? Your father's a big star."

"Yep," Sabrina answered happily. "I took your picture
to school."

"Wow. Show-and-tell, huh?" Cody said. "Well, that's
good. That makes me feel special. Did anyone say anything
about it?"

"Not about the picture," Sabrina told him. "One of the
boys—Frankie Mitchell—said he heard you on the radio,
on that tape they're talking about. He said you sounded
goofy."

"Goofy? Like Goofy, the dog?"

Sabrina laughed, a sharp, curling squeal of delight. "No.
Just goofy. Silly goofy."

"Your mother said I sounded that way, too, only she
had a better description for it."

"That's enough," cautioned Millie. "How's the fettucine?"

Cody sampled the food. "Great. Best ever," he said.
"Good wine, too. Expensive, I'd say. A gift?"

The question surprised Millie. She busied herself with
her salad.

"A little too close for comfort, was it?" Cody said, smiling. He enjoyed watching Millie suffer sudden distress. It
was a rare experience for her.

"Well, yes, it was a gift, if you must know, and, yes, it
is a little expensive, but it's mine and I'll do with it as I

please, and I wish to share it with you," Millie said matter-of-factly. She lifted her glass and saluted him and sipped with exaggerated pleasure from the rim.

"So, my little one, let's have a father-daughter talk, shall we?" Cody said to Sabrina. He rolled the fettucine with his fork.

"Okay," Sabrina replied gladly. She loved the attention from her father.

"First question: Who is Mama dating these days?"

"Cody!" Millie said curtly.

"What? It's a fair question. A little father-daughter talk covers anything. It's in the rule books."

"That's ridiculous," Millie said. She resumed eating and tried to appear uninterested.

"Who, baby?" Cody asked, leaning to Sabrina, whispering.

"Well, Mr. Lucas," Sabrina said shyly, glancing tentatively at her mother.

"Lucas, huh? I like that name. That's a good name. And what does Mr. Lucas do, baby?"

Sabrina squirmed in her chair. She tilted her head and mugged an expression that meant she did not know.

"He's a computer programmer," Millie said stiffly. "He has his own company."

"Ah," said Cody, nodding seriously. "A computer programmer. That's money. Lots of money. I like that."

"He just started the company a few years ago. There's not much money. Not yet. But—"

"Wait a minute," Cody interrupted. "Did I say this was a father-daughter-mother talk or a father-daughter talk?"

Millie sniffed theatrically. "As you wish," she said.

"Now, baby, my sweet, loves-her-daddy-more-than-anyone baby, is Mr. Lucas as handsome as your father?"

Sabrina looked up and grinned and shook her head.

"Of course, that's a silly question, isn't it?" Cody continued. "I mean, if your father is more handsome than

Tom Cruise, or Joel Garner, then he must be more handsome than Mr. Lucas. Right?"

Sabrina snickered again.

"And does he bring Mama flowers?"

"Sometimes," Sabrina said.

Millie raised her wineglass and saluted Cody triumphantly.

"Candy?" asked Cody.

"I don't know," Sabrina answered hesitantly. "I don't think so."

Cody returned the salute with his wineglass.

"Cody, stop this," Millie said bluntly. "It's unfair."

"You're right," Cody said. He thought of Freda. How would he describe Freda to Sabrina? Or to Millie?

"Let's eat in peace. I know you must have things to do."

"Yeah. Yeah, I do. I've got to put together a story for tomorrow."

"On the kidnapping?" asked Millie.

Cody told her of the new tape and of Menotti's suspicion that he was more involved in Aaron Greene's disappearance than the use of his voice. They finished dinner and sat at the kitchen table and had coffee while Sabrina shared candy in the lighted backyard with friends in the neighborhood. Cody knew that Millie was eager for him to leave; he knew also that he would be stubborn about leaving.

"Nothing serious going on with this Lucas fellow, is there?" he asked at last.

"No, Cody. Nothing serious. He's a nice man. I actually met him a little over a year ago, when we had a new program written for the hospital."

"Is he good to Sabrina?"

"Very. He likes her a lot. He's never been married, if that's the next question."

"What about the professor?"

"What professor?"

"Sabrina told me this week that you had a date with a professor from Emory," Cody said. "I figured him for philosophy."

Millie laughed. "Eddie Campbell came by for dinner. He teaches sociology. You remember him."

"The little bald fellow?"

"That's Eddie."

"My God, I didn't know you were seeing him," Cody said.

"I'm not. We're working on a project together. One of those case studies about the impact of urbanizing rural areas. We've got some patients at the hospital who're caught in the middle of it. We're just interviewing them, that's all."

"God love him," Cody mumbled. "Quaintest little fellow I ever saw. You ought to slip into your bikini the next time he drops by. Poor little bastard would have cardiac arrest."

A car door slammed outside the house and Millie looked up quickly. A blush colored her face, then vanished. She glanced at her watch. "Look at the time," she said lightly. "It's eight-thirty. I didn't know it was so late."

"Company?" Cody said. "Mr. Lucas?"

Millie stood and took the coffee cups from the table. She avoided Cody's eyes. "He said he might drop by. I don't know. Maybe it's him."

"You should have told me. I could have done this another night."

"Don't be ridiculous," Millie said. "Sabrina's been looking forward to this for days. I didn't realize it was this late, that's all."

"That's okay," Cody told her. "I've got to run anyway. I'll slip out the back and say goodbye to Sabrina."

"No, of course you won't. I want you to meet him. I think you'll like him."

Cody forced a smile. "I'll behave," he promised.

The man at the front door was tall. A relaxed smile

rested in his face. His eyes beamed with good nature. A neatly trimmed beard, reddish bronze in color, covered his jowls and chin.

Millie greeted him with a quick, awkward embrace, then stepped back.

"Cody, I want you to meet Robert Lucas. Robert, this is my former husband, Cody Yates."

"Good to meet you, Robert," Cody said, extending his hand.

"And it's a pleasure to meet you, Cody," Robert said in a lilting, merry voice, with a faint British accent. His grip was strong, confident. "Indeed it is." His smile broadened. "I've heard the voice, of course—all the radio play, I mean—and I knew there was a good man behind it."

EIGHTEEN

JOEL GARNER WAITED IN HIS SUITE AT THE
Buckhead Ritz-Carlton for the arrival of Ewell Pender.
He had spent an hour secluded in his bedroom studying
the dossier that Qwen McMillan had prepared on Pender.
Joel was impressed. Ewell Pender was the kind of man Joel
wanted to be—wealthy yet giving, quiet yet powerful. He
was especially impressed by the funding of major symphony orchestras throughout the world, and by Pender's
own accomplishments as a pianist. In the material that
Qwen had gathered, there were three reviews of concerts
that Pender had played as a special guest artist in 1968. The
reviews expressed surprise over his clean, aggressive keyboard technique and his thorough understanding of the
music. Joel knew the tone of the reviews. They were not
obligatory offerings of appreciation for his financial support, nor were they without criticism—small nicks short-
changing his inherent talent. The reviews were plain but
sincere paeans to an artist whose dedication had matured
into obsession. Yet, curiously, the three concerts were the
only ones ever performed publicly by Pender. It was as
though he had rehearsed a lifetime for the splendor of a
moment and the moment had been a triumph as pleasing,
and as fulfilling, as the dreams that made such triumphs
godlike. It was the same power as that of a conquering

general, or king, the same power of vengeance fully mea-
sured, fully completed.

If it was true, Joel thought—if Ewell Pender had taken
his moment and lived it uninhibitedly, freely, lived it as
an act of vengeance against those who had condemned
him to failure—then Joel understood more than Pender's
passion in helping Aaron Greene; he also understood Pender's soul. The act of perfect art was always an act of vengeance, a Mephistophelian treaty between hate and love,
possibility and accomplishment. It could be realized over
years, over a lifetime, consuming the artist in small, dangerous sips of poison coated with the tongue-pleasing
sweetness of praise, or it could be achieved in a moment,
like the unveiling of a classic painting, and the artist could
die happily, swiftly, with the ringing of applause echoing
in the black tunnels of memory. It did not matter which
choice the artist elected; it was all a plotting of vengeance—vengeance against the inanity and crudity of an
indulgent, stupid world, spinning itself into oblivion over
greed. The human creature had the power of gods but the
appetite of pigs. Only a few—Ewell Pender among them,
perhaps—knew the cool feel of silver goblets on their lips
and the earth-taste of blood-colored wine in their mouths.

Ewell Pender arrived at ten-thirty, as agreed, in the company of his chauffeur and his assistant, Alyse Burton. Joel's
breakfast tray had been removed and a special blend of
Colombian coffee had been delivered for his guests.

The meeting of the two men was cordial and purpose-
ful, conducted by rules of etiquette that both understood
and practiced. There were introductions, exchanges of admiration, positioning of the seating—the principals facing
one another in comfortable chairs, the assistants near the
fringe of the conversation—and the careful building of
dialogue.

"As you know, Mr. Pender, I have petitioned my associates in the entertainment industry to vigorously sup-

port the fund for Aaron," Joel said sincerely. "As of this morning, my secretary in Los Angeles tells me the response has been promising. At least another three hundred thousand has been pledged, and I believe that means we're gaining momentum. Additionally, I'm pleased to report that Miller Williams, the music composer for a number of the films I've done, is composing a song for the Wake Up America campaign. I've heard a little of it. It's quite rousing."

Ewell Pender smiled politely and thought of the secretary in Los Angeles staying awake to report the progress of Joel Garner's fund-raising campaign. "That's extremely pleasing," he said. He turned his head slightly to Alyse. "Would you give Mr. Garner a brief rundown of the response we've gotten?"

Alyse opened a folder. "The amount we have doesn't begin to match what you've just told us," she said in a business voice, avoiding Joel Garner's eyes, "but it perhaps represents a broader cross-section of the public. In total, we know we can count on an additional one hundred and fifty thousand, but that's from only two days of the campaign, essentially. The bulk of it, of course, is from business and industry, but approximately sixty thousand has been pledged—directly or indirectly—by individual or civic groups. These range from Boy Scout troops to—believe it or not—a motorcycle gang. The Jewish response has been particularly encouraging, as we anticipated. The talk shows have been promoting the fund with—well, more vigor than usual—and we're already seeing the results of that. I anticipate a large mailing of contributions today."

Joel was impressed with Alyse's report, and with Alyse. "Is all of this local?" he asked.

"Most of it," Alyse replied, glancing into his eyes, then back to the report. "Of course, that's to be expected, but we've also had calls from virtually every state in the union, and several international inquiries have been received as well. The fact is, we've been severely undermanned, but we've got volunteers working today. Mr. Pender has rented a suite of offices in the Farley Building and the telephone company has installed a bank of telephones."

"Excellent," Joel enthused. He turned to Ewell Pender. "Small wonder you've accomplished all that you have," he said. "Efficiency. I like that."

Ewell Pender blinked acceptance of the praise. He said, "I think people understand what we're doing. It's something of a classic dilemma, wouldn't you say, Mr. Garner?"

"It is, yes," Joel replied thoughtfully. He looked at Alyse, held her in his gaze. "The plot-writers in Hollywood would call it the plight of the downtrodden. A trite phrase, I think, yet the truth." He drank from his coffee, then motioned for Qwen to refill the cups. "There was another tape, I understand," he added.

Ewell Pender nodded. It was agreement and a signal to Alyse.

"Yes," Alyse said quickly. "A short message. Supposedly there'll be a tape from Aaron released sometime today."

"Nothing at all from the FBI or the Atlanta police?" Joel asked.

"Nothing concrete. We understand that a number of people have been questioned, but it's more a matter of routine investigation than serious suspicion," Alyse said. "Apparently they've never handled anything quite like this."

"I would think not," Joel agreed. "I've never heard of anything quite like it. Usually, an abduction involves people of wealth, unless it's politically motivated, of course. But this seems money-driven. Qwen tells me the bank is getting a lot of pressure because of its decision not to meet the ransom demand."

"Some," Alyse acknowledged. She smiled warily.

"Well, I want to do what I can," Joel said with vigor. "I've canceled all my appointments for the next few days, and plan to stay here. I'm at your disposal. If I can make appeals, I will. In fact, I think I should start today by dropping in on your volunteers. Let them know how much I admire them."

"Very well," Alyse said. "I'll arrange it. I'm sure they'd be delighted."

"Good," Joel said. "Mr. Pender, do you have any suggestions?"

Ewell Pender moved forward in his chair. He touched the handle of the china coffee cup with a slender finger. His clear blue eyes stared at the steamcap over the freshly poured coffee. He said, after a moment, "I would like you to be the guest of honor at a reception in my home on Friday evening." He looked up. A smile lifted in his face. "If you wouldn't object to being presented in such a manner."

"I'd be honored," Joel said earnestly.

"Please understand, we would solicit contributions, and you, of course, would be the attraction," Ewell Pender added. "I'm certain you would be surrounded the entire evening by admirers."

"Mr. Pender, I spend almost all of my life as a billboard," Joel said politely. "It's the one thing I'm truly good at doing. I know the expectations."

The old man nodded, held his smile. "From what I know of you, I believed you would agree." His eyes moved to Alyse. "Please give Mr. Garner a copy of the guest list, as we now propose it." To Joel: "If you wish to add any names, please feel free to do so. I'm sure you're familiar with a number of entertainers who have settled permanently in Atlanta. Alyse will be handling all the arrangements and will communicate with you, or"—he indicated Qwen with a nod—"your associate."

"Call me personally, anytime," Joel said eagerly. "Qwen will have to return to California tomorrow. Unfortunately for me, she has other clients to attend."

"Really, Joel, I could stay if you want me to," Qwen said.

Joel shook away the offer. "No. This is not your job. I'll handle it."

"If you like, I'll provide a secretary for you," Ewell Pender said.

"Thank you," Joel told him, "but that won't be necessary. Ms. Burton can keep me informed, I'm sure. There's really nothing I can do but place myself in your hands. This is your campaign. I want to be a worker in it, that's all."

"That's kind of you," Ewell Pender said quietly. "You can't imagine what it means."

Olin McArthur's call surprised Cody. They were not friends, or enemies. There was no hostility between them, no wars of bitter rivalry, no petty jealousies. If anything, they demonstrated a silent, yet obvious respect for one another, and they shared the distinction of being the most experienced reporters of their respective newspapers— Olin for the *Constitution* and Cody for the *Journal*—before the two staffs were merged into a single, around-the-clock newsroom. Olin and Cody still functioned with the mindset of separate newsrooms and pretended competition. Yet, they were different. Olin was quiet and serious and meticulous. He was organized, worked within the system, though the system annoyed him. Cody was a rebel. Both were old-school journalists, but Olin had Ivy League polish while Cody's behavior was that of a graduate from a correspondence course advertised on a matchbook cover. Once, in a benefit performance sponsored by Sigma Delta Chi, Olin and Cody had been described in a skit as the Odd Couple of the Atlanta media. The comment made both Olin and Cody smile.

"Why don't we get lunch?" Olin said.

"Sure," Cody responded. "Where?"

"There's a pleasant little restaurant on Juniper, near Colony Square," Olin said. "Why don't I drop by about eleven-thirty and we'll drive over together."

"Good enough," Cody said. "All I'm doing is waiting to hear about the new tape."

"No word on it yet?" asked Olin.

"Nothing. But it'll be past our deadline in a few minutes. You guys will have first shot, I'm guessing. See you at eleven-thirty."

Olin's promise of the pleasant restaurant was not exaggerated. Both ordered a chicken breast which simmered in a sour cream sauce. Olin had a glass of chardonnay; Cody had coffee. They talked of Aaron Greene as they ate, and when the plates were removed, Olin pushed back from the table and reached inside his coat pocket and withdrew a folded sheet of paper. Cody played with an unlit cigarette while watching him. He knew that Olin possessed information he did not have.

"What do you know about Ethridge Landon?" Olin said quietly.

"Nothing. Amos looked into him, I think, but he hasn't said anything to me. But that may be deliberate. Harry wants me to keep a low profile; said it would give off the wrong signals."

"Harry's right, of course," Olin said. "I'm sorry you're being accused of grandstanding, Cody. Personally, I think they used your voice because you're rather well known. That's all."

"If that's true, they would have used you," Cody replied. "You're better known and a hell of a lot less likely to pull off a stunt like this one."

An embarrassed smile waved across Olin's face. He cleared his throat and opened the paper he held.

"Landon's a cute one," he said. "I've got it on pretty good authority that the bank examiners have popped in for a surprise visit."

Cody was interested. "Really? Anything different?"

"An old issue, I understand," Olin answered. "Several months ago, the feds issued a poor report on the bank's shabby participation in the Community Reinvestment Act, and Landon was at the center of it. Didn't want to see the money going for something as risky as improving the standard of life in the community."

"What is that—that reinvestment thing?" Cody said.

"It's like all government rules and regulations," Olin replied. "It simply means that financial institutions have to offer investment in the community. Highly risky at times. A lot of write-offs, I understand, but once in a while somebody makes it and they have a ribbon-cutting to celebrate American enterprise. Anyway, Landon was on the hot seat and his attorney—Jason Littlejohn's the name—gathered enough lawyers to invade China and they buried the government in paperwork and rhetoric about sound business practice, and sound business practice won the round. Got an upgrade on the finding, but, Cody, you know the government as well as I do. Tomorrow's another day. That's why they're back."

"What's all this got to do with Aaron Greene?" Cody asked.

Olin drained the wine from his glass, replaced the glass on the table. "Maybe nothing. Maybe everything. I get this funny feeling that Landon's the target here, and Aaron's merely the gun barrel. I'm not sure this is a kidnapping at all, but a very bold and dramatic game of wits. Then, maybe, it's all coincidence."

"It's still a puzzle to me, Olin," Cody admitted patiently. "Isn't there a piece or two missing in your 'funny feeling'?"

Olin looked at his paper, folded it again, and slipped it back into his inside pocket. He said, "A lot's missing, Cody, but when it comes to Landon, guess what name keeps popping up for me? Pender."

Cody thought of Victor Menotti. He said, "Pender? Why?"

"Part of it's obvious—his crusade to raise money for Aaron, and his resignation from the board of the bank. But it was also Pender who fought Landon over the bank's failure to be leading the pack for community improvement, and I don't believe Pender's the kind of man who likes to lose."

"Who the hell is?" Cody said in a mumble. He broke his unlit cigarette in half and dropped it into his coffee saucer. "We also know Pender can afford to be a little more generous with his sentiments than the average man on the street."

"True," admitted Olin. "I've thought about that. Even checked into his philanthropic habits. You wrote about it in your magazine story on him, if you remember. That man ought to be knighted, Cody."

"So I understand," Cody said. "I only wish he had a soft spot for aging newspaper hacks. I could use a grant."

Olin's smile was one of tolerance. He continued, "From what I gather, the real battle lines were drawn over the board's decision to reward Landon with a bonus after the dust had settled over the reinvestment question. And *that* is what Pender can't abide. Landon's predecessor was a giver, not a taker, and he was in Pender's camp. With Landon, it's a little like Robin Hood fleecing the poor to pad the condos of the rich."

"My God," Cody said in astonishment. "Can they do that?"

"They did. Oh, it was under some pretense or another. The rewards of a good job, I think they'd call it."

"In my neighborhood, we call that a mugging," Cody said. "I can't believe it. No damn wonder the feds are back."

"Cody, it's the day of the lawyer, believe me," Olin said dryly. "If there had been one single corporate lawyer present when Moses came down from Mount Sinai, there would have been ten thousand commandments instead of ten, and the Israelites would still be staggering around trying to find the Promised Land because of condemnation proceedings."

Cody laughed. Humor from Olin was unexpected. It was also humor laced with truth.

"Why are you telling me all of this?" asked Cody. "Seems you've got a pretty good angle working. Why share it?"

Olin fingered the knot in his silk tie, perfecting it. He said calmly, "You and I have been in this business too long to start playing games with one another, Cody. It so happens I have a, ah, personal interest in Landon. It could cloud my judgment."

"Want to tell me what it is?"

"Not particularly, but I know you'll spend more time trying to figure it out than you will following up on what I've told you, so I'll share it with you. A few years ago Landon foreclosed on a small business venture that belonged to a man I like immensely, a black man, Cody. His mother once worked for my mother as a maid. Sounds like one of those weary Southern clichés, doesn't it? Rich white boy, poor, pitiful black boy." Olin shrugged. "That's what it was. So be it. Anyway, we grew up as casual playmates. I went to college; he didn't. But we stayed in touch over the years, and he took a chance, at my urging. He started a small painting firm, doing interiors of new homes mostly. He was about to show some profit when Landon's boys stepped in. Frankly, I despise the bastard."

"You've got pull, Olin. Why didn't you intervene?"

The smile on Olin's face was sad, small. "I tried," he explained. "Even scheduled a meeting between my friend and Landon. Landon told him that he'd reconsider the proceedings if my friend would paint his house—without compensation, of course. We rejected the offer and the proceedings proceeded."

"Son of a bitch," Cody whispered. "Why didn't you call me when that happened, Olin? You forget: I know the criminal element. I could have enlisted some of those boys to paint his house fire red, and I mean fire as in smoke and flame."

"Thanks, Cody," Olin said. "I'll remember that. Next time, maybe."

"So, you're giving me the story?" Cody asked.

"No, Cody. I'm sharing information with you. I want the story, but I also want your help, and I want your promise—your *professional* promise—that whatever you find out regarding problems at the bank, if anything, you'll bring to me. And I want you to review me, to make sure I keep a clear picture of things. In return, whatever I find out about Aaron Greene, if anything, I'll give it to you."

"You've got a deal, my friend," Cody said. "And to show how generous I really am, you can also have the check."

"My pleasure," Olin replied. "You may leave the tip. Ten dollars should cover it nicely. I want to be remembered as an appreciative diner."

"Ten dollars? Jesus, it wasn't that good."

"Ten dollars, Cody."

"Wait a minute," Cody said suddenly. "What the hell was on that sheet of paper you pulled out of your pocket?"

"Nothing," Olin said after a moment. "I just wanted your full attention."

On the drive back to the newspapers, Olin turned on his car radio for the one o'clock news. The lead story was of the promised tape from the kidnappers of Aaron Greene. The tape had been delivered, said the announcer in a proud voice, by courier to WJES. "And now, the contents of that tape," the announcer intoned.

Cody's voice crackled over Olin's car radio: *"For those who think we are not serious about our demands, here is the voice of Aaron Greene. Listen to it."* There was a pause, a static scratching, and then the boyish voice of Aaron Greene said, *"Uh—I'm—I'm in a fence. Do whatever they tell you. I don't want to hurt anymore."*

"Jesus," Cody whispered. He stared at the radio.

"They went all out this time, Cody," Olin said softly. He turned off the radio. "They pulled their thumb out of the dike. We're about to get flooded."

"Jesus," Cody said again.

Because Philip Oglesbee had been prompt in informing the media of new developments in the Aaron Greene kidnapping, Bernie Niles, the news director of WJES, had called him immediately upon receiving the tape with Aaron's voice. Philip had listened to the tape over the telephone, mumbled his appreciation, and promised a conference by three o'clock.

"It's all right to run this, then?" Bernie had asked.

"You'd better, before somebody else gets it," Philip had advised. "There's nothing hiding behind closed doors about this one. Whoever's got the boy wants the world to know, and we couldn't stop that if we wanted to."

"Thanks," Bernie had said enthusiastically. "We're ready to roll with it. I'll make some copies for you if you want to send somebody to pick them up."

"No, you keep the copies," Philip had instructed. "I'll take the original, and if it hasn't already been fondled by everybody over there, how about using a handkerchief to handle it."

"Oh," Bernie had said. "Fingerprints. I got you. Sure."

Philip had killed the call with a push of his thumb, then buzzed his secretary and ordered a pickup of the tape. He had swiveled in his chair and turned on his radio and dialed WJES. The lead-in to the playing of the tape was already being announced. *"Exclusively on WJES,"* the announcer had crooned, drawing lines under "exclusively" with his voice. Goddamn circus freaks, Philip had thought.

A half hour later Tito Francis entered his office. Tito had been dispatched from the FBI office in Washington to assist Philip. He was a veteran of abduction cases and a master strategist, particularly in manipulating pressure through public resentment and anger. The Aaron Greene case was tailor-made for Tito Francis.

"You know about the tape?" Philip asked.

"I heard it on the way over," Tito told him.

"They've punched it up a notch," Philip said wearily.

"No shit," Tito said. He sat heavily in a chair in front of Philip's desk. "You got any ideas?"

Philip wiggled a no with his head and rubbed his eyes with his fingertips. He was numb-tired. "I'm going to hold a news conference at three," he answered. "Feed the lions. Maybe keep them off our ass for a few more hours. The boys picked up the tape, but they won't get anything off it. It's what's on it that concerns me. What the boy said was scary, but he didn't sound that way to me."

Tito blinked an agreement. He sat slouched back in the chair, his elbows on the armrests, his hands in front of his chest, his fingertips touching. He did not agree with Philip Oglesbee's constant posturing before television cameras, delivering deep-voiced concerns over Aaron Greene's disappearance. The African Prince liked the camera too much, Tito believed. Liked the way he looked on replay, the way he sounded. Tito would have diverted attention from the tapes and offered rewards to bounty hunters eager for cash and notoriety. There was always someone willing to sell information, or fragments of information, especially in the drug-habit culture of the nineties.

"You've got something on your mind, Tito," Philip said. "Either that, or you need a face-lift."

Tito sighed. He ran his fingers through his thick red hair. His large, athletic face, dotted with pin drops of freckles, furrowed in thought.

"I think we'd better move them," he said after a moment.

"The Greenes?"

"Yeah. This new tape will have those lions of yours grazing on their front yard before sundown—especially since the number's been changed out there—and they're not the kind to take much pressure."

"I guess you're right," Philip conceded. "Let me make a couple of calls. See if I can line up some rooms somewhere."

"Don't bother," Tito told him. "It's taken care of."

"What the hell's that supposed to mean?" Philip demanded.

Tito stood and stretched his shoulders. "It's one of my own little procedures," he said. "You've been busy. I was going to tell you about it later."

Philip stared suspiciously at Tito. He said sternly, "Tito, I don't give a damn what your past record is, or if you've been decorated by the president with a cluster of gold magnolia leaves draped over your genitalia. This is my responsibility, and you will not run a separate program. Do you hear me?"

Tito flushed with anger and embarrassment. "Just trying to be helpful," he said.

"Fine, but goddamn it, tell me. I don't like surprises, and I don't tolerate end runs."

"You want them moved?" Tito asked.

Philip walked to the window of his office and looked out. It was a bright, clean day. "Yeah," he said. "Tell them we'll see them in a couple of hours."

Tito reached for the phone, punched numbers in a rapid succession, then spoke: "Take them to the inn, now. Keep them away from radio and television. We'll see you there as soon as we can."

The inn was a La Quinta Inn off Piedmont Avenue. Tito had registered for a suite of rooms two days earlier under the name Straiton Irish of Irish Imports. He had promoted his stay as a sales conference with regional sales managers to introduce a new line of cookware from South Korea. Each day, Tito visited the rooms and left evidence of occupancy—mussed beds, damp towels, filled ashtrays, half-empty bottles of whiskey, literature about the South Korean cookware. In his years of experience, Tito had learned it was always necessary to have privacy and secrecy.

For Nathan and Ruth Greene, the move was swift. They were given ten minutes to pack, and the questions they asked out of confusion were answered with a polite but firm "You'll know soon." Neighbors peering from windows—as they had for days—saw them rushed to the unmarked government car to be driven away quickly. Ten minutes later, the first television remote unit arrived at the house. Within thirty minutes, the street was jammed with media vehicles.

Nathan and Ruth Greene sat together on the sofa in the suite assigned to them at the La Quinta Inn. They sat close, their bodies touching, their faces pale with the certain knowledge that they were about to be told of the death of their son. A film of tears moistened their eyes.

Philip and Tito entered the room, and Philip nodded for the agent guarding the door to leave. When the door closed, Philip took a chair from the small conference table and moved it to face the Greenes. He sat and leaned forward, his elbows on his knees. He rubbed his hands together. A soft scrubbing sound floated faintly in the room. He knew the Greenes were frightened, could see it in their faces. He spoke in a quiet, comforting voice.

"First, let me tell you that Aaron's all right—"

Ruth Greene gasped. She pulled her husband's hand to her throat.

"No, I mean it. He's all right," Philip continued. "We moved you because we wanted you to avoid another rush by the media." He smiled. "They can be pretty persistent, as you already know. But this time, I don't think they would have been as cooperative about leaving when we asked them."

Philip looked at Tito, then back to Nathan and Ruth.

"There's been a new tape," he explained, "and this time it has Aaron's voice on it."

A moan caught in Ruth's throat. She held her husband's hand in a vise grip.

"Don't get distressed," urged Philip. "We knew it was coming. The reason we've monitored media reports for you is that we know they do nothing but increase anxiety, especially some of the talk radio shows. You've been very cooperative, and we're grateful. We're going to play this one for you, but before you hear it, let me tell you that our experts listened to it and they all agree it's an edited version. It's their opinion that Aaron is not in any danger at all. In fact, they think the tone of Aaron's voice says much more than the edited words. They believe Aaron had an entirely different message, one meant to comfort you. So does Mr. Francis." He turned to Tito. "You've met Agent Francis from Washington, I believe. Tito."

Tito pulled a small cassette player from his pocket. "I do agree," he said. "But we want the media to think it's real. When you hear it, you'll understand. We want public pressure. Lots of it. Maybe we'll get someone talking if we get enough pressure." He handed the player to Philip.

"There's one other thing you should know," Philip said. "The reason we've been taping telephone calls at your home is a caller—the same person each time—who keeps making anti-Semitic threats. But we've had it profiled and we're reasonably certain it has nothing to do with the abduction. I don't believe we'll get any more of those calls, however, since we've changed the number and left it unlisted."

"That kind of thing always happens," Tito added. "A lot of sick people are wandering around out there, as you both know. We'll probably never find out who was doing it, but that doesn't matter right now. What we're doing is trying to find Aaron."

"Are you ready to hear the tape?" Philip asked softly.

Nathan Greene turned slowly to his wife. A bewildered

look was on her face. "Yes," Nathan whispered.

"Remember, what you hear is edited—brilliantly edited," Philip said. "Only an expert with some very sophisticated equipment could do this. It may frighten you, but it encourages us. We know a lot more about them than they think we do. Most of all, we know we're dealing with some highly intelligent, gifted people, not some idiot making up the rules as he goes. The idiots are the ones who are really dangerous."

Philip studied the couple sitting before him on the sofa. God, they hurt, he thought. They don't believe a damn word we're saying.

"All right," Philip whispered. "I want you to hear this and we'll answer any questions you may have." He pushed the play button on the recorder and held it up in his hands.

NINETEEN

———◆———

MENOTTI KNEW THE NINE O'CLOCK REVIEW meeting was one of Philip Oglesbee's strategy moves, a detail of the art of deception and manipulation: He who schedules the meeting runs the meeting. And the timing was perfect. By nine o'clock at night, the huddle of waiting reporters would be thinned by hunger, or by boredom, or by the clicking sound of bar glasses calling seductively to them. Menotti admired Oglesbee's understanding of the media. Oglesbee had learned, to his benefit, that few reporters had the gift of patience. Their training, their instinct, was that the latest probability—the *quintessence* of story—must be spread often and quickly, and that innuendo was as legitimate as truth as long as it had been oiled with the slippery qualifier of being *alleged*. It was one hell of a word—this "alleged." It had the pliability of putty and the strength of steel. Menotti had once seen a cartoon of a reporter in Roman armor, holding his shield against the broadsword of public opinion. The bastardized Latin on the warrior's escutcheon read *Allegitis Maximus*. Menotti also knew that as much as Oglesbee preened before the cameras and as confidently as he answered questions flung at him from obnoxious people, he considered the media as dangerous as assassins. They were, however, often helpful, like good hunting dogs whose loud yelping flushed out more game than the hunter could bag.

The African Prince did not mind the yelping, but he did not want to become the game. And that meant having his meeting at his time, without a microphone suspended before his face like an unlit cigar.

Menotti arrived at eight fifty-five and was directed to a conference room leading from Philip Oglesbee's office. He spoke to the men already gathered—Oglesbee, Tito Francis, and Homer Auchmuty and Archie Day of the Georgia Bureau of Investigation.

"Didn't see your boss anywhere, did you?" asked Philip.

"Who?" Menotti said.

"Your boss: Russell."

"Is he coming?"

A sour smile cracked on Philip's face. "Insisted on it. Wants to say a few words."

"Shit," Menotti mumbled.

"You can say that again—for me," Philip said.

Menotti poured coffee from a pot on a hot plate and settled into a seat at the conference table next to Tito Francis. Archie Day and Homer Auchmuty were telling of a break in a drug-smuggling operation from Miami, but Menotti did not listen with interest; he wondered what message Clifford Russell had been dispatched to deliver. Whatever it was, it would be political. As the police commissioner for the City of Atlanta, Clifford Russell performed his duties with the passion of a political appointee posing as an ambassador to a foreign government. He was the mayor's puppet, a fact so obvious no one ever commented on it, other than to joke about the twitch that Clifford Russell had in his shoulders. A twitch was a yank from the mayor. Still, he played the role. He was haughty and demanding and, worse, he was two-faced. Publicly, he supported his officers; privately, he believed they were little better than the criminal element they supposedly controlled. Clifford Russell's threat of an internal investigation loomed like a plague over every arrest, regardless of the evidence. Among the officers of the Atlanta Police

Department, he was known as the Albatross.

It was ten minutes after nine when the commissioner arrived and took his seat at one end of the conference table. He spoke only to Philip Oglesbee, mumbling an apology for the delay. Menotti knew better: The Albatross was purposely late. Delaying a meeting was a way to assert his importance.

"No problem," Philip told him. He sat at the opposite end of the table. "I think you know everyone here," he continued. "Now, you have something you wanted to say, I believe."

"It'll just take a minute," the commissioner replied gruffly. He scanned the men sitting silently around the table. His eyes paused on Menotti, blinked in distrust, then moved to Philip. His shoulders twitched once. He began, "I've been in meetings this afternoon with the mayor and the governor, and, frankly, they want to know what in the name of God is going on. They can't see any obvious progress in finding this boy, and, to tell the truth, neither can I."

Philip gazed at the commissioner in his calm, African Prince manner. He did not speak.

"I guess all of you know damn well the kind of pressure we're getting, and I don't want to shovel it your way when you've got enough to keep you busy," Clifford Russell continued. "But we've got to be able to say something pretty soon. My God, whoever's doing this is doing one hell of a good job of making us look like amateurs. They've got the upper hand, and with that tape they released today, they've got the whole damn country—no, make that the universe—in an uproar. We've been getting calls by the goddamn wagonload—from the Anti-Defamation League, the unions, the NAACP, and every church large enough to have a collection plate that's not the preacher's hat, and that doesn't include every three-watt radio and television station in the world, and every newspaper with enough ink left in the bottle to print another edition."

"We can't control those things," Philip said indignantly. "You know that."

The commissioner nodded. "Yes, I do. But I also know the roar in this uproar is the loudest I've ever heard. I think we can keep it controlled for a short time, but with Pender and that actor and a few other people with big names out beating the drums, we need something concrete as soon as we can get it."

Menotti watched Philip's face freeze at the insult.

"You see the reports," Philip said curtly. "I think you could tell them what we're doing."

"They don't understand reports," the commissioner shot back. "They understand results."

Philip shifted in his chair. His fingers rubbed the surface of the table, like a pianist. "What they should understand," he countered, "is that we've got people all over this city working this case. The same with the GBI and every other law enforcement agency with enough money to have walkie-talkies. They should understand that we're looking at every piece of editing equipment we can find, and that we—all of us—have interviewed everyone we know who has ever uttered the word 'kidnap.' They should be told we've chased calls from drunks and idiots that take up hours because we want to be sure. They should be told that we've all got people who've been without sleep for so long they can't give you their home address or the names of their children. What we've done, Mr. Commissioner, is what we have to do, and if they want to make it worse by unreasonable demands, then, goddamn it, that's their doing. I will not compromise a federal investigation for local political comfort. Do I make myself clear, or should I repeat what I just said?"

Clifford Russell's eyes blinked in surprise, then defeat. He was not accustomed to resistance. "I don't think it's political," he said defensively.

"Then what is it?" demanded Philip.

"They're—anxious, as we all are," the commissioner said. "They simply wanted me to encourage the efforts being made."

There was a pause. Menotti fought a smile. Finally, Philip spoke: "Look, Commissioner, tell them we're grateful for their support. Now, will you stay for the meeting?"

The commissioner nodded. "I'm here to help," he said in a quiet voice.

Philip rose from his chair and walked to the chalkboard and picked up a piece of chalk. "There's nothing formal about this," he said. "I think we need to go over things, compare notes. Anything any of you want to say, say it, and I don't give a damn how stupid it may sound to anyone else." He drew a square in the middle of the chalkboard and wrote Aaron Greene's name in it, then he began to draw lines from the square.

"What's that supposed to be?" asked Archie Day. Archie was a small man with a thin, weak face, but he was one of the GBI's best investigators.

"Call it a picture, if you want," Philip replied.

Menotti smiled. He thought: Son of a bitch. He does it my way. Lines. Lines leading to something, or someone. Or nowhere.

"The thing I still don't understand in all of this is why in the name of God did they pick Aaron Greene?" Philip said. "I've tried to put names with him, and the only ones I can come up with are his parents"—he wrote *Parents* at the end of one line—"and Ethridge Landon"—he wrote *Landon* at the end of another line. "And that doesn't make any sense, except for the fact that Landon's president of the bank. We don't think he ever even saw the boy, and we know damn well he didn't know who we were talking about when we mentioned Aaron's name."

"Friends at the bank?" asked Archie.

"Didn't have any," Philip answered. "Some of them

knew him, but nobody ever spent any time with him. He kept to himself. Had lunch alone, took breaks alone, didn't horse around. When we asked about him, the most common answer we got was 'Aaron who?' He was your classic loner. Didn't seem to fit in, but he didn't rock the boat and he seems to have done a good job, so nobody ever paid any attention to him."

"You need to add a couple of names," Menotti said quietly.

"Who?"

"Pender, for one."

"All right," Philip said. He wrote Pender's name at the end of a line. Then: "Anybody got any ideas about him?" He looked at the commissioner.

"He's got money and nothing better to do," Clifford Russell said. "He's old, but he's still a power. He was with the mayor this afternoon. Had that actor with him. Said he had an appointment with the governor. It's a grandstand play, we figure. Nothing more."

Philip turned to Menotti. "You think that's right?"

Menotti could feel the glare of the commissioner's eyes, daring him. He said, "Maybe. I understand he's had some problems with the management of the bank over the past few years. But I'm sure you know that."

Philip rolled the chalk in his hands, smearing his fingers with the dust. A small grin wiggled across his mouth. "It's—well, coincidental that federal bank examiners happen to be looking at a few things over there," he admitted. "We've had a chat with them, but there's nothing to report. At least, not now."

Clifford Russell swiveled nervously in his chair. He said, "We've considered that—coincidence, but I'd be careful about barking up the wrong tree. Pender's the Pied Piper. The management of the bank and the kidnapping of the boy who worked there are two entirely different things, in our opinion. Any link would be too circumstantial. Anyway, that old man's always been a little off-the-wall, if you know what I mean, and you've got to remember that he's given more money to this city than anybody alive. That buys him some courtesy, if nothing else. Our position is, if he wants to wake up America, let the roosters crow."

Archie Day laughed. He asked, "How much money has he raised?"

"Around a million," Clifford Russell answered. "Including his own contribution, which was matched by the pretty boy from Hollywood."

"He put up two hundred thousand, didn't he?" Archie said.

"Correct," Philip replied. "Plus, he's picking up some pretty hefty expenses."

"Why didn't he make it a reward?" Archie said. "Good God, that would be tempting. No names. No questions. Just information."

"We asked him that," Philip explained. "He said it was an issue for the people, not just one man. He also believes it wouldn't work. Why would someone give up millions for a few hundred thousand? I think he's got a point. Our people who profile these things tell us this is a highly sophisticated group. They've been patient and deliberate, and they're not likely to crack under the pressure of a little temptation, and I'd bet a dollar to a dime that every last one of them has seen *Ransom*. They're not about to make a real-life mistake."

"*Ransom?* What's that?" asked Archie Day.

"It's a movie," Philip explained. "About a kidnapping where the victim's father offers a reward."

"Oh," Archie said. He was still confused.

"What do they say about the boy?" asked Clifford Russell. "Your profilers, I mean? How much danger is he in?"

Philip glanced at Tito Francis. Tito looked bored. "Agent Francis and I believe he's safe," Philip said. "In fact, he may be in Hawaii as we speak, surfing with some grass-skirted teenage hooker, having the time of his life."

"Hawaii?" the commissioner said seriously.

"It's a figure of speech, sir," Philip explained patiently. "It means we think he's in good hands, being well cared for. We know the last tape was edited. The experts say there's no cause for alarm in the voice."

"Any leads on the delivery of the tape?" asked Homer Auchmuty.

Philip shrugged. "Unfortunately, no. It was dispatched under a bill-to number for a music store in Marietta, but we can't find a connection, other than a stolen number from a receipt. It happens all the time, a hell of a lot more than people think. The people at the courier service don't remember anything about it. False return address, of course. Everybody thought it was a press tape. No prints, except for the ones from the station. The boys with the microscopes and chemicals are still looking at things, but it's all long-shot guesswork at this point. Personally, I'd say the tape was purchased in some small store in some place like End-of-the-World, Utah. I promise you, these guys are good. Damn good."

"Damn gutty, at least," Archie Day said.

"Or stupid," the commissioner suggested. He added, "Anything new on the Jewish angle?"

"Nothing," Philip reported. "We're sure the caller was a loner. Muffled voice. Calls from all over—downtown, on the south side, out on Roswell Road, in Vinings, all over. We had caller ID and the tracer system working, but they were all from pay phones. Menotti, you looked into that. Anything to add?"

Menotti thought of Howard Edwards and his shop of premium sleaze. He shook his head. "We're still talking to a few people," he lied.

Clifford Russell muttered, "The bastard." He glanced restlessly at his watch.

"I'm going to remind everyone in here to keep quiet about the calls," Philip said forcefully. "That gets out, we may as well throw in the white flag, and we all know it."

He turned to Menotti. "You said there were a couple of names. Who else?"

"The reporter," Menotti replied. "Yates."

Philip mugged a half-interested expression with his mouth. He wrote the name Yates at the end of the line. "You really think there's a connection?" he asked.

"I don't know," Menotti admitted. "Nothing that Yates knows about, but it's his voice they're using. There's got to be a reason for that."

"You've checked him out?"

Menotti's fingers played over the rim of his coffee cup. The question was too direct. "Yes," he said. "Have you?"

The African Prince's eyebrows arched. A smile began on his lips, then vanished. A little boy's smile. Little boy with his hand shoved into the cookie jar. "A little," he said. "But I don't think we know him as well as you do. You're friends, I understand."

"We are," Menotti answered calmly.

Clifford Russell sat forward. "What?"

"Cody Yates is a friend of mine," Menotti replied. "Has been for years. He's a police reporter, and he's been more than helpful to the department a number of times."

"And you're handling the case for the City of Atlanta?" Clifford Russell snapped.

"Yes sir," Menotti said. "I was assigned to it, with your approval, I believe."

"Nobody told me you were friends," the commissioner mumbled.

"We think it's an advantage," Philip said firmly. "If you remember, Commissioner, I made the request, and I can assure you that Lieutenant Menotti has conducted himself in an exemplary manner. We agree with his analysis: Yates has no idea why his voice is being used. But if there's anything to be found, it's going to be found by someone he trusts, not by forcing the issue. He may be a reporter, with a reporter's failings, but he's been around a long time and he's a bullheaded son of a bitch."

"The media could take us apart on that one," Clifford Russell complained.

"We'll take the risk," Philip said. "No matter how many press conferences we hold, we don't need public relations at the moment. We need answers. We think Lieutenant Menotti is our best resource with Yates, not to mention other possibilities."

Menotti put his coffee cup on the table, pushed it away from him with his fingers. He stared at the African Prince. There was compliment in Philip's voice, but it was compliment coated in a condescending tone. Philip Oglesbee was telling him that he was being watched, evaluated, or it was bluff to control the commissioner. If bluff, it was damned effective. He wondered if Philip knew about Freda Graves, or if Philip had his own men following the City of Atlanta policemen who had been following Cody.

"We'll leave it for the time being," Clifford Russell said, rolling his shoulders, "but if we start to get heat on it, I'll have to consider a change. The city won't tolerate the suspicion of collusion in an investigation."

"If it comes to that, we'll take the responsibility," Philip said easily. He turned to face Menotti. "You comfortable with that, Victor?"

Victor Menotti shrugged.

TWENTY

———◆———

WHEN HE AWOKE, STILL DRUGGED BY A DEEP, muscle-tiring sleep, Cody reached for Freda, but she was not in the bed. He stretched and yawned. She must be in the shower, he thought, but he did not hear the running of water. He looked at his watch on the night table. It was seven-thirty. He had overslept. Freda was already gone. He remembered that she had an early-edition sidebar to complete on her homeless series. He pulled from the bed and slipped into his running shorts and pulled a T-shirt over his head, and then he went into the kitchen. Freda had left a note on top of a clean coffee mug beside the coffeepot. Cody poured coffee, sat at the table, and read the note. It said: *You look like a small boy when you're sleeping. Thanks for the night. If you ever need references, please include me. I believe in supporting my local gigolo. Stay in. I'll call later. Don't smoke.*

Cody smiled at the note. It had been a memorable night, a lingering, discovering night. He could feel it in the tenderness of the muscles of his shoulders and abdomen and thighs and in the slight bruise of his mouth.

He took his coffee and went onto the deck and lit a cigarette and watched the smoke swirl in the still-cool breeze of the morning. Freda would be disappointed, but he needed the cigarette. To have the cigarette was an act of celebration.

He had promised Harry Dilliard that he would spend the day with Menotti, trying to con Menotti out of high-level details about the kidnapping of Aaron Greene. It was a foolish assignment and Harry knew it. Menotti had the one quality that reporters despised in their contacts: Menotti had integrity.

To hell with it, Cody thought. Harry only wanted him out of the office, away from the glare of the spotlight, and any assignment was sufficient. He'd give Menotti a call in an hour or so, ask him if he had any news, and Menotti would say no in his annoyed voice, and that would be that. Assignment completed. He could take a long, hot shower. Turn the shower head to massage and let the water beat down on his sore shoulders. And then maybe he'd go back to bed and rest for the return bout with Freda Graves. And he would try not to think of Aaron Greene, and the gnawing need to be out looking for him. What could he do? Every agency in America—possibly on earth—had someone out looking for Aaron. If they couldn't find him, what good would his poking about be?

And to hell with Harry Dilliard and Harry Dilliard's orders, Cody reasoned. He had his own life, and that included doing nothing on occasion. Maybe he'd call Millie at work and tease her about Robert Lucas. Ask how her sex life was with Robert. Did he have staying power? Was he patient in foreplay, as she preferred? Did he know about the one small, secret spot at the curve of her back, the one that needed only the tip of a fingernail or the tip of a tongue to release her like a sudden geyser breaking through the soft sponge of damp and cracked earth? Not likely, Cody thought. Smiling Robert Lucas would have to find that one on his own; Millie would not guide him there. She had too much pride to surrender secrets.

Cody drew hard from his cigarette and crushed it in the ashtray on the deck table. He thought of Millie and the ease of their sex, the perfect, accustomed fit of their bodies, the practiced rhythms, the sighing signals of peace. Their sex had been remarkable. Sadly, it was the only agreement they had had in the last years of their marriage. With Freda, it was different. They were exploring one another in bed, and that, too, was remarkable, but also there were long talks about writing and stories untold, stories without endings. Freda understood perfectly the fragile nature of journalism, that nothing was ever completed, that all stories were merely excerpts plucked off an assembly line of mundane living.

The coffee was cooling in his cup, and Cody returned to the kitchen and poured it into the sink and took a fresh cup. He was not hungry, but he made toast and ate it. He thought of Aaron Greene, of Aaron Greene's voice on the tape. It was small and tense contrasted to the casual, conversational sounds of his own voice. The sons of bitches who had Aaron were smart. They were playing it like a soap opera in prime time.

The telephone rang once. There was a pause and it rang again, twice, before Cody picked it up.

"You remembered the signal," Freda said in a covered voice, a controlled whisper that could have been a serious, but muted, conversation if overheard by a passerby in the constant movement of the newsroom. Cody knew her expression: a look of absolute concentration, a bearing-down professional look.

"I told you I could count to two," he replied. "How are you?"

"A little tired, but happily so," Freda answered. "Listen, Olin McArthur was at your desk a few minutes ago. He asked if I had seen you. I told him I didn't know where you were and didn't care. He left a note."

"Thanks. Did he believe you?"

"He smiled. You know—that smile he has. It's in his eyes. I've always thought he had Merlin's eyes, anyway. Does he know anything?" She sounded uncomfortable.

"Not that I'm aware of," Cody answered. "Olin's good, though. Too damn smart to be doing what he does for a living. He could have talked to one of Menotti's men. But what if he did? We're adults, and Olin couldn't care less. Trust me. Anything else?"

"I glanced at your desk when I went by a few minutes ago. There's an envelope with the Pender Foundation's name on it. Looks like an invitation."

"Wonder what that's about?" Cody said.

"Want me to take it when no one's looking?"

"Why not? If anyone says anything, tell them I called my own line and you answered, and I asked you to check my desk for something—my calendar. How about lunch?"

"Not today," Freda said. "I've got an interview."

"Cancel it. I'll make an omelet."

"I can't. Really. I've got to meet with the supervisor of one of the homeless shelters."

"It'll be a small omelet," Cody said. His voice was boyish, teasing.

Freda laughed quietly into the phone. "I'll bring you the envelope tonight," she said. She hung up without waiting for the whining plea she knew she would hear.

It was past eight-thirty. If Olin McArthur had been at his desk so early in the morning, it must be important, Cody reasoned. He picked up the telephone and punched in Olin's office number. Olin answered promptly.

"Jesus, you're already there?" Cody said, pretending surprise. "I was going to leave you a message. You got anything for me?"

"Are you at the office?" Olin asked.

"Nope. Trying to stay away. Like I told you, Harry's orders."

"Well, then, this is a coincidence, I suppose," Olin said dryly. "I was by your desk a few minutes ago. Freda Graves said you weren't in. I left a note."

"Really?" Cody said. "What's up?"

"I'm not close to confirming it—though I believe I will—but one of my sources at the bank tells me the examiners are making our friend perspire rather freely. Seems one of the directors said more than he should have about Landon's bonus."

"Pender?" asked Cody.

"No," Olin told him. "This one's still on the board. A big supporter of Landon. Tell you the truth, I don't know his name yet, but I've got a pretty good idea. Anyway, he was in there when the examiners were talking to some people and he started popping off about the great job Landon had been doing, and how they were justified in giving him the bonus. You know the kind, Cody. Power fools. They think they can shout and snort and get away with anything they damn well please. Happily, they don't faze the boys from the government. They just piss them off."

"What'd Landon have to say about it?" Cody said.

"Not a lot. Laughed it off, but hustled his man out. I understand Landon's scheduled some time off to get away from the pressure. His lawyer's behind that. Wants him to disappear for a while."

"I don't blame him," Cody said. "I wonder if he needs company."

"Maybe you could teach him a trick or two," Olin said casually. "You're rather accomplished at disappearing. I tried you at your apartment half the night."

"Yeah, well, I need my sleep, Olin."

"I hope you've found pleasant quarters," Olin said.

"Better than the Y," Cody replied. He could sense the smile on Olin's face. He knew. The bastard knew.

"You really should get a beeper, Cody," Olin advised.

"Had one," Cody said. "Every time it went off, it scared the shit out of me. I put it on vibrate. Every time it went off, I got aroused. So I threw it away."

There was a pause. Cody could hear a small, weary sigh. "By the way, do you know about Pender's reception?" Olin asked after a moment.

"No. What's that?"

"Tomorrow night. A big fund-raiser for the Greene boy. Joel Garner's being promoted as the guest of honor."

Cody thought of the envelope with the Pender Foundation's name on it. He said, "Where's it going to be?"

"At Pender's estate. Don't worry, Cody, you've got an invitation. I saw the envelope on your desk."

"You get one?" asked Cody.

"To my surprise, yes. I think Pender remembers that I was incensed over the Landon thing."

"How much will it set us back?" Cody said.

"A couple of hundred, but the paper's picking up the tab. At least, that's what I've been told."

"The drums are rolling," Cody mumbled.

"Indeed they are," Olin replied. "Well, I've got to go. Thought I'd stop in at the bank. Maybe we should have a drink later."

"Sure. I'll give you a call. Any idea where Landon's hiding?"

"None. But he'll pop up. Believe me, he'll pop up. What are your plans?"

"Nothing special," Cody told him. "Got to talk to Menotti and a few other people. See if you can find out where Landon's holing up."

"I'll try. Talk to you later."

"Sure," Cody said.

TWENTY-ONE

—————————◆—————————

JASON LITTLEJOHN'S CABIN ON LAKE LANIER was on a secluded knoll that swept down an incline into a land jetty jutting into the lake. It was an expensive, modern log structure, with a kitchen, a dining area, an open-ceilinged great room, a first-floor guest room and bath, and a large master bedroom and bath in the upstairs area. There was also a basement with a third guest room. A large front porch lipped the cabin like the bill of a cap. Hemlocks and water oaks—massive, imposing trees—crowded the driveway and yard. The cabin was used for entertainment in the summer and an occasional weekend retreat in the winter. It was also used by Jeanne Littlejohn to escape the boredom of Atlanta when her husband was in New York or Washington to confer with law firms retained by the bank. Jason Littlejohn did not know about the trips to the lake by Jeanne; the trips were part of her private life that she did not share with anyone except the young, strong-muscled men she found tending luxury boats or estates. The young, strong-muscled men were her relief from the boredom.

Jason had not offered the cabin to Ethridge Landon as a retreat; Ethridge Landon had insisted on using it, and Jason had quickly made the arrangements.

"I'll need some time to pack," Ethridge had said. "I can get there by two."

"It'll be ready," Jason had promised.

He then had called Jeanne and instructed her to go immediately to the cabin and open the windows and to stock the refrigerator and cabinets with food. "You don't have time to call in the maid service, so you'll have to do it yourself," he had said. "It'll need airing out, and he's got to have something to eat. Make it simple. I'm guessing his cooking skills are limited to grilling hamburgers and boiling water."

"Why so sudden?" Jeanne had asked, annoyed by the demands.

"He needs to get away," Jason had answered in his business voice. "If he stays around here, they're going to press him into saying something I don't want him to say. And by the way, no one's to know where he is. No one."

"I'm not sure I can get everything done by two," Jeanne had protested.

"You'll have to," Jason had insisted. "Believe me, if he said two, he means two."

"Will Lydia be with him?"

"I don't think so. The kids are in school."

"All right," Jeanne had said. "I'll try."

"Don't try," Jason had ordered. "Do it."

The cabin was opened and airing in the clean lake breeze that slithered off the water and through the hemlocks and oak. In the kitchen, Jeanne was storing the supplies she had hurriedly purchased when Ethridge Landon's Mercedes rolled into the yard and stopped beside her Porsche. She went to the door and waved as Ethridge got out of his car and crossed to the house. He was dressed in slacks and pullover shirt.

"It must be two o'clock," Jeanne said cheerfully.

Ethridge glanced at his watch. "Five after," he replied. "I'm late." He stepped to the door and gave Jeanne an embrace that pulled her breasts to his chest. It was the way he always embraced her, and she had learned to play out the tease with a slight rubbing against him when he pulled away. Both knew that one day they would make love, because the teasing would become a dare.

"I understand you like being punctual," she said.

"Rumors from your husband, no doubt," Ethridge said.

"Actually, from your wife," Jeanne countered. "We had a late lunch last week and she was worried about being at home when you got there."

"She should have been. She's always late. Is Jason here?"

Jeanne was surprised by the question. "No. He didn't say anything about coming up. I think he had a meeting this afternoon."

"Oh, yeah, I forgot," Ethridge mumbled. "We talked about having some work sent up. I thought maybe he'd bring it. No problem. I'll call about it later."

"Come on in," Jeanne said brightly. "Is it too early for a drink?"

"Not after the day I've had. What've you got?"

"You like scotch, if I remember correctly. Over ice, slightly disturbed by bottled water."

"Good memory."

Ethridge followed Jeanne into the kitchen and watched as she prepared the drinks. She was dressed in a pair of tight jeans with an old flannel shirt, opened at the top.

"Looks like you've been busy up here," he said. "Hope the short notice didn't screw up any plans."

Jeanne exaggerated a playful shrug. "Nothing special." She turned to him. "I had nothing on the calendar but another lazy day of shopping. The place is still a little musty, but it'll air out in an hour or so. The wind's up." She handed him his drink.

Ethridge raised his glass toward her. "To you," he said easily. "Thanks. I owe you."

"Pay my husband more money so I can indulge my madness for the sale of the day, and we'll be even," she said. She smiled a teasing smile and sipped from her drink.

"I've stocked some things, but if you need anything else, I can get it for you by tomorrow."

"Don't worry about it. I'll run out if I need to," Ethridge told her. Then: "So, what should I know about this place?"

"Nothing you don't already know, I'm sure," Jeanne said. "It's a getaway place. No television, no radio, and no telephone. So if you want to communicate with the outside world, I hope you've got your cell phone."

"I think it's grafted to me," Ethridge said, "but I turned it off when I got to the driveway. I've got to have some peace. I'll check in later."

"If you'd like, I can give you a tour," Jeanne said. "But I think you know your way around, don't you?"

"I guess. We've spent a few weekends up here, but Lydia did most of the work."

"Of course she did. You're a spoiled man, Ethridge Landon."

Ethridge laughed comfortably. "The fruit of labor. I pay for it, believe me."

"Will money buy everything?"

"Just about," Ethridge said. "Where do you keep the booze? That's the main thing."

"Under the cabinet," Jeanne answered. She opened a door. "You'll find that it's pretty well stocked."

"Good. I like a selection. Any house rules?"

Jeanne smiled coyly. She closed the door to the cabinet and turned back to him. "Just one," she said. "If any of the local wood nymphs happen to seduce you and you use my bed, wash the sheets. As my husband can smell the fibers of a dollar bill from a hundred yards away, I can smell the heat of sex. I don't mind if it's my heat, but I get terribly envious if it belongs to someone else."

Ethridge's eyes narrowed on her, studied her. He licked his lips involuntarily, and a small smile broke over his mouth. "I'll remember that," he said. He added, "To wash the sheets, I mean."

"Do you smoke?" asked Jeanne.

"Cigarettes? Can't stand them."

"I don't mean cigarettes," Jeanne said calmly.

"The other stuff? Once in a while, when I kick back. Why?"

"I keep some. Quality leaf, all of it. Jason doesn't know about it, though."

"You're kidding?" Ethridge said.

"He doesn't approve," Jeanne replied.

"Lawyers," Ethridge said, grinning.

"My sentiments exactly. Anyway, if you want some, it's in the fondue bowl in the back of the cabinet, behind the bottles. We never fondue."

"The wrappings?" Ethridge asked.

"It's all there. Want help getting your things in?"

"Later. Let's go sit on the porch and enjoy the scenery."

"You're the guest," Jeanne said. "I'm here to please."

"Jesus, I wish you wouldn't say things like that," Ethridge sighed.

Jeanne looked at him. She could see the blood pumping in his neck. "I never say anything I don't mean," she whispered. She walked past him, through the living room, and onto the porch.

It was three-thirty when the BMW pulled into the yard of the cabin and stopped beside Ethridge Landon's Mercedes. Ethridge and Jeanne were still sitting on the porch, sipping their second drink of the afternoon.

"Who's that?" asked Jeanne.

"My public relations person," Ethridge said. "Miriam Finch. I think you know her."

Jeanne smiled. "I've met her. Jason talks about her occasionally."

"They can't stand one another," Ethridge whispered. He waved to Miriam as she got out of the car. "If I left them alone in a room, one of them wouldn't make it out."

"Why is she here?" Jeanne asked.

"Bringing me some work, I suppose," Ethridge replied. His voice was too casual. "She and Jason and my assistant are the only three people who know where I am."

Miriam crossed the yard with a briefcase in her hand. She was dressed in a business suit, her blond hair pulled back in a severe bow.

"Hi," Miriam said pleasantly as she reached the porch.

"You remember Jeanne Littlejohn, don't you?" Ethridge asked.

"Of course," Miriam said. "How are you, Jeanne?"

"Fine, thank you," Jeanne answered. "But you look as though you could use a drink."

"A soda, if you have one. The traffic's awful out of Atlanta. I'm beginning to understand rage killings."

"Sit down," Jeanne told her. "I'll get it for you."

"Thanks," Miriam replied. She turned to Ethridge. "I brought you some papers to look over and sign. I think they need them for tomorrow."

"Later," Ethridge said. "It's too pleasant to think about work. Right, Jeanne?"

"For me, it is," Jeanne said. "But I don't keep the wheels turning on the world of finance. Lime with the soda, Miriam?"

"Please."

Miriam sat in a chair near Ethridge and waited for the sound of Jeanne's footsteps to fade into the house. She said quietly, "I tried to call you."

"I turned the phone off."

"How long is she going to be here?"

"It's her house," Ethridge said.

"Get rid of her," Miriam said bluntly. "I have to be back early. I think Olin McArthur's asking about the examiners."

"I'll handle Jeanne. You handle Olin," Ethridge said. "Let me see the briefcase. Is anything in it?"

"Of course. I had to bring something. Some letters you've probably already seen."

The briefcase was open and Ethridge was examining the letters when Jeanne returned.

"You're sure you won't have a scotch?" Jeanne asked, handing the soda to Miriam.

"Thank you, no. It's a little early."

"We made an executive decision and arbitrarily cut short the afternoon," Jeanne replied. "It seemed a pity to wait."

Ethridge did not look up from the papers. He muttered, "Damn it, I thought this had already been handled. Christ, I didn't come up here to be buried in this stuff." He sounded irritated.

Miriam drank from her soda. She blinked an embarrassed smile toward Jeanne, then looked at Ethridge. "They said you needed to see it. I don't know."

"It'll take some time. I hope you've got a couple of hours."

"Things are a little testy back at the office, but sure, if that's what you need. You're the boss."

"It'll take at least that long," Ethridge said. He looked at Jeanne, mugged in surrender to the briefcase in his lap. "I'm sorry. I was just beginning to relax."

Jeanne smiled at the charade. It was poorly played, but it was also a signal that she understood.

"Just as well," she said. "I really have to be going, anyway. I think Jason has dinner plans with one of your visiting lawyers."

"Don't rush," Ethridge said.

"No, really, I should be running along," Jeanne replied. She looked at Miriam. "If you want to slip into some jeans and take a walk while he works, I've got a closetful of them. Sandals, too. Whatever you need. Help yourself."

"Sounds tempting," Miriam said, "but I'm afraid it'd spoil me. It's really beautiful up here. If I had it, I'd slip away every chance I got and not tell anyone."

"I do," Jeanne said in a purr. "Anyway, it's good to see you again."

"And it's good to see you," Miriam cooed. "Why don't you stop in for lunch one day when you're down to see Jason? We'll steal some time and go shopping."

"Ummmm, inviting," Jeanne said. "I'll do that." To Ethridge: "If you need anything, call." She turned to leave, then turned back. "By the way, if you need to do any laundry, remember that the washer and dryer are in the basement. You'll find detergent there, somewhere."

A rose blush swept across Ethridge's forehead. "I'll find it if I need it," he said.

Jeanne Littlejohn could not keep the smile from her face as she drove along the tree-lined road. She knew that Ethridge Landon and Miriam Finch were already in bed. No time wasted, she thought. She had primed him with her playful teasing and now he was taking Miriam. But it would be quick pleasure, Jeanne mused. The feeding of a great ego was always a matter of gorging. She smiled triumphantly. He was such a fool. He would be easy. Too easy. But it would happen. Both of them knew it.

TWENTY-TWO

———————◆———————

THE TELEPHONE CONVERSATION WITH CODY had been brief—"I don't know anything new, Cody, and you can quote me. Now, stay the hell out of my hair. Goodbye."—and Menotti had left his office to drive to the Atlanta-Fulton Public Library. He needed peace. A warning from Clifford Russell had been delivered earlier: Any lapse in the investigation resulting from his friendship with Cody Yates would be a matter of inquiry from Internal Affairs. The son of a bitch, Menotti thought. He was covering himself with an official warning, with another memorandum-to-file that he would pull out like a rabbit from a magician's hat at the first rumbling of discontent from his higher-ups. There was more fiction in Russell's memoranda-to-file than in afternoon soap operas, and he used them like hand grenades. Marty Keeler. Russell had gotten Marty Keeler with one of his memoranda-to-file. Had had Marty escorted from the building over paperwork failure, and Marty had been a damn good cop for eighteen years. But Russell didn't want good cops; he wanted his will obeyed. The son of a bitch was incredible.

Menotti found an isolated table in the monastic silence of the library. He opened his notepad and wrote *Ewell Pender*, and below that he wrote *Aaron Greene*. He held the point of the pen over the two names, waiting for the pen to move on its own, like a divining rod. It did not. "Shit," he muttered. He slashed X marks through the names. Then he wrote *Jew-boy*, and beside it he drew a crude rendering of a telephone. His fingers quivered and he placed the pen on the table and leaned back in his chair. He had listened that morning to the recorded tapes of the muffled calls that someone had made to Nathan and Ruth Greene's home, threats against the "Jew-boy," and there was something disturbing about the disguised voice. It seemed almost familiar—not in tone, but in arrogance. The profile-makers from the FBI had said it was the voice of an educated adult, most likely middle-class Caucasian, and not the ranting of someone like Howard Edwards. They had guessed his age between thirty-five and forty-two. His profession was a dart-throw against a wall of possibilities—anything from doctor to actor. Certainly he was someone accustomed to public speaking. The profile-makers were sure of one thing: The calls were carefully planned; the calls were meant to distress or distract, or both.

The profile-makers from the FBI were remarkable people, Menotti reasoned. Compared to them, Sherlock Holmes would have had trouble finding his pecker with a road map, a Seeing Eye dog, *and* Dr. Watson. The profile-makers could take a single strand of hair or a clipped fingernail and build a scale look-alike out of modeling clay. They were far superior to the courts that heard their astonishing discoveries, or to defense lawyers who hissed bitterly about inadmissible evidence.

Menotti rocked his body close to the table and placed his elbows on it and tucked his head in his hands. He closed his eyes and tried to remember the voice on the tape. Had he heard it before? Maybe, he thought. Somewhere, among the thousands of voices, maybe he had heard this one. At least it wasn't Denny Harlow, the boy who had taunted Aaron in Peggy Burns's class. According to his parents, and army records, Denny Harlow was in

Germany. And it wasn't Howard Edwards. Howard was not so careful in his abuse. Howard would call from his own telephone, never realizing how simple it was to trace a number. Or maybe he did realize it. Maybe all that Howard wanted was the recognition of his friends, and being arrested for harassment was as good as a ticker-tape parade.

The image of the tape recorder floated into Menotti's mind, then the image of the single-sheet report from the FBI's profile-makers. He could see them on the screen of his closed eyes—serious men huddled over a machine, listening intently, making notations on paper. Their imagined faces were those of doctors deliberating a chess game with death. The caller was between thirty-five and forty-two, an educated man, one accustomed to speaking in public. How did they know that? Menotti wondered. Why did they say forty-two? Why not forty-five or forty-seven? More important, why did he believe them?

He opened his eyes and stretched. He checked his watch. It was four-thirty. He looked at his pad and circled the X'ed-out names. Then he wrote Ewell Pender's name again. A muscle in his hand twitched. He underlined the name twice. Again the muscle twitched. He drew a block around the name and closed the notepad and pushed away from the table.

At the desk, a librarian with a gray, tired face asked, "Help you, sir?"

"I'd like to see any information you have on this man," Menotti told her, handing her a slip of paper with Ewell Pender's name written on it.

Cody watched Olin McArthur sniff the wine casually before delicately sipping from it. Smooth, thought Cody. Smooth as velvet. As neatly and as reverently done as a quiet communion in an ornate church. Not one man in a thousand could drink wine like Olin—properly, but without pretension. And it was a good show, something Olin enjoyed. At least he wouldn't eat the popcorn the waitress had left in the small straw bread basket. Not Olin. Not popcorn and wine. The popcorn was for Cody. He needed it. Since breakfast, he had only eaten a package of potato chips and an apple that he had found in Freda's refrigerator. Let Olin sniff and sip his wine. Cody was interested only in the popcorn and his beer.

"Acceptable?" asked Cody.

Olin wagged his head. "Not bad, really," he replied casually. "California, I'd guess, or perhaps Washington State. Actually, some of the California cabernets are as pleasing as those from Bordeaux."

"Always thought so myself," Cody said. "It's a little like Milwaukee beer and German beer. They're both wet."

Olin suffered a smile. "Did you hear *The Katie Harris Show* today?" he asked.

"No," Cody told him. "She still leading the Greene orchestra?"

"She was in the brass section today," Olin replied. "As in brass balls. Seems she can't get Joel Garner on her show. Must be driving the poor child crazy."

"As long as she stays off my case, I don't care if she pumps old Joel on Peachtree, with five o'clock traffic rubbernecking the action."

"That's precisely the point, old friend," Olin said. "She jumped off Joel's bandwagon and began to defame your good name again."

"What?"

"You've made the leap from innocent participant to— let me see, now—'a practitioner of shallow journalism,' if I remember correctly. Of course, I think she meant yellow instead of shallow."

"She said that?" Cody asked incredulously.

"Among other things," Olin answered. "Apparently she tried to get you after Joel went mum, on advice from Pender's people, I believe. Anyway, you've become incommunicado—without explanation from your loyal cohorts, I might add—and Katie believes you're either dodging the issues because you know more than you've told anyone, including the police, or have suddenly become a haughty celebrity."

"That's incredible," Cody sighed.

"Not really," Olin countered. "That's Katie. I would never have thought of accusing you of dodging the issue." He smiled and tilted his head smugly. "The celebrity thing has a nice touch, though."

"I'll be damned," Cody whispered in exasperation. "Can't they find anything else to beat to death?"

"It's the temporary hot topic, my friend," Olin said. "Flavor of the month. No, this won't die until something shakes loose, one way or the other. But you'll survive it. And when it's over, you can go on her show and play the violin and she'll be organizing a Cody Yates Fan Club. Now, to more important things." He pulled a sheet of paper from his inside coat pocket and handed it to Cody. "Here's where Landon is relaxing."

Cody examined the paper. "Lake Lanier?" he said.

"That's it. Do you know the address?"

"Not exactly," Cody answered. "But I've been on Lanier a number of times. It wouldn't be hard to find."

"You see who owns the place?" asked Olin.

Cody read from the description. "Littlejohn?"

Olin nodded. "You know him?"

"Sure," Cody said. "Used to be a public defender, then got out with one of those firms with an arm-long title. I always thought of him as one of the septic-tank crowd."

Olin's face furrowed in a question.

"Kept the scum running free," Cody explained. "I'd forgotten about him leaving the firm to go with the bank. He must have hit the jackpot to have a place on the lake."

"It's a corporate fringe, Cody. You'd be surprised how many of our former colleagues have a little cabin tucked away up there. It's one of the things we sacrificed."

"Tell me about it," Cody said. He chuckled wearily, looked at Olin. "We ought to get out before we get too damned old, while people think we still have some pull."

An amused smile cracked on Olin's face. He said, "Cody, we *are* too damned old. Anyway, you wouldn't like it. You've got so much ink in your blood it bleeds out on your shirt pockets."

"That's because the shirts are as old as I am, Olin." He wiggled the sheet of paper over the table. "How did you come up with this, anyway?"

"Looking for Littlejohn," Olin replied. "They told me he wasn't at the bank, so I called his home. The maid said he wasn't there, and then she volunteered that his wife had gone to the lake to open the house for Mr. Landon. I called a contact in the county office up there and he gave me the address. I owe him some Braves tickets this summer."

"Think we ought to pay Landon a visit? Interrupt his rest?"

Olin sipped again from the wine, held its taste in his mouth, then swallowed it. "Not me," he said. "Maybe you. He would never speak to me. We have a mutual dislike. But you're different. You're a figure in all of this. He loves that sort of thing. Mingling with notoriety, you know."

"Thanks," Cody mumbled. "I need all the praise I can get these days. Did you find out anything about the bank examiners?"

"Not much," Olin confessed. "It's all a little murky at the moment, but I gather they're suspicious of a couple of loans that Landon tagged for community reinvestment."

"Explain," Cody urged.

"Like I said, it's murky. I don't know any details," Olin said. "There seems to be a whisper that Landon cracked the whip to have more money going to the community after last year's hassle, and in so doing may have set up a bogus company or two to benefit, perhaps with the assistance of one of the directors. It would be easy enough to do, I suppose. Sit tight for a time, then declare it a bad investment and write it off. Meanwhile, the money flow clogs up a couple of offshore bank accounts."

"Where?"

"Only God and Landon know at the moment," Olin said. "But it's been my experience that the feds aren't afraid to pry into anyone's storehouse of information—Landon's or God's. If there's something to it, they'll flush it out, Cody. Trust me."

"Could they remove Landon from office?" Cody asked.

"Absolutely. I told you the government never forgets. If they get a confirmation, something solid, Landon's out of his job and into the cushy confines of a federal prison."

"Who's the director? Did you find out?"

"A man named Curren. Walter Curren. His family was in textiles and he inherited a warehouse full of money, give or take a few dollars. He's been a major stockholder in the bank for years, chairs the committee for meeting community reinvestment standards. Dumb as a stick, and Landon leads him around like a poodle on a gold leash. He thinks the whole thing with Aaron Greene is the work of the Jewish underground."

"Good God," Cody said in astonishment. "Have you ever heard of a Jewish underground?"

"Not me, nor has he," Olin replied. "That, of course, doesn't mean much. It sounds good."

"Doesn't Landon know how hot things are?" asked Cody.

Olin shrugged. He thought of the question, then answered, "I doubt it. Littlejohn would keep it from him, if possible. Remember, he's military. The best way to become a general is to leave the general that's in power alone. Solve the problems yourself."

"But why?"

"Why? I think that's obvious, Cody. Don't you? Makes him more heroic if he resolves it before Landon knows about it. And if he fails and they give Landon the boot, then Littlejohn stands a more than even chance of taking over as interim president."

Cody smiled. "Then maybe Landon should know," he said.

"Maybe you're right," Olin agreed.

TWENTY-THREE

———◆———

AARON SAT ALONE IN THE LIBRARY, GAZING at the thickening darkness of the garden. It did not seem to him that night descended on the garden; rather, it seemed to seep out of the ground, out of the plants and trimmed grass, out of the pebbled walkways—night, rising up and up, coating tree trunks and the underbelly of leaves, until it folded like a closing dome over the tips of the limbs. It was the only place Aaron had ever been where night appeared to rise from the earth, rather than fall over it, and he remembered a children's story about the Queen of Night who lived at the tip of the earth and kept night hidden in a silver chest. Each evening, the Queen of Night released small puffs of darkness to chase away the light of day and to bring slumber to the earth. Aaron had always imagined the Queen as a beautiful, lonely woman. From the window, he could see the statue of the nude woman, the marble Alyse, and he could see night rising from her lifted face like a dark blush. He thought: Queen of Night.

Alyse had asked him to dress in the sports clothes—gray slacks, blue jacket, patterned shirt, brown loafers—left in his closet earlier in the day when he was outside working in the garden with the old man named Ewell. "We have a surprise for you," she had said kindly. The outfit felt strange, but comfortable, and he had stood for a long time in front of the mirror examining himself, wishing that his mother could see him so finely dressed. His mother would smile with pride.

There had been an early light dinner of broiled tuna and a salad, delivered by Carla. She had seemed especially excited, but had not stayed to eat with him. "I'll see you later," she had promised, and when he had asked what was happening, she had replied, "You'll see. You'll like it. You're going to learn something tonight."

It was dark in the garden when Aaron heard the knock at his bedroom door, and then the sound of the unlocking. He stood.

"Aaron?" It was Carla.

"Here," he said softly.

Carla closed and locked the door and crossed to the library.

"You look wonderful," she told him. "I like that outfit." She smiled. "You look like a movie star."

Aaron could feel the heat of a blush on his face. "It's— nice," he stammered. "I've never had a coat like this."

"Well, you should. You should have a closet full of them. All colors. Want to go for a ride?"

The question stunned Aaron. "A ride? Where? Home?"

"Not home, but out," Carla answered. "You've been cooped up long enough. We thought it was time to get you out."

"Where—are we going?" Aaron asked suspiciously.

"Oh, I don't know. Downtown. Alyse has it planned. I didn't ask."

"Are we coming back here?"

Carla laughed easily. "Of course." She reached for Aaron's shirt collar and straightened it. "We're not taking you off to dump you somewhere, if that's what you think. Believe it or not, Aaron, we're not that sort. We just thought you'd like a night out."

Aaron did not reply. He turned slightly away from Carla and looked again into the garden, at the statue. The statue's face was veiled in shadows.

"Are you afraid?" Carla asked gently.

Aaron shook his head.

"You are, aren't you?" Carla said. She stepped to him and embraced him. She whispered, "Sometimes I forget how I felt. Don't be afraid. Nothing's going to happen to you. I promise."

"You said I was going to learn something," Aaron said.

Carla stepped back. "I did, didn't I? Well, you will. Come on." She caught him by his hand and led him to the door leading into the garden. "We'll go this way," she said.

The gate leading from the garden to the front of the house was slightly open, and Aaron could see through it to a car with dark-tinted windows. Alyse stood beside the open back door. Another figure he could not distinguish was in the car, in the driver's seat. Carla stopped him at the gate.

"I hope you don't mind," she said, "but we'll need for you to put this on. Not for long." She handed him a mask to cover his eyes. "I know it may seem silly, like games, but it's best. I promise you, Aaron, nothing's going to happen to you."

Aaron slipped the mask over his head and tugged it down to cover his eyes. He felt Carla's hand on his hand, guiding him through the gate. "He looks wonderful, doesn't he?" Carla said gleefully. "Like a movie star."

Aaron heard Alyse's easy laugh, and her reply: "Very nice. Do you like the outfit, Aaron?"

"Uh—yes," Aaron said. He felt Alyse touching his arm.

"I'm sorry about the mask," Alyse told him. "We'll take it off soon. Come on, we'll guide you."

Aaron obeyed the hands of Alyse and Carla, and slipped into the car and sat. He could hear the opening and closing of two doors, then the car pulled away.

"In case you're wondering, you're with me and Carla and Robert," Alyse said easily from the front seat.

"And how are you, Aaron?" Robert said.

"Uh—fine," Aaron replied softly.

"That's a sharp outfit, my boy," Robert continued. "It's an outfit for a ladies' man."

"Where—are we going?" Aaron asked.

"I thought we'd drive downtown," Alyse told him.

"Here's a vote for the Varsity," Carla said. "I love Varsity hot dogs and onion rings."

"You'll get no argument from me," Robert said. "How about it, Alyse?"

"Maybe next time," Alyse answered.

"We'll hold you to the promise," Robert boomed. His laughter filled the car. "But don't tell Maria. She'd pout for a week."

Aaron sat and listened to the easy talk swimming around the car. Relaxed talk. The cackle of laughter. The kind of talk of television families on vacation. He felt the car dipping and rising gently, then running smoothly. He heard the cutting slaps of wind as the car met other cars on what Aaron believed was a two-lane road, and he knew by the sound they had entered a congested area. The car slowed to a stop. He could hear the clicking of the turn signal and then he felt the car turn left, slip down an incline, and gather speed. Aaron knew by the acceleration that the car had merged onto an expressway.

"Won't be long now, Aaron," Robert said merrily. "We'll have that mask off your face."

"Oh, I think it's fine now," Alyse said. "Go ahead, Aaron, take off the mask."

Aaron removed the mask slowly and looked up. He blinked at the sharp strobes of light from cars and security poles, leaving a yellow-and-silver contrail of scratches floating across the wet membrane of his eyes.

"Know where we are?" Carla asked lightly.

Aaron shook his head. He saw an interstate sign with 75 on it, then an off-ramp sign for Howell Mill Road and, immediately, another for Northside Drive. In the distance he could see the skyline of Atlanta trimmed in night lights.

The skyline was a silhouette, dark against the sienna of the burning lights, the pointed spire of One Atlantic Center jabbed into the halo suspended over the city. Aaron could not remember ever approaching Atlanta from that direction—north, or northwest, he reasoned. He had always lived in the same house, which was east of the city.

"Pretty, isn't it?" Carla said softly.

"Big," Robert said. "That's what it is. Big."

Aaron sat against the backseat, in the corner away from Carla, and watched as Robert exited on Williams Street and drove into the city, maneuvering through the streets until he turned left on Forsyth and pulled to a stop at the curb in front of the Journal-Constitution Building.

"Aaron, I want you to do something for me," Alyse said quietly. "I want you to go into the building, into the lobby, and buy a newspaper."

Aaron did not speak. He stared at Alyse, remembering the day of rain and the heavy, angry woman crowding him on the street, and the car that stopped for him.

"Would you do that for me, Aaron?" Alyse asked. She extended her hand and offered him some coins.

"We'll be right here," Robert promised.

"It's all right, Aaron," Carla whispered. She touched his arm. "I told you that you were going to learn something. This is it. When you come back, we'll explain it."

Aaron took the coins and opened the door and got out and walked through the heavy glass doors of the building and approached the guard desk. On the desk, he saw a picture of himself on a stand. Beneath the picture were the words HAVE YOU SEEN AARON GREENE? It's me, he thought. They'll know me. He looked back through the glass doors and saw the waiting car and the faces of Alyse and Carla watching him from the open windows.

"Help you?" the guard said. The guard was heavy, with sleepy, bored eyes.

"Could—I get a paper?" Aaron asked.

"Sure."

The guard reached behind him to a stack of papers and placed one on the counter. He said, "Fifty cents."

Aaron placed two quarters in the guard's hand. He looked again at his picture. Three people stepped from an elevator that opened near him. They were laughing. One looked at him—quizzically, Aaron thought—then walked away with his companions.

"Anything else?" the guard asked.

Aaron glanced again at his picture in the poster stand on the desk. He was only inches from it. Mirror-close. The eyes of the picture, covered in a caul of fear and uncertainty, stared blankly at him. The thin, straight lines of his lips seemed death-still. Aaron blinked and looked away from the picture to the guard.

"Anything else?" the guard said again.

"I—I'm—" Aaron stuttered. He glanced back at the picture.

"Yeah?" the guard said impatiently.

"I—"

"Did you get the paper?"

Aaron turned to the voice. It was Robert. He was standing in the doorway, smiling at Aaron.

Aaron nodded. He tucked the paper under his arm and looked once again at the guard.

"That the one you want?" the guard asked.

"Yes sir," Aaron said meekly. He turned and walked through the glass doors with Robert. They got into the car and Robert pulled back into traffic.

No one spoke for a block, then Alyse said, "Did the guard know who you were, Aaron?"

Aaron shook his head. He looked out of the window. The Century National Bank was on his left.

"How did you feel?" asked Alyse.

Aaron did not answer.

"Invisible?" Alyse said.

Aaron lowered his head in a nod.

"Do you think there's a feeling on earth worse than that,

Aaron? People looking at you, but not seeing you? I don't
think anything could hurt as much, and yet everyone does
it. Look out of the window, Aaron. Look at all the people
out there, walking with their heads down, not looking at
anyone. Do you know why? It's not really because they
don't want to see someone else, but because they're afraid
that someone else won't see them."

Aaron could feel Carla touch his arm. The car rolled
slowly along the street, trapped in the sluggish crawl of
night traffic. Aaron looked out of the clouded window.
He saw people rushing along the sidewalk, their heads
tucked. He wondered how many of them felt invisible.

"That's the first lesson, Aaron," Alyse said gently. "They
looked at you, but they didn't see you. They didn't know
you. The first lesson is to understand that most people
recognize only what they want to recognize, or what
they're told to recognize, and everything else is invisible.
They overlook so much, so very much. When you know
that—really know it—you can do anything, because you
learn that it isn't that important how other people see you,
or if they recognize you. It's important for you to see
yourself, for you to recognize who you are."

Victor Menotti looked at the papers spread across the
dining-room table. Reports from the FBI, the GBI, other
investigators with the Atlanta Police Department, messages
and queries from county agencies surrounding Atlanta.
Notes hastily scribbled. Names. Names crossed out.
Names underlined. Call reports from meetings. Clifford
Russell's warning about Cody Yates. Two telephone messages from Cody. Philip Oglesbee's report on Nathan and
Ruth Greene. Random sentences he had written from his
research on Ewell Pender. Words, he thought. A senseless
puzzle. None of it fit. It was oil and water. Even when
stirred by a paddle of possibilities, it separated. What was
missing? What in hell's name was missing?

He lit a cigarette and sucked the smoke deep into his lungs.

"Victor, don't smoke in the house," Arlene Menotti said from the kitchen. "You promised me."

"All right," he said. "I'll go outside."

Outside, in the front yard, it was cool. The air of the March evening rolled briskly across the lawn, and Menotti watched a candy wrapper tumble over the grass and lodge against a tree in the island of oaks that his wife kept immaculately clean and sculptured. She'd be pissed, he thought. He crossed the lawn and picked up the wrapper and slipped it into his pocket. Across the street, he saw a door open and Lyn Ramsey stood for a moment silhouetted against the door light, dressed in her nightgown. Against the light, the gown was transparent, and the nude outline of Lyn's body was like a mannequin covered in flimsy gauze. Menotti smiled. The men in the neighborhood had said among themselves that Lyn Ramsey was the most sensuous woman east of Cindy Crawford. Watching her for the brief moment against the backlight of the door—hearing her chirp for her poodle to come inside— Menotti thought they were right. Lyn Ramsey was a goddess. He saw a small dog scurry past Lyn's legs, and the door closed quickly. Menotti wondered if she had seen him standing among the oaks. Probably not, he decided. He would know the next time they spoke. Her eyes would tell him.

He dropped the cigarette and stubbed out the burning tip with his shoe, then he gouged a small hole in the soft dirt and buried the butt.

Damn it, he thought angrily. Why can't I put it together?

He walked back into the house, closing and locking the door.

"Want to watch the news, honey?" Arlene called from the family room. "There's supposed to be something about trouble at the Century National Bank."

Menotti walked into the room. "What?"

"The news. You want to watch it?"

"What did you say about the bank?"

"I saw a promo on it earlier," Arlene told him. "Something about an investigation."

The spirited jingle of an advertisement sang from the television. Animated cookies danced in rhythm, then rolled magically into a cellophane wrapper. Menotti slumped beside his wife on the sofa.

"I hope they're about to burn the assholes," Arlene said. "I can't believe their arrogance."

"It's business," Menotti said. "Just business."

"Then, thank God you're not in it. I think I'd prefer somebody shooting at you."

"Thanks."

"You're welcome."

They watched a second commercial, then a report on an accident on I-285, near the Roswell Road exit, and then Curtis Rawlings, the anchor, announced, "Charges against the Century National Bank for mishandling of corporate funds may be filed by the U.S. Attorney, according to informed sources, complicating an already-sensitive public reaction to the bank's position on the kidnapping of Aaron Greene. For an update, we switch now to Ken Masters, who has been covering the story for WJES television."

The screen snapped to a shot of the lobby of the Century National Bank. Jason Littlejohn waited nervously to be interviewed, as Miriam Finch stood helplessly at his side. Ken Masters, who was television-handsome, turned to the camera, furrowed his brow to his television-serious look, and said in his television-deep voice, "Thanks, Curtis. As you mentioned, informed sources have revealed today that federal bank examiners now feel confident they can confirm that Ethridge Landon, president of Century National Bank, is involved in the misuse of bank funds supposedly earmarked for community development projects. Though no details have been released, it has been learned that Mr. Landon, and perhaps one member of the board of directors, was allegedly involved in setting up bogus companies which received an undetermined amount of money from the bank, with the plan to ultimately write off those loans as poor investments. If so, Landon may be removed from his position and a further investigation by the U.S. Attorney's office could result in prosecution. Mr. Landon is unavailable for comment, but with us now is Jason Littlejohn, the corporate counsel for Century National." He turned to Jason. "Mr. Littlejohn, could you clarify any of these rumors for us?"

Jason Littlejohn cleared his throat. His face colored in a blush. He blinked rapidly and his small eyes darted over Ken Masters's face. "First," he said, "I think you've used the correct word. What you're hearing is rumor. We do not believe Mr. Landon has received any money that would not constitute sound and sensible business practice. We've received no direct notice from federal bank examiners, the U.S. Attorney's office, or any other agency that the Century National Bank has in any way violated any law or banking standard. Other than that, I have no further comment."

"Mr. Littlejohn, where is Mr. Landon?" Ken Masters asked.

"He's on vacation—a well-deserved vacation, I might add," Jason replied irritably. "His whereabouts are private."

"Doesn't it seem a little irresponsible to be on vacation during one of the most critical times in the history of the bank?" Ken Masters pressed. "Not only is this investigation occurring, but the kidnapping of Aaron Greene is certainly on the minds of every American, as well as the rest of the world."

"Mr. Landon has expressed his concern and sorrow over the abduction of Aaron Greene," Jason said tensely. "He is as concerned as anyone over the safety of a valued employee, and he is keenly bothered by the innuendos suggesting otherwise. In fact, it has been the stress of Mr. Greene's disappearance that caused a number of us—myself included—to urge Mr. Landon to get away for a few days of rest. I don't think he's slept many hours at all since learning of the abduction. As to other speculations, I can only say that Mr. Landon will be eager to clear his good name and the good name of the bank if, and when, such speculations become charges. Now, I must excuse myself. I have a meeting to attend."

"One last question, Mr. Littlejohn. One of the bank's directors, Walter Curren, has suggested publicly that the kidnapping of Aaron Greene may be linked to activities of a Jewish network seeking attention. Would you comment on that?"

Jason blinked, then stared indignantly at Ken Masters. "Mr. Curren has the right to express his personal opinion, of course," he said curtly, "but that does not mean it is the opinion of the bank or of the other board members. To my knowledge, there is no hard evidence at all that this matter is related to any organized group—Jewish or Protestant or any other religious or fanatic affiliation. Personally, I think it is inadvisable to discount any possibility, but until there is proof substantiating such charges, the abduction remains, to us, the work of terrorists, because we believe kidnapping is an act of terrorism. Now, if you'll excuse me."

Ken Masters turned back to the camera. "We've been talking to Jason Littlejohn, corporate counsel for Century National Bank, addressing the rumors of possible federal charges, and the absence of Ethridge Landon during one of the most trying times in the history of the bank. Back to you, Curtis."

"The bastards," Arlene Menotti snorted. She felt her husband push against her, felt his body stiffen as he pulled to the edge of the sofa. "Victor? What's the matter?"

Menotti whispered, "Goddamn it."

"What?"

"I'll be a son of a bitch," Menotti said softly.

"I don't know what you're talking about, Victor."

"But I do," Menotti said. "I do."

TWENTY-FOUR

———————◆———————

AMOS TEMPLE'S STORY ON THE KIDNAPPING of Aaron Greene for the first edition of *The Atlanta Journal* was a repeat of the stories he had written for a week: nothing of substance to report from anyone. Law enforcement officials were turning over grains of sand and could find nothing. Tips flowed in like a high tide with thundering, whitecapped waves, but all evaporated under the heat of questioning. It was a thin story padded with the filler of terse comments from Philip Oglesbee, from Clifford Russell, from the mayor's office and the governor's office, comments repeated again and again, like a dulling chant, and the comments said the same thing, but in different words—words that Amos had pulled from the mouth of his interviewees like a maniacal dentist extracting teeth. The comments said, "We don't know. We're working on it. We hope to get a break soon." It was as exasperating as the investigation in the Centennial Park bombing during the Olympic Games. With one exception. The bomb over Aaron Greene had not yet exploded.

Yet, as the shock of Aaron Greene's abduction soured in its static, no-news repetition, the Wake Up America! campaign to rescue him became a spectacle that changed hourly, and the stories of that spectacle, which accompanied Amos's daily, solemn announcements of investigation, became far more intriguing than the suspense of

Aaron Greene's well-being. Ewell Pender's crusade to raise ten million dollars—with Joel Garner's presence providing glamour—fit easily into mouths, fell easily from slippery tongues. The abduction was a matter of horror; the rescue was a matter of heroism and celebrity and gossip.

"It's a goddamn circus," Amos complained in the ten o'clock staff meeting in Harry Dilliard's office.

"It's human nature," Harry told him.

"Fine," Amos growled, "but why in hell's name are we running a front-page thermometer on the contributions? Jesus, Harry, we're supposed to be a newspaper, not a goddamn lottery sheet. It looks like one of those campaigns for Jerry's Kids."

"We're supposed to be what people want us to be," corrected Harry. "They want it quick and easy. They want pictures. That's what they're getting."

"I don't believe it," Amos said sadly. "Here we are with a chance for the Pulitzer and we're running a bloody contribution thermometer."

"That's bullshit," Harry snapped. "We're doing more than that, and you know it. We've got the bank story. We've got sidebars on everybody that sneezes or wipes his ass more than twice a day. We've got six people working exclusively on this. What the hell do you call that?"

Cody could not resist. He said, "Overkill."

"Don't be a smart-ass, Cody," Harry hissed. "If you'd get back to work, we'd have seven people working on it."

"I didn't think you wanted me doing anything," Cody said. "You want me on it, fine. Tell me. I'll do something."

"Then do it," Harry ordered.

"Fine," Cody replied angrily. He pushed away from the conference table and stood.

"Where do you think you're going?" demanded Harry.

"To do it," Cody answered.

"What does that mean?"

"You told me to go to work. I'm going to work."

"You want to give us a clue as to what that means?"

"I've got a couple of things to chase down."

"All right," Harry mumbled after a moment. "You find anything, you get on the horn." Then: "Are you going to the Pender thing tonight?"

"You paying?"

"Of course we're paying."

"Then I'll be there. Who else is going?"

"Me," Harry said. "And Amos and Olin and Freda Graves."

Cody could feel the pulse of surprise in his face. Freda had said nothing to him about attending the Pender reception. He said, "Who?"

"You heard me: Freda. I had an at-large ticket, so I gave it to her this morning."

Cody forced his voice to sound irritated: "Why?"

"Because she's the best damn sidebar writer I've got, and I don't want that idiot society editor out there doing one of those gowns-by-Faggot pieces. In the unlikely event you ever get around to reading what this newspaper publishes, I recommend the story she's got today on her homeless series. It's the best thing we've run in a long time. She picked up that the residents of one of those shelters are collecting money for the Greene kid, put a twist in it that grabs the gut, and, God knows, we don't get a lot of that anymore."

Cody frowned a question.

"Yeah, Cody, " Harry said. He picked up a section of the early edition of the *Journal* and slid it across the conference table.

Cody read the headline of Freda's story: HOMELESS JOIN GREENE CRUSADE. He blushed with embarrassment. He had not read Freda's story. He knew she had worked late and was tired when she finally arrived at her apartment. They had had a quick glass of wine and she had fallen asleep with only a soft hand touch to his face and a promise for the morning. The promise had been magnificent.

"I'll read it," Cody said. He picked up the paper.

"Do that," Harry snarled. He twisted his body to face Amos. "And whether any of you believe it or not, I don't want what we're doing to become a circus, either," he added.

"Then let me go put the elephants back in the barn," Cody said. He opened the door to leave.

"Cody," Harry said.

"What?"

"I know there's not a hell of a lot of love lost between you and Freda. Frankly, I don't blame her one iota, and I don't give a damn how you feel personally, but tonight you will be civil to her. In fact, you're going to glow in her presence, and she's going to be as giddy as a schoolgirl at a spin-the-bottle sleepover after I have a little talk with her. You can fight in the office. You can even slip little capsules of cyanide in each other's coffee when no one's looking. But when we walk out of these doors, we are one big, happy family. You understand me?"

Cody swallowed a smile. Maybe Olin McArthur knew about Freda, he thought, but no one else did. He thought of Freda working at her desk, her face wearing the earnest look of business. Four hours earlier, he had lifted her to his body. "I'll be civil," he said. "I'll even escort her, if that'd make you happy."

"That would make me extremely happy, Yates. Extremely."

"Then you tell her," Cody suggested. "Tell her it's an order."

"I will," Harry said smugly. "If you think I won't, you're sucking wind."

"Harry, I never doubt you," Cody mumbled wearily, fighting the laughter that would leap from him when he left the building.

★   ★   ★

It took Cody an hour and ten minutes to drive to Lake Lanier and another thirty minutes to find the turnoff to Jason Littlejohn's cabin. He had stopped to ask directions at a service station.

"Can't see it from the road," the blond young man had said cheerfully. "It's stuck back up in the woods a couple hundred yards." He had added, "Nice place. You see Mrs. Littlejohn, tell her Wade said hello."

Cody stopped at the turnoff, obeying an instinct that tempered his reporter's impatience. It was something he had learned early: Instinct was more valuable than information. He parked his car and followed the road until he saw the cabin on the knoll above the water, then he slipped into the woods and moved carefully among the trees. He saw two cars—a Mercedes and a Porsche—and he heard from the house the rolling squeal of a woman's laughter. His eyes scanned the cabin. Wade was right, he thought. Nice place. No, better than nice. Damn nice. He saw a movement from the upstairs window and the flash of a woman skinning a blouse from over her head, her breasts springing loose and free. Then she dropped down out of sight. The laughter raced again from the house, then stopped abruptly. Son of a bitch, Cody thought, whistling silently. He wondered who the woman was. He looked at his watch. Twelve-forty. A nooner. Ethridge Landon was having a nooner to relieve his terrible stress over Aaron Greene and federal bank examiners.

Cody sat beside the tree, in the shadows, and watched the window. Incredibly, in fewer than five minutes, he saw Ethridge Landon rise up in front of the window. He heard a distant, hollow laugh, like an echo, and saw Landon wave his hand in a mock refusal, then stumble away out of sight. In a moment the woman stood and ran her fingers through her blond hair. He heard her voice, but did not understand the words. She moved away, toward the unseen Landon. Cody smiled and shook his head. In-

stinct, he thought. He turned and moved through the
woods, back to his car.

Cody waited until ten minutes after one before driving to
the cabin. It would be enough time for Landon to com-
pose himself, yet still be forced to scramble to dress before
answering the door. He wanted Landon off-guard, wanted
to watch Landon's face as he lied about the presence of
the woman. He parked behind the Mercedes and got out
and loudly closed the door to his Pontiac. He smiled at
the image of Ethridge Landon leaping up at the sound.

When he answered the door on the third round of
knocking, Ethridge Landon was dressed in a pale blue V-
necked sweater and jeans and tennis shoes. His hair was
damp. He glared suspiciously at Cody.

"Yes?"

"Ethridge Landon?" Cody said casually.

"Who wants to know?" Ethridge asked.

"Cody Yates. I work for the *Journal-Constitution*. You're
a hard man to find."

"That's because I don't care to be found, Mr. Yates. I'm
on vacation."

"I know," Cody said. "Sorry to interrupt, but you know
how it is. World keeps turning."

"And so do the presses," Ethridge replied curtly. "I'm
sorry, Mr. Yates, but I have nothing to say. You should
call Miriam Finch."

Cody smiled easily. "I don't think she can answer what
I have to ask."

"Why don't you try her?"

"Sure," Cody said. "If that's what you'd like. Only
problem is, she may not be working for you by the time
I get back to Atlanta."

Surprise flickered across Ethridge's face. "What does
that mean?" he asked.

Cody let a pause build and pulse across the space that
separated him from Ethridge Landon. He could see Lan-

don's face twitch with irritation. "It means," he said slowly, "that you may not have a job. At least the rumor's on the street."

"What?" The question was almost a scream.

"I just wanted to see if I can confirm anything," Cody said.

"Come on in," Ethridge mumbled. He turned in the doorway.

"Are you sure I'm not intruding?" asked Cody.

"Does it matter?" Ethridge said coolly.

"I guess not," Cody answered. He stepped into the room and followed Ethridge to the kitchen. He could smell the faint odor of marijuana, like the smoke of sweet incense, weaving through the room.

"Want some coffee?" Ethridge asked.

"If you've got it," Cody said. "That would be good." He sat at a stool near the serving counter and watched Ethridge Landon pour coffee into two cups. He wondered where the woman of the blond hair was hiding, waiting for him to leave.

"Just tell me what you've heard," Ethridge said. He put the coffee before Cody. His glare was hard on Cody's face. "And believe me, I'll know if you're bullshitting me, and if you are, I'm going to call the sheriff of this good county and have your ass hauled away from here like last week's garbage."

The threat made Cody smile openly. Olin McArthur had been kind: Ethridge Landon was more than arrogant; he was an asshole, a small, posturing bully who wore his steamrollering accomplishments like gaudy medals on a dictator's chest.

"You don't have television up here?" asked Cody. "Or radio?"

"Or newspapers," Ethridge said evenly. "That's the purpose of getting away, I believe."

"And no one's called you from your office?"

"The only phone I've got is my cell phone, and I've

had it turned off," Ethridge said. "They don't call me. I call them. I told you, Mr. Yates, this is a getaway for me, and I'd like to continue it, so get to the point."

"It was announced last night that federal bank examiners had enough evidence to remove you from the bank," Cody said. "And there's some talk about prosecution. But maybe that's just talk. You know how it is with the media."

Ethridge's eyes blinked in shock. The blood drained from his face. He sat heavily on one of the stools at the serving counter. His eyes stayed fixed on Cody. Disbelieving. "What the hell are you talking about?" he said hoarsely.

"Just that," Cody told him. "I saw an interview with your lawyer last night. Since you're here at his place, I thought surely——"

Ethridge spun from the chair. He muttered, "Goddamn it." Then, in a loud, calling voice: "Jeanne."

Cody heard footsteps from upstairs. He turned to see Jeanne Littlejohn appear at the top of the stairs. She was dressed casually, in jeans and the pullover blouse Cody had watched her remove.

"Where's Jason this morning?" demanded Ethridge.

"At work," Jeanne answered. She glanced nervously at Cody. "Why?"

"Did you talk to him last night?"

"No. We were supposed to have dinner, but he had to cancel, so I went to a movie and didn't get in until late. He got in about one, I suppose, and he left early."

"You didn't talk to him at all?"

"No. I was still asleep when——"

"You didn't read a paper this morning, or listen to the news on the drive up?" Ethridge asked in a hard voice.

"No. I played some CDs. What's wrong?"

"I'd like to know the answer to that myself," Ethridge growled. He glanced at Cody. "This is Cody Yates. He's with the newspaper." He motioned with his head toward

Jeanne. "This is Jeanne Littlejohn, Jason's wife. She brought up some fresh bed linens."

"Just finished putting them on the bed," Jeanne said quickly.

Cody bit the smile. "Pleased to meet you," he said.

"Thank you," Jeanne replied. She looked at Ethridge. "I think I'll run along. Do you need anything else?"

"No," Ethridge said irritably. "If you talk to Jason, have him call me. I may not be able to reach him."

Jeanne descended the steps quickly. She paused as she passed Cody. "It's nice to meet you," she said. "Of course, I've heard a lot about you lately."

Cody smiled. "It's good to meet you," he said pleasantly. He added, "By the way, I spoke to a young man at the service station down the road. I believe he said his name was Wade. Said to give you his regards."

A blush, like a shadow, rushed into Jeanne's face. "Oh," she said. "Yes. He—does some odd jobs for us occasionally." She turned to Ethridge. "Keep your phone on. I'll call later." She flashed a quick smile to Cody and left the house.

Ethridge sat again on the stool. He drank from his coffee and listened to the Porsche leave the yard, then he looked up at Cody.

"I know what you're thinking, Mr. Yates," he said. "I can see it in your face, and, frankly, I don't like it. Jeanne Littlejohn is the wife of my attorney and that's all. We've been friends as couples for several years. She was simply delivering some bed linens. Nothing more." He paused. "Sometimes you people make me wonder what in the hell ever happened to dignity."

"You don't like reporters, I take it," Cody said calmly.

"You're right. I don't."

"And I don't like you, Mr. Landon," Cody said. "I don't like your face. I don't like your voice. I don't like the air you breathe. I don't like the way you do business. I don't like your goddamn haughty attitude. I hope they nail your ass to a rotten chinaberry tree and leave you there until the maggots come to dinner." His voice dropped to a rumble. "I'm here as a reporter, to ask you some questions. I don't give a damn what you did or didn't do with your lawyer's wife. But the fact is, I saw it, Mr. Landon. I was out in the woods, before I drove up. I'm surprised you didn't have enough sense to close the curtain. She's got great tits, Mr. Landon, and she giggles like a teenager. And you, you've got the staying power of a bull in heat. Slam, bam, thank you ma'am. Now, are you going to answer a couple of questions, or not?"

Olin McArthur would be proud of him, Cody thought as he guided his Pontiac away from Jason Littlejohn's cabin. Olin would smile with amusement and satisfaction as he told of Ethridge Landon's blubbering excuses about the rumor of charges impending against him. There was nothing to the rumors, he had contended bitterly. It was nothing but political pressure, resulting from the abduction of Aaron Greene.

"The fact is," Ethridge had declared, "I'm up here working on a way to have the bank put up a reward for information about the boy. I'm going to put fifty thousand dollars of my own money on the table and try to get the board to match it out of their personal funds. There's no damned way the bank can go along with a ten-million-dollar ransom, regardless of what Ewell Pender thinks, but we can show our concern. Besides, I think reward money will get the right people talking. It's pretty damn obvious the cops don't know what the hell to do."

"If the board matches, that's a hundred thousand," Cody had said. "That's a lot of concern."

"It's nothing compared to what we're losing in withdrawals," Ethridge had admitted weakly. "But it's not all business, either. I want the boy found—alive and well. It's personal, and I don't give a damn what you think, Mr. Yates."

"I think you're covering your ass," Cody had replied. "I think you're dead meat, and you know it. I think you're looking for a little sympathy."

Yes, Olin McArthur would be pleased, Cody thought. He laughed aloud in his car. He wanted to stop at the service station and tell Wade that he had seen Jeanne Littlejohn and she was doing well and looking fine. Looking fine indeed. He imagined the smug smile on Wade's face. Wade would know exactly what he meant.

TWENTY-FIVE

————◆————

MENOTTI SAT IN THE ARMCHAIR IN PHILIP Oglesbee's office, his aching shoulders pushed deep into the billowed chairback. He had been ushered into the office by a secretary with the explanation that Mr. Oglesbee would join him in a few minutes. By the slow, mesmerizing sweep of a long, needle-thin second hand on the wall clock behind the African Prince's desk, the few had labored away to ten, then fifteen, and now twenty. Typical, Menotti thought. Making people wait was an exercise of the bureaucratic process, a requisite instruction for candidates of federal jobs. Waiting implied importance, and importance was an excuse for impatience if the occasion demanded it. Surely someone had studied it, Menotti reasoned: the percentage of times a federal employee had said to a citizen, "I can only give you ten minutes." Or, worse, "That's not handled by us. You need to contact So-and-So in Washington." It was nonsense to believe the federal government would ever crumble; it was too well supported by the compacted clutter of policies and procedures and confusion. Menotti was used to the waiting, however. The waiting did not bother him. He was bothered only by the sign on Oglesbee's desk: THANK YOU FOR NOT SMOKING. He wanted a cigarette. The sign annoyed him, teased him, dared him. But he did not smoke.

Philip Oglesbee swept into his office twenty-three

minutes after his secretary had left Menotti alone. He was followed by Tito Francis.

"You nailed him," Philip said enthusiastically, sliding into the chair behind his desk. He added, "Sorry we're late."

"They're certain?" asked Menotti. "No doubts?"

"It's a match," Tito said. "Just listening, our guy agreed with you: The way he said 'Jew' fit like the proverbial glove. Then he ran it through his little voice machine, and he was right. We need to double-check it, but we've got at least one confirmation. Jason Littlejohn made the calls."

"The question is why he did it," Philip said. "You got any ideas?"

"Who knows?" Menotti replied. "Maybe it's his hobby. Maybe he hates Jews. I'd guess he wanted a distraction to keep the heat off the bank. Fizzled on him."

"You're probably right," agreed Philip. "I had a talk with the boys in charge of the bank exam. They tell me they're ready to pull the rug on Landon, and Littlejohn's up to his ass in alligators on how he's been covering. My guess is he's been trying to keep Landon in the dark while he wiped out his own tracks. If we had jumped on the scent of the anti-Semitic trail, he might have made it work."

"There's a bigger question," Tito said. "Did he have the boy snatched?"

Philip wagged his head. "Possible." He turned to Menotti. "Victor?"

Menotti laced his fingers across his chest and stared at the THANK YOU FOR NOT SMOKING sign. After a moment, he said, "Why? What did he have to gain from it?"

"Ten million, for one thing," Tito answered dryly.

"In his position, he didn't need it," Menotti said. "He makes a pretty decent wage, I'd say. Why take that chance?"

"Maybe he was making a play at being named the president of the bank," Philip suggested. "Stir up a hornet's nest, get Landon ousted, and get himself installed."

"Too big of a risk," Menotti argued. "Especially since he's a party to everything that would get Landon kicked out. He may not be brilliant, but he's in the highly intelligent range."

"Frankly, I don't give a shit what made him do it," Philip said. "We want to pick him up."

"When?" asked Menotti.

"Today. No reason to wait. He won't call again, not with the number changed."

"I'd like to be in on it," Menotti said.

"Any particular reason?" Philip said.

"Yeah. A good one," Menotti told him. "I've just never liked the man. I'd like to see him squirm."

"I'll buy it," Philip said. "Tito?"

"Ought to have some pleasure in every job," Tito said. He smiled. "When can you go?"

"Tomorrow would be better for me," Menotti answered. "I'm ass-deep right now. Can it wait a day?"

"Sure. Why not?" Philip said easily. "We'll put a shadow on him for tonight. Just to make sure he's around. He may even screw up before tomorrow. Make it easier."

"You going to the Pender reception?" asked Menotti.

Philip smiled. "Didn't get an invitation. Did you?"

"I don't need one," Menotti said. "The mayor offered police coverage. Somebody volunteered me."

Philip laughed his African Prince laugh—good-natured, lacquered in cynicism. "Bring me a Joel Garner autograph," he said. "My wife's a fool over that man, and damned if I understand it." He laughed again. "I keep telling her, 'Honey, that's a white boy,' and she keeps telling me, 'Honey, there's some men that make a woman color-blind.'"

The whispered call from Miriam Finch at two-thirty had angered and then frightened Ethridge Landon. An emergency meeting of the board of directors of Century National Bank had been scheduled for four o'clock.

"Without me?" Ethridge had asked.

"I'm not supposed to know myself," Miriam had replied. "I wanted to use the boardroom for a meeting with Olin McArthur, but it was booked for the board."

"Where's Littlejohn?"

"He's with the chairman."

"Cary Wright?"

"Yes."

"What the hell's going on?"

"I have no idea, Ethridge, but I thought you should know. I tried calling you last night and this morning, but you didn't answer."

"Yeah, well, I screwed up. I'm on my way in."

"Remember, you didn't hear this from me," Miriam had cautioned.

"Fine, fine."

It was four-ten when Ethridge arrived at the bank and hurried into his office, speaking brusquely to Brenda Patterson as he passed her desk. "Get in here."

"Yes sir," Brenda said in a startled voice. She threw a puzzled look at Rachel Segriest. Rachel shrugged her shoulders and walked away.

In his office, Ethridge dropped his briefcase on the conference table and turned to Brenda, who stood at the closed door. "I don't want any bullshit, not one word of it," he said bitterly. "What's going on here?"

"I have no idea," Brenda said, her voice quivering. "Mr. Littlejohn has been meeting with Mr. Wright since this morning. They're in with the board now."

"Why didn't you call me?"

Brenda's eyes moistened. "Mr. Wright instructed me not to," she confessed. "Mr. Littlejohn, too."

Ethridge dropped heavily into his chair. He swiveled and looked out the window. "Where's Miriam?"

"She left for the day," Brenda said. "Her mother's ill.

She'll probably be gone for a couple of days. South Carolina, I think."

Ethridge nodded. Bitch, he thought. First rat to leave the ship.

"The bank examiners have been here all day," Brenda added. "And someone from the U.S. Attorney's office. He met with Mr. Littlejohn and Mr. Wright."

Ethridge laughed softly. "They've got me, Brenda. That's what it's about. The sons of bitches are deal-making. What's Littlejohn's mood?"

"I—don't know, sir."

"No bullshit, Brenda. We've been together too long for that."

"He—he seems happy. I was in your office earlier and he came in to ask if I would arrange for lunch to be served in the boardroom. He kept looking at the walls, at your pictures. It was like he knew something."

Ethridge swiveled back to face Brenda. "He was seeing himself in here. The little bastard's been after this job since he walked in the door."

"Yes sir," Brenda said simply. "Yes sir, he has."

"Well, I think I'll pay them a visit."

"I—I'm not sure you should," Brenda said hesitantly.

"Why not?"

"I just don't think it would be a good idea."

Ethridge studied his assistant carefully. She was trying to warn him, but did not know how. He said, "All right, Brenda. But I want you to do this: I want you to go into the boardroom and give Mr. Littlejohn a note. You write it. Tell him I'm in my office."

"That's all?"

"That's all."

Ethridge Landon stood by the window and watched the traffic on the street below—barely moving traffic, tightly packed between the jerky stop-and-go of traffic lights and the commands of a lone policeman, his arms spinning in

the air, hands pointing, palms snapping up, a street per-
former in an artful pantomime of burlesque humor. Ethridge despised the street. It was a clogged, polluted cement
stream, slow-moving into the wasteland of the suburbs.
He would be on it soon, he thought. He would drive away
from the Century National Bank and not return. He knew
what the meeting in the boardroom was about, and he
knew that within minutes the door would open and Jason
Littlejohn and Cary Wright would enter his office and
deliver his fate.

His instinct was correct. The door opened as he stood
looking out the window. Jason Littlejohn entered, followed by Cary Wright. He saw them in the reflection of
the window.

"Gentlemen," Ethridge said. He turned to face them.

Cary Wright spoke first. "Ethridge," he said. He sat
heavily at the conference table.

"You don't look well, Cary," Ethridge replied.

"I'm not, goddamn it," growled Cary Wright.

"And you, Jason. How are you?" Ethridge said.

"Worried," Jason answered seriously. "We've got to
talk."

Ethridge sat at his desk and leaned comfortably in his
chair. He said, "Fine. Obviously, you know something I
don't, so I'll ask you to begin."

"The board just met," Cary Wright said wearily. "It's
unanimous, Ethridge. You can either resign, effective immediately, or the bank examiners are going to remove
you."

Ethridge laughed quietly. "Well, you've never avoided
the nitty-gritty, Cary. I don't suppose there's any reason
to argue the point."

"None," Cary Wright replied bluntly. Then: "Goddamn it, Ethridge, they've got our backs against the wall.
The board feels that you left us hanging. Somebody should
have kept us informed. None of us had any idea how
serious things were."

The smile was fixed in Ethridge's face. He watched Cary Wright's frightened, darting eyes. Cary Wright, he thought. The evil son of a bitch. Cary Wright had squeezed more debit money from anxious holders of worthless insurance than any man in the world's history, and now the great hypocrite was cowering behind the pitiful excuse of ignorance. He had been drunk with Cary Wright in New York, had watched Cary Wright make insane, perverted demands of prostitutes hired as escorts to dinner and theater.

"Well, that's why we had a lawyer, I thought," Ethridge said easily. He looked at Jason. "I thought we'd covered everything pretty well after last year. At least that's been my impression from your reports."

Jason Littlejohn shifted his weight and stood forward on the balls of his feet, a military habit of assuring his presence. "Some new things have come to light," he said professionally.

"New things?" asked Ethridge.

"Apparently there was a letter from Walter Curren to you, referring to one of the companies you've been accused of fronting."

Ethridge had never seen such a letter. He said, "And let me guess what was in it: Walter informing me that he wanted nothing to do with such a deal."

"Essentially, yes," Jason replied. He touched the knot on his tie, cleared his throat, waited for a response.

Ethridge shook his head slowly. "That's a new one on me," he said. "But I'm sure it's useless to plead innocent."

Jason's eyes leveled on Ethridge. He said, "I think you'll have an opportunity to defend the matter."

"That means?"

"The U.S. Attorney has indicated that he'll press charges," Jason told him. His eyes flashed.

"I see," Ethridge said. He stood at his desk. "All right. If you gentlemen will excuse me, I'll draft my resignation.

Then I'll have Brenda help gather my personal belongings and I'll be on my way."

Cary Wright stood quickly. He nodded and turned for the door.

"Thanks for being direct, Cary," Ethridge said.

"Sorry it turned out this way," Cary Wright mumbled. He walked through the door. Jason turned to follow him.

"Could I speak with you for a minute, Jason?" Ethridge asked.

Jason hesitated. "Of course," he said after a pause. "I'll be out in one minute, Mr. Wright," he called. He closed the door.

"It's bad, is it?" asked Ethridge.

"Yes." The reply was calm and haughty.

Ethridge smiled. "I guess I'll need a good lawyer."

"I would advise it," Jason said.

"You seem to be taking things pretty well, though."

"I did everything I could," Jason said. "I've negotiated around the clock. As the corporate attorney, I'm accountable to the board of directors and the bank. It's business."

"I understand, Jason. Yes. Yes. Business. And you're good at it. Damned good. I suspect they'll consider you as my replacement."

"I don't know what their plans are," Jason said.

"Well, I'm sure somebody's already thinking that way," Ethridge replied.

"I can assure you that nothing will happen anytime soon," Jason said with authority. "I think the feds will run things for a while."

"Hell of a way to retire," Ethridge mumbled. He sat again in his chair and gazed out the window. After a moment, he said casually, "Oh, by the way, Jason, I think I should tell you something."

"What's that?"

Ethridge looked back at Jason and smiled. "In banking

language, I opened an account with your wife this morning. She's got great assets."

Jason paled. "What?" he demanded.

Ethridge laughed.

TWENTY-SIX

CODY STOOD UNDER THE STREAM OF WATER spewing from the shower head, pounding over his shoulders. The water felt good and Cody felt good. If he kept a journal, it would be a day worth writing about. Conning Harry Dilliard into making him escort Freda to Ewell Pender's fund-raiser. Discovering Ethridge Landon and Jeanne Littlejohn. The confrontation with Landon. His call to Olin McArthur and, most important, Olin's praise. ("That's what I can't do; bully the bastards," Olin had said. "I admire that, Cody. I truly do.") The spilling laughter from Freda when he called from his apartment. ("Harry told me. I don't believe it. I told him I'd go with you, but only because he insisted. By the way, wear that ridiculous tuxedo I've seen you in. I don't want you to appear underdressed.") A good day, all in all, Cody thought. Mark one up for the kid. It was about time. It had been years since he had considered a day even a close draw in the combat that he called living.

He dressed slowly in the tuxedo—old, but well-preserved—and then he called Millie.

"What is it?" Millie asked impatiently.

"Well, hello, for starters," Cody said. "You sound rushed."

"I am. I'm trying to dress and get Sabrina ready to spend the night with Jennifer, and nothing's going right. The faucet in the bathtub's still leaking. I thought you were going to fix that."

Cody smiled. I will not let Millie's carping get to me, he thought. "This weekend, I promise. You going out?"

"Yes," Millie said wearily. "At least I'm supposed to."

"Where?"

"In the first place, Cody, it's none of your business. In the second place, I don't know. Just out. Robert said he had a surprise."

"Surprise?"

"Surprise, Cody."

"Maybe it's the question," Cody said.

"What question?"

"The big one, love."

"Stop it, Cody. You know damned well I'm not about to get married. Not now."

"Yeah, I know," Cody said in a teasing voice. "You've got to get over the trauma of losing the big boy—namely me."

"Cody, that took exactly fifteen minutes. I timed it."

Cody laughed. "Where's Sabrina?"

"In the tub with the leaking faucet. I'll tell her you called. Call back tomorrow afternoon."

"Sure," Cody said. "Give her a kiss for me. And, Millie, if it is the big one, let me know. I'll send roses."

"Cody, you don't know what a rose looks like. I've got to go."

Cody smiled as he dropped the telephone back onto its cradle. There were times when he missed Millie with sadness; other times, he understood why they were divorced. He looked at his watch. It was six-fifteen. He had promised Freda he would be at her apartment by seven. If he left now, she would still be dressing when he arrived. He smiled. Why not? he thought. He enjoyed watching her dress. And maybe he should stop at the florist and buy her a dozen roses to celebrate her story. Harry had been right: it was brilliant, a story with power and compassion. He stood and slipped into his jacket and inspected himself in the mirror of his dresser. Handsome fellow, he thought. A little gray. A few pounds heavier than the last time he had worn the tuxedo, but not so heavy that the suit fit uncomfortably. Not bad. Not at all bad for his age.

Freda did not open the door at her apartment: Menotti did. He smiled smugly and said to Cody, "You'll have to wait in line."

"What the hell are you doing here?" Cody asked sourly.

"Looking for you."

"Why didn't you try my apartment?"

"I thought you'd abandoned it for better quarters," Menotti said. His eyes swept the room. "And believe me, Cody, these are better quarters." He dipped his head toward Freda's bedroom. "She's getting dressed. She said she expected you around seven. You're early."

"I like being early," Cody mumbled, pushing past Menotti into the room.

"In this case I can understand why," Menotti said. "You look presentable, by the way. It's amazing how long a tuxedo holds up."

"You're wasting the charm," Cody said. "And the sarcasm."

"It's called practicing good manners. I'm trying to get into the spirit of the evening. You wouldn't happen to have an umbrella, would you? It's going to rain, and I forgot mine."

"So drown," Cody said. "Even if I had one, you wouldn't be sharing it." He moved to the hallway leading to the bedroom. "I'm here," he called. He put the flowers on a hallway table.

"You're early," Freda said from behind the closed door.

"So I've been told," Cody said. "Don't rush. I'm with the entertainment committee." He heard a laugh from behind the door.

"I'm having a scotch," Menotti said. "Want one?"

"No," Cody replied. "So, why are you looking for me? Let's cut to the chase."

"The chase?"

"Christ, Victor, I know you," Cody grumbled, dropping into an armchair. "You don't drop around to have a chat with anyone. If you're looking for me, you've got a reason."

Menotti sat on the sofa, drank from his scotch, his eyes studying Cody. "The fact is, I need your help, " he said after a moment.

Cody gazed suspiciously at Menotti. "The last time you asked for my help, it almost got me fired. Harry didn't think much of running a bogus story to set up one of your sting games."

"Worked, didn't it?" Menotti said. "But this is different. It won't involve the paper."

"So, what is it?"

"Pender."

"Pender? What about him?" Cody asked.

"I want to know if he was aware that Aaron Greene once had considered going to his school, and I want to know how he feels about Jews."

"What?" Cody said incredulously.

"His grandfather founded Carlton-Ayers. Remember? You told me about it earlier, but you didn't mention the name of the school. Aaron's parents thought about sending him there. Connection, Cody. Connection."

"Where did you get that?"

"In case you've forgotten, I'm a detective. It's in the job description. I was also good at arithmetic. One plus one equals—"

"All right," Cody replied. "I don't know much about the school, except that it's his one great passion, other than music."

"Maybe it's all coincidental, but maybe not," Menotti said. "The fact is, there's nothing wrong—morally or legally—about what he's done, even if he's kept quiet about that little touch of irony. But to be honest, Cody, if it got out that he was trying to help a onetime candidate for his school, it could pin another feather in his cap, not to mention increasing enrollment."

"I think it's interesting, like trivia," Cody said, "but I don't see that it has any bearing on anything."

"Maybe it doesn't," Menotti admitted

"Let's jump to the other question," Cody said. "Why do you want to know how he feels about Jews? Because Aaron's Jewish?"

"It's just a long shot," Menotti answered. "Pender's grandfather was anti-Semitic."

Cody could feel his forehead furrowing with surprise. "And where did you dig that up?"

"I found it in the library," Menotti answered smugly. "You missed it when you did the story on him. Surprised me. Very careless of you. His grandfather despised the Jews. Thought they were trying to take over his business. Fact is, he ruined a couple of Jewish businessmen along the way. And there was some suspicion that it was one of those victims who did the poor fellow in."

"So? He ruined a lot of people," Cody countered. "That was his specialty. Why this interest in Pender?"

"Intuition, Cody. Intuition."

"I know you better than that, Victor. Why use me? Why don't you just haul him in and ask him yourself?"

Menotti shrugged nonchalantly and sipped from his drink. "For one thing, you've interviewed him before, and you wrote a damn fine story, with the exception of a few holes. I read it. He'll be more comfortable with you. For another, they'd hand me my head if I pulled one of the city's leading citizens in for questioning. For still another, I'd like to get rid of this gnawing feeling that you're more of a character in this little drama than an offstage voice."

Cody shook his head in astonishment. "My God," he said. "Are you still on that?"

"Nothing personal, old friend. Fact is, I don't think you

have the slightest idea of what's going on. But I think there's something there. Now, are you going to help me or not? I want to put a wire on you and I want you to con yourself into an interview with him tonight."

"A wire?"

"That's right. Call it procedure."

"Victor, I would crawl through a foot of elephant shit in this tuxedo, with my mouth pried open, if I could get you off my back. Fine. You want me to do a number on Pender, I'll be happy to, but I think you're braying at the moon."

"That's possible," Menotti admitted casually. "But one good deed deserves another. Want some news?"

"Sure. Why not?"

"They got to Landon. The feds. I got a call from Philip Oglesbee about an hour ago. Landon resigned today. It'll be made public tomorrow."

"I'll be damned," Cody whispered. "How'd they do it?"

"Found the link they needed between Landon and Walter Curren on the bogus community investment companies."

"What was it?" Cody asked.

"Curren broke like a piece of crystal when they dangled the right deal in front of him, and to put icing on that little cake, we even know who made the calls to the Greenes," Menotti said.

Cody looked up in surprise.

"Can't tell you right now, though," Menotti said. "Tomorrow."

"Damn it, Victor," Cody muttered.

"Don't start on me, Cody. We've been together too many years. You'll be the first person I call. You've got my word on it. I thought you'd be interested in the Landon thing, but you have to keep a lid on it, or if you do leak it, make damned sure it didn't come from me."

"Don't worry," Cody said. "It's not my angle anyway,

but I know someone who may be mildly interested."

"Olin McArthur?" asked Menotti.

Cody smiled. "They ought to call you Dick Tracy," he said.

"They do," Menotti replied. He turned his head to a sound from the hallway. "Steady yourself," he whispered. "I think she's ready."

Freda stepped into the living room. She was dressed in a tight, full-length white gown with thin shoulder straps. Her hair was swept to one side and a narrow headband with a design of tiny pearls circled her forehead like a crown. She stood as though posing for a fashion photographer. Both men stared at her in awe.

"Gentlemen," Freda said softly. "I will accept the rather silly expressions on your faces as a sign of approval."

The two men stood.

"My God," Cody whispered. "I can't be seen with you. Nobody would believe it."

"Cody, I'm the one risking the reputation," Freda said playfully.

"There's no question about that," Menotti said. "You look lovely," he added in a quiet voice.

"Thank you, Victor," Freda cooed. She turned to Cody. "I saw the flowers. They're beautiful. Thank you. I need to put them in some water before we leave. It won't take but a minute."

"Sure," Cody said.

"Take your time," Menotti told her. "We need to borrow your bedroom for a couple of minutes, anyway."

A puzzled look spread over Freda's face.

"I'll tell you later," Cody said. Then, to Menotti: "Let's get it over with."

Menotti laughed easily. He said to Freda, "It's business. Just business. Believe me, I don't like being with the man in public, much less behind closed doors."

*   *   *

The reception at Ewell Pender's mansion was as spectacular as the elite who had giddily accepted invitations believed it would be—a gala, a worthy-cause gathering of the wealthy and the famous, dressed in tailored suits and fashionable gowns, the women flashing jewelry and benevolent smiles, the men posturing like dignitaries attending a state function, moving in small gatherings from grouping to grouping, flowing slowly through the massive rooms of the Pender mansion. The controlled noise of their greetings and laughter and practiced conversation was a hum, a quaint musical note tuned to the size of the rooms. For most, it was an accustomed ritual, with one exception: Their faces were transfixed in awe, in a reverential expression that might have been a subtle shading of makeup, but was not; it was the intimidation of the Pender mansion, and in the eyes of the guests—eyes that seemed always to be looking up at something majestic above them—there was a respectful surrender that confessed they were humbled by what they saw. Few of them had ever been in the mansion. Indeed, few had ever seen Ewell Pender in person. The whispers told their secrets: "Have you seen Ewell Pender? I don't really know him."

Cody's whisper to Freda was more direct: "Can you believe this place?"

And Freda's whispered answer was, "It's a palace. An absolute palace."

"Yeah, well, they've put some spit and shine on it," Cody replied. "I don't remember it being this impressive when I came out to interview Pender."

"I feel sorry for you, Cody," Freda said. "You're the kind of person who would call the Champs Elysées a waste of space, needing a shopping center. This is a palace compared to anything you've ever seen."

"Fine. It's a palace and there's the palace bar," Cody mumbled. "What're you drinking?"

"Champagne, Cody. What do you want? A beer in a bottle?"

"I want *you* in bed, *with* a beer in a bottle," Cody whispered. He smiled a leering smile. "But I'll settle for champagne. Stay here, and watch out for these rich old farts. They'll be sneaking a pinch if they can, especially when they find out who you are."

"I hope so," Freda said. "If you see Harry, send him over. He needs to see how splendid we are together."

"Why don't we invite him back to your place to see that?" Cody teased.

"Cody, leave."

Cody crossed the room lazily, smiling, nodding to faces he recognized from photographs that ran regularly in the newspaper. Curious, he thought. He knew their faces, but what the hell were their names? Doesn't matter, he decided. Maybe they didn't need names. Maybe all they needed was their faces in photographs. He paused at the end of a line waiting at the bar. The small Nagra recorder at the pit of his back, with the two wires running up and over his shoulders and taped to his chest—"Stereo," Menotti had said—irritated him, and he involuntarily touched one of the wires with his finger and wondered if the recorder had been activated. Jesus, he thought, I should have remembered it when I made that remark to Freda. He imagined Menotti laughing when he heard the tape.

Across the room, he saw Menotti and Clifford Russell standing together solemnly, not talking. He saw Olin McArthur in a polite conversation with a tall, handsome woman with striking silver hair. Amos Temple and Harry Dilliard—obviously uncomfortable in his sports ensemble of gray slacks and blue blazer—stood near Olin, like misfits. Cody lifted a hand and waved and pointed across the room to Freda. Harry frowned, then moved in the direction of Cody's wave. Amos followed. Cody turned his head, scanning the room. At the foot of a wide, curving staircase, he saw a servant holding a tray of hors d'oeuvres to be inspected by a slender, elegant woman wearing an off-shoulder gown that shimmered like soft gold. The woman's deep blond hair was pulled up in the carefully casual way that women hand-combed and pinned their hair after a shower, leaving it fresh and sensuous and perfect. From the distance, the woman was strikingly beautiful and, Cody thought, familiar. He watched a man approach her and speak, saw her smile pleasantly. Cody knew the smile. My God, he thought, that's Alyse Burton. It had to be. He did not remember her as a blonde during his interviews with Ewell Pender three years earlier, but as a brunette. The miracle of the hairdresser's bottle. Nice touch, though. Alyse Burton was radiant as a blonde.

"Cody?"

The voice came from behind Cody. He knew who it was before he turned: Millie. He watched Millie and Robert Lucas weave through the crowd toward him. Millie's black cocktail dress hugged her body seductively. Robert wore a trim tuxedo with a blue cummerbund.

"Hello, love," Cody said, embracing Millie. He extended his hand to Robert. "Good to see you again, Robert."

"And it's good to see you, Cody," Robert replied, beaming. "Quite a place, isn't it?"

"It's—ah, cute," Cody said.

"Don't be an ass, Cody," Millie whispered. Then: "I didn't know you were going to be here. Why didn't you tell me?"

"You didn't exactly give me a chance when I called," Cody said. "So, this is your surprise?"

Millie blushed. "Yes," she said. "Robert does some work for Mr. Pender."

Cody turned to Robert. "You do? What sort of work?"

"Boring stuff, I assure you," Robert answered. "I keep his computers running between his private office here and his downtown headquarters. He doesn't get away from this place very often, you know."

"I gathered that. Don't blame him. If I had this place,

I'd sit on the front porch and guard it with a shotgun," Cody said.

Robert laughed robustly. "Have you met Joel Garner yet?"

"Nope. Just got here a few minutes ago. Frankly, I'm more interested in speaking with Mr. Pender. I did a magazine story on him a few years ago," Cody said.

"Ah, yes, I've read it," Robert replied. "Excellent. Excellent. Of all the things written about him, it's his favorite, I believe. I've heard him remark about it. He said it was honest, and he respects honesty. I believe he and Joel Garner are in the library, with some radio and television reporters. I think I can get you a few minutes alone with him, if you'd like."

"Yes, I would, Robert. Thank you," Cody said. "That's kind of you."

"Let's say that I owe you," Robert replied.

"Owe me?"

"If you hadn't had the poor judgment of leaving this lovely lady, I wouldn't be in her company tonight."

Cody looked at Millie. She was beautiful, he thought. God, she was beautiful. "My loss," he muttered. He looked back to Robert. "Your gain."

"Cody, that's sweet," Millie said gently.

"But, come now, let's have some champagne," Robert urged. "You've got to get about, Cody. Mingle. There're people here who'll be eager to meet you. You're the voice. You could say you're one of the stars of this occasion. Joel Garner's got nothing on you."

"Oh, yeah, sure," Cody said with a soft laugh. He added, "By the way, Millie, I'd like you to meet some of the people from the paper."

"Who's here? Harry?"

"Harry and Amos and Olin McArthur," Cody answered. "And Freda Graves. I think you may remember her. I was always bitching about her. Believe it or not, Harry made me escort her tonight. One of his object lessons about behavior. I think he believes if we speak outside the office, we'll be a bit more friendly in the newsroom."

A cloud flashed in Millie's eyes. "Oh? I read her story today. It was excellent. In fact, it's the reason I finally wrote a check for Aaron. What she wrote put it in better perspective than anything the rest of you have done. I'd love to meet her. Maybe later."

"Sure," Cody said.

TWENTY-SEVEN

———————◆———————

FROM THE WINDOW OF THE LIBRARY, AARON
could see the spraying of car lights against the trees lining
the walled garden, and there was the sound of car doors
being closed in dull thumpings and cars being driven away
and parked nearby. It was all unusual—so many cars, so
much disturbance at the place that seemed to Aaron se-
cretively remote and hidden from the outside world. He
wondered if, somehow, the police had found him and the
cars were police cars, but there were no twirling blue lights
spinning in colorful strobes across the trees, no blaring of
sirens. The cars were not from the police, he decided. No.
There were too many.

He leaned against the windowsill and studied the garden. Why were the lights off in the garden? he wondered.
All of them, except for a pinspot that covered the statue
with an odd fluorescent coloring. And why did the lights
not work in the library? And why had he eaten dinner
early, served hurriedly by Alyse? Why had she left him to
eat alone? It was only the second time he had eaten alone
since he had arrived. And Carla. Where was Carla? He
thought of lifting the telephone that would summon
someone from somewhere in the front of the great house,
but he did not. He had never used the telephone. More
than anything, the telephone that could not be used to call
the outside world reminded him that he was a prisoner.

He wandered from the library back into the bedroom. Earlier, Robert had installed a television set with a VCR, and Alyse had provided him with a collection of movies on videotape. The television had been disabled; it would not receive broadcasts. "You're not missing much," Robert had said cheerfully. "Between the gloom and the trash, there's not much worth watching, anyway." Aaron had watched two movies—*A Man for All Seasons* and *Sense and Sensibility*. Tomorrow, he thought, he would ask Alyse for *Moby-Dick*. He stood by the television and read the titles on the videotape cartridges, then selected *Fiddler on the Roof*. He had seen the movie with his parents. The movie had made his mother laugh and then cry joyfully, emotions that had surprised and pleased him. He slipped the videotape into the VCR and pushed the play button. A soft rapping struck the door, and he pushed the stop button and walked to the door.

"Yes," Aaron said.

"Aaron, it's me," Carla said from behind the door. "May I come in?"

"All right," Aaron replied.

He heard the key trip the deadbolt lock and the door opened and Carla stepped inside. She was dressed in an off-shoulder green gown. A string of pearls circled her throat. Her short hair was pushed up and straight back. Her face was tinted softly with a bare blush of makeup, highlighting the small green cups of her eyes. Aaron stepped back in surprise, causing her to smile.

"Yes, it's me," she said playfully.

"You—look—different," Aaron stammered.

"Do I look like a princess, Aaron?"

Aaron smiled awkwardly.

"Of course I do," Carla said. She closed the door and locked it, then she did a dancer's turn in the room. "I look like a princess because I am one." She curtsied. "And how are you?" she asked.

Aaron nodded. "I've been—watching some movies."

"Great. Do you hear all the noise outside?"

"Some," Aaron said. "I saw car lights from the library."

"The place is overrunning with people," Carla said. "That's why we've got the lights out in the garden and in your library. We don't want people wandering around back here. The garden's always off-limits to visitors." She smiled. "With a few exceptions, of course."

"The light's on the statue," Aaron said.

"That's never turned off. Haven't you noticed it at night?"

Aaron shook his head.

"It's always on. Always. But it won't matter. No one can see it from downstairs anyway," Carla said.

"Why are they here?" asked Aaron.

Carla did another dance step, another turn. She stopped in front of a mirror and gazed at herself. "It's a party," she said after a moment. "A benefit. Just a lot of stuffy people. You know the kind. They don't breathe; they sniff the air. Boring people. All the women have little compacts they carry around with them and every few minutes they take them out and look at themselves. It's like they can't believe who they are. And the men are worse. They look at themselves in windows and in the glass frames of photographs. No one ever sees anyone else; they're too busy looking at themselves."

"I—don't know," Aaron mumbled.

"There's a big actor out there: Joel Garner. Have you ever seen him?"

Aaron's face lifted in surprise. Joel Garner was his favorite actor. "He's here?"

"You should see the women, Aaron. They're following him around like puppies. All the men just stare at him and smile. Big, like this." She mugged an exaggerated grin. "Oh, they won't stay long. It's supposed to start raining later, and they'll start leaving then. They always do. Sometimes I think it's because they don't want the dye in their hair to start running, so they leave before they take a chance."

"Are you going to the party?" asked Aaron.

"I have to," Carla replied lightly. "Alyse wanted me to look in on you, to make sure you're all right. I'll come back later, if you'd like."

Aaron looked away.

"Would you like that, Aaron?"

Aaron tilted his head. "I—guess."

"Good. I'll do that. I'll find us something from the kitchen, maybe a bottle of champagne, and we'll celebrate. It's very expensive champagne."

Aaron smiled foolishly. "I never tasted champagne," he said.

"It's really not very good," Carla told him, "but everybody should at least taste it." She leaned up quickly and kissed him lightly on the cheek. "I'll see you later."

The adhesive on the wire over his left shoulder pinched him and Cody pulled at it gently as he followed Robert Lucas up a wide staircase. Menotti owes me, he thought. The little news snippet about Ethridge Landon was not enough, especially since he had passed the information on to Olin McArthur, as he had promised to do. At least Olin was pleased. More than pleased. Olin had laughed aloud and strolled away to find a telephone. A few minutes later, he had seen Olin leaving and he knew what the lead story on the front page of *The Atlanta Constitution* would be the following morning.

But maybe there would be something from the information that Menotti had let slip—deliberately, probably—about the telephone caller to the Greenes. He would have that at least. Yet, knowing Menotti, it would not be worth what he was about to endure.

"I told Mr. Pender it wouldn't take long," Robert said at the top of the stairs. "He has a number of guests, you know."

"Of course," Cody replied. "I promise."

"Actually, he's delighted to see you," Robert continued. "He saw your name on the acceptance list earlier and remarked about it."

"He did?"

"Yes. Said he was glad you would be able to attend. I think he's feeling a bit sorry for you, what with the abuse you've been taking the last day or so from the electronic media."

"Oh, the radio stuff," Cody said.

"Have you listened to any of it?" asked Robert.

"Not much," Cody told him. "I'm not masochistic."

"Not kind at all, the things they've been saying," Robert said. He clucked his tongue and wiggled his head comically in disgust, then started walking toward a door at the end of the corridor. "It's Mr. Pender's personal study. He suggested you meet there, where you won't be disturbed."

"I get the feeling that everything above ground level here is off-limits," Cody said casually.

Robert smiled. "Oh, it is," he emphasized, stopping at the door. "Mr. Pender's very conscious about privacy."

"But you seem to have—well, roaming privileges," Cody replied.

"At times," Robert said easily. "At times. There's a rather extensive computer setup scattered about. Please, go on in, but remember the other guests." He paused. "Or perhaps you should remember the look on your lady's face when she met Joel Garner. Better still, remember the look on Joel Garner's face when he met your lady."

"You've got a point," Cody said. "I won't be long. You have my word on it."

"In the meantime, I'll watch after Millie," Robert said. "I think I heard a small gasp out of her in front of our Hollywood celebrity. And I'm not sure she's completely comfortable with your companion for the evening, regardless of how she feels about the story Freda wrote. I can sense a bit of tension."

"You're a good man, Robert," Cody said. "A good man."

The laugh stayed on Robert's face, hidden in his beard, as he walked away.

Ewell Pender was standing beside the window overlooking the garden, holding a brandy snifter in his hand. He turned as Cody opened the door and entered the room.

"Mr. Yates," Ewell Pender said cordially. "We meet again."

"Thank you for seeing me, Mr. Pender," Cody said, crossing the room, extending his hand.

The two men shook hands. Cody was surprised at the strength in the older man's grip.

"It's good to see you again, Mr. Yates. Could I pour you a brandy?"

"Thank you, no," Cody replied. "I had champagne earlier. One glass. I'm a one-glass guest these days, and I find that my hosts are usually grateful."

Ewell Pender smiled patiently. "It's a civil thing," he said. "Too many people use these, ah, little occasions to prove how barbaric they can be." He turned his face to Cody. It was an old man's face—kind, wise, benevolent. "I believe you wanted to speak to me."

"Yes. Thank you for taking the time. I know you have guests to attend."

Ewell Pender waved his hand in front of his chest, a dismissing gesture. "Not at all. Mr. Garner's the attraction, as you've certainly seen. As he should be. No one ever misses an old man at such times. I'm sure they believe I've slipped off to take some bedtime medication and to retire beneath the sheets." He turned to the window. His eyes gazed at the lighted statue. "It's beginning to mist a bit, I see. They'll be leaving soon."

"Still, I promise not to bother you for too long," Cody said politely. "I'm intrigued by what you're doing for

Aaron Greene, particularly in light of your grandfather's regard for Jewish people."

Ewell Pender's face turned slowly from the window to Cody. "I'm sorry," he said. "I don't understand what you mean."

"Your grandfather was anti-Semitic, wasn't he? At least that's what some of the stories I've read have suggested."

Ewell Pender shook the brandy snifter and stared into the light amber liquid that swirled in the glass. "Perhaps he was," he said at last. "My grandfather, Mr. Yates, was not a very civilized man." He smiled again. "He would have taken his brandy from the bottle."

"I understand, sir. It's easy for legends to grow with powerful people."

Ewell Pender moved to the chair behind his desk and sat. He motioned for Cody to sit in the chair in front of the desk. "My grandfather was a man who loved to see others defeated, in pain, perhaps," he said. "Did he hate the Jews? I'm sure he did. He also hated most other men. Or, he found them incompetent. He wasn't a very pleasant fellow. I believe you know that he was killed by someone."

"Do you know who?" Cody asked directly.

A soft laugh rose from Ewell Pender. "No. No, I don't. There were enough people with—understandable motives. Even I, Mr. Yates. My grandfather treated my father shabbily. As a child, it used to anger me greatly to see my father cowering as he did, and, of course, he eventually committed suicide. I think that's one of the reasons I chose the life I did."

"I was never quite clear about it," Cody said, "but did you find your grandfather's body?"

Ewell Pender's clear blue eyes calmly searched Cody's face. He said, after a pause, "No. I discovered my father's body. Oscar discovered my grandfather. I believe you met Oscar."

"Oscar?" Cody said.

"Like me, an elderly gentleman. He attends the house."

"Yes, of course, " Cody said. "I remember him from the time I came out to interview you. He found your grandfather?"

"He did."

"I didn't know he had been with you that long," Cody said.

"Oh, yes. He began service with us right after the war— the Second World War. He was my grandfather's driver. My grandfather had a Duesenberg, I believe. A classic. Oscar and I became friends at an early age. He was a very cultivated man, even then. It's a quality I appreciate, Mr. Yates."

"Yes, I think you do," Cody said. Then: "Do you believe there's an anti-Semitic group behind the kidnapping of Aaron Greene, sir?"

"Oh, I don't think so. No, Mr. Yates, I don't think so. And I don't think there's a radical Jewish underground involved, as has been suggested by some irresponsible members of your profession, and, incidentally, by at least one member of the board of directors of Century National Bank. I find that humorous, in fact. But it's a grand example of the absurdity we wallow in, isn't it?"

"Perhaps," Cody said. "But why are you doing this? I mean, all that you're doing for Aaron Greene?"

"I think he deserves it, Mr. Yates. Don't you? I've known many young people like him. No one ever pays any attention to them. No one ever cares, really. What is it they call Aaron on those radio programs? Aaron Who? A nobody. Isn't that sad, Mr. Yates? Still, I think it's an appropriate word. That's why I keep the school going— Carlton-Ayers. It was the one good thing my grandfather did, establishing the school. Of course, he was trying to buy my favor in those days, but it turned out well. It helped me, and I, in turn, have been fortunate enough to help others. In fact, every member of my staff, with the exception of Oscar and a few with domestic duties, attended the school. Once, they were all nobodies."

"Were you aware that Aaron once considered attending Carlton-Ayers?" asked Cody.

"Certainly," Ewell Pender answered. "It was called to my attention immediately by an assistant. I think you may remember her: Alyse Burton. She stays directly involved with the school. Indeed, she spends much of her time as a counselor to our young people there."

"I spoke to her a few minutes ago," Cody said.

"Good. I asked her to watch for you."

"Did that information—about Aaron and your school, I mean—have anything to do with your actions?" Cody said.

"Perhaps it did. I have a great interest in such people, as you know. Do you think that's wrong?"

"Of course not," Cody said quickly. "And I think you're right about Aaron being thought of as a nobody. I've heard the Aaron Who remark, also. I have a friend, a police officer, who says the reason so many people are caught up in this, the reason they're giving money, and the reason they've been demanding Ethridge Landon's head on a platter, is because they, too, understand what it's like to be a nobody, a victim of some sort."

Ewell Pender rolled the glass of brandy in his hand, gazed at it. He said slowly, "You have a wise friend, Mr. Yates. That's precisely why." He looked up at Cody. "But do you know what will happen, Mr. Yates?"

"No, I don't. Do you?"

"Yes. This, too, will pass, to borrow from a rather eloquent statement."

"Meaning?" Cody asked.

"Meaning that nothing lasts, Mr. Yates. Time does that, you know. It blurs things that once were perfectly clear. It's like having a cataract on memory."

"Then all of this means nothing?" Cody said.

"I hope it will mean something to young Mr. Greene," Ewell Pender replied.

"Mean what?"

Ewell Pender placed his brandy snifter on the desk and touched the tips of his fingers together like a man in prayer. For a moment, he gazed at his fingers, as though his fingers held answers. Then he said, "If he's alert to it, he will learn to look to himself and to be pleased with what he sees. And it won't be the young man everyone is fretting over now, but the young man who becomes a conqueror. When he understands that, he'll be able to do anything he's capable of doing, because he will have learned that caring—true caring—is the center of living. That's what we teach at Carlton-Ayers. It's a cure, Mr. Yates. The problem with people like Aaron, like me, and, may I suggest, people such as yourself, is that we need to please people, to trust them, and every small offense we commit drives us deeper and deeper into uncertainty, and then, somewhere along the way, we are bound to discover that those people we think we have offended have little concern for how we feel. They have other agendas, other, newer interests. It's a very frustrating experience, but from it we may learn that we have the power to be different, the power to be caring people. It's a very persuasive lesson, sir. It's the kind of lesson that makes great, bold warriors, don't you think?"

Cody sat back in his chair and looked at the aging man sitting behind the desk across from him. What he had said was confusing, the uttering of someone seized by the kind of dogma that ruled cults, yet it also contained great truth.

"It's a thought to ponder, sir," Cody said quietly. "I'm not sure I understand it, but it's interesting. Still, it doesn't seem like a philosophy that would come from your grandfather, and he was the founder of the school."

A small smile settled on Ewell Pender's face. "My grandfather never knew what was going on at the school," he said. "He left it to the headmasters—a Mr. Carlton and a Mr. Ayers—to run the program. It's probably the only thing he never interfered with that had his financial support. And do you know why, Mr. Yates?"

"He didn't care," Cody replied.

"Precisely. Is that all you wanted to ask, Mr. Yates?"

"Yes—no. There's one other question, if you don't mind."

"By all means, ask it."

"Why do you think the kidnappers used my voice?"

Again the old-man smile rose in Ewell Pender's face. "I think it was a clever little diversion. A publicity stunt, I believe they call it. You have a certain reputation, if I might be so bold. You're a nonconformist. You write about crime and you annoy those in power with your inquiries. That's another thing people find fascinating— those people who think of themselves as nobodies. They like nonconformists. I think the kidnappers knew that. I think at least one of them is a rather spirited tease, someone who loves a good time in his, or her, work."

"I think you're right," Cody said. He stood. "Thank you for your time, Mr. Pender. It's an honor to see you again."

Ewell Pender did not move. "The honor's mine, Mr. Yates. I truly enjoyed your story about me."

"Thank you," Cody said. "Not everyone accepts my words so well."

"You're not always so kind, I would guess."

Cody smiled and turned to leave, then stopped. He turned back to Ewell Pender. "A moment ago, you said that all of your staff had been students at Carlton-Ayers. Does that include Robert Lucas?"

"Robert? Oh, yes. A bright gentleman. Since he has his own business, technically I suppose you could say he isn't a full-time member of my staff, but sometimes it's hard for me to remember that, I'm afraid. He used to stammer, you know, but we got him out of that. He studied in England for quite a time. I'm sure you've heard it in his voice."

"I wondered about that," Cody said. "He dates my former wife, you know."

A soft smile creased Ewell Pender's face. "Yes, I believe he told me that. I met her earlier. A lovely young woman. Millie. Is that her name?"

"Yes. Millie. Well, good night, sir, and again, thank you," Cody said.

"Good night, Mr. Yates."

Ewell Pender watched Cody cross the room and leave through the door leading to the corridor. The merriment of the reception drifted into the room, then died away as Cody closed the door. For a moment Ewell Pender gazed thoughtfully at the door, then he reached forward and touched a button concealed under the lip of his desktop. A door leading into an adjoining room opened and Oscar stepped into the library.

"Yes sir?" Oscar said.

"Did you hear the conversation?" Ewell Pender asked.

"Quite clearly, sir," Oscar replied. "I have it on tape."

"Why do you suppose he asked about my grandfather?"

"I wouldn't know."

"Does it bother you?"

"No sir," Oscar replied calmly.

"Where is the gun now? I haven't seen it in years."

"The Luger, sir?"

"Yes."

"I have it. It's well hidden."

"How old are we, Oscar?"

"I'm seventy-nine, sir. You're seventy-eight."

"We've been together a long time, haven't we?"

"Yes, we have," Oscar said.

"I've always felt protected, knowing you were close at hand."

"Thank you. And I feel the same. I know you protect me."

"Have you heard from Morris?"

"Yes. He completed his task."

"And where is he now?"

"Posted out front, I believe."

"Good. He seemed a little restless, don't you think?"

"It was the risk," Oscar replied. "He believed it was too great."

Ewell Pender nodded agreement. "There's always risk, Oscar."

"Yes. Always."

"And Carla? Is she prepared?"

"I believe so, sir."

"Do you think she objects?"

"No sir. I think she's become rather attached to the young man."

"Of course, I've left that part of it to Alyse to explain. Still, it's a very great asking of one so young."

"Yes sir."

Ewell Pender was quiet for a long moment, then he pulled up from his chair and crossed to the window and gazed out of it. "Have you heard any talk of Landon among our guests?"

"No sir, I don't believe his resignation is generally known."

"I would think not," Ewell Pender said. "Still, it's a small community and such information spreads rapidly."

Oscar tucked his head once in agreement. He did not speak.

"He reminded me very much of my grandfather," Ewell Pender said quietly, still gazing through the window. "He inflicted pain." He turned to look at Oscar. "He should be grateful that he did not suffer my grandfather's fate, but we are not as young as we once were, are we?"

"No sir," Oscar answered.

"Do you think we've accomplished our mission, Oscar?"

"I believe so, sir, but that's your decision."

"I sense that a lot of good is coming out of it. I'm rather enjoying that."

"Yes."

"Our young people are becoming warriors."

"Yes."

"Soon," Ewell Pender said. "Soon."

Cody saw the sweep of the television light as he descended the staircase. A hard, glaring light that cut across the room like the beam of a broad laser, and he thought of a story he had covered years earlier—deer hunters with spotlights. It had not been sport, though the deer hunters had posed proudly with their kills, like men on safari standing godlike beside the gray mountains of elephants. It had been slaughter. And maybe that was what the lights from television cameras did, Cody decided: caught people in a startling moment, sized them up for some sort of kill.

He waited until the light passed below him, off the bottom steps of the stairs, and then he eased himself back into the crowd, looking for Freda. She was across the room, talking with a short, portly man. The man's face was red. Cody could see the shine of perspiration from his balding forehead, could see the man's eyes darting wildly over Freda's breasts, could see his tongue licking his lips involuntarily. Freda seemed slightly annoyed, but pleasant. Perhaps the man was important, Cody thought. A contact. Someone to be tolerated. Or perhaps he was simply a fan, someone gushing over Freda's story about the homeless. There were many gushers present. Many awed looks from warm, unguarded eyes, praises in eyeblinks. Many hands reaching to touch Freda, or the air around her. Many confessions that, like Millie, admirers of Freda's story had given money to the Aaron Greene Fund because the story had humbled them. Cody had listened happily to the compliments; Freda had shied from them.

He saw Menotti near a window, standing with Millie. They were engaged in awkward, polite chatter. Victor doing his good deed for the evening, Cody thought. Spending time with an abandoned woman at a party. He could see Millie flash smiles, nod. He could also see her glancing anxiously toward a gathering near the piano.

Robert was among the gathering. Robert and two other men and a tall woman with streaked blond hair that had a billowed, windblown look above a face that a plastic surgeon had kindly, but obviously, improved. She wore too much lipstick, too much rouge. The woman was talking. Or lecturing. Even from across the room, Cody knew that Robert was agitated, struggling to be patient. He needed rescue.

The room was crowded, clogged with people caught in webs of conversation that had more noise than voice. As he moved among them, Cody heard his own name mentioned. Tidbits of sentences, lost in other tidbits. Strange, he thought, hearing his name like that. Like some code word. He wondered what they were saying about him.

He knew the art of rescue. It was simple. Touch the person you want to rescue on the arm, apologize for the interruption, then tell a grand lie. *Excuse me, but we just received a call. Your prize Holstein is in labor and it looks like a breech birth. They need you at the stables as soon as possible.* Anything would do, as long as it was grand enough to be remarkable.

He touched Robert on the arm and smiled at the woman.

"Excuse me," Cody said. "Mr. Lucas has a phone call from a guest who seems to be lost in traffic."

The woman's eyes flashed to Cody. She wore contact lenses that were seaweed green.

"Cody Yates," the woman exclaimed.

And Cody knew her voice: Katie Harris. He thought, Oh shit. He nodded.

"I'm—" Katie gushed.

"I know," Cody said. "Katie Harris."

"I don't think we've ever met," Katie said. The tic of a smile bobbed across her mouth.

"We haven't," Cody replied.

A shrill laugh peeled from Katie. "I've been looking all over for you."

Cody smiled. "It's a big crowd."

The two men standing with Robert, also trapped, eased away.

"Miss Harris has been inquiring about our—participation in all of this," Robert said. His voice was tense.

"Really?" Cody said.

"Oh, I'm just rambling," Katie countered, "but I'm afraid I'm making Mr. Lucas uncomfortable."

"And how's that?" Cody asked.

"Miss Harris wonders if there's not some ulterior motive in Mr. Pender's efforts to raise the ransom demand for Aaron Greene," Robert said.

"It's a natural question," Katie replied flippantly. "After all, we are getting calls about it—whether or not there's any monetary gain for Mr. Pender when all this is over. You're a journalist, Cody. You understand that."

Cody shrugged. "Personally, I've never questioned it. But I guess I'm old-school. Some things I think you take at face value."

"Oh, come on, Cody," Katie teased. "I'm sure that old adage about where there's smoke there's fire was around when you started."

Cody fought an urge to turn and walk away. He said, "You're right, but in the old days, no one started the fire just to look at the smoke."

For a moment, Katie did not reply. Then she said icily, "That's tacky."

"I'm sorry," Cody said.

"So I don't suppose you're yet willing to talk to anyone with a microphone?"

"You've got it," Cody said.

"Then you know your own role in this will continue to be a subject of serious speculation," Katie warned.

"I don't doubt it," Cody replied.

Katie Harris's seaweed-green-covered eyes glared hard

at Cody. "I hope you never really need us," she said after a moment. There was threat in her voice.

"Oh, God, me, too," Cody said.

Katie turned to Robert. "I thought you had a call."

Robert blinked surprise. "Oh, I forgot. Yes, if you'll excuse me."

"Of course," Katie said. She forced a smile. "Lovely party," she added.

As they walked away, slipping through the crowd, Robert whispered, "Bitch."

"Don't be so kind," Cody replied.

TWENTY-EIGHT

———◆———

THE DOOR OPENED WITHOUT A KNOCK AND
Aaron jerked forward in surprise from his bed. It was
Carla. She was now dressed in jeans and a red sweater and
sneakers, and she held two yellow rain slickers and a bottle
of champagne in her hands.

"Want to see Joel Garner?" she asked excitedly.

Aaron did not reply. He looked beyond Carla into the
corridor.

"He's not out there," Carla said, snickering. "He's
about to leave. Come on. You can help me. We'll celebrate with this later." She dropped the champagne on the
bed.

"What—are you doing?"

"It's raining," Carla said. "We'll be the umbrella bri-
gade, you and I. You know—escorting people to their
cars. We've got some giant umbrellas up front. Come on.
It'll be fun."

Carla handed him one of the rain slickers. She slipped
her arms quickly into the other one and pulled the hood
up over her head as Aaron watched in bewilderment. She
looked suddenly like a small boy.

"Aaron, you can be exasperating at times," Carla complained playfully. "Are you going to help me, or not?"

"I guess," Aaron said meekly.

"Then put on the raincoat and let's go."

*   *   *

Aaron was led by Carla down a corridor and through an unlit sitting room that had been closed for the reception. He could hear the din of voices from behind closed doors. He moved slowly, his eyes scanning the shadowed, unfamiliar room. It was very much like the library in his own suite—walls covered in books, heavy, comfortable furniture, a room meant for rest and reading.

Carla stopped and waited for him. "Come on," she urged. "I can see some cars pulling up." She went to a window and looked through it. "Joel Garner's limousine is already there." She rushed through a door, and Aaron followed her outside to a porch that covered the front of the house, and then to the front door, where an umbrella stand had been stationed. The stand was filled with large umbrellas.

"Here, you take one," Carla said, handing an umbrella to Aaron. She peered through the beveled glass bordering the door. "He's in there," she whispered. She opened the door and Alyse and Joel Garner stepped outside.

"I'm sorry we kept you waiting," Carla said cheerfully. "I had to find a raincoat."

Alyse looked at Aaron and smiled. "Don't worry. We've been busy talking." She turned to Joel. "Are you ready?"

"Ready," Joel said. He extended his hand to Alyse. "It's been a wonderful evening. Call me tomorrow." He looked up into the sky. "It's a beast of a night."

"A spring shower in the South, Mr. Garner," Alyse said lightly. She turned to Aaron. "Would you escort Mr. Garner to his limousine?"

Aaron opened the umbrella and held it over Joel Garner. Joel glanced at him pleasantly. He said, "Now, that's a generous thing for you to do, young man. I'm afraid you may get a bit damp before the evening's over."

Aaron smiled awkwardly. He moved with Joel to the

car. The limousine driver opened the passenger door, and Joel slipped quickly inside.

"Thanks a lot," Joel said to Aaron. "I don't think I'll drown, or melt, now." He looked at Aaron and a puzzled frown ripped across his eyebrows. He flashed a smile.

"I—" Aaron stammered.

"Oh, I'm sorry," Joel said. "You'd like an autograph, but unfortunately I don't have a pen." He looked around the backseat of the limousine, saw a stack of signed studio photographs. He picked one up and handed it to Aaron. "I promise you, I signed it myself," he added.

Aaron could feel the rain on his face, under the hood of the yellow raincoat. He pulled the umbrella closer to his head.

"Well, thanks again," Joel said. He pulled the door closed and the car began to move away.

Aaron moved back to the porch. He could feel the rain splattering steadily on the raincoat. Alyse smiled and touched his arm, and Aaron remembered what she had said about people seeing only what they wanted to see. She turned and went back into the house.

"You didn't believe me, did you?" Carla said giddily. "That was him, and you got his picture. Now that he's gone, they'll all leave. Are you okay?"

Aaron looked away. "Okay," he said. He watched a car approach, and a man wearing rain gear got out of it. The man looked up at Aaron, and Aaron blinked in surprise. He stepped back. The man in the rain gear was the brooding Morris.

"What's the matter?" asked Carla.

"Nothing," Aaron whispered. He could feel Morris's eyes firing into him.

Carla saw Morris, saw his glare. His glare was a threat, a command.

"Why don't you go on back into the sitting room— you know, the one we came out of," Carla said. "I'll be there in a minute."

Aaron dipped his head. He turned and walked away

quickly. He could feel Morris's eyes following him, watching.

The door to the house opened again and Cody and Freda stepped quickly outside.

"My God," Cody said. "Victor was right. I should have brought an umbrella."

"Is this your car, sir?" Carla said brightly.

Cody and Freda turned to Carla.

"Oh, hello," Freda said.

"Hi," Carla replied.

There was a moment, a pause. The expression on Freda's face narrowed quizzically. "I do know you, don't I?" she asked.

"I don't think so," Carla said. "Maybe we met inside earlier."

"No. I don't remember that."

"Oh, I changed clothes," Carla said. "I'm part of the staff here."

"Then perhaps we did," Freda said warmly.

"Let's go," Cody urged. "Before the bottom falls out."

Harry Dilliard wiped his palms over his pants legs to dry the dampness of the rain from them. The windshield wipers on his Ford slapped noisily. He said to Amos Temple, "Damn it, I just bought this coat."

"Yeah, I thought so," Amos replied. "You've still got the little strings on the sleeves, where the tag was."

"Jesus, why didn't you tell me?" Harry muttered irritably.

"I just noticed it," Amos lied. Then: "How much you think they picked up tonight?"

"A bundle," Harry said, examining the tag strings on his coat. "It was a goddamn check-writing frenzy there at the last. Rich people amaze me. I love rich people. And did you hear all that talk about Freda's story? It opened some wallets."

"I didn't see you make a contribution, Harry."

Harry cracked a laugh. "I gave at the office. What about you?"

"Twenty-five bucks," Amos answered. "I think of it as expense money."

"I see that on a report and I'll bounce your ass off the wall," Harry said. He added, in a mumble, "Damn this traffic."

The cars leaving Ewell Pender's mansion rolled slowly out of the driveway. Harry followed a white Cadillac.

"You ever see a place like that, Harry?" Amos asked.

"Yeah, once. In Paris. I think they call it the Louvre."

"God, I'd love to have that kind of money for one day," Amos sighed. He shifted in the seat, considered what he had said, amended it: "Make that two hours. That's all I'd need. Two hours. I've just got to believe being rich beats the hell out of being poor."

"Aw, you're young," Harry said. "You'll get out of this business one of these days. Get into something that'll pay you for doing nothing. You young guys are all alike. It's the Age of Gratification, and that's all that matters. If it's not a good time, it's nothing."

"Talking of good times, Cody looked like he was enjoying himself," Amos said.

"Yeah, he did, didn't he?" Harry mused. "But the way Freda was dressed, I think I would've been a little perky myself." He smiled smugly. "Way up. Never thought of her as being sexy."

"Hell of a punishment you put on him," Amos said. "Now I know why Brer Rabbit was laughing his ass off in the briar patch."

A frown wiggled across Harry's face. "Wait a minute. You think Cody's been diddling that?"

"Couldn't tell it from the way they treat each other around the office," Amos said.

"Could be a cover. Maybe that old boy's hung like a donkey. Two best-looking women in the place were Freda and his ex."

"Pretty woman, his ex," Amos said. "I met her once at a party of some kind. Smart as hell, Cody told me. Who was that guy she was with?"

"Some computer salesman or something," Harry replied. "He's the friendly sort. Big talker. Probably an asshole."

"Looked like he owned the place."

"They're the ones who rake it in, Amos."

The traffic picked up speed as it spilled onto the main road leading to the interstate and Harry leaned back against the seat and relaxed. "Is Tech playing tonight?" he asked.

"You got me," Amos said.

"I think they are," Harry said. "See if you can pick up the game."

Amos reached to turn on the radio. "What do you want me to do with the tape?" he asked.

"What tape?"

"The one in the player."

"I don't have a tape," Harry snorted. "Never played one."

"Well, you've got one now," Amos said.

"Where?"

"In the place where it's supposed to be."

"Play it," Harry ordered.

Amos turned on the radio and pushed the tape and watched the player swallow it. There was a scratching, static sound and then Cody Yates's voice.

"Now that the party's over you may think Aaron is safe. He isn't. Not until the ten million is raised. We want a story in tomorrow's paper. There's a new deadline. It's three days from now. Monday night. We want the money Monday night, and we want the rest of it to come from the bank. If we fail to get it, you will find Aaron in a most unlikely place."

The voice went dead. The scratching, static sound hissed from the radio's speakers.

"Jesus," whispered Harry. He could feel his hands shaking. He pulled the car to the shoulder of the road.

★   ★   ★

"Do you like it, Aaron? It's very expensive."

Aaron sipped again from the glass. He could feel the champagne sizzle in his mouth. Its taste was bittersweet, and it tickled and burned in his throat.

"Do you?" Carla pressed, holding her glass up. She was sitting on the bed with Aaron. Music rose softly from a compact disc player in the entertainment center.

"It's—all right," Aaron said.

"Good. Then I propose a toast. To us. To Aaron and Carla." She offered her glass to click against his glass, then swallowed some champagne. "Come on, you have to drink when someone makes a toast. Those are the rules."

Aaron drank. A small sip, but too quickly. He coughed, then laughed softly.

"And I propose a toast to Alyse," Carla cooed, again offering her glass against Aaron's glass.

The two drank.

"And to Joel Garner. Oh, make that two toasts to Joel Garner."

Again they clicked glasses, again drank.

Carla moved on the bed, tucked her legs beneath her, balancing the champagne bottle. "He didn't know you, did he, Aaron?" she said.

"No," Aaron answered.

"You remember what we told you? About people seeing only what they want to see? You need to know that, Aaron. It teaches you to see more than what seems to be there."

"I know," Aaron replied.

Carla studied Aaron's face closely. He turned his eyes from her and gazed into the champagne glass.

"Do you know why they had the party tonight, Aaron?" Carla asked quietly.

"No," Aaron answered. He did not look up.

"It was for you, Aaron. For you."

Aaron's face jerked in surprise. His fingers played on the stem of the glass. "What?"

"It was a party for you. All the people were there because of you," Carla told him. "A benefit."

A question formed on Aaron's face, but he did not speak.

"Everyone's worried about you. The whole world is. Joel Garner came to Atlanta because of you. We had this benefit to help raise the money to set you free."

"I don't—know what you mean," Aaron whispered.

"And I can't tell you everything now," Carla said. "But someday I will. I promise. I've got a scrapbook just for you. Someday I'll show it to you. There've been hundreds of stories about you, Aaron. From all over the world. Magazines and newspapers and television programs. The only thing anybody talks about now is you. You should hear the radio programs. People are calling in from everywhere, all kinds of people, Aaron. People like you and me. They're calling in because they think nobody cares about you, and they want to say they care. Everybody wants to know where you are and if you're safe. They don't know how safe you are."

Aaron's face paled. He stared at Carla quizzically.

"You don't believe me, do you?" Carla said. "Well, it's true. Do you know that Joel Garner gave a check for two hundred thousand dollars, just to help find you?"

"I don't believe you," Aaron said weakly.

Carla reached for Aaron's hand and stroked it gently. "Please don't be angry, Aaron. Please. Soon you'll know I'm telling you the truth. Soon you'll understand it all. But you must promise me something."

"What?" Aaron said.

"You must promise that you won't tell Alyse or anyone what I've told you. You're not supposed to know. Not yet."

Aaron looked away.

"Please. Promise me."

Aaron nodded slightly.

"Thank you." There was a pause. Carla's hand tightened on Aaron's hand. "I know you won't. I only want to help you, Aaron." Her eyes moistened. "I remember it so well: being like you. Being afraid. But you don't have to be. That's what I've learned, Aaron. That's what we've all learned."

"Are—they going to kill me?" Aaron asked in a whisper.

"Kill you? No, Aaron. No one's going to kill you. That's the first thing we all understood when we began this. No one's going to hurt you. We want you well, not hurt. One day you'll be free, but when you leave here you will be part of us, and you won't betray us. We know that. Someday you'll know it, too. People say you were kidnapped, but that's not really true, Aaron. You were *selected*. Selected to be one of us. Now, let's stop talking about it. I've said more than I should have."

"I won't say anything," Aaron told her.

"I know that," Carla said softly. "I trust you, Aaron. I do." She refilled the glasses from the half-empty bottle, then rolled off the corner of the bed. "It was a great party, Aaron. I wish you could have seen it. I've never been around such people, or at least so many of them at the same time. We should have had a band and a dance. I love to dance. Do you?" She began to move in a dreamy dance step.

Aaron smiled from the bed. The champagne was seeping into his senses. "I never danced," he confessed.

Carla stopped and turned to Aaron and stared incredulously at him. "Never?"

Aaron tilted his head in answer.

"I don't believe it," Carla said.

"I never went to a dance," Aaron told her.

"Well, you can learn how. Now."

"I—can't dance," Aaron protested quietly.

Carla reached for his champagne glass and took it from

him and placed it on the nightstand. Then she took his hand and pulled him from the bed.

"It's easy," she said. "You just move. Give me your hand. Like this." She placed Aaron's hands in the dance position. "You're the leader. Men always lead. Now, put yourself very close to me." She moved easily against Aaron. "That's right," she whispered. "We fit. Can you feel that, Aaron? Our bodies are just right for one another. That means we'll dance beautifully. Now, you move your feet to the music. The music's slow, Aaron. Come on. You can do it." Her face was against his face. Her voice was a purr. She began to move and Aaron moved awkwardly with her.

"I can't," Aaron said desperately.

"But you are, Aaron. You're dancing. Do you know that? You're dancing."

Aaron could feel the champagne swimming in his head. The music seemed far away. A smile broke across his face.

Carla pulled her face from Aaron's face and looked at him. "It feels wonderful, doesn't it?"

Aaron did not answer. He stared into Carla's face, into the blazing of her eyes.

"Oh, you'll be a grand dancer, Aaron Greene. A grand dancer," Carla said. "All you need is someone to dance with, someone who believes in you."

She leaned forward and pressed her lips to Aaron's lips. He could feel her mouth working against his mouth, her tongue touching his tongue. Her body began to curl against him.

"I'm going to teach you, Aaron," she whispered. "I'm going to teach you how to be loved."

They did not know that the small, flat glass eye of a hidden miniature video camera watched them.

TWENTY-NINE

—————————•—————————

"Hello, Ray, you're on The Katie Harris Show."

"Hey, Katie, I'm your number one fan."

"Thanks, Ray. What's on your mind?"

"That boy they took. Like I said last week—you remember me calling, don't you?"

"Sure, Ray."

"Anyhow, like I was saying last week, I still believe the whole thing's tied up with that newspaper fellow. You can't tell me he don't know nothing about what's going on, and if he don't, why don't he come on the air and just say so? You ask me, he's got one of them movie deals cooked up, and the reason we ain't heard nothing from him is he's off writing. And them finding that new tape last night in the car of that other newspaper fellow—the one who's the boss? You can't tell me that wadn't a put-up. That Yates fellow probably slipped it in there. I'm telling you, Katie, they playing around with a boy's life just to sell a few newspapers."

"So, Ray, you think something's rotten in Denmark, too, do you?"

"Well, I don't know nothing about Denmark, but I damn well know there's something wrong about that newspaper."

"Now, let's be patient, Ray. Let's presume that the tape was found exactly as it has been reported, that it was already in the car when Harry Dilliard left the Pender estate last night, put there by an unknown party or parties, with the police inside enjoying

299

the festivities. And let's presume that Cody Yates is telling the absolute truth, and nothing but the truth, when he says he has no idea why it's his voice that's being used by the kidnappers. If all of that is true, then what's going on here? Is this all a publicity stunt? Did someone set the whole thing up just to get Ethridge Landon to resign from the bank, as it was announced this morning? Is Aaron Greene still alive?"

"Well, I don't know, Katie. That's a good question. Seems to me there must of been something going on over at that bank if that fellow's quit his job. Don't know too many people that'd give up a do-nothing job like that."

"Of course, we're still trying to get to the bottom of that story as well, Ray, but from what we do know the U.S. Attorney has announced that he'll file charges against Mr. Landon for mishandling of bank accounts. We don't know what that means as of yet, but our news team is working on it. The only thing we have is a press release stating that Mr. Landon has resigned due to the pressure imposed on him as a result of the public's reaction to the kidnapping. And maybe that's it, but who knows? As I was saying to Cody Yates last night, I'm the kind of person who believes that where there's smoke, there's fire. I don't think Mr. Yates exactly agrees with me, but that's the difference between Stone Age and modern journalism. Thanks for the call, Ray. Let's see—Lottie in East Point, you're on the air."

"Katie?"

"This is Katie. You're on the air, Lottie."

"Well, I don't know about other people, but it scares me to death to think there's only three more days left to raise the money to save that boy's life. I know lots of people have been sending in money. I sent in ten dollars myself, but I don't know how they can get up enough to make ten million dollars in three days, not unless somebody like that Mr. Pender takes it out of his pocket and hopes they'll be enough coming in to pay him back. You think he could do that, Katie?"

"Good question, Lottie. Very good question. In fact, as I said at the lead-in to today's show, I was at the Pender estate last night for the fund-raiser, and I overheard several people wondering

why Ewell Pender was involved in this at all. Does he have anything to gain from it? Could it be that public response will make him even richer? Are his numerous business ventures floundering? Is he seeking publicity? Is that why he resigned his seat on the board of directors of Century National Bank—a bank his grandfather established? Is he, in any way, involved in the accusations the U.S. Attorney is leveling at Ethridge Landon? Like any decent reporter, I posed some of those questions to one of his associates last evening. He, of course, denied that Ewell Pender had any ulterior motive in helping raise the ransom for Aaron Greene other than being a concerned citizen—a concerned wealthy citizen, I might add."

"I don't know what to think about things like that, Katie. I was just worrying about that boy. I been praying all along. I just wish I could send in more than ten dollars."

"Don't feel that way, Lottie. Your ten dollars with a lot of other people sending in ten dollars, or whatever they can afford, may help persuade the kidnappers that we all care, and maybe they'll drop their demand about the bank paying the rest of it. The only thing I hope is that somebody reliable is responsible for auditing what's coming in. I'm glad you called, Lottie. Call again. Bill, in Duluth, what do you think—?"

Menotti switched off the radio with a violent twist and pushed hard on the accelerator and sped past a slow-moving Volkswagen van that had been artistically painted with kudzu vines crawling up its side door and over the top. He was late meeting Philip Oglesbee at the Century National Bank, but the day had been less than perfect. Clifford Russell had feasted on the metaphorical flesh of his ass since early morning. Where the hell were the officers responsible for security at the party? Clifford Russell had demanded. Had anyone checked for prints—finger or foot? Had anyone questioned the parking lot attendants? What about Harry Dilliard? Was Harry Dilliard lying about the circumstances of finding the tape? Could the tape have been in his car *before* he arrived at the party?

The answers Menotti had offered were feeble and unacceptable, and Clifford Russell had given him a grace period of twenty-four hours to find something concrete enough to take to the public.

Jason Littlejohn would be that something.

Menotti parked his car in a lot near the bank and crossed the street and tapped on the locked glass door. He displayed his badge to a waiting security guard, who opened the door. As he entered the lobby, Menotti saw the African Prince seated in a remote corner, impatiently waiting with Mike Ogden, the U.S. Attorney stationed in Atlanta. He had worked other cases with Mike Ogden and liked him.

"You're late," Philip Oglesbee said bluntly.

Menotti wanted to say, "Now you know how it feels." He did not. "Sorry," he mumbled. "I've been with Russell. Had to pick a few teeth out of my ass." He nodded to Mike.

"How are you, Victor?" Mike said.

"I've been better," Menotti answered. "Is he here?"

"Upstairs," Philip replied. "I don't think he liked being called in on a Saturday." He looked around the closed bank. "Don't think I blame him. Place is like a morgue."

"Do we know how we're going to handle it?" Mike asked.

"Something I probably won't agree with," Menotti said. He saw a smile rise in Mike's face. He added, "I'm not exactly in the mood to be gentle this morning."

"Press him, then," Philip said. "Mike and I have been talking. If we can get him to cooperate on the Landon thing, we'll scare him a bit and then offer a deal he can't refuse."

"Such as?" Menotti asked.

Philip sniffed dramatically, then tugged at the knot in his tie. "Forget the calls," he said. "No one knows about them but us. Make him resign, then hound him on the bank charges. See what we can get on Landon."

"You're kidding?" Menotti said in shock.

"No, Victor, we're not kidding," Mike said. "Maybe we could nail him on this, maybe not. Fact is, we've got two experts who disagree on the voiceprint. One says yes, the other says maybe. Not always easy to tell with a muffled voice. All it takes is one maybe, and you know that as well as I do. If we can get to Landon, we'll have done our Boy Scout deed for the year. We don't think he's involved at all in the kidnapping, but he's the slimy son of a bitch in this bank mess."

Menotti shook his head. He was astonished. How in hell could the profile makers get so close on speculation and the technical experts quibble over something as tangible as a voice track? Jesus, a voiceprint was as clean as a fingerprint. He wanted to argue, but he was tired. God, he was tired. He had slept two hours at the station, and even the early-morning shower and shave had failed to revive him. "Yesterday, it was positive," he said.

"Yesterday was yesterday," Philip replied.

"It's your game," Menotti said wearily. "I just wanted to come along for the show."

"Actually, I'm glad you're here," Philip told him. "We need to push, and you've been elected the pusher. We'll clean up." He leaned close to Menotti. "Mike tells me you're good at the bully stuff." He smiled. "I like to see a master at work. Make his ass pucker."

"Ought to be easy," Menotti said. "I've had mine puckered all morning."

The African Prince laughed quietly.

Jason Littlejohn greeted the three men in his office in a solemn mood. His eyes were puffed, his face splotched in pale, red dots. He wore the look of stress and fatigue.

"Please, gentlemen, sit," Jason said, attempting courtesy. He was standing behind his desk. "I'm sorry my secretary isn't here. I'd offer you some coffee."

"Thank you," Philip said curtly. "We'll stand. But you may want to sit."

The tone of Philip's voice sliced into Jason. He glanced nervously at Mike Ogden and then sat.

Menotti stepped closer to the desk. He said, in an even, hard voice, "You've been making some phone calls, Mr. Littlejohn. A number of them, in fact."

Jason's face furrowed in a worried question.

"Those phone calls constitute terrorism," Menotti continued.

"What are you talking about?" Jason asked fretfully.

"The calls to the Greene family. The Jew calls," Menotti snapped. "We've got a voice match, asshole."

"Victor," warned Philip.

Menotti whirled to Philip. "Back off," he growled. "I want this son of a bitch to know exactly how I feel. He's cost me a week of sleep and he's scared two good people shitless."

Jason slumped back in his chair. His face paled and his right eye began to blink rapidly. He opened his mouth to speak, but could not. He looked at Philip with a plea.

"You've been making calls to the Greene home, threatening the life of their son," Menotti said angrily. "Where is he?"

"I—I—"

Menotti leaned over the desk and slapped it with the palm of his hand. "Goddamn it, I asked you a question. Where is he?"

"I—don't know what you're talking—about," Jason stammered.

Philip caught Menotti by the shoulders and gently pulled him away. "He's a little overwrought, Mr. Littlejohn, but he expresses how we feel. Do you understand that?"

The pale red splotches on Jason's face deepened.

Philip continued calmly, "We know it was you who made the calls, Mr. Littlejohn. Now, I advise you to answer Mr. Menotti's question. Do you know where the boy is?"

Jason shook his head. The muscles on his jowls twitched. "I—don't know," he whispered. "I don't."

"Are you involved in the kidnapping, Mr. Littlejohn?" Philip asked.

"No," Jason answered. He repeated, "No."

"But you made the calls?" Mike Ogden asked.

Jason turned his face to Mike. He blinked once, then nodded.

"You will note that we have not arrested you or read you your rights," Philip said. "And nothing you have said, or indicated, could be held against you in a court of law, as you certainly know. This is not an oversight on our part. It's an opportunity for you."

Jason stared at him quizzically.

"We think we know why you made the calls," Philip continued. "We think you did it hoping they would be made public and, if so, they would divert attention from the bank, at least long enough for you to put together a plan of action to protect Ethridge Landon and perhaps your own involvement in questionable conduct."

Jason bowed his head at the mention of Ethridge Landon's name.

"But you know now that it didn't work," Philip said confidently. "You know now that charges will be made against Mr. Landon and possibly others, including yourself. Mr. Ogden and I have discussed this at length. We're prepared to offer you a way to avoid prosecution for the threatening phone calls."

Jason looked up. "How?"

Mike Ogden stepped closer to the desk. He said, "For your cooperation with federal agents, we will simply forget the phone calls. You will resign your position and take your chances with the investigation. If it's found that you were knowingly involved in whatever charges are finally delivered, you will also be charged and arrested. Your cooperation, however, should be a mitigating factor in your behalf. But you know how that works, I presume."

Mike Ogden's eyes stayed on Jason in an unforgiving gaze, forcing him to turn his head and to stare out of the window. After a moment, he drew a deep, nervous breath and nodded once. "All right," he said quietly. "I only ask for one thing."

"What's that?" Philip said.

"Give me some time. Today. Tonight. I'll talk to you tomorrow."

"Bullshit," Menotti snarled.

"Not so fast, Victor," Mike Ogden said. He looked at Philip. Philip made a slight, agreeing gesture with his shoulders.

"You understand that if you leave the city, you will immediately be arrested on all charges," Mike said. "Including the phone calls. And I assure you, Mr. Littlejohn, you will be prosecuted to the fullest."

"I understand," Jason said.

"We'll be back at nine o'clock in the morning," Mike added. "And one other thing, Mr. Littlejohn: If you speak of this to Mr. Landon or to anyone else, you will forfeit the agreement."

"I understand," Jason said again.

Menotti turned off Peachtree Street onto Ponce de Leon and headed east. Again he was late. He had promised to meet Cody at two o'clock at Freda Graves's apartment, and now it was two-fifteen. But Cody would be waiting, and even if Cody bitched—and he would—it would be gentle bitching, not the angry bellowing of Clifford Russell or the insistent questioning of the mayor. The day was not improving, Menotti thought, even with Jason Littlejohn's arrogant ass being nailed to the plush walls of his plush office. He had wanted to deliver the message to Clifford Russell that Jason Littlejohn had been arrested, but now he could not. There had not been an arrest. Not officially. And to even tell Clifford Russell of Jason Littlejohn would violate his agreement with the African Prince and Mike Ogden. The matter of the telephone calls to the Greene residence was closed. Officially, at some day in the distant and murky future, it would be reported as unsolved. The only other person who knew anything about the calls was Cody, and he would handle Cody by telling him the truth. Cody, thank God, had some years on him. He had written too many stories to worry about the value of another one.

Clifford Russell's twenty-four-hour grace period for something substantial to report was slipping away, and Menotti knew that he was striking blindly at moving targets. Perhaps there would be something on the tape from the wire he had placed on Cody. There had been no time to retrieve it from Cody, not with the furor caused by the tape Harry Dilliard had discovered in his car. The three-day deadline hanging over Aaron Greene like a teasing execution had kept Menotti busy, moving from briefing to briefing, hounding meeting to hounding meeting.

He pushed the heel of his hand against the steering wheel, stretching the muscles in his shoulders until he felt pain and the pain revived him. At least there was pleasure in watching Jason Littlejohn collapse under pressure like a whimpering teenager caught shoplifting, he thought. The memory of Jason's face—quivering, pale, frightened—made Menotti smile. The son of a bitch. Howard Edwards was a better man. Howard believed in his insanity, was passionate about it. Maybe he should go see Howard. Tell him what had happened. It would please Howard. Howard would laugh his ass off, then say something stupid about Jews and niggers. Howard was an idiot.

He pulled off Ponce de Leon and headed north on Briarcliff. Cody had said there would be nothing of value on the tape, but Cody could be wrong. Cody was a reporter. He had a reporter's tin ear. The tape could be crackling with messages—something small, some word or intonation, something left dangling that Cody would miss. He would not dismiss the value of the tape simply because

Cody believed it was worthless. His intuition about Ewell Pender had been too strong to ignore, and he had nothing else to pursue but his intuition. Let the African Prince and Tito Francis ponder the brittle pieces of evidence that Oglesbee had sketched out on his flip chart. Even their experts disagreed.

Cody was on the deck of the apartment, stretched across a lounge chair, reading the first edition of *The Atlanta Journal,* when Menotti arrived. He took one look at Menotti at the apartment door and softly whistled sympathy. "Jesus," he said, "you look like Peter Falk in an outtake of *Columbo.* Come on, I'll get you some coffee."

"Put some brandy in it, if she's got some hidden around here," Menotti said. "Where is she, by the way?"

"Went shopping. She'll be back later."

"You on the deck?"

"Yeah. Catching up on the latest crime gossip from the local rag," Cody answered.

"Must be reading yourself," Menotti mumbled.

"No, Victor. That would be literature. What I'm reading is trash."

"Yeah, sure," Menotti said. He walked onto the deck and fell into a chair and lit a cigarette. The sun fell on his face, warming him. It was a bright, clean day, sweet with the smell of the greening of spring.

"You been to bed?" Cody asked as he stepped through the door and handed Menotti the coffee.

"Got a couple of hours at the station," Menotti told him. He added, "Damned if I don't have as many clothes down there as I do at home."

"One of these days, old friend, you're going to show up at that place you call home, expecting a hug and a martini, and you'll find nothing left but a hooked rug that's too heavy to drag off."

"Don't even joke about it," Menotti said. "So, what's in the paper?"

Cody sat again on the lounge chair. "Rewrite of what Olin had this morning and a first-person by Amos on finding the tape in Harry's car. You guys know anything new about that?"

"Of course not," Menotti said, drinking from the coffee. Cody had found brandy. It was a soothing, pleasing taste. "Somebody tiptoed in there, put the tape in the car, and took off. No prints of any kind. Easy enough to pull off. It wasn't exactly a secret gathering."

"You talk to Pender's man? The guy who was taking care of the parking?"

"His chauffeur? Sure. He was inside most of the time. Says he didn't see a thing. And no, Cody, we didn't have anyone stationed outside. Pender's people didn't want it to seem like a policeman's ball. Besides, it was an invitation-only affair."

"Russell give you a medal this morning?" asked Cody.

"Pinned it on personally, right over my ass."

Cody laughed easily. "Three days," he said. "Not a hell of a lot of time to raise a few million, even for the bank."

"How much do they have now?" Menotti asked, spewing smoke from his lips.

Cody picked up the newspaper on the floor of the deck. He looked at the front page. "By the thermometer, a little over three mil, but that's inflated, I'd guess. Got to make it look good."

"How much actual, do you think?"

"I don't know," Cody answered. "Two and a half, maybe. There's been a pisspotful of it coming in. Some guy dropped in fifty thousand last night at Pender's party."

Menotti shook his head in amazement. "We're in the wrong business. We ought to be snatching people right and left."

"Yeah," Cody said. "We'd be great at it, wouldn't we? Before it was over, you'd have them riding out in a Porsche and I'd have their college education paid for, and

we'd both be in hock for twenty years. We're tough, Menotti."

"You pick up on anything else last night?" Menotti
asked. "Any little bit of gossip?"

"Nothing," Cody said. He picked up the newspaper he
had been reading and folded it against his lap. Then he
added nonchalantly, "Well, there was one little observa-
tion—not from me, but from Freda."

"What?"

"You know the young girl who's on Pender's staff—
not Alyse Burton, but the other one?"

A furrow wiggled over Menotti's brow. "Don't remember."

"She was at the ball. Pretty little thing. Bubbly."

"So?" Menotti said.

"She was helping escort people to their cars. Freda
thought she had seen her somewhere before, especially the
way she was dressed when she was handing out umbrellas."

"And?"

"That first day—the first message, I mean, the one they
left on my car tire—Freda saw someone running across
the parking lot in the rain, and that someone stumbled
near my car. She wasn't sure, but she thought it was a
young girl, and she thought the girl at Pender's looked a
little like her."

Menotti sat up. "How close was Freda to her in the
parking lot?"

"I asked her that," Cody told him. "Not very close."

"Did she see her face?"

"Just a glimpse. Freda said she was wearing one of those
old aviator caps, the kind with the earflaps. That's what
she remembered the most."

"Then what makes her think it was the same girl?" Menotti asked.

"I asked her that, too," Cody answered. "She said it was
the build, the body type. Personally, I don't think there's

anything to it. Even she doubted it after we'd talked. Said it could have been a boy."

Menotti slumped back in the chair and drank again from his coffee. He seemed far away. After a moment, he said wearily, "Shit, it's like a dog chasing its own tail." He rolled his head to Cody. "Where's my tape?" he asked.

"Here," Cody said. He pulled a small cassette from his shirt pocket and tossed it to Menotti. "Your little gizmo is in the kitchen."

Menotti slipped the tape into his pocket. "I'll listen to it later. Right now, I've got to talk to you about a story you can't write. Now, or ever."

"Don't tell me, then," Cody said.

"Wouldn't if I didn't have to. I told you I'd tell you about the Jew calls. We know who did it."

"Who?"

"Jason Littlejohn," Menotti said.

Cody's face jerked toward Menotti in surprise. "What?" he said incredulously. "I can't write about that? You're sucking wind, Victor."

"We struck a deal with him," Menotti explained.

"What kind of deal?"

"Ignorance for information. In this case, ignorance about the calls on our part in exchange for information on Landon. Quid pro quo, Cody. Quid pro quo."

"Aw, shit," Cody muttered.

THIRTY

———————◆———————

ALYSE BURTON STOOD PATIENTLY WAITING
for the elevator. She wore a dark blue business suit with a
white shirt blouse opened at the neck, showing a small
gold necklace ringing her throat. Her hair was gathered in
a bun. She held a briefcase. It should not take long, she
thought, and she glanced at her watch. It was four-twenty.
But the time did not matter. It mattered only that Joel
Garner believed her. He would. She knew it. She would
make certain that he did. She could feel a surge of excitement in her body, like a sudden, joyful song.

The elevator opened and Alyse stepped onto it and
pushed the floor button. Two men rushed up and entered
the elevator. They were laughing and they smelled of
whiskey.

"What floor we going to?" one of the men said.

"Tenth," the other said. He laughed again and pushed
the button.

"You here on business?" the first man asked Alyse.

Alyse turned her body to face him. She gazed at him
for a moment, then lifted her chin slightly. "Yes," she said.

"What business you in?" the man asked playfully.

"Mine," Alyse answered evenly.

The man's smile vanished and a blush covered his face.
His friend giggled, coughed, looked away.

"I'm sorry," the man apologized. "I'm being rude."

"Yes, you are," Alyse told him. "But I can forgive that." The elevator stopped and she stepped off and the door closed again. She could hear the fading rush of laughter from the men as the elevator rose.

She walked purposefully to Joel Garner's suite of rooms and knocked lightly on the door. He opened it immediately.

"Good afternoon," Joel said pleasantly. The scent of his cologne was strong.

"And good afternoon to you," Alyse replied. "Am I too early?"

"I'd call it late, but then I have to admit I tend to be selfish," Joel answered. "Please, come in."

Alyse entered the room and followed Joel to the seating area. She saw a stack of manuscripts scattered on the floor beside the sofa.

"Forgive the mess," he said. "I've been doing some reading."

"New scripts?" asked Alyse.

"New attempts at scripts. Nothing very appealing, I'm afraid."

"Keeps you busy, doesn't it?"

"Part of the job," Joel said. "Though, actually, I've been enjoying it. I think I'll make a practice of getting away to a good hotel room to read in the future. The isolation's good. Get you something to drink?"

"An orange juice, if you have one," Alyse said.

"Orange juice coming up. Find a seat. Relax." He went to the bar to get the orange juice.

"I suppose you've read the news about last night," Alyse said, sitting in an armchair near the sofa.

"Hell of an ending to a party, wasn't it?" Joel said, returning with glasses of juice. "That was gutsy, whoever did it."

"And a little frightening," Alyse added, accepting the glass from him.

"I guess so," Joel agreed. He dropped casually on the

sofa and lifted his feet to the edge of the coffee table, crossing them at the ankles. "Are you all right?"

"Oh, I'm fine. We all are. But we're a little more watchful than normal."

"Don't blame you. Anything new on it?"

"Nothing we know of. The police were at the estate most of the morning, but I don't think they found anything. The car was parked on pavement."

"I thought you might be bringing good news," Joel said.

"No. Not that kind of good news, I'm afraid. But I did bring you something."

Joel moved his head in a puzzling gesture. It was the same gesture he had used many times in movies. "What?" he asked.

Alyse placed the glass on the table beside her chair and opened the briefcase and took out a small box. "It's a gift from Mr. Pender."

Joel rose from the sofa and crossed to her. She handed him the box. "A gift?" he said. "Why?"

"For what you've done. He hopes you like it."

Joel opened the box and lifted a delicate gold pocket watch from it. He whispered, with astonishment, "It's beautiful."

"It belonged to Mr. Pender's grandfather," Alyse told him. "It's very old, an antique."

"I can see that," Joel said, holding the watch up to the light, cradling it in the palm of his hand. "This is marvelous, but I shouldn't accept it. He must value it greatly, since it belonged to his grandfather."

Joel did not see the smile on the mouth of Alyse. She said, "He wants you to have it. He's a very generous man, and when he cares for people, he believes in expressing it."

Joel leaned quickly to Alyse and kissed her lightly on the lips, surprising her. "Thank you," he said. He put the watch back into the box and placed it on the table. "I'll treasure it."

"You deserve it," Alyse assured him. "We picked up a lot of support last night, and it was due to you."

Joel turned back to the sofa and sat. His eyes flashed a soft blue light to Alyse. "No," he said quietly, "it's not due to me. It's due to an illusion, but an illusion that sometimes has its merits. I'm glad I could help. I'm glad I came here."

For a moment Alyse did not speak. Then she said, "So am I."

"Thank you for saying that," Joel said. "It—well, it sounds personal."

"It is," Alyse replied. There was a pause. "I've always admired your work," she added.

"See? Illusion. That's what I'm admired for—illusion."

"I don't mean it that way. I'm glad I met you."

"That's better. Now, could I invite you and Mr. Pender to dinner tonight? I meant to call earlier, but I started reading, and—"

"Thank you, but we can't," Alyse said. "And there's another reason for seeing you today."

"What?"

"Mr. Pender thinks you should return to California," Alyse said.

"Excuse me?" Joel said in surprise.

"He thinks that for your safety, you should return home."

"My safety? What's that about?"

Alyse sipped from the glass of juice. She deliberately waited to answer.

"I don't understand," Joel said.

She looked up, into his face. "We don't care to have anyone else know this," she said, "but this morning we received a telephone call, threatening to kill anyone involved in promoting the fund-raising. Of course, that's confidential."

"My God," Joel whispered. He sat up on the edge of the sofa.

"Please don't misunderstand us," Alyse continued.
"We're not concerned for Mr. Pender's safety, or for ours.
We have a rather good security system in place and I'm
sure we'll increase it, but we do have concern for others,
such as yourself. You're the most public person involved
in this."

"I just can't leave," Joel protested.

"I know how you feel. I wouldn't want to, either, but
I also understand Mr. Pender. He's a very old man now.
He feels a lot of responsibility, and that worries him. However, you should also know that it was I who made the
suggestion that you return to California, not Mr. Pender."

"You?"

Alyse's eyes held Joel's face, drew his face to her. "I
know him well. I don't want to see him become more
fretful than necessary. I hope you understand that."

"Of course. Of course I do," Joel said. "I just wouldn't
want anyone to think that I've dashed in here for publicity
and then caught the first jet back to Hollywood."

"They won't. Not about you. You've made a grand
impact. I think you could take the position that you've
returned to help raise money on the West Coast."

"I suppose," Joel mumbled.

"I don't want to see anything happen to you. Will you
do this for me?" Alyse asked gently.

Joel pulled himself up from the sofa, leaned forward, his
elbows dangling over his knees. Then he said, "All right.
I'll make arrangements to leave tonight."

"Thank you," Alyse said. Her face did not move from
him.

"I wish I could do more."

"You've done more than you know," Alyse told him.
"I—I'm sorry that it's worked out this way, that you have
to leave so soon."

"Me, too," he said. He stood and moved to the chair
where Alyse was sitting. He leaned to her and kissed her
again, a kiss with gentle force. "Forgive me for that," he

added quietly, "but I've wanted to kiss you since seeing you last night. I don't know if I told you, but you were beautiful."

"Were?" she asked.

"Are," he answered.

"Are you trying to seduce me?" Alyse said.

"Yes."

"Thank you. That's honest, and it's a compliment."

"I know it's inappropriate, under the circumstances," Joel said. "I'm behaving badly."

"I could say the same of myself," Alyse said.

"Do you want to leave?" asked Joel.

Alyse reached her hand to his face, touched his mouth with her fingertips. "No," she said softly.

The telephone on the bedside stand rang at nine o'clock, and Freda pulled from Cody and reached for it. "Yes?" she whispered. Then: "Oh. Just a moment." She pushed her hand against Cody and motioned with the phone. "It's Victor," she said.

"Christ," Cody mumbled. He took the phone. "Hey, I was just about to leave."

"Take my advice and put on some pants before you do," Menotti said. "It's cold out."

"What's up, Victor?"

"Jason Littlejohn."

"What about him?"

"He swallowed a bullet about an hour ago, but it popped out the back of his head," Menotti said.

Cody sat up in bed. "What?"

"Killed himself, Yates. But not until he'd taken the same liberty with his wife."

"Good God, why?"

"Stress, my lad. Stress. He left one hell of a note, though. Not the kind of thing that would please Landon—the poor bastard—but strong enough for us. Seems Landon was fooling around with his wife."

"Yeah, Victor, he was."

There was a pause. Cody could hear the heavy breathing of Menotti. "You know something I don't?"

"I know about the diddling. I saw it."

"When?"

"Yesterday. I found out that Landon was staying at Littlejohn's cabin up on Lanier and went up to see him. Arrived at an inconvenient moment, you might say."

"You son of a bitch," Menotti snarled. "I told you to tell me everything."

"Jesus, Victor, there wasn't anything to it. The guy was taking advantage of the opportunity, and the opportunity appeared to be enjoying it."

Menotti mumbled something Cody did not understand.

"Come on, Victor, I'm not holding out on you."

"Cody," Menotti said in a low, threatening voice, "you get your sorry ass out of bed and get dressed and meet me at that Waffle House up the street. In ten minutes. If you're not there, I'm going to pick up Millie and Sabrina and the three of us are going to beat down the door on that sweet little love nest you've made for yourself." He slammed down the phone.

"What was that about?" asked Freda.

Cody rolled off the side of the bed. "Menotti," he grumbled. "He wants to see me."

"Now? Why?"

"The lawyer at the bank—Littlejohn—just blew his brains out. Took his wife with him."

Freda sat up and pulled the sheet around her breasts. "What's that got to do with you?"

"Nothing," Cody said wearily. "Victor thinks I've been holding out on him. He's got his shorts in a wad."

"I heard what you said about seeing something. What was it?"

"Landon and Littlejohn's wife doing the dirty deed."

"How did you see that?"

"Through the window," Cody answered patiently.

"Forget it. It was nothing. I'm a sneaky bastard and Menotti's paranoid. My God, he thinks everything connects to everything else, like some dot-to-dot-to-dot picture." He pulled a sweater over his head.

"Maybe it does, Cody," Freda said softly. She pushed pillows against the headboard of the bed and settled into them with her shoulders. "You won't be long, will you?"

"I don't know. He's pissed. I'll be back as soon as I can."

The parking lot at the Waffle House had only two cars—Menotti's and a new Honda with the tag of a Conyer dealership still advertising its sale. Cody parked next to Menotti's car and went inside. Menotti had taken a remote booth and was drinking coffee.

"So, it's twelve minutes," Cody said defensively as he slid into the booth opposite Menotti. A second cup of coffee was on the table in front of him.

"I was about to leave," Menotti said. "Drink your coffee. It's decaffeinated. Wouldn't want you to stay up the rest of the night when you get back."

"I got here fast enough. Anyway, you're the one who's always late. Just where the hell were you when you called?"

"Near Lenox. Littlejohn lived up that way," Menotti answered. He smiled a disapproving smile. "And I didn't have to take time to dress," he added.

"Get off my back, Victor. My God, I deserve a little comfort as much as the next man."

"Sorry. You're right. Maybe I'm jealous. What did you tell her?"

"I told her I was meeting you. That was obvious, don't you think?"

"I guess," Menotti replied wearily. He looked closely at Cody. "You really see Landon banging Littlejohn's wife?"

"Not close-up and personal, but, yes, I did," Cody answered. "Landon and I had a little chat about it."

"Chat?"

"Nothing serious. He pushed. I pushed. I'd call it even."

"You should have told me," Menotti said.

"Come on, Victor, I didn't even think about it. A guy got laid. What difference does it make?"

Menotti sighed and shook his head. "I told you earlier today about the deal with Littlejohn over the calls to the Greenes. You remember that?"

"Of course I do. I now assume that deal is as dead as Littlejohn, and I can write about the calls."

"You'll have to get it from Oglesbee," Menotti said. "He knows I talked to you, and he also knows that Clifford Russell is breathing hot air down my neck because of you. Best it comes from him, not me."

"Fine," Cody said.

"The point is, Cody, if we had known about Landon and Littlejohn's wife, we might have played it differently when we nailed Littlejohn's ass to the wall. Now, what I want to know is this: Is there anything else you know that I don't?"

Cody poured sugar into his coffee and stirred it and took a sip. It was hot and strong and good. He said, after a moment, "I don't know anything, but let me ask you something."

"Ask."

"Was there anything on the tape I made with Pender that you could use? I'm sure you've listened to it a dozen times by now."

"You mean besides all that shitty nonsense about getting laid?"

"Yeah, yeah, Victor, besides all of that, which, incidentally, I said on purpose, just for your prurient pleasure."

"Maybe," Menotti answered. "I think that old boy's sharp as a tack. He played you beautifully."

"Thanks," Cody said sarcastically.

"You're welcome. And, no, there was nothing on the

tape that surprised me. He seems up front on everything, even about the boy going to his school. Frankly, that makes me feel a little better about him. It tells me he cares about something besides money. But there is one thing I want to know: How long has Millie been dating the computer wizard?"

"Lucas? I don't know. A year or so, I guess. I think that's what she said. Maybe less, maybe more. It's only been recently that he's become something of a regular fixture around the house, though. Why?"

"And you didn't know him until recently?"

"Millie and I made a promise when we divorced. We wouldn't snoop around on what the other was doing. We seldom mention our social life. Sometimes I kid Sabrina about it, but that's all. Why?"

"Because it surprised the hell out of me to see her at the Pender reception, and in the company of a computer genius who, coincidentally, happens to be close friends with Pender."

"Good God, Victor, you're letting your imagination get away from you. There must be thousands of people in this city who work with computers."

"Maybe, but let's play Sherlock Holmes," Menotti said seriously. "Suppose our Mr. Lucas is one jealous son of a bitch, and he's heels over ass in love with the ex-wife of a certain fading media celebrity. He's smart. He's talented. He knows computers inside out. He's got connections with the richest man on the continent. So he does his homework and snatches a kid that he knows will tug at the heartstrings of everybody possessing even a glimmer of a soul, and then he starts distributing tapes, using the voice of his lady friend's old bed partner, which he has conveniently taken from the longest-running wiretap since J. Edgar Hoover checked out Martin Luther King. Makes the faded celebrity sound like a blithering idiot. Then, to his great surprise, his rich old friend gets involved and starts throwing money around like it's confetti, and our Mr. Lucas gets giddy with greed."

"My God, Menotti, you need rest," Cody said in amazement.

"No, Cody, I need proof."

Cody leaned in exasperation against the booth. He fingered a cigarette from a package in his pocket and lit it with his disposable lighter. He looked at Menotti and shook his head sadly.

"You think it's picking fly shit out of pepper, don't you?" Menotti said bluntly. "Well, it's not, Cody. What if I'm right? What if everything I've said is the absolute truth? Wouldn't it explain why they used your voice? Think about Millie and Sabrina."

Cody drew hard from the cigarette and crushed it in the ashtray. "Look," he said, "why don't you go pick Lucas up? Go arrest a man who works for Ewell Pender. Take him down to the station and book him. Work him over. Beat the living shit out of him with a rubber hose. How long do you think you'd last, Victor? Good God, man, nobody in this town—in this state, in this country— would stand with you. You know what would happen, Victor? One day Clifford Russell would send you out to investigate a naked jaywalker and they'd find you a year later, pushing up cactus plants in the Grand Canyon. Victor, Victor, God almighty. If I were worried about Millie and Sabrina, I'd be over there with a chain saw, whacking body parts off smiling Mr. Lucas. Come on, old friend. He's a nice guy. The way he talks, he loves my ex-wife, and I've got a feeling he must be crazy about my daughter. Jesus, he reminds me of that guy out of *The Music Man*. He's the jolliest human being this side of Santa Claus. You're tired, Victor. Go home. Get some sleep. Tomorrow you'll feel better."

Menotti stared at Cody with contempt. He said in a whisper, "Tomorrow's too late, Cody. No, you go home. Go put your head between those pillows of tits and count leaping orgasms until you fall off to sleep. You're wasting my time."

Menotti pulled suddenly from the booth. He reached into his pocket and dropped two one-dollar bills on the table and then stalked away.

Cody glanced at his watch. It was nine thirty-three. He would be pushed to meet the deadline for the Sunday final edition on the death of Jason Littlejohn and his wife. He needed to find Oglesbee.

THIRTY-ONE

THE TRAY ON THE SERVICE CART THAT ALYSE pushed was warm and the breakfast scents of coffee and omelets and thin German potato cakes seeped through the cloth covering. She had been awake for two hours, had taken a short walk around the grounds, and then she had taken breakfast with Ewell Pender, and, later, she had helped Maria prepare Aaron's breakfast. Surprised with company, Maria had chattered noisily about the party and the guests. She had an autograph from Joel Garner, she had announced proudly, and she had pried into Alyse's relationship with the famous actor. The questions had made Alyse laugh. "No," she had said to Maria. "It was all business."

She smiled again as she guided the cart down the corridor to Aaron's room. She could still feel the pressure of Joel Garner on her, the frantic, hard laboring of the famous actor to please her. It was a gratifying memory. But he was gone. He would forget her. Yet, it did not matter. He had believed her lie about the threat and he would no longer be a distraction. There were enough distractions, some unexpected and unmanageable. Cody Yates's story about Jason Littlejohn's death and his anti-Semitic calls to Aaron's parents was one. It had bloomed that morning from the front page of *The Atlanta-Journal Constitution*, causing Ewell Pender to retreat to his study in silence.

324

She stopped at the door to Aaron's suite, tapped lightly on the panel, and waited for Aaron's asking voice, the timid "Yes?" She tapped again at the door. Waited. She called, "Aaron." There was no answer. Strange, she thought. He was always there, always waiting for her. Perhaps he was being cautious. He had been isolated in his bedroom during the police search of the property after the discovery of the tape in Harry Dilliard's car.

She unlocked the door with her key and opened it slightly. She called again: "Aaron."

There was no sound in the room, and Alyse pushed open the door and stepped inside and looked at the bed. It had not been disturbed. A sudden, sickening fear struck hard at her. She called, in a loud voice, "Aaron!" Still there was no answer.

She closed the door behind her and locked it and moved cautiously across the room to the bathroom. The door was open and the room dark. There was no sound of running water. She turned and moved quickly into the library, calling Aaron's name. He was not in the library. She went to the window and looked out into the garden. He can't be in the garden, she thought. Impossible. The door leading to the garden was on a time lock; it would not open until later, or until it had been manually disarmed. She went to the door and twisted the knob. It opened. "My God," she whispered. She reached for the phone that had been installed for Aaron for internal calls only, and she dialed a single-number intercom connection. There was no answer. She dropped the telephone back onto its cradle and rushed from the room back to the kitchen. Maria gave her a puzzled look.

"I need to use the telephone," Alyse told her.

"So, there it is," Maria said lightly.

Alyse picked up the receiver and tapped in a memory-dial code. After a moment, Robert Lucas answered. "Our guest is gone," she said in a whisper.

"Gone?" Robert replied with surprise.

"Yes."

"You're sure?"

"Yes."

"Maybe he's with Carla," Robert suggested.

"I just tried to call her. She didn't answer either," Alyse said.

"Check her room," Robert told her. "See if you can find Morris. I'll be there as soon as I can."

Alyse heard the click of the hang-up by Robert. She thumbed the phone to get a dial tone, then pushed the number for Morris. She counted the rings. Three. Four. Five. Six. Then she put the phone back onto its cradle and leaned against the wall of the kitchen. My God, she thought. My God. She knew what had happened.

"Are you all right?" asked Maria with concern.

"Would you please find Oscar for me?" Alyse said.

Ewell Pender sat behind his desk, his thin body leaning into the contoured leather back. Alyse stood beside the window, looking out over the garden. Robert sat in a chair placed near the desk. Oscar stood near the door.

"Do we all agree, then, that Morris has the boy and Carla?" Ewell Pender said in a tired, faint voice.

"It has to be that," Alyse said angrily. "He's gone and Aaron and Carla are gone. Besides, he's the only one who could have done it. He knew the security system better than anyone."

"The boy couldn't have escaped?" Ewell Pender asked.

"No," Alyse said firmly. "We checked the system. It was operative. Morris reset it. The only things turned off were the security cameras and the automatic lock on the door to the garden. Morris took him. And Carla. Carla would never have gone voluntarily."

"I'm afraid I have to agree," Robert said. He was nervous. He rubbed his hands together in an old habit of anxiety. "The question is: Why?"

"I'm sure we'll learn the answer soon enough," Ewell Pender said.

"He's been acting a bit strange lately," suggested Robert. "Tense. I noticed it a few days ago, after the tape was left in Rich's, and he didn't seem to trust Carla around Aaron."

Ewell Pender rocked forward slowly in his chair and picked up a thin cup containing tea from his desk. He tasted it absently. "I'll take the responsibility," he said at last. "I made a mistake in judgment. Now I need to think about it." He looked at Alyse. "I want both of you to be available today. And I don't want you to worry, or to let your imaginations overcome your good sense. I'm sure we'll learn something soon. I would suggest, however, that you dispose of any materials—clothing or anything else—relating to our recent activities. I think a thorough cleaning of his suite would be in order."

"The tapes, also?" asked Robert.

"Most definitely the tapes," Ewell Pender answered. "I assume you have disks in the event of further need."

Robert nodded.

"Do you think he would hurt Aaron, or Carla?" Alyse asked.

Ewell Pender shook his head calmly. He said in a consoling voice, "No, I don't think so. They're both too valuable to him. Please trust me. There's an answer and we'll find it. Now, please, go. All but Oscar."

Oscar waited at the door until everyone had left the room, then he closed the door and crossed the room and stood before the desk.

"Sit down, Oscar," Ewell Pender said.

"Thank you, sir," Oscar replied. He sat in a chair facing the desk.

"Do you know anything?" asked Ewell Pender.

"I'm afraid I don't, sir."

"He's either taken the boy to the police or he's kidnapped him from us and he's using Carla as insurance."

"I don't think he would go to the police," Oscar suggested.

"Nor do I. We'll hear from him, but not soon. He'll wait. He'll want us to be anxious."

"Yes sir."

"Have you searched his room?"

Oscar dipped his head in a nod. "I have."

"Did you find anything to help us?"

"I'm afraid not."

Ewell Pender shifted in his chair. He touched his finger to the rim of the teacup, gazed at it thoughtfully. "It has to do with Carla," he said. "I've been afraid of it. There was a small item in the newspaper a few days ago about a young boy who had been mugged and badly beaten. His name was Ron Eaton, the same young man who spoke to Carla when she made the call from the university. Morris was upset about it. He warned me that Carla might have been overheard, but that wasn't the reason he was angry. He was angry because he was jealous."

"You believe he was responsible for the attack?" asked Oscar.

"I'm afraid so. I looked at his profile again only yesterday. He had a fear of rejection. Apparently it's surfaced again."

"The young man?" Oscar said. "Will he recover?"

Ewell Pender nodded. "Thankfully, yes. He was one of our boys, Oscar. He went to Carlton-Ayers."

"I'm sorry, sir. Will that be all?"

"One other thing," Ewell Pender said. "I read Mr. Yates's story about the death of Jason Littlejohn and his wife, and the calls made to the Greene family. Have flowers sent to the funeral home." His eyes wandered up to Oscar. "It was despicable what he did, but we must be respectful. I would ask Alyse to take care of it, but she's too disturbed at the moment."

Oscar stood. "Of course."

"Thank you, Oscar," Ewell Pender said. He added, "We may be forced to amend things."

"Yes sir."

The blindfold that Morris had wrapped tightly around Aaron's face still covered his eyes, and his arms were still locked behind him, bound by duct tape, and his legs were still taped at the ankles. He sat in a corner against a wall, not moving. The great, thundering fear that had overwhelmed him when Morris stepped into his bedroom hours earlier, pushing Carla in front of him, still caused him to tremble.

Carla's hands had been bound at her back with duct tape, and duct tape was over her mouth. Her eyes had flooded and a tear-stream had rolled down her face and over the tape on her mouth. She had looked at Aaron with bewilderment and apology, and Aaron had known that she was trying to speak, but could only make guttural sounds.

Morris had said nothing. He had waved the barrel of the semiautomatic that he held, motioning Aaron to move from the chair where he had been watching a movie titled *Malone*, which starred Joel Garner, and Aaron had obeyed. And then Morris had guided him and Carla quickly and quietly through the library door, along the shadowed wall of the garden, and out of the gate. He had been forced to lie on the floor of the car beside Carla until the car was well away from the estate, and then Morris had blindfolded him and taped his hands and mouth. He did not know how long they had driven. An hour. Longer. He knew only that his body ached from the hard floor and the pounding of the car over rough roads.

He also knew that outside it was daylight. He could hear through the walls the singing of birds and, off in a distance, the occasional barking of a dog. He had not heard anyone moving about for a long time, and he wondered if he had been left alone. And he wondered where Carla was. He remembered that a door had closed, and by the sound of

it, the door was near him. It was cold. If there was heat in
the room, Aaron could not feel it.

Aaron rested his head back against the wall. The blindfold made his eyes burn, and against the black screen he
saw colors of purple and blood-red—splotches of color,
like small, slow-motion explosions, erupting soundlessly
in a faraway place. He tried to bring images to his mind.
Carla. Her thin girl-woman face waved through his memory, and then he saw her mouth close to him, opening,
and the moist, pink muscle of her tongue slipped across
his lips. Carla. He watched in his memory as she slowly
removed her blouse, revealing small, strong breasts, and in
memory, she took his hands and lifted them to her breasts.
He felt a violent shudder convulsing in his body and the
vision of Carla was gone. He then saw his mother's face—
the drawn, worn, timid face of his mother. He had believed he would see her again. Now he did not believe it.
He began to cry into the blindfold.

He did not know when he fell asleep, but he awoke to
the pull of the blindfold from his face. He recoiled instinctively, striking his head against the wall. The burst of light
on his aching eyes blinded him, and he closed them and
turned his head.

"Rise and shine," Morris crowed. The sound of his
voice was frightening.

Aaron opened his eyes in a painful squint. He saw Morris's face close to him in a blur of light. Morris was smiling
triumphantly. Carla was standing behind Morris. Her face
was puffed from crying. He could see a welt across her
mouth where the duct tape had been.

"Leave him alone," Carla said angrily. She pushed at
Morris and kneeled in front of Aaron and pulled away the
duct tape as gently as possible, and then she touched his
face. "Are you all right?"

Aaron's head quivered in a nod. He looked at Morris,
then back to Carla.

"I'm sorry," she whispered. She worked to pull the tape away from his hands. "I'm so sorry. I told you you wouldn't be hurt—"

Morris laughed.

"There's some food," Carla said. "That's where I've been. Morris made me go with him."

"Hamburgers," Morris sneered. "I hope you like hamburgers, boy. All you may ever eat again."

Carla turned her head to glare at Morris. He winked at her and smiled and turned away and crossed the room to the table.

"Come on, I'll help you up," Carla said. She pulled the tape from around his ankles and then took his arm and supported him as he stood.

Aaron could smell the thick odor of meat in the room. He looked over Carla's shoulder. The room was large. A log cabin, sparsely furnished. It had three cots and a table and four chairs. A kitchen area was along one wall, with a range and oven and, beside it, an aging refrigerator. A television set with a VCR was on a crate against the wall, near a rock fireplace. An open door led into a dingy bathroom. The antlered head of a deer was over the rough wood door. There were four windows. Aaron believed it was a hunting cabin, like the hunting cabins he had seen on television programs.

"Yeah," Morris said, glaring at him. "A little different from what you're used to." He motioned for Carla to lead Aaron to the table. "By the way, I wouldn't get any ideas about leaving," he warned. He touched the semiautomatic crammed into his belt. "Let me give you the same little speech I gave Carla: I know how to use this, and, believe me, I will."

Aaron saw a flash of anger burn in Carla's face, but she said nothing. She took Aaron's hand and led him to the table and sat near him. A bag containing hamburgers was opened.

"Eat," commanded Morris.

"Go on," Carla urged gently. "I had one on the way back. You need to eat." She took a hamburger from the bag and handed it to Aaron. "There's a Coke for you," she added.

The hamburger was tasteless, and Aaron chewed on it slowly, his eyes avoiding the gaze of Morris.

"I had nothing to do with this, Aaron," Carla said after a moment. "I want you to know that. None of us did. Only Morris."

"Who asked you to give a speech?" Morris snapped.

Carla whirled in her chair to face him. "Leave us alone," she said in a low, warning voice.

"Oh, I am," Morris said. He moved toward Carla. "Soon enough, I will. Soon enough."

"What does that mean?" Carla demanded.

"You'll see," Morris told her. He reached to touch her face, and she pulled away. Morris smiled, then turned to Aaron. "How about a little relaxation, Aaron? A little entertainment?"

Aaron did not answer.

"Hey, I asked you a question," Morris said roughly. He stepped around Carla, toward Aaron. "You like movies, don't you? Sure you do. You watched a lot of them. That's something else we knew about you. You watched a lot of television, didn't you, Aaron?"

"Morris—" Carla said.

"Shut up," Morris growled. He moved closer to Aaron, leaned to him. He whispered, "I've got a little show that you're going to love. I promise you. Guess who stars in it, Aaron?" He pulled back from Aaron, spread his arms, one toward Aaron and one toward Carla. "Tah-dah," he sang. "It's *The Aaron and Carla Show.*"

"What—are you talking about?" Carla asked.

A wide grin broke over Morris's face. "Did you like her?" he said to Aaron. His voice was low and threatening.

"How did it feel? Up on you like that? She showed you how, didn't she? Up on you. I saw it, Aaron. She showed you what to do, didn't she? Made your hands go where she wanted them to, didn't she?" He laughed suddenly, sharply, causing Aaron's arms to jerk. "You stupid damn fool. The man's supposed to be on top. But you didn't know. It was the first time. It was, wasn't it?"

"Morris—" Carla said weakly.

Morris whirled to Carla. He caught her by her hair and yanked. Carla gasped in pain. "Does he know you're a whore?" Morris growled. "Does he know it was all a setup, just to make him feel better?"

"No," Carla cried.

Morris jerked hard on her hair and then released her. "Bitch," he growled. He flicked his fingers across her mouth. She cried in surprise.

"Don't," Aaron said. It was not a command. It was a plea.

Morris's hand darted to the gun tucked into the waist of his pants. "Don't what?" he demanded. "You want to be a hero, Aaron? Come on, try it. Be a big hero. I'll blow your worthless brains out, you stupid little son of a bitch." His fingers played across the grip of his gun. He stepped to Aaron and caught him by the shoulder and pinned him against the chair. "And you know what, Aaron? Who would care if I did? You're a nobody. That's why you were chosen, you idiot. You're a nobody. That's what they keep calling you on the radio. How can you kill a nobody? If it's a nobody, then nobody's killed." He snickered.

Aaron lifted his arms in front of his face against the assault of Morris's voice. He began to weep quietly.

"You did this, not me," Morris growled, thrusting his face close to Aaron. "You had to have her. She's a whore. Don't you know that? She takes any man she can. That was what she was doing when we got her. When she was twelve, thirteen, she was a whore. Men are always around her, like a bitch dog in heat."

Aaron looked away, toward the door. He could hear Carla weeping.

"You want to see what it looks like, Aaron? I'll show you," Morris said. He moved angrily to the television and turned it on. He then slipped a tape into the VCR and tapped the play button. "Watch this, Aaron. Watch it carefully. I've got the good stuff on here. You didn't know you had a camera on you, did you? She didn't either." He cracked a sputtering laugh toward Carla. "I didn't tell her. I didn't tell any of them. I did it after Robert put in the television and you were outside with her. It was hooked up to the security system. All I had to do was watch."

The screen blinked once and a harsh, crimson line floated across the shadowed images of the darkened room. Aaron stared at it in astonishment. He could see Carla dancing with him, then kissing him. He watched her moving against him, picking at the buttons on his shirt, undressing him calmly, tenderly. He saw her face against his chest, saw her kneeling to brush her mouth against his stomach and then to embrace his legs. He saw himself push away at her shoulders and saw her stand again and hold him for a moment and then pull away and begin her own slow undressing. He saw her place his hands on her breasts, saw her pull him to the bed, saw the dark, gleaming hair growing at the parting of her legs, saw her position him, touch him, rise above him on her knees. He saw her bend to kiss him, a gentle, easy kiss. He saw her hands move like a pale, slow light to guide him inside her, saw her body rise up, her hands flying to her hair like the pose of the statue in the garden, saw her collapsing and rising against him, saw her move quickly away. He remembered the sudden, surprising hot spill coating his abdomen, and the flush of shame that swam across his chest.

Morris pushed the stop button. He turned deliberately to Aaron. "You son of a bitch," he hissed. "You stupid son of a bitch. You need to die." His fingers stroked the steel of the gun in his belt.

"Don't!" Carla screamed. She threw herself toward Morris, and Morris caught her and lifted her and shoved her across the table into Aaron.

THIRTY-TWO

THE TEMPORARY TRANSFER OF MANAGEMENT of Century National Bank had occurred, unofficially, on Sunday morning at nine-thirty in a special session of the eight sitting members of the board of directors. The members had met at the request of Wally Cogill from the Office of the Comptroller of the Currency, who had arrived at seven o'clock from Washington. There was no agenda. No reason for one. Wally Cogill had announced that the federal government would be operating the bank until "matters were resolved."

There had been only one question: "What are you going to do about the kidnapping issue?"

"Nothing," Wally Cogill had said bluntly. "This bank will not pay a ransom demand, regardless of the circumstances. That investigation is being handled by appropriate federal agencies, working with other law enforcement officials. That's all you need to know."

The meeting had lasted ten minutes.

At eleven-thirty, Philip Oglesbee met with the primary team of investigators assigned to finding Aaron Greene. The team had increased to twenty-five men and seven women, representing federal, state, county, and city forces. The meeting lasted until one o'clock, and by the notes Victor Menotti had taken, there were seven theories of

what might have happened, not counting his own speculation about Robert Lucas. Menotti had not offered the
Lucas theory. Menotti had said nothing at all. He had sat
beside Clifford Russell and listened and made notes. Menotti knew, without reason to know, that none of the
theories was correct. None of them would find Aaron
Greene. They would only make great memoranda-to-file,
a thick ass-padding for the Albatross when the mayor and
the governor and the media started finger-pointing, and
Clifford Russell would be as grateful for the protection of
the memoranda—"Look at what we've done!" would be
his cry—as he would have been for the safe delivery of
Aaron Greene.

The meeting ended with new teams assigned to chase
after the seven incorrect theories. Menotti was not assigned
to any of the teams. "Lieutenant Menotti will be coordi-
nating things with me," Philip Oglesbee had announced.
"If you get anything, contact either of us."

"Have those notes typed up for me by noon tomorrow," Clifford Russell ordered as he left Menotti alone
with the African Prince.

Neither man spoke until the conference room was
empty and the sound of voices in the corridor had faded
to silence.

"Want to take odds?" Philip asked.

"I don't think so," Menotti said. "Do you?"

Philip laughed easily. He folded a sheet of paper into a
paper airplane. "Well, it's better than sitting around with
our thumbs up our collective asses, but, no, I wouldn't
put any real money on anything." He sailed the paper
airplane the length of the conference table, watched it rise,
turn, then dive with a thud to the floor, smashing its needle
nose. "Could you believe the one about Aaron staging the
whole thing? Sometimes I wonder about our profession,
Victor."

"Yeah. Me, too," Menotti said wearily.

"Don't know why I should bitch about it, though,"

Philip continued. "You know how I spent my morning?"

"Not in church, unless you went early."

"You're right about that. Maybe that's where I should have been. Maybe I would have been better off. Maybe some divine wisdom would have popped up, rendering a miracle."

"So, where were you?"

"I was with two psychics," Philip answered.

"You're kidding?"

"Nope. There's a study going on in Washington about the use of psychics in finding the unfindable. I got a call from one of those boys. Said they'd appreciate it if I'd at least give it a shot, and they gave me a couple of names who mingle with the local spirits."

"Anything happen?"

Philip pulled out of his chair and poured a cup of cooked coffee and broke a stale doughnut in half. "I think one of them got a migraine," he said at last. "He went off babbling about stress. He called me later and told me he'd been trying to conjure Aaron up since the day he was kidnapped. Poor bastard. Feels like he's failed his calling. Said he couldn't see him, or sense him. The other one kept saying the only thing she could see was water. Said it was hot and bubbling. That was about it."

"Hell of a clue," Menotti said. "Maybe they've got him down at Warm Springs."

"And maybe they put him in a pot and boiled him. Maybe they're a bunch of cannibals," Philip said. He took a bite from the doughnut and chewed slowly.

"The boys in Washington will be disappointed," predicted Menotti.

"The boys in Washington will assume it was because of me," corrected Philip. "They swear by the power of the mind. I'm sure they must think my people practiced voodoo in some jungle in the Congo and therefore I refuse to cooperate with the more scientific approach to mysticism."

"Could be something to it, though," Menotti said. "I remember when I was a kid, there was a woman in our neighborhood who lost her diamond ring. Couldn't find it anywhere. She finally went to a fortune-teller—one of those operating out of a double-wide on the side of the road—and damned if she didn't tell her where it was. Under a rose bush the woman had planted."

"You suppose that double-wide's still in business?" Philip asked lightly.

"Wish I knew," Menotti replied. He stood, stretched. "I'd pay her a visit just to find out if I'm ever going to get to bed again."

Philip drank from the coffee. It was cold and bitter. "You look a little bushed," he said. "Go home. Get some rest."

"Maybe I will," Menotti said. "Nothing else I know to do."

"Give me your best guess," Philip said.

"My best guess? My best guess is we won't hear anything for a while. Maybe a week. Maybe a month. We know damn well the bank won't spring for the money—that was made clear this morning—and we know Pender's campaign couldn't come up with it, even if it didn't have strings attached."

"Will they kill him?" asked Philip.

Menotti thought for a moment. It was a question he had avoided. "I don't know," he said. "It's kind of strange, but they've never threatened to kill him. Do you realize that? They've said he was in jeopardy, that he may be found in an unexpected place, but they've never threatened death."

"That's true," Philip agreed. "I haven't thought about that."

"But I think they've got to do something," Menotti suggested. "They've made too much of a splash. Way it looks, the whole thing has to do with the bank. Somebody who got his balance screwed up and then got pissed off because the bank wouldn't take the blame." He shook his head. "If that's true, I know how he feels. I'm at the point with banks where I had rather deal with the ATM than with a teller. It's got a better personality."

"Theory number three, I think it was," Philip said. "Well, close to it." He paused and nodded agreement. "I think he's already dead, Victor."

"You could be right," agreed Menotti. "What about his parents? How are they holding up?"

Philip shook his head. "Not well. We had them on ice at one of the motels, but they missed being home, so I had Tito take them back. At least they now know the truth about the calls, and we've let some members of their synagogue in to help with that blight in human relations." He stretched his arms over his head, yawned, then added, "Someday, Victor, I'm going to get one of you Southern-bred Anglo-Saxon Protestants to explain just what the hell it is that's so damned irritating about the Jews."

"Better ask somebody who knows, then," Victor told him.

The African Prince laughed softly. "That's the point. I don't think anybody *does* know. It's just there. In the air, you know. But it's not the WASPs and the Jews, or the rednecks and the blacks, or the Asians and the Hispanics. Shit, Victor, it's everybody. I just don't understand why we make it so damn hard. Before God and the saints, I just don't understand it."

"Me either," Victor said.

There was irony to it, Morris thought. A collect call to Ewell Pender, and, yes, the old man would take the call. He would take the call and he would sound composed and righteous, but there would not be a lecture. Now it would be business.

Morris heard Ewell Pender's voice accept the charges on his private line, then: "Hello, Morris."

"I want you to listen to me," Morris said.

"Of course."

"Is this line clean?"

"Of course it is, or I wouldn't be talking to you."

"You know that I can and will dispose of the packages that I hold," Morris whispered. "If you want them back, and I know you do, I want the ten million."

"Are they well, Morris?"

"Yes."

"I think I should speak to one of them, just to verify it."

"You can't," Morris said. "I guess you just have to trust me."

There was a pause. The image of Ewell Pender sitting in his chair, the telephone close to his face, pondering, billowed in Morris's mind.

" 'Trust' is a strange word, don't you think?" Ewell Pender said. "But I am willing to do that. All right. You will have the money, but you must do two things. Today is Sunday. You must give me a day to put it together, and you must assure me that the boy and Carla will not be harmed."

"You can have the day. They won't be hurt," Morris said. "But I want something else, too."

"What do you want, Morris?"

"I want Alyse to deliver the money."

"No," Ewell Pender said firmly. "I will not do that."

"You want them to disappear?" Morris snapped.

"If you think to bargain with me, using a life for a life, you misjudge me, Morris. No, I will not do that. If you think you must dispose of them, that is your choice. If you do, you will forfeit the money and I assure you, for as long as I am alive, you will never have peace."

Morris squeezed the telephone angrily with his hand. He had driven east for two hours over the backroad ridges of the north Georgia mountains to make the call, in case the call was traced, and now he was tired. He cupped the mouthpiece and looked across the parking lot of the truck stop and cement-block motel. He saw a man wearing a cowboy hat walking from one of the rooms toward his truck.

"All right," he said, spitting the words into the telephone. "Get the money. Tomorrow."

"I'll have Oscar deliver it when we receive your instructions," Ewell Pender said.

"I don't care who brings it," Morris growled. "You've got twenty-four hours from right now. And I don't suppose there's any reason to warn you against going to the police."

"I think that would be foolish on my part, don't you?" Ewell Pender said.

"With what I could tell them, yes," Morris replied.

"Morris."

"What?"

"Why don't you bring them back tonight? Come home. We'll talk about this. Nothing will happen to you. I promise it."

"Nothing's going to happen to me," Morris said. He slapped the telephone into the cradle and stalked across the parking lot to the restaurant that separated the truck stop from the motel. In the restaurant he ordered coffee and sat at a remote table, away from a family still dressed for church. The family ate silently, as though mesmerized by the simple act of being in a restaurant. As he watched them, a quaint, unexpected sensation of pity fluttered through Morris. He shook it away and gazed out of the window. He needed two other things to complete what he had started, he thought. Two things that would make Ewell Pender bow in certain surrender. He needed some of the tapes of Cody Yates's voice, and he needed the one thing that Ewell Pender prized more highly than any of his possessions. He needed Alyse.

THIRTY-THREE

MILLIE YATES KNEW THAT WHEN ANXIOUS, she became annoyingly impatient. She had once taken a series of aptitude tests administered by a consultant psychologist, a cunning, dark-eyed, smiling, egocentric man hired by the hospital to evaluate management structure, and he had written two damning words on the front sheet of the results: *Too impatient.* In parentheses, he had added an editorial comment: (*Could be detrimental in corporate interpersonal relations.*) The analysis had angered Millie and she had stormed into the consultant's temporary office and had demanded a less negative summary. The consultant had merely smiled at her with a triumphant, you-just-proved-it smile, and Millie had retreated meekly to her own office to weep over her failure.

Millie could see her impatience in the face that gazed back at her from the mirror. There was an aura in the image—a thick, dusty aura, impenetrable and dangerous. And from within the aura, the face that Millie saw was angry and bitter.

Damn you, Cody, she thought. Damn you.

She shook her face from the image and the aura in the mirror and walked away to the kitchen and poured another glass of diet Coke and sat at the table. Why am I blaming Cody? she wondered. Habit. Of course. Habit. Cody had always been an easy excuse because Cody had been responsible for so many of her foul moods. But Cody was not the reason that she was now anxious and impatient. It was Sunday. Cody was with Sabrina.

She looked at the clock on the wall above the counter. Its digital numbers read 2:03; then, as she watched, the clock blinked to 2:04. Cody and Sabrina were at a movie or a shopping mall. They were laughing like children at play because they *were* children at play. It was not Cody's fault that Robert had called to cancel his afternoon date with her.

A surge of envy pulsed through Millie, filling her throat with a short, swallowing cry. She wanted to be with Cody and Sabrina, to laugh with them, to invade the privacy they shared with the gaiety of a warm secret. Damn Cody. Damn him. Why was he always there, always on the periphery of her emotions? She had divorced him, but she had never exorcised him. And, yes, damn it, it was possible to love two men. She loved Robert. Was certain she loved him. But she also loved Cody. It was as though she were possessed by dual personalities, by twin, quarreling selves joined with an umbilical cord too powerful to sever. One self loved one man, the other self loved another.

She picked up the glass and swirled the Coke and watched its lazy whirlpool, a miniature maelstrom, spin a cube of ice. At least Robert had never lied to her, she thought. Cody had. Cody still lied. He lied to disguise his nonchalant habits, his inattention to schedules and to the expectations other people imposed on him. His lies were gentle, almost childish stories, told with cleverness and with such grand exaggeration she had often laughed away her anger and resentment and had forgiven him with the same benevolent embrace she offered Sabrina.

Robert did not lie. She was certain he did not lie.

She moved restlessly from the kitchen table and stood by the window, gazing outside at the sunbright day. Damn you, Cody, she thought again. She picked up her purse and stalked quickly out the door.

It would surprise Robert to return to his home and discover it cleaned and orderly. If Robert had a fault, it was his casual attitude about his home. He did not clutter exactly—not as Cody cluttered—but he did not clean as thoroughly as she cleaned, especially in her impatient, energetic moods. She would clean his home and leave him a message. No. Not a message. A bill for services. She smiled as she drove. She had tormented Robert about getting a cleaning service, but he had always insisted that it was unnecessary and costly. "Soon," he had replied repeatedly. "Soon, I'll take a cleaning fever and put a shine on it, top to bottom. You'll think you're in a house of mirrors. It'll be that glittery." Soon had never arrived. Now she would surprise him and she would leave him a bill from Millie's Maid Service for a thousand dollars. She smiled again.

Robert had given her a key to his home two months earlier, a reluctant arrangement she had forced because she had waited one afternoon for a quick, passionate tryst, and she had complained to him that it was embarrassing to nod and smile to silver-haired neighbors strolling inquisitively past her car. He had given her the key with an awkward request not to use it except on their agreement. She had answered, "Why should I? I can always look at the four walls of my own home, if you're not going to be there." Then he had smiled and said, "If I know you're going to be there, it'll give me time to take down the pinups. Otherwise they might offend you."

Millie had never violated her pledge, but she had never wanted to surprise him, either.

He lived on the bubble of a cul-de-sac in a neighborhood of older, stately homes in Decatur, homes that were occupied by older, stately residents. Millie had seen only one child on the street, a solemn-faced young boy, who played silent, solitary games. She had often waved to him, but the boy had never returned her greeting. Once she had asked Robert about him and Robert had explained that the boy was deaf. "I've learned a little sign language and he visits me occasionally," Robert had said. "He's a great kid. I'm teaching him about the computer."

She slowed her car before entering the cul-de-sac, then stopped three houses away from his house. A car she did not recognize was parked in his driveway. Who's that? she wondered. An urge to turn her car and leave shivered through her. A chill. She sat peering at the car and the house, then picked up her cellular phone and punched the two-number code that would automatically dial Robert's home number. After the fourth ring she heard his voice: "Sorry for the machine voice, but I'm not available in person at the moment. Please leave a number after the beep and I'll get back to you." She pushed the kill button on the phone.

Maybe it's nothing, she thought, gazing at the car. A friend, or a client, who left his, or her, car, while he, or she, and Robert were away for a late lunch. She let a smile play over her lips. Better be a he, she thought.

It didn't matter. She was there. On a mission. She picked up her telephone and tapped in another two-number code for his cellular phone. Six rings later, she heard his voice again: "Please leave a message and I'll re-turn the call as soon as possible."

"You're an impossible man to find," Millie said in her chattering voice. "Just wanted to warn you that I decided to work off some energy by cleaning your home, but I see there's a car parked there. You and *someone* must be having a very late lunch, and if that someone is of the female variety, you'd better wait until I leave before you return." She paused, then added, "Whether you know it or not, I am the jealous, insecure type. Talk to you later."

She eased her car forward and parked in front of the

house and got out of the car and crossed the walkway to the door. The young deaf boy was sitting in a lawn chair under an oak in the yard across from Robert's home. She waved. The boy looked away. She unlocked the door and stepped inside.

The house was dim and cool and the still, captured air of the rooms had the faint odor of a man's cologne. She turned on the lights in the entryway. Strange, she thought. Why does he have all the curtains pulled? The house needs sunlight. She went to the dining-room windows and opened the curtains and raised the windows, and then she paused at the dining-room table. A film of dust coated the slick mahogany finish. She wrote in the dust with her finger: *Clean me before serving Millie.* She would clean everything except the table. He would see the message and smile, she thought. He would smile and immediately wipe away the dust. Cody would have laughed and left it alone.

She saw the man standing in the doorway of the family room as she turned from the table. A gasp flew from her throat. She stepped back.

The man laughed. "I'm sorry," he said. "There's just no way to keep from startling someone when you're in this situation."

Millie touched the wall with her hand. Her heart was thundering. She could not speak.

"Really, I'm sorry," the man said, stepping toward her. "But there's no reason to be afraid. You're Millie Yates, aren't you?"

Millie nodded. The man seemed familiar.

"I'm Morris Raines," the man said. "I'm Mr. Pender's chauffeur. I saw you at the reception we had, but we didn't meet."

"Oh," Millie whispered. She flicked a smile, glanced over his shoulder.

Morris smiled pleasantly. "Robert's not here. I just dropped by to pick up a few things."

Millie remembered unlocking the front door. "How—did you get in?" she asked.

"The back door was open," Morris answered easily. "I thought I'd have to sit around, waiting for him, but the door was open."

Millie again flicked a smile.

"Are you meeting him here?" asked Morris.

"No," she said hesitantly. "I—thought I'd surprise him and clean the house. But I can come back."

"No reason for that," Morris said. A broad smile flashed on his face. "I'm just leaving, and, to be honest, the place needs a cleaning. Especially his office. Boxes everywhere."

"His office?" Millie said. It was a question of surprise. The door to his office was always closed and locked. "It's a mess," Robert had explained once when she asked about it. "I keep it locked because of all the equipment I've got in there. Keeps people from toying with it, you know." And she had never inquired again about it. It did not matter what he had in his office, or how it looked. In fact, she envied him. If she could lock her own home office from intruders, she would. In her home, such a policy would have been treated with blatant disregard. Cody and Sabrina would have taken the door off its hinges merely to break rules and have fun.

Morris laughed softly, a friendly easy laugh. "I know. He's the kind of man you think of as having order, everything in its place. What's the saying? A cluttered mind, a clean office? Or is it a cluttered office, a clean mind? Something like that."

An uncomfortable pause simmered between them.

"I—" Millie began. Her voice was broken by the sharp ringing of the telephone. She glanced toward the sound and then back to Morris. She saw the smile disappear from his face.

"That's probably Robert," she said. "I left him a message, telling him I'd be here."

"I'll let you answer it," Morris said after a moment. "I never answer anyone else's phone."

"Yes," Millie whispered. She rushed past him to the kitchen and lifted the telephone from its wall stand and said, "Hello."

"Millie?" Robert said anxiously. "I got your message. There's a car at my house?"

"Yes," Millie replied. She turned toward Morris, then away. "Morris."

"Morris?"

"He said he had to pick up a couple of things."

Robert did not reply.

"Are you there?" asked Millie.

"Yes, yes, I'm sorry," Robert said quickly. "Listen, do me a favor, will you? Jump in your car and meet me at Lenox Square—no, make it Park Place, across from Perimeter Mall. In the courtyard. We'll get some coffee or tea at Intermezzo. I've got a short break."

"Now?"

"Right now," Robert urged. "Forget the house. I know it's a mess. I've been going through some old files."

"How long do you have?"

"Long enough for a leisurely cup of hot tea and a hug," Robert said. He added, "I need both."

Millie had never heard him sound so defenseless. In an odd way, he sounded like Cody in Cody's weaker moments. "Fine," she said.

"Leave now—please."

"I will," she promised.

"Is Morris still there?"

"Yes. He was just getting ready to leave, though."

"Let me talk to him for a moment," Robert said, "but you leave now. Don't wait to be polite."

"I'll see you in a half hour or so," Millie said. She turned back to Morris and offered the phone. "He wants to speak to you."

The smile eased back into Morris's face. "Thanks," he said, taking the phone.

"I'm going to run," Millie told him. "We're meeting for tea." She smiled. "Good to see you."

"It was good to see you again," Morris said. He cupped his palm over the mouthpiece of the phone and watched her hurry from the house. Then he lifted the phone to his ear. "Pretty woman," he mused. "Maybe I should keep her around for security."

"That's a threat that won't work, Morris," Robert said evenly. "You're not that stupid."

Morris sighed a laugh. "You're right, I'm not," he admitted. "My hands are full enough at the moment. Still, it's a thought. Yes, a thought."

"What are you doing there?" Robert demanded.

"I thought I'd pick up a few tapes for—well, a safety net," Morris answered. "Sorry about the back door and the door to your office."

"Where are they?" Robert asked.

"They?"

"Carla and Aaron."

"Oh, they're safe. Maybe a little uncomfortable, but safe."

For a long moment, Robert did not speak, and then he said slowly, "You know you can't do this, Morris."

"But I am," Morris replied calmly.

"If they're harmed, in any way, you know what will happen."

"You sound like the old man," Morris said.

"And, like him, I'm asking you to bring them home."

"I don't think so," Morris said. "Anyway, it's time to go. But before I do, I want you to hear something."

"What?"

"Be patient."

Morris put the telephone on the kitchen counter and moved swiftly through the house to Robert's office. The room was crowded with boxes and computer equipment on a computer table. He yanked back the top of one of the boxes and pulled an audiocassette tape from it. He turned the tape in his hand and studied the row of numbers penciled on the cover of the plastic holder. The coded numbers were 723/729. Seventh month, twenty-third day through seventh month, twenty-ninth day. Morris smiled, tapped the tape from its holder, and then slipped it into a cassette player that had been placed next to the computer. He picked up the telephone to Robert's fax machine. "For your listening pleasure," he cooed. "Just remember, I have some of these." He pushed the play button, placed the phone near it, then turned and left the house casually, whistling.

Robert heard the distinctive ringing of a telephone— three rings—jarring from the speaker of the cassette player, and then the sound of a telephone being lifted. Then he heard Millie's voice.

"Hello."

And he heard Cody say, *"Hi, what's up?"*

"What's up, Cody? My temper. You were supposed to call last night."

"Sorry, love. Got caught up down at the station trying to get some information on a drug bust that went bad."

"Don't play coy with me, Cody. You could have found a phone."

"I'm sorry. Really. The time just slipped by on me. How's Sabrina?"

"Oblivious to you, thank God. She's out playing."

"Come on, Millie. Goddamn it, I didn't call to get my ass chewed on again. Do you still want me to switch weekends with you?"

"Yes. I've got that conference at Callaway Gardens."

"Good. That's all I need to know. Tell Sabrina I'll pick her up early Saturday morning. That's day after tomorrow, by my calendar."

"Before eight, Cody. I mean it."

"Before eight."

Robert heard the clicking end of the conversation. His hand trembled as he closed his cellular phone.

THIRTY-FOUR

MORRIS HAD HANDCUFFED EACH OF THEM, with one end of the handcuffs snapped over a wrist and the other end looped through heavy trace chains that he had nailed high and secure on opposite walls of the log cabin. The chains were no more than eight feet long, enough length to sit on the floor against the wall, but not to move about the cabin.

"Try all you want," Morris had said of the chains before leaving, "but you'll never pull them off the wall."

"I know him," Carla had said to Aaron in an empty voice. "He wouldn't leave us like this if he thought we could escape."

They had slumped to the floor, opposite one another, and for a very long time they did not speak. Inside the cabin, it was still cold. Outside, a light wind billowed under the heavy limbs of hemlock and pine, and the sound of the wind was the sound of a sigh. The midafternoon sun streamed through two of the windows in a pattern dappled by the trees.

"Are you angry with me?" Carla said at last.

Aaron shook his head. "No," he mumbled.

"It's not true—what he said," Carla whispered. "I'm not a whore. They didn't find me that way. He just said that to make you feel bad."

"It's—all right," Aaron told her.

"I need for you to believe me, Aaron."

"I do." His voice was weak, barely audible.

"It doesn't sound that way."

"I do," Aaron repeated, more strongly.

"I hope so," Carla said. She looked toward the door. "I'm sorry about the tape," she added quietly. "I didn't know about it. I swear to you I didn't. But I'm glad we made love, Aaron. Are you?"

Aaron bowed his head and gazed at the floor. He did not answer.

"I don't want you to be ashamed," Carla said. "Nothing is as beautiful as making love, especially when it's with someone you care about. And I do care about you, Aaron." She paused, inhaled slowly. "More than I thought I would. I think I knew so much about you before we— before you came to us—that I liked you. I liked you a lot, but I didn't know that it would be different when I met you."

Aaron looked up at her. "How?" he asked.

"You needed me," Carla said softly. "I don't know why I believe that, but I do. Or maybe it wasn't that. Maybe it was just me. Maybe I needed you to need me. It's hard to explain, Aaron. It really is. The world I've lived in for the past few years has everything to do with that—with understanding what it means to be needed. All of us believe that. Or, I thought all of us did. Morris doesn't. He couldn't. Doing what he's done, he couldn't believe it. But Morris was always more like a shadow than a person. I've always been afraid of him."

"Me, too," Aaron said in a small voice.

"But he did say one thing that was true," Carla admitted, "and I have to tell you about it, so there will never be anything secret between us."

"What?" asked Aaron.

"When we made love: I was supposed to do that. Or something like it. I was supposed to make you trust me, because if you trusted me, it would not be as easy for you to tell the police about us when you were released. And you were going to be released. I promise you. That was always in the plan."

Aaron did not reply. He raised his shackled hand and rubbed his face. His body felt drained, exhausted.

"But I would have done what I did even if it hadn't been part of the plan," Carla said. "I would have. Because I wanted to, Aaron." She paused, then added, "Would you like me to tell you everything? From the beginning?"

"Yes," Aaron said.

"I will," Carla promised, "but I want you to do something for me first."

"What?"

"I want you to say your name."

A puzzled expression crossed Aaron's face.

"Say 'Aaron Greene.' "

"Aaron Greene," Aaron said quietly.

"No, Aaron. I don't want you to whisper it. I want you to say it aloud. I want you to remember that you're somebody. You're Aaron."

"Aaron Greene," Aaron said again, his voice raised slightly.

"That's still a whisper," Carla insisted. "You're more than a nobody. You're a *somebody*. You're Aaron. Say it aloud. Scream it."

"Aaron Greene," Aaron called.

"That's it," Carla cheered. "Do it again, Aaron. Do it again."

"Aaron Greene!" Aaron shouted. He could feel the strain of his voice in his throat, a tender aching. And he began to weep over the sound of his name.

"All right," Carla said gently. "Now I'll tell you."

On the days that he spent with Sabrina—days of shameless extravagance at shopping malls and movie theaters and restaurants—Cody was left always with an oppressive feeling of guilt and of failure. It did not matter how much money he allocated for their excursions together, he could not assuage the sense of loss that shadowed him to the car when he left her, smiling and waving, at the door of the home that had once been a place of family. He knew he could not ransom the periods of separation from her, yet he could not deny the laughing-pouting wishes of the child who made him giddy with joy.

"You've got to quit giving her everything she wants," Millie complained.

"It was just a stuffed animal, for God's sake. She collects them."

"Who told you that?" asked Millie.

"She did," Cody said. "She said she'd been collecting stuffed bears for a long time."

Millie sighed in disbelief. "Do you know why I worry about her being with you, Cody? It's because you're so damn gullible. She gets anything she wants from you, and then I have to play the villain by saying no to her. She does not collect stuffed bears. The one you bought her today is the only one she has."

"Maybe I misunderstood her," Cody said defensively. "Maybe she said she wanted to *start* collecting them. I think that was it, in fact."

"You're lying, Cody. You take her off for one Sunday afternoon and bring her back and she's a terror. It'll take me a week to get her back to normal. You know what she's doing right now? She's next door, telling Judy Hill's little girl that you're going to buy her a Mercedes or something equally ridiculous. She'll claim you paid a thousand dollars for that bear."

Cody kept the smile of pride from his face. He could not keep it from his eyes. He said, "Pretty close. And it's a BMW, not a Mercedes."

"You're funny, Cody. You're very, very funny."

Cody nibbled at the apple pie Millie had served him. It was hot and spicy with cinnamon. And it was also a signal that Millie was disturbed. She baked only to work off anger or frustration.

"Good pie," he said casually. "Still wish you had joined us for dinner."

"Pizza? God, Cody."

"Yeah. Well, it was a little heavy, but that's what Sabrina wanted. It's not my fault if she's developed such common tastes. I'm not the one who lives with her on a daily basis."

"Cody, it's all your fault. She's got your genes."

"Thanks. Now, tell me: Why are you pissed?"

"Me? I'm not."

"Of course you are. The pie's superb. That's a sure sign."

A blush bloomed quickly over Millie's face. She often forgot how well Cody knew her. "It's nothing important," she said.

"Robert didn't show up, did he?" Cody said.

Millie got up from the chair at the table and crossed to the coffeepot and poured another cup of coffee.

"Am I right?" pressured Cody.

"It's none of your business, but no, he didn't. I met him for tea. He was busy. Writing a new program for one of his clients or something like that." She poured fresh coffee into her cup and Cody's cup.

"Who's the client?"

"How should I know?" Millie answered in a testy voice. "He was upset about it, that's all I know. We were supposed to go to a movie and then to early dinner."

Cody finished the pie and swallowed some coffee. He watched Millie as she stared out of the kitchen window, a fragile, preoccupied look clouding her face, and he thought of Menotti's rambling Waffle House scenario about Robert Lucas. It was foolish babbling, but Cody had not been completely able to dismiss it. If he lived by his instincts and they were often right, how could he doubt Menotti's instincts? Menotti's instincts had kept him alive.

But Menotti had been tired and the pressure of doubting himself over the death of Jason Littlejohn had skewed his thinking.

"How well do you know him?" Cody asked gently.

"What does that mean?" Millie countered.

"Not what you think. I'm not prying into your night life. We made that a promise, and we've abided by it. No, love, I mean how well do you *really* know him? You looked surprised that he was so familiar with everyone and everything at the Pender estate."

Millie sat again at the table. She took Cody's empty plate and stacked the one with her own half-eaten portion on top of it. She did not want to talk about Robert Lucas. She said, after a moment, "I don't know where you get that. I've always known he worked for Ewell Pender. It's one of his best accounts. At least, I think it is. If anything surprised me about that night, it was the fact that he did seem to know everyone there, like you said."

"But if he works there, he should, don't you think?"

"I guess. Why are you asking me all these questions, Cody?"

Cody wanted to tell her of Menotti's theory about Robert Lucas, but he knew it would erupt into an argument. He said, instead, "Just curious. We've never talked about it. When did you meet him?"

"I told you before. Almost two years ago," Millie answered. "The hospital had hired him to link our records with medical records. I dreaded it, but Robert was so pleasant it turned out to be a good experience. We talked a lot, and then, one day, after he'd finished the job, he invited me to dinner. I guess you could say that was the start of it."

"Did he know that we had been married?"

Millie took a swallow of coffee from her cup, looking away from Cody's gaze. "He was most impressed," she said, after a moment. "He said he thought you were a splendid writer." She turned her eyes back to him.

"You're still a star, Cody, but I don't think you need to ask anything else about Robert."

"Just jealous," he said. He flicked a smile toward her and winked.

"You? Come on, Cody. I did meet Freda Graves, if you remember. I doubt if you spend very much time being jealous over Robert." She looked at him suspiciously. "I thought the two of you had been conducting a cold war for the past several years."

"I was forced to take her," Cody said meekly. "Harry's orders."

Millie cracked a laugh. "Sure you were, Cody. I also know you, and I can tell you that the cold war probably melted into a puddle after she showed up in that hot little number she was wearing. Don't you think it was a little obvious?"

"I thought it was—well, interesting," Cody replied. "But I thought the same about you."

"Flattery will not put off the question, Cody."

"What question?"

"Have you negotiated a peace treaty? And if you have, is it an 'ea' or an 'ie' agreement?"

"You're getting vulgar, Millie. That doesn't become you," Cody said.

"I'm sorry. You're right. It was vulgar. I'm sure she's a nice person. She has to be, to write the way she writes. It's none of my business what goes on between the two of you."

"It's not, but I'll answer it anyway. Yes, we are more friendly than we have been. She's a different person outside the newsroom. The two of you are alike in many ways—very likable ways."

"Jesus, Cody, spare me," Millie said, looking away. "I don't care to know the graphic details. I have an overactive imagination as it is."

"Fine. By the way, did you catch the early news?"

"Yes," Millie said. She added peevishly, "I had nothing else to do."

"Anything of interest on the kidnapping?" Cody asked.

"There was something about that lawyer's suicide and his calls to the Greenes, and something about the bank affirming that it wouldn't come up with the money and something else on the charges against Landon. Some agency's taking over operation tomorrow. And there was still something else about an announcement expected from Pender."

"That's a lot of something," Cody said, teasing.

"You asked me. And quit making fun of me."

"Couldn't resist it," Cody told her. He rose from his chair. "Pender's full of surprises for an old man. I think I'd better drop by the newsroom." He leaned to Millie and kissed her lightly on the forehead. "Thanks for letting me spoil her, love. I'm sorry you have to mop up after me."

"It's all right, Cody."

"I love you," Cody said softly.

"And I love you, too. Now, leave me alone. I also love my misery."

It was twenty minutes before nine o'clock when Cody arrived at the newspaper. He knew there would only be a skeletal crew in the newsroom. Sunday-quiet people, people who moved about like shadows, happy for the peace they found in the off-day atmosphere. He found Olin McArthur at his desk, reading from the monitor of his computer.

"Well, there you are," Olin said with surprise. "You really do need a beeper, Cody." He punched the screen blank.

"What's up?" Cody asked.

"You know about the bank, I suppose," Olin replied.

"About the feds taking over? Yep, sure do."

"And about the firm 'no' on the money for the boy?"

"What I expected. Didn't you?"

"It's the only thing they can do, Cody, no matter what any of us think about it. You know that."

"I know," Cody said heavily. "I feel for the boy and for his family. They're good people. Christ, they're good people."

"Pender made an announcement about an hour ago. That's why I was trying to reach you."

"What'd he say?" asked Cody.

"He's requesting people to stop sending in contributions, since the last tape warned that it wanted the money from the bank. He's also inviting the kidnappers to negotiate directly with him—without interference from law enforcement. My guess is he's ready to take the hit himself."

"All ten million?" Cody said.

"Discounting what's already been raised," Olin answered. "He didn't say that, but I think that's what he's planning."

Cody whistled softly and shook his head. "Wake up Ewell Pender. When he wants to make a point, he makes it, doesn't he? How did he make the announcement? In person?"

"Sort of a news release. More like a letter. He had his assistant deliver it."

"Alyse Burton?" asked Cody.

"Yes. I met her at the party. Very pleasant," Olin said.

"Then you haven't been out to the estate?"

"Not today," Olin told him. "I went out yesterday morning when the police were looking around. Why?"

"You remember a large, bearded fellow? Jovial type. Robert Lucas."

"The man with Millie?"

"Yes," Cody said. "The man with Millie. Was he at the estate yesterday?"

Olin's brow wrinkled in thought. "I think he was. Why do you ask?"

"No reason in particular," Cody confessed. "Just wondered. I didn't know he was associated with Pender until the party."

"Any problems?" asked Olin.

"No. Not really. Just one of those odd circumstances."

"The world's a small place full of small events, Cody," Olin advised. He smiled. "Especially when it comes to an ex-wife, I imagine."

"That's an understatement," Cody admitted. "Well, I've got to go. Leave us something to nibble on tomorrow."

"After your story today on Littlejohn, I think I'll even keep the crumbs, Cody."

From a telephone in the lobby of the Journal-Constitution Building, Cody called Freda and explained that he was working.

"How late?" Freda asked. She sounded impatient, or anxious.

"Maybe another hour, maybe longer," Cody told her.

"Are you coming over?"

"Just waiting for the invitation."

"I'll be here. I've missed you today," Freda said quietly.

Cody did not know why he had the sudden compulsion to drive to the Pender estate. He did not want to see Ewell Pender or Alyse Burton or anyone else. He wanted only to be there. Or maybe he was lying to himself. Maybe being at the Pender estate had nothing to do with Aaron Greene. Maybe it was his curiosity about Robert Lucas. Would Robert Lucas be at the mansion? And if so, why? Another coincidence in the small events of a small world?

From the narrowing of the road leading past the estate, Cody could see bubbles of lights covering the grounds and the buildings. He parked his car on the side of the road and got out and crossed a shallow roadside ditch and moved along the massive, clipped front lawn, staying in the shadows of the tree line. He stopped beside an oak with powerful, hanging limbs and stared at the house. A quick flicker of memory, of standing in the woods at Jason Littlejohn's cabin, passed through him, and a smile lifted his lips. He was doing it again: spying. He could see lights from windows of the Pender mansion, and he moved closer, staying in the trees, then he stopped suddenly and lifted his head. He could hear the faint, distant sound of a piano. The music was forceful, commanding. Cody stood, listening, until the music stopped abruptly, ending on a note as absolute as death. Around him, from the trees, he could hear the piercing hum of night bugs, so shrill the sounds seemed to scream from inside his head.

A side door at the mansion opened and a woman that Cody knew immediately as Alyse Burton stepped outside and crossed slowly under the lights covering the grounds to a bench in a small, oval garden. She sat on the bench and lowered her head and wrapped her arms to her body. After a moment, she stood and moved back toward the house, pausing to bend over and pick something up from the lawn, something too small for Cody to see from his distance.

Cody stayed only a few minutes longer. A chill swam on the dark surface of night, making the night seem old and tired. Like me, Cody thought. Old and tired. He moved quietly away, back along the path he had taken from the road. He did not see the man standing in the black pit of tree shadows thirty feet from him.

THIRTY-FIVE

———————◆———————

MORRIS WATCHED CODY'S CAR TURN IN THE road and leave. He looked at his watch. It was nine-fifty. In ten minutes, the outside floodlights would automatically turn off, leaving only dim pools of landscape lights to play ghostily over the grounds. Unless, of course, Robert had deprogrammed the system. Morris smiled confidently. No, he thought. Robert believed in order and habit. Robert would not bother with the system, because Robert—because none of them—would think of him returning to the mansion with so much at stake. Yet, it was a risk worth taking. He had the tapes, but having Alyse with him would force the old man not to play tricks. The old man would not toy with Alyse's life.

The night was cool in the tricky way of Southern spring weather, and Morris turned up the collar of his pea jacket. He thought of Aaron and Carla in the cabin. They would be cold. Shivering cold, even with the blankets he had thrown at each of them before leaving. He should have tied them together, body to body. Should have taken their clothes from them and tied them together nude and let them try to keep warm from body heat on the floor of the cabin. A grin broke on his face, and he wiped at it with his hand. Patience. He had to have patience. He pulled the suppressor from his pocket and fastened it to the barrel of his 9mm.

At ten o'clock, the floodlights covering the grounds snapped off, leaving the grounds in deep shadows, accented only by landscape lights, but Morris knew where the lights were and he knew the shadows. He studied the house. There were lights in the kitchen and in the downstairs study. On the second floor, he saw the lighted window of Alyse's bedroom. He knew Robert was not at the mansion. He had seen Robert leave earlier. To be with the woman, he guessed. Robert was always with the woman. He wondered if the woman would ever discover the truth—that Robert had suggested using Cody Yates's voice after meeting his ex-wife at the hospital. At first, it had been a smiled-at joke, patiently endured by the old man. Only the joke had turned like a twirling boomerang. Robert had fallen in love with Millie Yates, and that announcement had very nearly stopped the project. Would have if the old man had not been so committed to Robert, and if he had not admired Cody Yates. Still, it had worked. Cody Yates's voice provided mystery and mystery provided attention.

From where he stood, Morris knew he could not see the rooms that Ewell Pender and Oscar occupied. It did not matter. He knew their habits. They were harmless old men. Their habits never changed.

He began a slow, deliberate walk toward the house, staying close to the trees. He crossed in the cover of shadows to the small oval garden where Alyse had been and hunched down beside a bush and watched the house. He could see the movement of Alyse behind the sheer curtain covering her window. Excitement pumped in his chest. He had watched Alyse and Carla dozens of times, carelessly undressing behind their curtains, their nimble bodies moving like silhouettes in dance. Taking Alyse would be easy. She would fear the gun, and she would fear for the safety of Aaron and Carla. She would go quietly and quickly. He stood and began striding across the lawn to the house.

The door leading into the study opened easily to his

key. He reached for the light switch and turned off the light, then slipped across the room to the door leading into the kitchen. He pulled at the door soundlessly and peered through the wedge of the opening. He did not see Maria. Good, he thought. Good. She's in her room. He stepped into the kitchen and turned off the light, then crossed it and opened the door leading to the back stairwell. The stairs led to the corridor outside the suite of rooms occupied by Alyse. Morris paused and listened. He could hear the muted playing of Latin music from Maria's downstairs bedroom, and the smile broke again on his face. She would not hear him. He mounted the stairs and opened the corridor door slightly. He did not see anyone. He eased into the corridor and crept along the wall, his gun raised. Twenty feet down the corridor, he stopped at Alyse's suite. He drew in a deep, full breath and placed his hand on the knob and turned it and pushed the door open and stepped inside.

His eyes scanned the room in a flash. Alyse was near her bed at the window. She wore a terry-cloth robe pulled tight to her body. Her hair was damp, gleaming from the light of the room. Her face had the just-showered freshness of a young girl's. Ewell Pender was sitting in the wheelchair he occasionally used, close to an ornate desk. A small blanket—an afghan—covered his lap and legs. Why is he here? Morris wondered.

"Morris—" Alyse said in surprise.

Morris waved the gun in front of him. "Stay there," he ordered.

"What are you doing?" Alyse asked.

"Shut up," Morris hissed. He could feel his face flaming with heat.

"Morris," Ewell Pender said in a quiet voice. "Put away the gun. Talk to me."

Morris pivoted to the voice.

"Put it away," Ewell Pender said again.

The gun in Morris's hand quivered.

"Did you bring them back?" asked Ewell Pender.

A short, hard laugh broke in Morris's throat. He licked his lips, glanced back to Alyse. "Not yet," he sneered. "I thought they needed company."

"And I thought we had an agreement."

"We do," Morris snapped.

"Then why are you here?"

For a moment, Morris did not answer. Then he said, "For an insurance policy."

"Alyse, you mean?"

Morris grinned in answer.

"I can't let you do that."

"I don't think you're in any position to stop it," Morris said.

"Do you want the money, Morris?" Alyse asked angrily.

Morris swept the gun toward Alyse.

"If you do, then leave," she ordered. "Now. This very minute. You can't get it if I go with you."

Morris laughed again. "Oh, I think so."

"No," Alyse said. She paused, glared at him, then turned her face to look at Ewell Pender. "I know my—husband," she said slowly. "He will not let you take me. You would have to kill him, and then there would be nothing. You know that."

Morris's face jerked in surprise. "Husband?" He whirled to face Ewell Pender.

The old man smiled gently, nodded once.

"Does that surprise you, Morris?" asked Alyse.

"It's a lie," Morris growled.

"I'm pleased to tell you it's not," Ewell Pender said. "It's been our secret. Now you share it." He crossed his hands in his lap, looked at Alyse, smiled again. "Two years ago, when we went to Nevada on business." He looked back at Morris. "Of course, it's a marriage with—certain agreements." He coughed softly, touched his chest with his hand. "You really must learn to be more observant, Morris. We've talked about the meaning of possibility so many times, and still you haven't learned. Reality exists in every possibility."

"I—don't believe you," Morris stammered.

The old man rested his head against the pillowed back of the wheelchair. An amused expression played on his face. "That's better," he said. "And you may be right. It's a possibility that I'm lying." He turned to Alyse. "That we're lying," he amended.

"Why do you think we've done what we've done?" Alyse said harshly. "For amusement? My husband . . ." She paused, then continued, "My husband wants to be certain that someone can continue what he started, that someone cares enough to take great risks. He wants to know that there are people who will stand with me. Taking Aaron was not a game, Morris. It had—it *has*—purpose. What you're doing is a game, and you're a fool." She stepped toward him.

"Get back," Morris snapped.

"No, you get out," Alyse ordered angrily.

The gun flashed toward Alyse in a sudden motion of Morris's hand, and he pulled the trigger. A spitting pop echoed in the room and he heard the shattering of window glass. He glanced at the gun in disbelief. He had missed her.

"Morris!" The shout from Ewell Pender was strong, demanding.

Morris fell instinctively to the floor, swinging the gun toward the voice. He pulled the trigger once and saw Ewell Pender's throat flower in a brilliant red. He saw the old man slump back into his chair, his head thrown up, his eyes open, his mouth moving in an involuntary begging for air.

Morris stood slowly, his eyes holding on Ewell Pender. A great surge of pity and sorrow flooded him. Ewell Pender had been the only father figure he had ever known, and now he had killed him. He looked at Alyse, his face contorted in bewilderment.

From the hallway, he heard a crying voice, and he turned. It was Maria, standing in the doorway. Her hands covered her face, and the shrill scream in her throat was muffled by her fingers. Morris raised the gun and fired twice, and Maria slammed against the wall of the corridor and rolled clear of the door.

He stood, trembling, holding the gun tight in both hands. He shook his head numbly. He had killed them. He had killed them. So sudden. He had not wanted to kill anyone, but he could not stop his finger on the trigger. His finger had moved and they were dead. He glanced again at Alyse. She stood frozen, her eyes locked on him in disbelief.

"I—" Morris mumbled. He stepped back into the corridor. He thought he could hear a soft escape of air from Ewell Pender's throat.

"Morris." The voice was from the end of the corridor.

Morris knew the voice. It was old and cultivated. Oscar. He pivoted his body slowly. He could see Oscar standing with the erect, perfect bearing of the proud servant.

"Morris," Oscar said again. He took a step toward Morris.

Morris tried to raise his hands, but could not. He stared in astonishment at the gun he held. He could not lift it. His hands trembled and a short, skittering laugh rippled in his throat. He let his hands fall to his side, then he rolled his body against the corridor wall and rushed toward the stairs.

He heard Oscar bellowing his name: "Morris!"

Robert Lucas was tired. The muscles of his back ached from the tedious work of erasing the contents of the audiotape cassettes of Cody Yates's voice with a magnetic eraser. Detail. It was detail. The boxes were being bound with a clear adhesive tape and would be moved to a landfill where they would be covered along with the tons of trash that were dumped daily for burial. Keeping the tapes had been a great mistake.

The ringing of the telephone—jarring, unexpected—startled him. It was late. Too late even for Millie to call. He answered on the third ring.

"Mr. Lucas?" Oscar said.

"Yes," Robert answered.

"I think you should return to the estate," Oscar said calmly. "There's been some trouble."

THIRTY-SIX

——◆——

INSIDE THE CABIN, IT WAS COLD, THE WINTER of February lingering late into March, and though they had wrapped themselves in the blankets that Morris had left them, Aaron and Carla quivered from the chilling air that seeped into the cabin.

They had not talked for two hours, or longer, except for occasional mumbled questions, asked only to break the numbing silence, questions that were as simple as "Are you asleep?"

They were not conscious of the hour, for the room did not have a clock and Morris had taken Carla's wristwatch and put it into a counter drawer, studying it suspiciously as though the watch contained a secret transmitting device beaming distress signals. The hour was late, but the hour did not matter; the fact that Morris had not returned did.

"Something's happened, hasn't it?" asked Aaron.

"I don't know," Carla admitted. Then: "He'll be back— soon." Her voice was forced and it betrayed her. She did not want Aaron to know how frightened she was. "You know what we need?" she added in a rush. "A hairpin. Maybe we could work the locks on the handcuffs if we had a hairpin. I saw that in a movie one time." She ran her hand through her hair and laughed a hollow, skittish laugh. "I always thought movies like that were dumb. How long do you think it would take to pick a lock with

371

a hairpin if you've never done it before? Hours. But in the movies, they do it in about two seconds."

Aaron pushed his back against the wall, pulling the blanket up around his neck. He said, "I saw a movie one time where somebody used soap on their hand to slip out of handcuffs. It was a funny-looking hand, though. Kind of long and thin. I don't think it was real. Maybe it was plastic."

"I've been trying that—without the soap," Carla told him. "Doesn't work."

"Me too," Aaron said.

They sat in the silence of the dark room for a few minutes, listening to night sounds outside the cabin. It was not easy to tell if the night sounds were from the breeze raking through limbs or from singing bugs. Both, Aaron thought. Bugs mimicking the wind, knowing the wind had begun to tease spring from the ground and, later, would drag summer out of the valleys and leave it drying on the new-green tips of hemlocks growing high in the mountains.

"What time do you think it is?" Aaron asked.

"I don't know. What do you think?" Carla answered.

"Midnight," Aaron guessed. "Maybe one, or two. It's been dark a long time."

"It's getting colder," Carla said.

"You want my blanket?" asked Aaron. "I can throw it to you."

"No," Carla insisted. "I'm all right." She paused, peeked at Aaron from the cover of the blanket. "Did I tell you? You're a very warm person," she added softly. "I mean—touching you. You're warm."

After a moment, Aaron said, "You, too."

Carla leaned her head against the rough log wall and gazed at Aaron. She knew he was afraid, but he did not act afraid, or sound afraid. She knew also that he believed her story of his abduction—it had been the truth, or as much of the truth as she had understood—and she knew that he would not betray them. Ewell Pender had said Aaron would look weak, but, at the end, he would not be. At the end, Aaron Greene would be a warrior.

He did not look like a warrior, bundled in a thin blanket. She could see his legs shaking from the cold.

"I don't remember," Carla said. "Did you ever use the hot tub?"

Aaron shook his head. "No."

"It'd feel good now," Carla suggested.

Aaron did not reply.

"We'll do that," promised Carla. "When this is over, we'll do it. You're going to love it, Aaron. Makes your body tingle, and when you get out, it's like you've got a cloud of steam clinging to you. I remember seeing Alyse one night from my room. It was cold outside and she'd been in the hot tub and then she got out and walked across the garden, and the steam was clinging to her. She looked like a ghost."

Aaron moved against the wall, and the chain leading from the handcuffs clattered softly. He stood and looked out the window.

"What is it?" Carla asked.

Aaron lifted his hand toward her in a signal.

"You see something?" she whispered. She stood.

"I—don't know," Aaron told her. "I thought I heard—" He paused, tilted his head to look in another direction. "Maybe it was just—"

Carla saw his head jerk in surprise, saw him step away from the window.

"What is it?" she asked anxiously.

"I saw somebody," he answered.

"Where?"

"On the road. Coming this way."

Aaron stepped against the wall, his back to it. He could feel his heart thundering. His arms and knees were shaking violently.

The sound of a key slipping into the doorlock echoed

faintly in the cabin, and then the door opened and Morris stepped inside and closed the door. He flicked on a flashlight and swept its beam across the cabin, first to Carla and then to Aaron. He did not speak.

"We're cold," Carla said. "And hungry."

Morris gazed at her, then lifted a paper sack that he had in his hand. "I got some food," he told her. "I'll start a fire."

"Take us off the chains first," Carla insisted. "I've got to go to the bathroom."

Morris bobbed his head once. He reached for the wall switch and turned on the cabin lights, and then he went to Carla and unlocked the handcuff binding her to the chain.

"Aaron, too," Carla said.

Morris shrugged. "Sure," he said. "Why not? You're not going anywhere. You don't even want to think about it." He crossed to Aaron and unlocked the cuffs.

"Where've you been?" Carla complained, pulling the blanket around her shoulders. "We could have frozen to death."

"I thought you had to go to the bathroom," Morris snapped.

"I do. Start the fire—please." She turned and went into the bathroom and closed the door.

"It is being called the Greed Killing—the shocking news this morning of the murder of Atlanta philanthropist Ewell Pender last evening. And speculation already abounds that Pender's efforts to secure the release of kidnap victim Aaron Greene is directly responsible for the murder.

"I'm Katie Harris and this is The Katie Harris Show. What do you think? Why was Ewell Pender killed? Was it merely the work of a burglar who believed the contributions made to the Aaron Greene Fund were kept at the Pender mansion, or is it part of the kidnapping conspiracy itself? What happens now to all the money that has been raised on Aaron's behalf—money

contributed by thousands of citizens from all across the country? Do we really know the truth about any of this? And what about law enforcement officials? What are they withholding? Surely they know something. But all we've heard is a brief statement from Police Commissioner Clifford Russell, saying the murder of Ewell Pender is being investigated. Does any of this sound familiar, people? Are you getting as weary of runarounds as I am? Who killed Ewell Pender? Who kidnapped Aaron Greene? Franklin, you're on the air with Katie Harris."

"Katie?"

"This is Katie. Where are you calling from, Franklin?"

"Avondale Estates. I'm a second-timer."

"Glad to hear from you again, Franklin. What do you think about all of this?"

"I think a blind man could see through what's going on, Katie. That's what I think."

"What do you mean?"

"It don't make sense, is what I mean. You mean to tell me that these people go out and kidnap somebody and want ten million dollars for him, and then they go and kill the man that's trying to get it? Wadn't them, Katie. Ain't nobody that stupid. I'm laying odds it was somebody hopped up on drugs, thinking he was gonna set himself up for life, or it was an inside job."

"Could be, Franklin."

"I tell you one thing, Katie, I can't see it no other way. Unless it was that Aaron boy, hisself. You ask me, somebody ought to take a good hard look at that angle. Maybe that he's smarter than anybody ever gave him credit for being. I'd bet a week's pay that if you unscrewed the cap on his head, you'd find somebody that's one of them computer nerds, and maybe he's been pulling the strings all along. I mean, you think about it: Where'd the boy work? The bank. Who was supposed to pay off his ransom? The bank. Now, I ain't a rocket scientist, but I did pass third-grade arithmetic, and this sounds a whole lot like one and one adding up to two."

"That's a pretty strong opinion, Franklin."

"Well, I ain't saying it happened that way, Katie, but it's worth looking into."

"Well, stranger things have happened, and you do bring up an interesting point: Just why did the kidnappers choose Aaron Greene? And what do we really know about him? Maybe we've all been so sympathetic to his cause that we haven't examined him as well as we should."

"What I'm saying, Katie."

"Something to think about. Thanks for the call. Rebecca, in Athens, what do you think?"

"I think you should leave the dead to rest in peace. Why add to everyone's hurt?"

"Well, Rebecca, that's sweet, but it's a little simple, isn't it? There's more at stake here than greeting-card mentality. So, I think I'll let you leave the dead to rest in peace. On The Katie Harris Show, we believe the issues are more important than sentimental little observations of gush and mush. So, let's see— Eugene, line four. Speak to us, Eugene."

"My God, Katie, who was that woman—Sister Teresa? I'm glad you cut her off."

"Be kind, Eugene."

"That's what's wrong with this world, Katie. Bleeding hearts. Who does that woman think she is? I guess I feel just as much as she ever did, but it don't mean I'm gonna swallow everything I hear and read, hook, line, and sinker. Let me tell you how this all comes down. I'm kind of like Franklin: I ain't sure about that boy, either, but I'm a lot more interested in what's going to happen to all that money that was sent in to that Pender fellow, because I sent some of it in. Now, I know he ain't gonna be using it—not unless they shovel it in the grave with him—but what about other people? You think the police are looking into that?"

"Are you talking about the Keystone Kops?"

"That's what they seem like, don't it?"

"You're right. Sometimes it does."

"Just what are they doing, anyhow, Katie? You know anything?"

"Well, according to our reports—and they are sketchy—the

police are still investigating the scene and interviewing people. What they've discovered is anybody's guess. The commissioner said he would have a news conference sometime today, but all that means to me is they need some time to have the spin doctors write a script."

"You're probably right. It's just like everything else. In a couple of weeks, they'll put all of this in some file and just let it disappear. But I hope you don't do that, Katie. I hope you keep after it. If you don't, I don't know who will."

"Don't worry, Eugene. I'm not jumping ship on this. Not at all. And one of these days, someone will say the right thing—or the wrong thing. Thanks for your call, Eugene. We'll be back after these messages."

You will, but I won't, Menotti thought as he pushed the off-on button of his car radio. He shook his head in slow disbelief, the same sensation he always had when listening to talk radio. It wasn't news; it was legalized gossip. Usually it was nothing more than slightly annoying nonsense, loudly babbled by egomaniacs such as Katie Harris, who, sadly, believed that her voice and the voices from her personal Greek chorus had the power to declare truth without proof. But the Katie Harrises of the world could also be persuasive. And they could bring pressure. By God, they could do that.

He glanced at a billboard, cornered to face northbound traffic at Piedmont and International Boulevard. A weary laugh caught in his chest. The billboard was an advertisement for Katie Harris. It showed Katie sitting on a gilded throne dressed as royalty out of the Victorian period, a jeweled crown balanced tentatively on her billowed hair, a haughty look painted on her face. A single line shot across the top of the billboard in underlined block letters: QUEEN OF THE AIR.

"My God," Menotti mumbled. Queen Katie. The bitch. Queen Katie making cracks about the Keystone Kops. He smirked, let the smirk hide a small smile. The

Keystone Kops might have an easier time of it. Maybe the Keystone Kops could cut through all the bullshit of politics, where appearances were as important—or *more* important—than forensic evidence.

He remembered what an old detective—Dalton Bruce—had said about a particularly frustrating case during his first year of homicide investigation: "Sometimes you just ain't gonna get Aunt Sally to lift her skirt."

"What does that mean?" Menotti had asked.

"Well," Dalton had explained, "one time, over in South Carolina, there was this cranky old woman that everybody called Aunt Sally. She was from old stock, if you know what I mean. Had money back to Adam and was married to another old-stock family going back to the Revolutionary War, but her husband was a lowlife in his soul, and Aunt Sally finally had enough, so one night she shot the sorry son of a bitch dead at the dinner table, with two or three servants looking on. Anyhow, when the sheriff showed up, he asked Aunt Sally what had happened and Aunt Sally insisted her husband had died of a heart attack so bad his heart had blown its way out of his body. The servants told a different story, of course. They said Aunt Sally had shot her husband just after he'd put away a bowl of potato soup, and that she'd pulled up her skirt—this was when they wore those long dresses, with all those slips—and she hid the gun there in some kind of pocket or something. Wadn't nobody going to ask Aunt Sally to lift up her skirt, not being who she was. So they declared her husband dead of excessive heart failure, or, as one of them put it, a blowout."

Everyone had laughed at the story. Afterward, any tough case was called an Aunt Sally.

The murder of Ewell Pender was an Aunt Sally. No one was going to push anyone who worked for Ewell Pender too hard, regardless of how much Katie Harris yammered about it. It would be undignified.

He glanced at the digital clock on the instrument panel of his car. It was 1:17. He shook his head. Monday, wasn't it? Yes. Monday. He had slept only three hours, after getting the call twelve hours earlier of the death of Ewell Pender. He knew there was a connection between Ewell Pender's murder and Aaron's kidnapping—*everyone* knew it—but he did not know how, or why, or who was involved, and he knew there would not be any easy answers.

And maybe he would never know the answers, he thought—even if he had had moments so intuitively clear he believed he could touch them, lift them up like torches burning brightly in a parade.

Everything was out of sync. He seemed always early or late. A continent of bodies seemed in his way, too dense to go around, or over, or through, or under. The Pender mansion had been mobbed, and he had watched in silence as Philip Oglesbee took command, his voice booming orders, the flash strobes of police cameras popping around him like holiday fireworks. Being at the Pender mansion was a waste of time, but the order had come from Clifford Russell, an order Menotti understood: The African Prince would have his army of investigators, and Clifford Russell would have his army. The two armies would spend as much time watching one another as they would searching for evidence in the death of Ewell Pender.

He had arrived late at Aaron Greene's home, yet being late did not matter. He did not believe the killing of Ewell Pender meant the impending release of Aaron. It was merely guesswork on the part of Philip Oglesbee, echoed by Clifford Russell. Probably one of the African Prince's tricks, in fact. A diversion to chase Clifford Russell down a thorny path.

"Get over there," the commissioner had ordered in a whisper, "but sit in on Oglesbee's strategy meeting first."

The strategy meeting had been attended by as many note-takers as investigators. Ass-covering note-takers. Oglesbee was no fool. There would be a finger-pointing day when his memoranda-to-file would be matched against Clifford Russell's memoranda-to-file. Menotti did not remember the strategies discussed. He did not care. A homing device was singing in his mind, and he was following it. It was the only strategy he truly trusted.

The two armies that had gathered at Aaron Greene's home were smaller, less intense, their duties simple: Keep the media at bay. Let Aaron's parents have some peace. Oglesbee had dispatched Tito Francis to be in charge of the Greene location, and Tito had been in a sour mood. "I was thinking maybe we could shoot a couple of the bastards," Tito had muttered to Menotti. "See if that old shark-to-blood theory works."

"Anything going on?" Menotti had asked.

"Shit," had been Tito's disgusted reply.

Aunt Sally, Menotti thought. Aunt Sally wearing her thick crinolines and covering skirts. He turned left onto Clairmont Road, off Ponce de Leon, easing into the traffic headed toward Decatur, the homing device in his mind crying in a high-pitched hum.

Menotti could feel himself waddle as he walked, the muscles in his legs wanting to sleep, and it was a strange, almost frightening awareness—his legs dead from too many hours without sleep, yet the rest of his body was jittery with energy. He was burning the volatile, quick-heat fuel of adrenaline, and he knew from experience that it would last only a short time and then his body would collapse and he would close his eyes for the dark sleep that would have no memory. And he would awake in pain, his body lead-weighted and weak, his mind sluggish and distorted.

Still, the adrenaline burned and the humming in his mind was deafening.

He had gotten the address for Robert Lucas from a dispatch operator at the police department, who had pulled it out of a computer with a few casual finger strokes across a keyboard. Computers astounded Menotti. Computers ruled the world. Ask and it shall be found. Nothing could hide from the lightning mind of a computer. Little electric brains, they were, he believed. How in the name of God could such small electric brains hide so much information? So much information, and so few answers.

Menotti wanted answers.

The car parked in Robert Lucas's driveway had been backed in from the street, and the trunk was open. Two boxes, heavily taped, were on the ground beside the car. Menotti paused at the walkway to the front door, studied the boxes for a moment, waited for his mind to ask a question about them.

"Hello."

Menotti turned to the voice at the front door. It was Robert Lucas. Robert was holding a box like the boxes beside his car.

"Lieutenant Menotti, I believe," Robert said, crossing the yard toward his car. He sounded cheerful.

"That's right," Menotti answered. He followed Robert to the car.

"We met at the Pender estate, at the Joel Garner reception, though you may have forgotten. It was pretty crowded," Robert said. He placed the box he was carrying on top of one of the other boxes.

Menotti faked a smile of acknowledgment, then casually raked his shoe against one of the boxes. A clicking sound, like a faint rattling, rose from the box.

"I'm sorry. I'm being rude," Robert said. "Would you like to go inside? After last night and this morning, I needed to do something physical, so I decided to attack the house and thought I'd get rid of some of this stuff on my way out." He laughed easily. "Millie came to visit and left a message in the dust—one of those 'Wash me' things you see on trucks. Thought I'd better start making a better impression. I think we can find a couple of empty chairs."

Menotti could feel a cooling of the blue heat. His eyes suddenly began to burn. He gazed numbly at Robert. "That's all right," he said. "You mind a couple of questions?"

"Not at all."

"It's really nothing but routine," Menotti explained, "and I know you've answered the same questions a dozen times or more, but I haven't read any of the reports. Were you at home when Mr. Pender was killed?"

Robert smiled warmly. "Sure was. Doing this cleaning. Believe me, I've been living in squalor, and I don't like the thought of losing a good woman over it."

Menotti could feel his body bobbing, like an old man lost in a wandering thought. After a moment, he said, "You got any ideas about this? Who might have done it?"

"Not at all," Robert answered.

Menotti's head stopped wagging. He squinted at Robert. "The talk shows are on the insider-job bandwagon."

Robert smiled again. A weak smile. "That's sick. And sad."

"I'm sorry about Pender," Menotti said. He glanced again at the boxes beside Robert's car.

"Thank you," Robert replied. "This city lost a very great man. I lost a very great friend—a father figure, really."

"So you were close to him?"

"In a manner of speaking, yes," Robert said. "I attended the school his grandfather founded. Mr. Pender later advised me on my career and was charitable enough to help me get started in business. In fact, his was my first account."

"What time did you hear about his death?"

"Ten-thirty or so, I think. Maybe earlier. I'm sure you can verify the time of the call from phone records."

"And you went straight there?"

"Yes."

"I understand the killer wore a ski mask," Menotti said. "Is that what you were told?"

"It was, yes. I don't think the descriptions were too good, but it must have been a horrible few minutes. Perhaps Alyse and Oscar will give better accounts when they gather themselves."

Menotti felt a frown wiggle over his forehead. He thought of the taped conversation that Cody had had with Ewell Pender. Robert Lucas sounded exactly like Pender. The same language, the same speech pattern.

"Did you know that Mr. Pender was married to Alyse Burton?" Menotti asked.

Robert smiled. "I didn't until last night. Believe me, it took me by surprise. All of us have respected the special relationship between them, but none of us knew about the marriage."

"Special relationship? What do you mean?" Menotti asked.

"She was his personal assistant. He shared many matters with her that were otherwise private."

"Such as the threats that she told Joel Garner about?"

A quizzical frown cut into Robert's face.

"Mr. Pender had received a phone call, threatening retaliation," Menotti explained. "Garner called this morning, when he learned of the murder. He told us about it."

"I wasn't aware of that," Robert answered. "Not personally, but it's possible. If Mr. Pender did receive such a call, he may have shared it with Alyse, but not with the rest of us. That's what I mean by their special relationship."

"Well, thanks," Menotti said. "I think that's all the questions I have." He turned back to his car, stopped, did a half-turn back. "I've been too busy to ask, but when's the funeral?" he asked.

"Tomorrow afternoon," Robert said. "He always wanted to be buried as soon as possible, and we're honoring that request, even though a number of people from out of the country may not be able to attend. There's going to be something of a wake, or a reception, for him tonight at the estate. You're welcome to attend."

"Thanks," Menotti said. "I have a feeling I'll be tied to my desk."

"It's a little unusual, I know," Robert admitted. "Having a wake so soon at the site of the murder. But Mr. Pender long ago planned the details of his funeral. I asked the commissioner if it would interfere with his investigation. He assured me it wouldn't."

"And the woman, the cook? Maria. When will she be buried?" Menotti asked.

"Thursday," Robert answered. "There weren't any surviving family members. At least, none we know of. We had to find a suitable site."

Menotti shook his head. "Sad, the way it all happened." He motioned toward the boxes. "You need help loading anything?"

The smiled dimmed in Robert's face. "No, not at all," he replied quickly. "Thanks, though. I'm about finished."

Menotti shrugged with a shoulder roll. "I think I'm glad you can manage it. I'm almost too tired to stand up. Oh, one other thing: I didn't see the chauffeur or the young girl that was at the reception. Where are they?"

"Unfortunately, both are away for a few days. Morris, I suspect, is on a river somewhere. He's a woodsman. Carla, I believe, is in Florida." He smiled. "I'm sure we'll hear from both of them as soon as they learn of Mr. Pender's death. It won't be easy for either of them—especially Carla. She loved Mr. Pender very much, as we all did. I'll probably even urge her to stay away until after the funeral. Frankly, she's rather fragile."

"Uh-huh," Menotti mumbled. "Probably a good idea. When they come back, I'd like to talk to them." He reached into his pocket and pulled out a business card and handed it to Robert. "They can find me at either number."

"I'll tell them," Robert said.

THIRTY-SEVEN

IF MORRIS HAD SLEPT, CARLA DID NOT KNOW it. He seemed numb, drugged. He had not eaten from the orders of fried chicken that he had purchased somewhere from a KFC franchise. He did not talk. He sat in a chair in front of the fire, occasionally adding split pieces of wood to the flame.

Carla and Aaron watched him in silence, realizing the danger of the brooding. Morris, Carla had warned during the night, was dangerous. She had always been afraid of him, she had admitted.

Morris had refused to talk about where he had been in his long absence from the cabin, and when Carla asked to watch television, he had simply ripped the power cord from the back of the set, disabling it.

Late in the afternoon, Morris rose suddenly from the chair, like someone jolted awake from a sleep of exhaustion.

"Come on," he ordered. "Time for the chains."

"Are you leaving again?" Carla asked nervously.

"Why do you care?" snapped Morris.

"Because I remember last night," Carla said. "I remember how long you were gone and how cold it got."

"I'll be back before the fire goes out," Morris told her, slipping the handcuffs from his pocket. "Now get over here."

386

*   *   *

Because he knew that Morris would call and he knew the call would come to him on his cellular telephone—an agreement of communicating to cover emergencies in the kidnapping of Aaron—Robert left his home in late afternoon and drove to Park Place and sat alone at a table inside Café Intermezzo, drinking coffee and reading Amos Temple's story on the murder of Ewell Pender. It was a bold, dark story, one that spilled over the front page of *The Atlanta Journal* like the announcement of a war. A sidebar by Cody Yates repeated elements of the magazine story he had written years earlier—the Pender legend. Events. Dates. The spotlight moments of a great man. It was written with surprising tenderness, and as he read it, a sense of loss fell over Robert with the power of the childhood fears that Ewell Pender had assuaged with kindness.

He had spoken with Cody briefly at the Pender estate in the early stages of the investigation of Ewell Pender's death. Cody had been subdued, quiet, watchful. He had asked only one question, and Robert was not certain if it was direct or rhetorical: "Who did this?" Robert had answered with a shake of his head. And then Cody had said something odd: "Jesus, this makes me feel old."

Or maybe it was not at all an odd statement, Robert realized, folding the paper and putting it on the small table. Perhaps death did make some people feel old. He looked at his watch. The digital numbers read 6:13. He could not wait much longer. The reception—the wake—to honor Ewell Pender had been planned for seven-thirty. I, too, feel old, he thought. He remembered the last counsel of Ewell Pender, less than a week past. *Someday, you're going to have to make the courageous decisions. Never act in haste.*

A crowd of young Asians—students, Robert guessed— entered the restaurant. They were laughing, and Robert could see self-assurance blazing in their eyes. They wandered to a table in the smoking section, jammed themselves into chairs surrounding the table, lit cigarettes in an act of celebration. Their laughter was like a song. One of the girls was spectacularly beautiful.

He motioned for a second cup of coffee. As his hand was in the air, he heard the low, dull chiming of the telephone that he carried in the inside pocket of his jacket. He fished the phone from the pocket, snapped open the mouthpiece.

"Hello," he said.

"It's me," Morris replied quietly.

"I thought it would be," Robert told him.

"Where are you?" Morris asked.

"At Café Intermezzo, near Perimeter Mall."

"You alone?"

"Yes. Are they all right?"

"They're fine."

"We have to settle this," Robert said. "What do you want?"

"Nothing," Morris answered. He paused. "No. A little money."

"How much?"

"Two or three thousand. I don't care. Enough for a few weeks."

"Why don't you bring them in? You'll never outrun this. You know that."

"Don't start on me," Morris snapped.

"Fine," Robert said. "It's your life."

"When's the funeral?" Morris asked softly.

"Tomorrow. You know he wanted to be buried as soon as possible after his death."

"You can get them tomorrow night, then."

"All right," Robert said. "I'm going to trust that you'll keep your word. I want you to call me tomorrow, this same time," Robert said.

"Fine," Morris replied. He added, "You know not to talk to the police."

"Of course," Robert said. Then: "Morris, I want to say something to you."

Morris did not reply. Robert could hear his labored breathing.

"I'm sorry," Robert whispered. "About everything. I'm deeply sorry. I'll never forget you. Inside of you is a very fine person, one I'm grateful to have known."

There was a pause. "Me, too," Morris mumbled. "I'm sorry. I didn't mean to do it. Not to hurt anyone."

"I know that."

The phone clicked dead.

Harry Dilliard had not ordered Cody to attend the wake for Ewell Pender. "If you want to go, fine," Harry had said, "but it's up to you."

"I'd rather not," Cody had replied.

"Fine," Harry had said. "Amos and Olin can handle it. Besides, I don't think we'll make too much of it. Those sorts of things ought to be private, but I expect you to be at the funeral tomorrow."

And Cody had left Harry's office and had taken the stairs to the sixth-floor newsroom. He had crossed the room to Freda's desk and had said in a strong voice, "Could you go to dinner with me?"

The question had startled Freda and it had stunned their coworkers.

"Yes," she had answered.

"Son of a bitch," Amos Temple had whispered.

The only light in the bedroom was from the scented candle. Its teardrop flame waved in the warm air that blew up from a floor vent near the night table. On the wall, and across the bed covering, the candlelight was the soft color of straw. A faint, sweet scent of vanilla floated in the room.

Freda lay with her head in the cradle of Cody's shoulder, her body turned and draped against him in after-love quietness. He could feel her breath on his chest. Warm, moist, even. The fingertips of her left hand played lightly over the skin of his right shoulder, and the touch, he thought, was like the touch of silk skimmed across his body. He let his tongue brush his lips, tasted her again. The taste was the same as the faint, sweet scent of vanilla.

"Do you hear it?" she asked in a whisper.

"What?" he said.

"The rain."

He rolled his head on the pillow, listened. The sound of the rain against the building was the sound of a waterfall he remembered from his childhood visits to his grandfather's farm. Hypnotizing. Numbing in its beauty.

"Nice," Cody said. He added, "By the way, thank you."

"For what?"

"Tonight. I needed you."

"Why?"

"It's been a long day."

"Yes, it has," she agreed. "Tell me something, Cody: Why the big move today?"

"What big move?"

"Breaking our standing rule of behavior at the office."

Cody shrugged, touched her face, traced his finger over her lips. "It's time," he said. "I'm getting too old to play games."

"I'm glad."

"Tomorrow, I think we should strip naked and make love on your desk."

"Don't tempt me."

Cody laughed. "We did cause some heads to spin, didn't we?"

"And tongues to cluck," Freda said. She added, "I thought you'd go to the wake for Pender tonight."

"Nope."

"Why not?"

"I have a thing about death. I don't want to get too close to it prematurely, and I sure as hell don't want it to get too close to me. Besides, I've been ordered to the funeral tomorrow. That's enough."

"That's not the answer."

"I liked that old man," Cody said simply.

"Thank you."

"For what?"

"Being truthful."

"That's not the whole truth."

"What is?"

"I didn't want to be around Robert Lucas."

"Why not?"

"I get the feeling he's about to ask Millie to marry him."

"That bothers you?"

"A little," Cody admitted. Then: "I'm sorry. That's not fair to you."

"It's fine, Cody. Believe it or not, I understand that. I know you still care for Millie, and I'm glad you do. I think you'd be a real bastard if you didn't."

Cody rolled his head to kiss her cheek. "I love you," he told her.

"I love you, too."

He massaged her shoulder and she moved to the touch, rooting her body into him, and then she lay quiet and in a few minutes she was asleep.

The rain whispered against the window of the apartment, and a wind-sigh blew softly. As he listened, a sad flutter of loss settled over Cody.

Millie.

Millie making love to another man.

He could hear her happy laugh, could see light dancing in her eyes.

He inhaled slowly, deeply, let the air seep from his mouth. He closed his eyes. No reason to be jealous, or queasy. No reason at all. He liked Robert Lucas. He wanted Millie to feel as grand as he felt, holding Freda.

He was at peace with the sleeping woman curled against him. For the moment, at least. In the candlelit, vanilla-scented room, the sleeping woman was the best part of his life.

THIRTY-EIGHT

———◆———

EWELL PENDER HAD PREPARED INSTRUC-
tions for his funeral five years before his death. The instructions were simple: a meek service in the majestic
setting of the First Presbyterian Church.

An elderly minister with a soft New England accent
spoke a few words. Ewell Pender, the minister said, had
been a remarkable man, a giver, someone blessed with
tender sensibilities and uncompromising goodness. He did
not mention Ewell Pender's money. He did not mention
Aaron Greene.

There were no eulogies from grief-stunned friends.

There were no flowers. Oddly, no flowers.

Ewell Pender, the minister recited, had wanted to remember flowers growing in gardens—alive and vibrant—
not wilting in a ceremony for the already dead.

Only one selection of music was presented—a pianist
from the Atlanta Symphony Orchestra playing "Amazing
Grace." It was, the minister announced, the first selection
that Ewell Pender had played in public and had remained
his favorite. In the church, heads leaned to heads, mumbling surprise. No one had ever heard Ewell Pender play
"Amazing Grace."

The service lasted twenty-two minutes, barely long
enough for those who had crowded into the church to

become properly solemn for such a properly solemn occasion.

Outside, it was a threatening day of low clouds, dark in the underbelly, wind-foamed, ugly, the kind of clouds that caused television weathercasters to rush before their weather maps and make swirling motions with their hands, imitating the image of satellite photographs sliding across the outline of America. El Niño, the weathercasters would suggest, was playing its unpredictable tricks, and out of the dark, wind-foamed, ugly clouds, tornadoes were dropping to earth like spinning, string-pulled toys.

Cody listened to the whispered acknowledgments of people in their slow recession from the church.

Lovely service, the people said, not knowing what to say.

So simple.

So very like Ewell Pender. Quiet. Dignified.

Simple.

Better to remember him that way, rather than for his wealth, the people said in whispers.

A stern breeze slapped at the faces of the people as they left the church, glancing skyward, wondering if they could outrace the rain that would surely fall.

"They'd better get a rush on if they're going to get him buried before the bottom falls out," judged Harry Dilliard.

Harry stood with Cody and Amos Temple and Freda Graves. He was dressed in a new dark blue suit, purchased for the occasion. His wingtip shoes, always scruffy, were shined to a mirror finish. His shirt was new-white, his tie deep red with small starbursts of blue. The stories of Aaron Greene and Ewell Pender had injected new life into the newspaper and into Harry Dilliard. Harry could no longer sit behind his desk and let the news flow to him; he had to get outside, away from his office, and meet the news head-on, as he had done as a young reporter. It was both an invigorating and humorous change for those who worked with him. Harry's Second Wind, they called it.

They also knew it was only a temporary compulsion. Harry's Second Wind would be quickly exhausted.

"You going to the gravesite?" Harry asked Amos.

"I guess so," Amos answered patiently. Harry had ordered him repeatedly to cover the gravesite.

"Good enough," Harry said. "It'll be crowded out there. You take it. We'll get back to the office. If you see our photographer out there, make damn sure he gets enough stuff."

Amos did not answer. He was staring across the driveway that circled in front of the church. "Jesus," he said softly, "can you believe that?"

Harry and Cody and Freda turned to look.

A woman in a bright green dress, wearing a waist-length mink fur coat, stood on the edge of the grass, scanning the departing crowd. A swelling of blond hair, lemon-bright, seemed precariously balanced on her head. A proud, look-at-me smile bloomed on her face. She held a microphone with a small wire knob in one hand and a tape recorder in the other. Her voice sliced across the churchyard: "Hi, I'm Katie Harris. Could I ask you a couple of questions?"

"Oh, dear God," Freda whispered painfully.

The questions from Katie Harris stunned people.

"How did you feel about Ewell Pender? . . .

"Did you do business with Ewell Pender? . . .

"Why are you here? . . .

"Who do you think killed him? . . .

"Do you think there's any credibility to the speculation that someone close to Mr. Pender might have committed his murder? . . .

"Do you think the police are doing all they can do? . . .

"What do you think will happen to the contributions to the Aaron Greene Fund?"

No one stopped to answer her questions. They stared at her incredulously, walked away from her. Still she asked, her voice cutting harshly into the tender flesh of the uneasy moment. She did not want answers, Cody reasoned. She wanted the performance, something she could talk about with bravado. She would broadcast that she had tried to inspire truth at the funeral of Ewell Pender, and then suggest that no one seemed to care about truth. That would be her platform. And the people would listen, and believe. And her ratings would soar in the broiling heat of controversy.

"Somebody should make her stop," Freda said angrily.

"It's just show," Cody told her.

"I don't care what it is," Freda quarreled. "It's insulting."

They watched an older woman pause in front of Katie and glare at her. And then the woman broke into a sob and a young man took her arm and led her away.

"Am I the only person here who believes the Ewell Pender story is just beginning?" Katie shrilled. "If you're his friends, you should want to talk about him."

A woman wearing a black dress suit with a matching full-length coat moved from the crowd toward Katie. The woman's head was covered with a thick black scarf. She wore sunglasses. She stopped in front of Katie. Katie raised the microphone toward her.

"You're Alyse Burton, aren't you?" Katie said brightly. "We met at—"

Alyse reached and folded her hand over the knob of the microphone. She said, "Please leave. This is embarrassing."

A blush rushed over Katie's face, and then she composed herself and replied, "I'm sure you've heard of the First Amendment."

"I have also heard of respect and dignity," Alyse answered. And then she turned and walked away.

From the crowd someone applauded. Then someone else. The applause spread.

Katie's eyes swept the crowd. Her smile disappeared, then blossomed again. She lifted the microphone to her mouth. "And that's the mood at the funeral service for Ewell Pender," she cooed. "Strikes me as a little strange.

Here we are on the grounds of one of Atlanta's most honored churches and that biblical admonition about 'Seek and ye shall find' seems not to fit. We have been seeking, but not finding." She paused. A twinkle seemed to flash from her eyes. "But we haven't finished seeking, either. More later." She twirled and pushed through the crowd.

"Harry," Freda said in a bitter whisper, "I want you to give me an assignment."

"What?" Harry replied.

"I want you to tell me to do a profile on Katie Harris."

"Why?"

"I haven't written an obituary in a long time," Freda said.

The answer amused Harry. It was spirited, and mean. "You sound annoyed," he said.

"No, Harry, I'm not annoyed," Freda said. She looked at Cody. "I'm angry." She turned back to glare at the disappearing Katie Harris. "I can't believe how angry I am."

Harry patted her on the arm in a patronizing gesture. "We'll talk about it," he promised. "But I like your spirit. Yes, I do."

The vibrating beeper signal from Augie Haygood jiggled across Menotti's waist, startling him, even though he knew it was coming.

Augie was a uniformed officer, motorcycle patrol, for the City of Atlanta, and he had been assigned escort duty for the funeral of Ewell Pender. He was also one of Menotti's best friends, and a man who knew when to ask questions and when to ignore them. Menotti had asked Augie to signal from his cell phone at the conclusion of the church service, before the slow procession to Oakland Cemetery.

"You got it," Augie had said, and he had grinned mischievously, a code of secrecy.

Menotti reached for the beeper, pressed the button to

clear Augie's number. He glanced at his watch. Two twenty-five. Jesus, he thought, that was quick. He had guessed the church service for Ewell Pender would last an hour, maybe longer. The weather. It must be the weather, he decided. A short service to beat the rain that had been moving steadily toward Atlanta since early morning—rain following rain. Still, he had time. The drive to Oakland Cemetery from First Presbyterian would take at least thirty minutes, and then there would be a gravesite service. He had an hour, or an hour and a half. Plenty of time. It was not a large house, and it would be a hell of a lot easier to get out than it had been to get in.

Picking the lock to Robert Lucas's back door had taken time, annoying Menotti. He had never been good at such things, but it wasn't as simple as people believed. Not like the lock-picking in movies or on television cop shows. Those assholes could slip a dog hair into a lock and it would spring open. It was not that simple, and Robert Lucas's back door had already been damaged. The jamb around the lock had been splintered—recently, it seemed—and hastily nailed together. The door was tight in the jamb, dragging against nailheads. Something to re-member, Menotti had noted.

He had scouted the house carefully, had found one door locked—a door that had also been damaged and roughly repaired—and was in the process of picking it when Augie Haygood's signal came.

Be calm, he thought.

"Calm, my ass," he mumbled to himself. If Clifford Russell, or the African Prince, ever discovered what he was doing, he would find himself demoted to the motor pool, changing the oil in Augie's motorcycle.

But Clifford Russell and the African Prince could not hear homing signals, or, if they did, they dismissed them as brain static.

The door opened to Menotti's touch and he stepped inside Robert Lucas's office.

It had been a small bedroom—ten by ten, Menotti guessed—with a small folding-door closet. One wall of the room was covered with three tall bookcases, book-stuffed. A large computer desk with a recessed monitor was against another wall. Two steel file cases were at each end of the desk. There was one chair. The chair faced the desk at a three-quarter turn, as though someone had pushed it back to open one of the lower drawers.

Menotti stepped close to the desk and examined it. The desk was cluttered with papers and an array of silver disks spilled over a plastic in-and-out container box. Sheets of notes, coded in the language of computers, were taped to the shelves of the desk. A Christmas-patterned hand towel of holly leaves and berries was lumped on the flat hard drive.

Odd, Menotti thought. A day earlier, Robert had been working feverishly to clean his house, but the desk looked like the desk of a sloppy teenager, not someone like Robert Lucas. Everything about Robert had seemed orderly, even his casual, jolly nature. Not this. Not his office. He was not the kind of man to make blundering mistakes. Yet here was a place where he was obviously careless, a place where he felt secure. There was always such a place for everyone, Menotti reasoned. A closet for a child or a woman. A man's workroom. A locker. Barns. Sheds. A personal place.

He leaned over the desk, examining it. A scattering of envelopes lay on top of an open checkbook. Bills. Three computer magazines with strips of torn paper marking pages. Menotti picked up one of the magazines, opened it to a marked page. It was a story about legislation to protect use of the Internet. A few paragraphs had been highlighted with bright pink swipes from a felt-tip pen. He replaced the magazine exactly as he had found it, and picked up one of the disks. It advertised an encyclopedia. Christ, Menotti thought. He was holding thousands of words—hundreds of thousands of words—in his hand. He replaced the disk and kneeled in front of the desk and slowly tugged at a lower drawer, expecting it to be locked. It was not.

The drawer contained alphabetized file folders, and Menotti quickly thumbed to the G label. G for Greene. He spread open the folder. Inside was a four-page dossier on Aaron. "Son of a bitch," he whispered.

He was holding the homing device.

He read quickly. It was an astonishingly complete summary of Aaron Greene, from physical characteristics to habits and temperament. Classroom achievements. Hobbies. Books he had read. Movies he had seen. There was a brief history of his mother and father.

Menotti's hand quivered as he read. He glanced at his watch. Still plenty of time. Yet, he felt a chill over his shoulders and back, a premonition that he had to get away from Robert Lucas's house. It was a warning he never ignored.

He replaced the file and closed the drawer and stood at the desk and slowly scanned the room, examining it. The window wall was bare. Why? he wondered. He walked along the empty-space wall, crouched over, studying the floor. In the film of dust covering the wood flooring, he could see two distinct outlines—square-shaped—side by side. Something had been there, but recently moved.

The boxes, he thought. Jesus, the boxes. The boxes that Robert had been loading into his car. He remembered scraping his foot along one of the boxes, remembered the faint clicking sound. Not metal against metal, but plastic against plastic. Cassette tapes in their casing. The boxes had been full of cassette tapes.

He stood erect and laughed a short, quiet laugh of astonishment.

"Son of a bitch," he said again.

The boy smiled gratefully as Robert placed the steaming cup of hot chocolate before him at the kitchen table.

"It's hot," Robert warned, then, remembering, flashed the signing of what he had said.

The boy grinned. He leaned close to the table, picked up the cup, sipped carefully from it.

Robert sat opposite him, stirring sugar into the cup of tea he had prepared for himself. He watched the boy's glad eyes. All the boy wanted was attention, someone to care, he thought. He placed his spoon on the lip of the saucer and lifted his hand and began the slow signing of words:

What did he look like?

The boy answered: *Dark hair.*

He was here today?

The boy's head bobbed once.

Have you seen him before? Robert asked.

Again, the bobbing.

When?

Yesterday.

Here?

The boy bobbed yes. He signed, *With you.*

Robert smiled. "Menotti," he said aloud.

The boy looked puzzled.

A friend, Robert signed.

The boy smiled. He glanced eagerly at the laptop computer on one end of the table.

Robert pointed to his watch. He could hear the wind sighing from outside. The after-storm wind. It was ten minutes after six. He signed, *It's late. More tomorrow.*

The boy nodded again—happily.

Robert motioned for the boy to follow him, and he led the boy to the front door and opened it. He pulled an umbrella out of a stand and signed to the boy: *Rain.* The boy looked, grinned. Robert popped the umbrella and handed it to the boy. He stood in the open doorway and watched the boy cross the street and run to his own home. The boy turned and waved, and Robert returned the wave.

"Menotti," Robert said softly.

He glanced up the street, saw a car parked in front of a home owned by an elderly man who lived alone. He had never seen the car before.

He turned and closed the door and walked back into the kitchen and sat at the table and drank from his tea. He wondered if he would be able to lose a surveillance car in traffic, or if Menotti had assigned a watch at the Pender estate, and, if so, how would Oscar handle it? It was a risk, but one that had to be taken. He could not change the plan now.

The cellular phone that he had placed on the kitchen table rang. Robert glanced at his kitchen clock. It was six-fifteen. Punctual, he thought. He picked up the phone, opened the mouthpiece and spoke.

"Hello."

"What are your plans?" Morris said.

"How are they?" Robert asked.

"They're fine."

"Where are they?"

"At the cabin."

"What cabin?"

"The Boy Scout cabin," Morris said.

Robert laughed quietly, a jittering laugh. Jesus, he thought. The cabin. He had forgotten about the cabin. So many years had passed since his boyhood at the cabin.

"All right, I believe you," Robert told him. "I want you to do this: I want you to lock the place and leave the keys outside, under a rock near the door. Then I want you to drive into Atlanta. You know the nature trail along the Chattahoochee, at Powers Ferry Road off the perimeter expressway?"

"Yes."

"I want you to go there. Walk north on the trail. Oscar will be there with the money. He'll find you."

"I don't like that," Morris mumbled. "You could be lying. You bring it to me."

"You know I'm not lying," Robert said calmly. "I'll get

them. It'll be easier to handle if you're not there."

Robert could hear Morris inhale, then sigh. After a moment, he said in resignation, "All right."

"I'm leaving now," Robert said. "You should, too."

"All right."

"I wish you'd change your mind about this, Morris," Robert said quietly.

"I can't."

"We'll always be there if you need us."

"Tell Alyse—"

"What?"

"Nothing."

THIRTY-NINE

THE DRIVE TO THE CABIN TOOK ALMOST three hours, an hour longer than it should have, but Robert had deliberately exited twice, each time cutting dangerously across traffic. If a car followed him, he was not able to spot it, and once in the mountains he knew he was safe. He had pulled onto a side road and parked and waited ten minutes, watching, but he saw nothing.

It was strange returning to the cabin. As a young boy, part of the Boy Scout troop sponsored by Carlton-Ayers, he had enjoyed jubilant moments at the cabin. Long hikes and fishing. Canoe rides down a narrow river. Campfires and cookouts. Ghost stories told under the blanket of night dotted with the spectacular light of stars. Some of his happiest days had been at the cabin.

Now he would destroy the place of tender memories.

He killed the lights to his car a hundred yards from the cabin and drove cautiously over the ribboned tracks of the woods road. He could hear the crush of the tires on the bed of fallen pine needles, and he could smell the clean, rich moisture of the trees. He should have remembered the cabin, he thought, should have known it was where Morris would take Carla and Aaron. Morris had loved being there also. Once, Morris had cried desperately when leaving it. "I want to stay here!" he had protested. "Here!"

He could see a dim light coming from the cabin, but

he did not see a car and he was glad. Morris had not changed his mind. Like Carla, Robert had always been slightly afraid of Morris. There had been times when hiding the fear had been almost impossible.

He stopped the car under the canopy of a hemlock's branches and got out and quietly closed the door. He paused for a moment, studying the cabin, listening, and then he crossed to the front door and squatted and saw a rock that had been moved from its dirt bed. He lifted the rock and found a small ring of two keys. He stood, eased the larger key into the door and opened it and stepped inside. He saw Carla first.

"Thank God," Robert said in relief. He turned to Aaron. "Thank God," he repeated.

"How did—?" Carla asked in astonishment.

"I'll tell you all about it," Robert said, moving quickly toward her. "First, let's get the two of you out of here."

He unlocked their handcuffs and stood for a moment looking at the cabin, studying it, and then he said to Aaron, "Take a look at it, Aaron. A good look. Memorize all you can."

A puzzled expression clouded Aaron's face. "Why?" he asked.

"You'll understand," Robert assured him.

Aaron's eyes swept the cabin.

"Take your time," Robert said. "Tell me if you could draw a rough sketch of it on a sheet of paper."

Aaron nodded tentatively. "I—I think so."

"Good. Now let's go," Robert said.

Carla caught Aaron by the arm and urged him toward the door. Then she stopped, turned, and rushed back to the VCR and ejected the tape from it.

"What's that?" Robert asked.

"Something that shouldn't be left behind," Carla told him.

Robert shrugged. Carla's voice had warned him not to

push the question. Later, she would tell him, and that would be good enough.

"Where's the car?" asked Carla.

"At the edge of the woods," Robert said. "I had to be sure you were alone."

"Let's go, before Morris comes back," Carla said urgently.

"Don't worry," Robert told her. "He won't be coming back."

"What's going on?"

"I'll tell you in a few minutes," Robert answered. He glanced around the room. "Is there a lantern here?"

"There's one hanging on a wall peg," Carla replied. "By the bathroom door."

"Get it," Robert said. He glanced at Aaron. "What I'm about to do is for the best. I want you to know that. I don't like doing it, because I don't like destroying things that have a good place in my memory."

Robert took the lantern from Carla and opened the filler cap and began to pour the kerosene along the baseboard of the cabin.

"You're going to burn it?" Carla asked nervously.

"It's best," Robert answered. "You and Aaron go on. You'll see the car."

Carla took Aaron's hand and pulled him through the doorway. They walked rapidly toward the car.

"He knows what he's doing," Carla said. "He's a very smart man."

"The woods could burn," Aaron said quietly.

"I don't think so," Carla replied. "It's too wet." She stopped at the car and looked back. She saw Robert running after them. Behind him, an orange sheet of fire rose up behind the windows of the cabin.

"Get in," Robert said. Carla opened the back door of the car and pushed Aaron inside and ducked in beside him. Robert closed the door and slipped quickly into the front seat and drove away, leaving the lights of the car off until he was well away from the cabin.

No one spoke for a few minutes, and then Robert slowed the car to a stop and turned to the backseat and said, "Aaron, would you do me a favor?"

Aaron answered with a hesitant nod.

"Would you close your eyes for now, and keep them closed until I tell you it's all right?"

"Why?" asked Carla.

"It's best," Robert explained. "I want him to be able to describe the cabin, but I also want him to say honestly that he doesn't know its location, and the way these roads twist and turn, if his eyes are closed, it'll make it all the more confusing."

"All right," Aaron said quietly.

"It'll be better than a blindfold," Carla said.

"No more blindfolds," Robert insisted. "There's been enough of that."

"Where are we going?" asked Carla.

"You'll see," answered Robert. "Right now, we've got to talk about things."

Aaron listened to the conversation between Robert and Carla, or half listened. He kept his eyes closed, and on the deep lavender screen of his mind he could see his home, could hear the voices of his parents, could feel the warmth, the familiarity, of his own room. Still, the words from Robert were telling an urgent story.

Morris had called and an exchange had been arranged, Robert said. Oscar would meet Morris on a walking trail near Atlanta and give him money, and Morris would then disappear.

"How are you going to explain that?" asked Carla.

"I don't know yet," Robert admitted. "Maybe nothing more than he left."

"Will Oscar be all right with him?"

"Yes. Oscar will be fine."

"Morris scares me," Carla said.

"Did he say anything when he left?" Robert wanted to know.

"Nothing. He—" Carla paused. She glanced at Aaron, then away.

"What?"

"He—kissed me. Very lightly. It was—gentle. And then he left."

"Was he angry, or did he seem despondent?"

"Despondent," Carla answered. "Sad. You know—melancholy."

Robert did not speak for a moment, then he said, "Did he—talk to you about anything?"

"No. For two days, he didn't talk at all. Nothing, really. He would leave and get food and bring it back, but he didn't talk at all. He just sat and stared into the fire, or sometimes he'd get up and go outside."

"I saw a television set there," Robert said. "Did you watch anything?"

"We couldn't," Carla answered. "He pulled the cord out of it."

Robert rolled his hands on the steering wheel. He glanced in the rearview mirror. Aaron rested his head against the backseat, his eyes closed. "I have to tell you something that's going to be very disturbing to hear," he said.

Carla sat forward. "What?"

"Mr. Pender and Maria are dead."

Aaron heard a sharp gasp from Carla. "Oh, my God," she whispered. And then she began to sob openly. He opened his eyes, looked at her, reached his hand to touch her arm. She caught his hand and clutched it. Her crying echoed in the car.

Aaron closed his eyes again and rested his head against the back of the seat. The power of Carla's grip crushed his hand. The movement of the car rocked them, and Robert drove for a long time without speaking, waiting patiently for Carla to spill the shock of her grief. Finally, he said, "It was Morris who killed them. I don't think he meant to; it just happened. I'm sure that's why he's been depressed. I could hear it in his voice when we talked."

"When—when did it happen?" Carla asked.

"Sunday night," Robert said. "We buried him today, according to his wishes. Maria's funeral won't be until Thursday."

"I—"

"I know. You weren't there. I'm sorry. We had to do it."

"Did anyone ask—?"

"Yes. A few people. I told them you were on a short vacation in Florida, and that I had advised you to stay away until after the funeral."

Aaron could feel Carla's hand massaging his fingers.

"And what about Aaron?" she asked. "Now, I mean."

Robert inhaled slowly. The pause was long, fragile. He said, "We have to make a decision."

"What does that mean?" Carla demanded.

Robert did not answer. He turned the car onto a freeway.

"What does that mean?" Carla repeated forcibly.

"Aaron, you may open your eyes now," Robert said.

"What happens to Aaron?" Carla demanded.

"Alyse and I think it's time for Aaron to go home," Robert said. "But we have a few things to do first." He again looked at Aaron in the rearview mirror, saw the look of surprise in Aaron's face. "Aaron, what happens really depends on you, and how much you trust us."

It was wet-dark from the afternoon rain that had swept over Atlanta like a restless mood, and the walking trails that wiggled along the Chattahoochee River in the national forest park were mostly deserted under the dull light of a half-moon. The few walkers who were out moved at a brisk pace, their heads down, their eyes focused on the ground in front of them. A cool wind seeped through the trees, and the river, swollen with rain, spilled monotonously down the wide trough of the waterbed.

Oscar stood hidden in an unlit cove that dipped off the trail and rose gradually to a level granite formation, giving a clear view of the trail in both directions. He wore laced rubber boots with his suit pants tucked inside, a long, dark raincoat turned up at the collar, and a rain hat that was pulled low over his face. If anyone saw him, he would be remembered as an old man, probably eccentric, who appeared to be resting during a tottering late-evening stroll. He smiled at the thought. He was certain no one had seen him leave the trail. He knew also that Morris would exercise the same care.

He was, he realized, surprisingly alert after the tiring day.

The image of Ewell Pender lying in his coffin flashed, held, faded, and Oscar shuddered involuntarily. He closed his eyes, took even, calming gulps of air into his lungs.

Patience, he thought.

He opened his eyes and looked down on the trail. He saw a lone figure, a man, moving slowly, approaching from the direction of the parking lot. The man wore a heavy jacket with a hood that was pulled up over his head. He knew by the walk that it was Morris.

He waited until Morris was even with him, and then he spoke softly: "Morris."

Morris stopped abruptly and whirled toward the voice.

"Where are you?" Morris said.

"Here," Oscar replied. He stepped forward one step, out of the shadows.

Morris did not reply. He stood, gazing at the old man.

"Did you see anyone on the trail?" Oscar asked.

"Just a woman with a couple of dogs," Morris answered. "She was headed to her car."

"Good," Oscar said.

"It was the only car I saw," Morris said suspiciously. "How did you get here?"

"Miss Burton—" Oscar paused, corrected himself. "Mrs. Pender drove me out."

"How are you getting back?"

"I hoped you'd be good enough to drive me," Oscar told him. "But if you wish not to, I've been instructed to call Mrs. Pender."

"Have you got the money?"

"Yes."

"Let me see it," Morris demanded.

Oscar moved cautiously down the slope to the trail. He reached into his pocket and handed Morris an envelope. "I hope the amount is sufficient," he said cordially. "Five thousand dollars, I believe."

"I didn't ask for that much."

Oscar smiled. He did not reply.

Morris squeezed the envelope with his hands, feeling the bulk of the money. He looked away, then back at Oscar. "Come on," he said. "I'll drive you."

"That's kind of you."

"Any police out there?"

"Not at the moment."

"What does that mean?" Morris asked irritably.

"They've been there, of course," Oscar replied. "For investigative purposes, but they left earlier today."

"You're sure they're not watching the place?"

"I don't think so," Oscar said. "But if they are, it shouldn't matter. You've long been a resident."

"Where do they think I've been?"

"On holiday. Mr. Lucas explained that you were most likely on a fishing trip."

Morris shoved the envelope into the pocket of his coat. His head bobbed in a nod. "I don't want to see Alyse," he mumbled.

"Of course. I understand," Oscar assured him. "I took the liberty of gathering a few of your things that you might need—hoping you would return with me."

Morris nodded again.

"Shall we go?" Oscar said.

They did not speak on the drive back to the Pender mansion. Morris slumped beneath the steering wheel of his car, staring at the road. He drove cautiously, still deliberating, Oscar thought. In the car, with the light of the dashboard, it was easy to see that Morris's face was puffed, his eyes red with fatigue.

At the driveway entering the estate, Oscar suggested, "Why don't you go to the side entrance, by the garden gate? It would be easier to get to your quarters from there."

"Yeah," Morris mumbled. He hesitated, wondered if he was being led into a trap. No, he decided. He knew too much. He pulled himself forward on the steering wheel and studied the massive home. Only a few lights were on, all in the upstairs rooms. Then he eased the car through the side entrance and parked near the garden gate and turned off the motor. He sat for a moment, staring at a dim shaft of light glowing behind the garden wall. He knew it was the pinspot covering the statue, Salome.

"Shall we?" Oscar said calmly.

"Yeah. Yeah, sure," Morris replied quietly.

The two men got out of the car and walked to a side door leading into the mansion. Oscar unlocked it with a key and stepped aside and motioned for Morris to enter. He followed Morris, closing the door behind him, and then he touched a switch to turn on the stairway lights. He stood, waiting, until Morris began to climb the staircase hesitantly.

"I assure you, there's no one in this part of the house," Oscar said.

"Is my door locked?"

"Yes," Oscar answered. "I have the key if—"

"I have mine," Morris said.

At the top of the stairs, Morris paused and studied the

corridor, then he turned left and walked quickly to his room. He opened the door and stepped inside.

A clothes bag, ballooning with contents, was on the bed.

"You may wish to see what I've packed for you," Oscar said in the doorway.

Morris shook his head. His eyes were moving across the room. It had been his home for more than a dozen years.

"Of course, you may want your hunting equipment," Oscar said, closing the door quietly.

"I don't need it," Morris whispered.

"What did you do with the gun?" Oscar asked.

Morris turned to him.

"Do you still have it?" Oscar said.

Morris touched his chest, felt the gun in the inside pocket of his jacket. He nodded numbly.

"I remember when Mr. Pender gave it to you, because you admired it so much," Oscar continued. "It's a remarkable weapon."

Morris turned back to the bed and took a step toward it.

"This one I think is superior, however," Oscar said.

Morris glanced over his shoulder. Oscar was holding a German Luger with a suppressor attached to its barrel.

"It's very old," Oscar said, lifting the gun as if admiring it. He looked at Morris. "I don't think you've ever seen it, have you?"

Morris twisted his body to face Oscar. A look of terror was on his face.

"I'm so sorry, Morris. I've always liked you. Truly, I have," Oscar said sadly.

He stepped toward Morris, and Morris stumbled backward until his legs touched the bed, collapsing him to the floor.

"You were always the most fragile of all. Do you know it was I who persuaded Mr. Pender to make you one of his chosen few?"

Morris opened his mouth to speak. "I—"

"You should not have killed such a fine man," Oscar whispered. "He gave you so much, so very much."

Morris threw up his hands and covered his face.

"So very much," Oscar said again. He took a long, quick step to Morris, raised the gun in his hand, placed the barrel against Morris's right temple, and fingered the trigger. The *pfffttt* of the shot echoed dully in the room, and Oscar stepped away, letting the body roll against the bed and onto the floor. He stood for a moment, gazing down at Morris, and then he removed a handkerchief from his pocket and began to rub the Luger clean.

He crossed the room to the telephone on the nightstand, lifted the receiver, pushed a coded number, and waited. After a moment, he heard Alyse's voice.

"Yes," she said fearfully.

"I regret to inform you that our friend Morris has just taken his own life," Oscar told her. He paused, then added, "It seems he was deeply depressed over Mr. Pender's death."

For a moment, Alyse did not speak. Oscar could hear her swallowing air. Then she said, "I'm sorry. We should inform the police."

"May I suggest we wait until morning," Oscar said. "Reasonably, that's when one of us would discover him. And we do need a few hours tonight to complete the other details."

"I'm sure we would be asked about hearing a shot," Alyse said.

"It is a very large home, well insulated for sound. With the television playing, it would be difficult to hear anything. Also, the gun he used was equipped with a silencer. Apparently he was concerned about disturbing us."

"Whatever you think is best," Alyse told him.

"Thank you. If you need anything, I'll be in the laundry room for a few minutes."

"Yes," Alyse whispered.

He replaced the telephone on the cradle, crossed back

to Morris, kneeled beside him, and removed Morris's gun and the envelope with money from his jacket. He shoved the gun and the envelope into his own coat and then he forced the Luger into Morris's right hand, squeezing the hand over the grip. He released his grasp and let the gun fall free to the floor. He stood slowly, gazing down at the body. After a moment, he pushed the gun closer to the body with the toe of his shoe. He went to the bed, removed the clothes bag and unzipped it, and pulled out two sheets that had been crammed inside. He crossed to the closet, opened it, and hung the clothes bag inside on the closet pole. Then he tucked the sheets under his arm and quietly left the room.

FORTY

AARON STOOD NEAR THE WINDOW AND gazed out at the garden. He could see the narrow tube of light on the statue named Salome, her uplifted face peering into the dome of night. A security light at the far end of the garden glowed dimly, like a weak yellow moon. It was, Aaron thought, the most peaceful place he would ever see. A sensation of warmth, like a blush, swam through him. He was in the room where he had been held captive for days, and he felt safe.

He turned slightly. Carla stood at the far corner of the window, as someone who did not want to be seen from the outside would stand.

"Do you know what surprised him the most about you?" Carla asked.

Aaron shook his head.

"It surprised him that he liked you so much. That first day you saw him, in the garden, and you helped him with his planting, that was why. He didn't expect you to help. Sometimes when we were in the garden together, I could look up and see him in the window of his study—barely see him, but he was there. He was watching you. He liked you from the first time he saw you."

Carla paused, touched the windowpane with the tips of her fingers, then turned and moved to stand beside Aaron. She took his hand in both of her hands and began to stroke it gently. "So did I," she said. She looked up, her eyes peering into Aaron's eyes. "We've told you everything, Aaron. Everything. I think you know we're telling you the truth. If—if Morris had not done what he did, you would have been released to your parents, with our faith that you would not reveal us. We believed that from the very beginning. We still do."

She lifted his hand to her face, brushed it with her lips. "Please believe me," she begged. "I don't know how the others feel, but I think Mr. Pender knew he wouldn't live very much longer, even if he hadn't been killed, and I think he wanted us to understand how important it was to care, regardless of the risk, and that's why he did what he did. It was for us. For me. For Robert. For Alyse. And, now, for you."

Aaron did not reply. He could feel the warmth of Carla's breath on his hand.

"Do you want to go outside?" she asked softly.

"No," he told her.

"Will you promise me something?"

"I guess," Aaron answered.

"Will you promise that you won't forget us?"

A grin, barely visible, shy and boyish, crossed Aaron's face. He dipped his head. "I'll never do that," he said.

"You will think about us?"

"Yes."

"Who will you think about the most?"

"You," Aaron said quietly. "I'll think about you."

Carla stepped to him and folded her arms around him and rested her face against his neck and shoulder.

"I do love you, Aaron Greene."

"I—"

"No, you don't have to say anything," she whispered.

"But—"

"No," she insisted. "Not now. You're going home, and I want you to leave here tonight with something unsaid."

"Why?" he asked.

She pulled her face from him to look into his eyes.

"If you leave with something unsaid, that means you'll have to come back to say it, doesn't it?"

"I guess."

A soft knock fell on the door leading from the bedroom to the corridor, and Carla stepped away from Aaron.

"Yes?" Carla called.

The door opened and Alyse stepped inside. Robert stood behind her.

"Are you ready to go home?" Alyse asked.

Aaron nodded.

"Sure he is," Robert said in a bright voice.

Carla moved back to Aaron, tilted her face, kissed him gently. "Remember what I told you in this room, the night we danced," she whispered. "You were *selected*. You've always been one of us."

"Yes," Aaron said quietly.

Menotti drew from his cigarette and blew the smoke out the crack of his car window. He did not like smoking in his car—knew it would draw complaints from Arlene—but he needed the jolt of the nicotine. His mind and body were still partially asleep, still mesmerized by the soft cushioned mattress of his bed and by the wash-scented freshness of Egyptian cotton sheets. He had not slept well for days, and, being exhausted, he did not find it easy to force himself awake to answer the curious late-night phone call from Robert Lucas.

Robert had apologized for the call, then had said, "I think it's important that you meet me as soon as you can."

"What's going on?" Menotti had asked sleepily.

"I'd rather not say," Robert had replied. "I'd really rather see you in person."

And Menotti had agreed.

"My house," Robert had suggested. "You've been there."

It was twenty minutes after one when Menotti stopped

in front of Robert's house and got out of the car. He dropped the cigarette and stepped on the burning tip. He stood for a moment, studying the house. A few hours earlier, he had picked the lock to Robert Lucas's back door. Returning to the scene of the crime, he thought. He wondered if Robert knew he had been there. No, he decided. Not possible. He pulled up the zipper on his thin windbreaker and walked quickly to the front door.

The door opened before Menotti could knock.

"Come in," Robert said pleasantly, a tired smile lodged on his face.

Menotti stepped inside the house.

"I'm sorry to call so late, but I thought it best," Robert continued. He gestured toward the kitchen. "Coffee?"

"Sounds good," Menotti told him.

In the kitchen, Robert motioned Menotti to a chair at the kitchen table. He poured coffee and put the cups on the table and sat opposite Menotti.

"I really don't know where to begin with all of this," Robert said. "But I think it's important to be up-front."

"Go ahead," Menotti said.

"I know you were in my home today," Robert said. "Without a warrant, of course, and that's all right. I don't know what you saw, or found, but I would be happy to discuss anything with you."

Menotti blushed.

"A young boy who lives across the street from me—a deaf boy—saw you. We're friends," Robert explained.

"Well, you got me," Menotti said. "I don't know why, Mr. Lucas, but there's something about you that rings bells. I wanted to see if you were concealing anything."

"Could it have anything to do with your friendship with Cody?" Robert asked casually.

"I hope I'm better at my work than that."

"I'm sure you are," Robert said, "but I do want to put you at ease on that. No, I'm not using Millie. I'm going to marry her, Lieutenant Menotti. I asked her after the funeral today. She accepted."

"Congratulations," Menotti said.

Robert beamed. "Thank you. Now did you find anything in my house?"

"Not much. A detailed dossier on Aaron Greene, for one thing," Menotti answered.

"In my files? Of course you did. All of us had the same thing. It was Mr. Pender's practice to know as much as he could about anything, or anyone, he was involved with. Aaron was no exception, and there was a great deal of information already available, since he had made a preliminary application to Carlton-Ayers. Did you find anything else?"

Menotti thought of the outline of dust where the boxes had been. "No," he lied.

"Good," Robert said. "Now, I can talk to you."

"About what?"

"I'm sure you know that Mr. Pender had been in contact with people who were taking credit for kidnapping Aaron. They had my number as well as Mr. Pender's. Late this afternoon, I got a phone call from them."

"And?" Menotti asked.

"It was from a woman—at least I think it was a woman. It wasn't easy to tell. Anyway, whoever it was said they were holding Aaron and wanted to arrange an exchange."

"What kind of exchange?"

"You're going to find this very strange," Robert said.

"Try me," Menotti replied.

"Aaron for a single blank cassette tape."

"What?" Menotti said. His voice was a mix of humor and disbelief.

"That's exactly what I thought," Robert replied, "but it's a lot less expensive than ten million dollars."

"What did you tell them?"

"I told them it would be my pleasure. All they had to do was tell me what to do."

Menotti drank from his coffee and waited.

"I was to go to the parking lot of the Dunwoody United Methodist Church," Robert continued. "There I was to leave the tape in a paper grocery bag in the middle of the lot, and then to park across the street and wait until I saw a car retrieve the bag. Aaron would be released there, in the church lot. He would be blindfolded and he would be instructed not to move until I picked him up."

"That's an—incredible story," Menotti said slowly. "Did you tell anyone else about this?"

Robert smiled patiently. "I called Alyse and told her, and Carla. Carla just arrived home tonight from Florida. They're extremely relieved."

"The chauffeur—Morris, isn't it? Did he also return?"

"Yes, in fact, he did. Alyse said he was extremely despondent over Mr. Pender's death. She was very concerned about him. She said she would tell him about Aaron in the morning."

"You believed the call you received?" Menotti asked. "A story like that?"

For a moment, Robert did not answer, then he said, "Yes, I did. I know it all sounds a little far-fetched, but it also seemed possible."

"And you haven't called the police?"

"Only you."

"No one else? The FBI? No one?"

"No. They warned against it, of course."

"So when are you supposed to make the exchange?" Menotti asked.

Robert leaned back in his chair. A look of satisfaction rested in his face. "Aaron is on his way home now," he said. "I put him in a taxi a few minutes before you arrived."

"You did what?" Menotti demanded.

"I sent him home. That's where he wanted to be, and I wanted him to have some time with his parents before all the questions started. If you disagree with that, I'm sorry, but it was my decision and I don't regret it."

"You mean it happened—the exchange?" Menotti said.

"Exactly as they said it would," Robert replied. "A car—a white one, a Saturn, I think, though I was too far away to be certain—pulled into the parking lot and stopped at the spot I'd left the bag. I saw the door open on the driver's side, then close again. After a moment, Aaron got out on the passenger's side, and the car drove off. That's when I got him."

"Did he say who was driving?"

"I think you should ask Aaron," Robert said. "The only thing he told me is that a woman was driving the car—the same woman who picked him up on the street in Atlanta the morning he was taken. I didn't press him for answers to anything."

Menotti sat for a long moment staring at Robert Lucas. The story he told sounded outrageous, bizarre. Yet, curiously, it also sounded plausible. Everything about the kidnapping of Aaron Greene had been theatrical.

"A blank tape?" Menotti said finally. "That's what they wanted?"

"A TDK, ninety-minute play," Robert replied. "I bought it at a Kmart on Buford Highway."

"That's the kind they've been using," Menotti admitted.

"If they use this one, you'll know it," Robert told him.

"Why?"

"I marked it."

"How?"

"With a tiny nail-file scratch on the edge of the plastic covering—on the A side. In fact, it aligns with the A that's stamped on the covering."

Menotti nodded. It amused him that people wanted to play detective. "Why do you think they went from ten million dollars to a blank tape?"

"I don't know," Robert said. "Maybe they ran out.

Maybe it's symbolic. Maybe they're telling us they've got something else to say."

Menotti stood. He looked at his watch. It was twenty minutes before two. "I'd better go," he said. "I think I have a long night ahead of me."

"Sorry to get you out," Robert said.

"It's all right," Menotti mumbled. He looked back at Robert. "Do you think this is it?" he asked. "Do you think it's over?"

Robert bit the smile that wanted to ease into his face. "I don't know," he replied seriously. "They taught us a lesson, I think, so I'm not sure." He let the smile free itself. "They do have another tape, don't they?"

"Yes," Menotti said. "Yes, they do."

He had never ridden in a taxicab and he realized that he was nervous as the driver—a squat, heavy man with a pockmarked face—drove lazily along Ponce de Leon, going east.

"Let's see, Willow Branch," the driver said. "That near downtown Decatur?"

"No sir," Aaron said. "It's near Suburban Plaza."

"Oh, yeah," the man said. He cocked his head to look into the rearview mirror. "Say, that's on the same street where that boy lived that was kidnapped, ain't it?"

Aaron dipped his head in a nod. "Yes sir."

"You know him?" the driver asked. He added, in a mutter, "Shit, I can't never remember his name."

"Uh—yes sir," Aaron said. He added quietly, "Aaron Greene."

"What's that?" the driver said.

"Aaron Greene," Aaron said. "His name is Aaron Greene."

"Yeah, yeah, that's it. Just couldn't remember it," the driver said, pulling onto Lawrenceville Highway. He glanced into the mirror again. "Guess you heard about that old man getting killed two or three days ago?"

Aaron mumbled, "Yes sir."

"Well, the son of a bitch that done that was about as stupid as they come," the man declared. "Everything I been hearing, that old man was about to dish out ten million dollars for that boy, and the goddamn kidnappers put a hole in him. They might've got away, but they left the money behind. Don't make a damn bit of sense, does it?"

Aaron wagged his head. He could see the man's eyes studying him from the mirror.

"I'm telling you, boy, people don't give a shit about nobody no more," the driver continued. "I been driving this cab for more'n twenty years and I seen it all. Used to be you could trust anybody. Nowadays, you got to think twice before you let somebody in your car. What they been saying about that boy's right: You a little man, you ain't nothing but a nobody and you're gon' get your ass kicked around. Don't nobody care nothing about the little man no more. If it ain't somebody ready to knock you over the head to take what little you got, it's the goddamn government finding some way to steal you blind. I'm telling you, boy, you still young. You'll find out what I'm talking about. What was it they was saying? Wake Up America? Well, America better damn well wake up, or there's going to be hell to pay. Don't nobody care about the little man no more."

The driver snorted, coughed, laughed.

"I still can't believe those dumb bastards. Killing that old man like that and leaving that ten million dollars lying on the table," the man said. "If they was the ones that did it," he added quickly. "Some people think it wadn't them at all. They think it was just some damn fool trying to rob that old man, since he was in the news all the time, and everybody knew he was raising all that money."

The car slowed and turned onto the street where Aaron lived.

"This the right road?" the driver asked. "Willow Branch?"

"Yes sir," Aaron said. He could feel his heart pounding.

"Looks like a nice neighborhood," the driver said. "Don't think I ever had a fare out here, though."

"Yes sir," Aaron said again. He sat forward on the seat.

"You remember what I'm telling you," the driver advised hoarsely. "Them that's got, keep on getting; them that ain't got, they drive taxicabs." He laughed. "Aw, what the shit. Maybe we ought to put together a Nobody Union. That's what I told my wife."

Aaron could see the corner of his home.

"Which one?" the driver asked.

"That one," Aaron said. He saw two cars parked on the driveway. One belonged to his father. He did not recognize the other car.

The driver pulled the cab to the curb in front of Aaron's home. He glanced at the meter. "That's twelve dollars," he said.

Aaron handed him the twenty-dollar bill that Robert had given him and opened the door to the car and got out.

"Hey, son, you got some change coming," the driver said.

Aaron turned back to him. "That's all right," he said. "You keep it."

"Well, damn," the driver exclaimed. "That's nice of you, boy. Enjoyed talking to you." He sped away quickly.

Aaron turned to his home. The lawn was cluttered with Styrofoam cups and paper wrappers. It had the look of being played on, like the football field of his high school. He saw a light click on from inside the house. After a moment, the door opened and a man he did not know stepped outside.

The man said, "Aaron?"

"Yes sir," Aaron answered.

"Jesus," the man whispered.

EPILOGUE

IT WAS MENOTTI'S SUGGESTION THAT CODY meet him at the Bar-S Corral, but Menotti was late—as usual, Cody thought—and Cody sat at a table in a dim, remote corner, facing the door.

Nothing in the bar had changed since his first visit five months earlier. It was as though he had simply walked outside, turned, and then walked back inside. The lapse of time could have been a minute, or a month, or a year. The Bar-S Corral was the same. Looked the same. Smelled the same. Was the same. The waitresses with the uplift bras cupping breasts that quivered when they moved. The customers—loud, laughing, beer-drinking men, dressed in workers' clothing, bearded, caps with insignias jammed on the crown of their heads. The bartender in cowboy dress. The jukebox songs of country lamentations—lovings and leavings and lonely nights. The haze of cigarette smoke. The clinking glass sounds, like sharp-pitched bells. The Bar-S was a constant in an inconstant, frantic world that sped past it on Steward Avenue.

Cody had asked the waitress for six plastic swizzle sticks, and he held one and struck his lighter and played the stick over the flame until it began to curl, and then he picked up a second swizzle stick and carefully fused it to the first. In a few minutes, he had fashioned all of the sticks together in a rough likeness of Don Quixote, and it caused the waitress to say, "You the fellow that made that little stick man not long ago?"

"Guilty," Cody replied.

"Lord, I loved it," the waitress gushed. "I took it home and gave it to my daughter. She had it setting on her dresser, but the cat knocked it off and it broke."

"Sorry," Cody said. "I'll leave this one on the table for you."

"You're so sweet," the waitress shrilled, then whirled away to boast to the bartender about her good fortune in replacing her broken swizzle-stick man.

There was irony in Menotti's phone call, Cody thought as he gazed at the awkward figure of twisted plastic standing beside his glass. It had been months since Aaron Greene's return to his home. Months. And still the FBI searched for his kidnappers and for the killer of Ewell Pender—having concluded they were looking for the same person, or persons. Yet, the panic had subsided and the investigation had assumed an almost casual, routine pace. It was aftermath, Cody believed. Nothing but aftermath. Almost dull.

But not all of it was dull. Ethridge Landon had been indicted by a federal grand jury. Robert Lucas had slipped an engagement ring on the slender waiting finger of Millie, a diamond that dwarfed the dim, glasslike glitter of the one she had once worn. And Aaron Greene had been hired by Robert to work in his computer business, an act of generosity that Menotti had classified as bribery.

Not all of it was dull.

Cody had ordered his second drink when Menotti arrived, complaining about a late, unexpected meeting with Clifford Russell. "Someday," Menotti said as he signaled his order, pointing to Cody's glass, "I'm going to kill the son of a bitch."

"Who, honey?" the waitress asked.

"Your ex," Menotti said, grinning.

"Well, honey, you'd have to get in line behind me," the waitress cooed.

Menotti glanced at her body. It had the flabby look of swelling yeast. "At least I'd have something lovely to look at while I was standing there," he said.

"Lord, honey," the waitress exclaimed. "You could make a girl blush. I'll see if I can't get him to pour you something out of the good bottle." She waltzed away.

"You're a tiger, Menotti," Cody said.

"I'm Italian. It's in the blood," Menotti replied. He gestured with his face to Cody's plastic sculpture. "I can see by your little swizzle-stick man—"

"Don Quixote," Cody corrected. "It's called art, something you will never understand or appreciate because you are basically an uncultured sadist protected by the law."

"Whatever," Menotti said. "Anyway, I see you've been here awhile. Sorry."

"I didn't expect you to be on time," Cody told him. "You never have been. Why here, by the way?"

Menotti replied languidly, "Because I like this place. No pretension. It's a pigsty, one of the great lowlife places in the western world. It reminds me of you, Cody."

"From you, I consider that a compliment," Cody countered. "Is this going to be one of those harassing encounters, Victor, or are you going to let me drink in peace and then chauffeur me home?"

Menotti laughed. He took the glass offered by the waitress and saluted Cody with it. "To you," he said, drinking.

"That's the good stuff, honey," the waitress said proudly.

Menotti smacked over the inferior taste of the scotch. "Smooth," he said. The waitress smiled and left.

"How's Freda?" Menotti asked.

"Fine."

"I understand the newsroom gossip has the two of you toddling off into old age together."

"Who told you that?" demanded Cody.

"I'm a detective, Yates. You keep forgetting that."

"We've got a good thing going," admitted Cody.

"You moved in with her?" Menotti asked.

"Yeah. Yeah, I have, asshole. Does that please you?"

"Makes me envious, Cody. That's all."

Cody picked up his Don Quixote and twirled it in his fingers. One of Don Quixote's legs fell off. He put it down with resignation.

"Art," Menotti snickered.

Cody leaned his elbows on the table and looked at Menotti. He said, "You know, I'm glad we had this little get-together, Victor, but I've got this annoying feeling it's not to talk about my sex life. Nope, it's not about me, this time. You've got something to tell me, haven't you? Some little tidbit of steamy information that delights you because it won't delight me, something you've come upon that sends shivers of delight straight to your pecker. Am I right?"

"Close," agreed Menotti. "Damned if you're not getting more perceptive by the day."

"What is it, Victor?" Cody's voice was impatient.

Menotti struck a light to a cigarette. "They executed Ewell Pender's will today."

"And, so?" Cody said. "How much did we get?"

"We should be so lucky," Menotti said. "In the final tally—and it was one hell of a tally, by the way—the widow, Alyse, took home the bacon, but our friend Mr. Lucas was a comfortable second."

"Lucas? What do you mean?"

"He was named president of the Pender Foundation."

"Bullshit," Cody exclaimed.

"No, Cody. Bull's-eye. Dead center. That old boy has just landed a spot in the hall of fame."

"Why him? Why not the widow?"

"She didn't want it. From what I understand, she's going to be the fairy godmother at that school Pender put so much money into."

"Carlton-Ayers," Cody said. "And the other girl— Carla?"

"She and the butler both got tidy sums, enough to keep a couple of accountants busy," Menotti said. "She's also going to work with Lucas." He reached for Cody's broken Don Quixote and stirred his drink with it. "That's a smart man, Cody. But I guess you know that. Millie's going to marry him, and we both know what that means. Throbbing gray matter between two intellectuals is like sweat musk to somebody as constantly horny as you are. And— not to discount the working between his ears—he was one of Pender's all-time favorites. Has been for years, it turns out. Pender was the money behind his computer business, which, by the way, is totally legitimate and lucrative. I checked it." Menotti smiled smugly. "You're losing her to an inventive man."

"You still think he snatched Aaron, don't you?" Cody said.

"Sure do, but I also think Elvis is alive and I'm willing to let both of them abide in peace," Menotti answered.

"It's not what Aaron said," Cody argued. "He said he never saw anyone's face, that they always wore masks, or heavy makeup and sunglasses. And if I'm not mistaken, you and the rest of the Gestapo have been grilling the poor little bastard for months and he hasn't changed so much as a comma. My God, Victor, he talked about that cabin in detail."

Menotti pulled from his cigarette and let the smoke seep from his lips. He studied Cody. Cody wanted to believe Aaron—needed to believe him. He said, "Funny thing about that cabin. Used to be a Boy Scout camp before it was turned into a hunting lodge. Did you know that?"

"I read the report," Cody said. "What are you getting at?"

"I also know something that wasn't in the report," Menotti replied. "Once upon a time there was a Boy Scout troop at Carlton-Ayers and all those happy little campers used to make excursions up there, including our man Robert."

"That's reaching, Victor. If you're so hell-bent on nailing Aaron's ass, why don't you give him a polygraph?"

Menotti laughed softly. "Shit, Cody, do you think I'm crazy? Talk about your bad PR." He shook his head. "When you've got half the world lined up against you, you learn to go silently into that good night, my friend."

"They ever find anything at the cabin?"

"Nothing much. The sort of stuff Aaron mentioned. They hauled the ashes in and I suppose they're still sifting through them just to look busy, but I don't think they'll get much out of it. They taught the boy well."

"Jesus, Menotti," Cody said in disgust. He drained the scotch from his glass and signaled to the waitress for another round. He thought of Aaron Greene. Three weeks after Aaron's return he had been in a restaurant and had overheard two men at a nearby table discussing the kidnapping. One of the men had said, "Christ, what was that kid's name? I can never remember it." And his friend had replied, "Me either. Aaron somebody. I heard that Aaron Who line so much I forgot his real name. Anyway, you know who I'm talking about."

"You look pissed off," Menotti said. "Did I offend you?"

"No," Cody answered. "I just think the kid's been through enough."

"Well, I guess it doesn't matter. He's home and he's safe. And he's got one hell of a job with your soon-to-be husband-in-law."

"Kiss my ass, Victor."

"You are pissed," Menotti said in mock judgment. "You shouldn't be. All I'm saying is that I admire a good con job, and I think old Robert's a master of the craft."

"I admire kindness," Cody said.

"I guess it's all in the eye of the beholder," Menotti

replied dryly. He grinned, and added, "Or in the beholder of the eye."

The waitress put fresh drinks on the table and picked up the two empty glasses. Her breasts bulged over the tight uplift bra. "Y'all want something else?" she asked cheerfully. "Some nachos?"

"Not for me," Menotti said.

"Nothing here, either," Cody added. "Get me the bill when you get a chance." The waitress winked at Menotti and walked off.

"You know, Cody, if she took that bra off, her knockers would hit her knees," Menotti mused. "I've got to find out how those things work."

Cody ignored the comment. He asked, "Was there any truth to the trust fund for Aaron?"

"Two hundred thousand, the same amount Pender pledged to keep the flames burning," Menotti said. "He'll get it when he's twenty-one. In the meantime, he gets his college paid for out of a new scholarship fund. Not bad. Good job. Education. Money waiting. The victim finally gets a payoff. That's the part I like, Yates."

"So it's over, except for picking up the pieces," Cody said. "Is that what you're telling me?"

"I didn't say that."

"It's not over?"

Menotti shrugged.

"Jesus, Victor, you can be exasperating, do you know that?" Cody grumbled. "What is it you're leaving out?"

Menotti broke the tip of his cigarette in the ashtray and gazed for a moment at the whiplash of dying smoke. "One other thing," he said quietly. "But, for the time being, it stays with us." He looked at Cody. "Do you understand me?"

"All right," Cody said wearily.

Menotti took a shallow swallow of the scotch, then pushed it aside. He reached into his coat pocket and pulled out an audiocassette tape and dropped it on the table.

"What's that?" Cody asked.

"The tape," Menotti answered.

"What do you mean?"

"Do you remember that I told you about Robert marking the tape he exchanged for Aaron? A nail-file scratch on the A side?"

"It's that tape?"

"Yep."

"Where did you get it?" asked Cody.

"It was mailed to the police station, addressed to me."

"You?" Cody said in a surprised voice.

Menotti smiled, blinked a yes.

"When?"

"Today," Menotti answered behind a crooked grin. "Great timing, wouldn't you say? I get the tape on the same day the Pender will is executed." He touched the tape with his finger, tapped it twice. The grin dimmed to a smile. "Coincidence, of course."

"Why did it come to you?" Cody asked.

"I'd say it's a warning, or maybe just a tease," Menotti told him.

"What does that mean?"

Menotti leaned forward to the table and leveled his eyes on Cody. He said, "It means he knows that I know." He paused, then added, "He likes to play God."

"God is good, I thought," Cody said.

"Playing God is the not the same as *being* God, Cody, and this tape tells me he's *playing* God. When you hear it, you'll know what I'm talking about."

"My voice?" Cody asked.

"Of course. Why break old habits?"

"What does it say?"

"One sentence. Are you sure you want to know?"

"Try me," Cody said irritably.

Menotti again reached inside his coat pocket and withdrew a cassette tape player barely larger than his hand. He pushed the tape into the slot and fingered the play button, and then he handed the player to Cody.

Static hissed from the small speaker.

And then Cody heard his own voice.

"In the beginning, there was Aaron . . ."